Chudwell Hall

A LIGHTHEARTED NOVEL OF DARK ACADEMIA

Jeffrey L. Buller

Signed, Sealed, & Delivered
Raleigh, North Carolina

Copyright © 2023 by Jeffrey L. Buller

All rights reserved. No part of this publication may be reproduced, distributed or transmitted in any form or by any means, without prior written permission.

Jeffrey L. Buller / Signed, Sealed, & Delivered
9154 Wooden Road
Raleigh, North Carolina 27617
www.jeffbuller.com

Publisher's Note: This is a work of fiction. Names, characters, places, and incidents are a product of the author's imagination. Locales and public names are sometimes used for atmospheric purposes. Any resemblance to actual people, living or dead, or to businesses, companies, events, institutions, or locales is completely coincidental.

Book Layout © 2016 BookDesignTemplates.com

Chudwell Hall/Jeffrey L. Buller. — 4th ed.

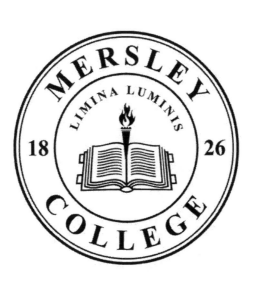

CONTENTS

The Garner Problem 7
The Department of Imminent Scholarship 13
P. Bradford Townsant III 19
The Scipionic Circle 25
The Caretaker 31
"The Road Up and the Road Down Are the Same" 37
The War on Whiteheads 45
The Department Chair 49
A Theory on Theories 59
"Cold ... Soooooo Cold" 69
An Advocate for Mersley College Students 73
The Bad Boy of the Scipionic Circle 79
Barbara the Barbarian Librarian 89
Esmé 95
Professor Fitzgerald 99
The Dean's Den 107
The Catacombs 113
The Golden Mean 119
The Transmundane Codex of Berossus 125
"Problem Solved" 131
Fall Break 135
Final Exams 143
"The First Annual Hallothankmas Party" 149
"The Flowers That Bloom in the Spring, Tra la!" 153
The Revenant 159
Interlibrary Loan 163
The Strategic Plan 169
The One-Hundred-Percent Solution 173
The Phantom 179
The Golden Ideal 183
The Spirit of Tolbert Fitzgerald 191
The Cabal 197

Winter Refuge	201
The Waiting Game	205
The Best Kind of Research	211
When One Door Closes	215
The Rat Pack's Pack Rats	221
"Painful and Divisive Experiences"	227
The Nightly Excavations Continue	231
The Strange Interlude	237
The Covington Prize	245
The Aurelian Club	253
La Tanière Dorée	259
Scholars Night	263
The Peeling of the Belles	269
The Consuls	277
Bloodstains, Bound Books, and Bastian	281
Suite 16	287
Faith and Confidence	293
A Fool's Errand	303
The Natatorium	307
A System and a Schedule	311
Back at the Diogenes Club	317
The Tabula Rasa	325
Thalatta! Thalatta!	337
No Arguments	345
Lillian Hawthorne	349
Front of House and Back of House	355
The Clearinghouse	361
Sexton	367
The Troubles	373
Count No One Happy	379
Acknowledgements	387

CHAPTER ONE

The Garner Problem

Professor Winton Garner was widely regarded as a difficult man. He was difficult in his grading, with students in his courses averaging a C-, well below the A-/B+ that had become the de facto standard at Mersley College. He was also difficult as a person, as nearly anyone who had ever met him might attest. Those who wished to be kind might say of Garner that he didn't suffer fools gladly. Yet, since he considered almost everyone besides himself at the college to be insufferable fools, the number of those who were disposed to be kind could be counted on one hand.

One of Garner's many peculiarities was that, despite the low grades he assigned, some students absolutely worshipped him. They regarded his arrogance as proof of his intellectual acumen, and they vied with one another over the degree to which they could adopt his mannerisms. Not that *all* the students at Mersley College felt this way, of course. If thirty students enrolled in one of his courses, four or five might stick it out to the very end. The withdrawal rate for students who enrolled in his classes sent shivers down the spines of the administration's bean counters. And yet, the fact that almost no one completed a course with Professor Garner led to a strange irony. Because student course evaluations were typically completed on the last day of the semester, only those who idolized Garner ever evaluated him. As a result, Garner had the lowest completion rate but also the highest approval rating of any professor in Mersley's history.

That turn of events created endless problems for Jefferson Woolridge, the college's longstanding (and long-suffering) president. A typical year meant that his desk soon became filled with petitions from faculty members, parents, and aggrieved local citizens, all of whom called for Garner's termination. But how could the president dismiss a tenured full professor who not only had the highest student ratings of anyone at the college but who had also been awarded the Covington Prize for Outstanding Scholarship in the Classics, only the second Mersley faculty member to do so? A thorn in the president's side he may be, but Garner was, for all intents and purposes, untouchable. Unless he committed a serious crime or stopped showing up for work altogether, Garner could remain on the faculty as long as he desired. And he desired to remain. With no surviving relatives and no interests outside of his professorial duties, he really had nowhere to go.

"The Garner Problem," as it was commonly called, came to a head one Friday in May, a few weeks after graduation, at the closing faculty meeting of the year. Recollections differ as to precisely what occurred on that momentous day. Garner himself insisted that he had simply called President Woolridge's most recent budget cuts "niggardly," adopting a term that *Roget's Thesaurus* describes as an innocently Anglo-Saxon synonym for "stingy" or "miserly." Roughly half of those in the room swore, however, that Garner had uttered a *different* word, one derived from Spanish and regarded as an ethnic slur so unforgivable that we dare not repeat it here. The uproar was immediate, and the outcome seemed clear: Winton Garner would have to be "released from his contract," to use the euphemism that the college's lawyers insisted on.

But precisely *how* Garner would be made to leave proved trickier than even President Woolridge had imagined. In a meeting with Mersley's aged and often irascible dean, Dr. Dawn McDaniel, it was suggested that the professor's behavior constituted "moral turpitude," one of the three reasons for which, according to the Mersley College Faculty Handbook, a tenured professor could be terminated. Upon examining the school's policies, however, Woolridge discovered that professors accused of moral turpitude were entitled to a hearing and to be represented at that hearing by legal counsel.

"Any decent lawyer would make mincemeat of us if we went that route," Woolridge told McDaniel. "After all, there's precedent at another university here in the state back in the late '90s. Those who cried 'racism' were broadly ridiculed the moment someone bothered to look up the etymology of 'niggardly' in the dictionary, and the whole affair proved to be a major embarrassment. No, much as I'd love to make Mersley a one-hundred-percent Garner-free campus, claims of moral turpitude simply won't get us there."

"What about dereliction of duty?" McDaniel asked, citing the second of the three reasons for which a tenured faculty member could be terminated.

"Dereliction of duty? Garner? Seriously?" Woolridge replied. "The man positively *lives* here. He never misses a class and puts in two to three times the number of office hours required under his contract. And good luck claiming that he's derelict in his duties because he turns in his grades late. It doesn't take long to grade your finals when you only have five students left in the class."

"What about financial exigency?" McDaniel suggested, proceeding to the third reason why Garner's contract could be voided.

"In order to do that, I'd have to terminate the entire Classics Department, and that would leave you out of a job if you ever stepped down from your administrative position," Woolridge reminded the dean.

As the president had alluded, Dawn McDaniel was also a classicist, a specialist in Eleatic philosophy, and the only other member of the Mersley faculty ever to have received the Covington Prize.

"I have no intention of stepping down," she replied.

"Well, even so, I need the Classics Department. It's the only reason we ever got our Phi Beta Kappa chapter, and besides, it's a cash cow. Salaries in that department are the lowest at the college and, apart from Garner's classes, enrollments are strong. Classical Mythology alone fills Radford Auditorium four times a day/three days a week, and that means that the cost per student credit hour in the department is next to nothing."

"It's too bad *all* the underperforming faculty members aren't in the same department. Then the decision would be easy."

"It would, wouldn't it?" Woolridge asked with amusement. But then he got a devilish look in his eye. "I mean, it *would*, wouldn't it? Hear me out for a second. Who else do we have on the faculty who doesn't pull his weight?"

McDaniel thought about it for a moment. "Ralph Briggs teaches the philosophy of language over in the Humanities Department, and his numbers aren't much better than Garner's. Oh, and then there's Wilda Dittman in English. She teaches postmodernist literary theory to classes that never number more than ten. Why? What do you have in mind?"

"Suppose—just *suppose*, hypothetically speaking—we created a new department. Just the three of them. Virtually no one signs up for their classes or, if they do, they drop them at the first opportunity. As dean, you can make changes in faculty assignments as long as you have a good enough reason for doing so. All we have to do is come up with a reason. Then, after a semester, the financial exigency case becomes easy to make. We eliminate the new department almost as quickly as we created it and ... " Woolridge wiped his hands. " ... our three worst-performing faculty members are history."

"Speaking of history, can we put Sabrina Pope in this new department, too? You know her. She's the 'problem child' at Faculty Senate Meetings."

"Oh, that one. She's a nightmare, all right. What does she teach, anyway? I never could tell from her remarks."

"The history of art, music, and literature."

"*All at once?* Can she do that? Well, no matter. I agree she's awful. Her enrollments must be abysmal, too."

"Actually, they aren't, but she's a royal pain in the ass, and I'd dearly love an excuse to void her contract before I have to endure even one more Faculty Senate meeting with her."

"All right, then. Consider it done. The Four Horsemen of the Apocalypse. It almost sounds too easy."

"Horse*persons* of the Apocalypse," McDaniel corrected the president. She was at least thirty years the president's senior and had no compunction at all about correcting him, even in open meetings. "Must keep in mind the board's multiculturalism, diversity, and inclusivity initiative. But you're right: It *is* too easy. Board policies state that, if a department's going to be eliminated for financial exigency, we have to show at least three years of tuition not covering the professors' salary."

Woolridge seemed disappointed, but then said, "Okay. So, it takes us three years. At least, in the meantime, they'll only have one another to annoy at department meetings. We'll just need to find some name for the program that sounds prestigious enough to keep them from complaining about the reassignment."

"Oh, they'll complain anyway. It's in their DNA."

"But what'll we call this new department? The Island of Misfit Toys?"

"Tempting, but it's a bit too on-the-nose. Don't worry. We'll think of something. The bigger problem is *where* we'll put them. Space is tight as it is. It has to be somewhere out of the way, somewhere no one else wants to be. It has to be ... "

The two administrators caught each other's eye and had the same idea simultaneously.

"Are you thinking what I'm thinking?" President Woolridge asked.

"I am, indeed," Dean McDaniel answered, a haunting gleam in her eye. "It looks as though we've finally found a use for Chudwell Hall."

CHAPTER TWO

The Department of Imminent Scholarship

Chudwell Hall, named after General Uriah Casperson Chudwell, would have been demolished decades ago if the Mersley City Council hadn't declared it a "structure of vast historical significance." Unheated in the winter and un-air-conditioned in the summer, most rooms in Chudwell were tolerable only in April and September. Since the academic year began in mid-August and ended in mid-May, that meant that the classrooms were stifling when the fall term started and when the spring term ended, reasonable for only two months, and bitterly cold the rest of the time.

Most people who entered the building said, however, that it wasn't so much the temperature of the building as its aroma that bothered them. Variously described as "musty," "what you'd expect a mummy's tomb to smell like," and "just plain evil," the fetid atmosphere of Chudwell had caused more than one student to drop a course for no other reason than because it was scheduled to be taught in the building. No one had done that, of course, during the past twenty or more years because the registrar no longer assigned courses to Chudwell. And so, the building simply sat on the far edge of campus, too historically significant to tear down and too freakishly awful to fill up.

By assigning Garner and the others office space in Chudwell, the president and dean thought they'd found the perfect solution. They weren't inconveniencing anyone else for the simple reason that no one in their right mind would ever *choose* to enter the building. And being forced to spend their days in such an inhospitable environment might even encourage one or more of the Four Horsepersons to resign even before their department could be abolished.

The question of what to call the new unit answered itself somewhat unexpectedly. As a way of making the four problematic faculty members willing to be reassigned, President Woolridge allotted each of them a ten percent increase in salary, extended their contacts from nine to twelve months a year, and bestowed on them the title of "eminent scholar" ... on the condition that they would agree to the move. He then proposed that, since the disciplines represented by the faculty members had relatively little in common, the new unit be called the Department of Eminent Scholars.

Whoever created the new signs for the building did not, it seems, know the difference between the words *eminent, imminent,* and *immanent*. As a result, a bronze plaque beside the front doors of Chudwell Hall now read *The Department of Imminent Scholarship*, which made it sound as though important new research would be forthcoming there momentarily. Beneath the names of each faculty member, the sign on their doors informed anyone who happened to pass by (i.e., almost no one) that the office belonged to an *Immanent Scholar*. Ralph Briggs, the philosopher in the group, was rather pleased to learn that the administration of Mersley College apparently thought his scholarship was not merely accidental but one of his inherent qualities. Garner, who hadn't yet found any new cause for grievance that day, regarded the malaprop as though it were a declaration of war.

He decided to respond to the perceived insult by a means that, he believed, was certain to produce immediate action: He fired off a strongly worded letter of complaint and emailed it to the dean. In this particular instance, Garner's assumptions were correct. His note of grievance did indeed produce an immediate response. The dean deleted his email the very moment she saw it.

The reason for Dean McDaniel's fit of pique was that she was now upset, not only with the eminent scholars themselves, but also with the president's decision to tap into her limited faculty salary budget by not only giving the four troublemakers a raise but also extending their contracts through the summer. With the money used for this purpose, McDaniel reasoned, she could have hired well more than a dozen temporary instructors of English composition to help improve the student body's notoriously poor writing skills or, alternatively, have paid one month's salary to an assistant professor in the Department of Business Administration.

What she didn't know was that President Woolridge had acted as he did for a specific reason. Typically, the salary savings accrued on faculty lines reverted to the dean's budget. But when a department was dissolved for financial exigency, that money reverted to the *president* so that it could be used for any pressing need the college might have. And President Woolridge regarded his own insufficient salary of barely $400,000 a year to be an indisputably pressing need.

There was also an additional reason why it made sense for the eminent scholars to work through the summer: As a newly-created unit, their department had no curriculum, no requirements for anyone choosing to major in the discipline, and no schedule for the coming fall term. The faculty was instructed, therefore, to overcome these deficiencies as rapidly as possible, and doing so would require every moment they had until the fall term began. Since the college's curriculum committee didn't meet over the summer, the eminent scholars were informed that whatever curriculum and schedule they developed would simply be rubber-stamped by the president and dean. "How could anyone dare question the decisions of such an elite group?" the president asked. Inwardly, however, he was thinking, "No one's going to take these courses anyway, so what does it matter?"

The first challenge facing the department, therefore, was what their course offerings should look like. What did the Classics, the history of art and music, post-modernist literary theory, and linguistic philosophy all have in common? Milton Schmidt, the head of Mersley's accounting program, might have answered that question by saying, "The likely unemployment of any choosing to major in those fields," but such an answer never occurred to the four faculty members themselves. Instead, they agreed that the focus of their new program would be "the human condition from Democritus and Demosthenes to Deleuze and Derrida." Garner was quick to point out that some of the authors he intended to include on his syllabus lived earlier than Democritus, and Wilda Dittman noted that her sources often postdated Jacques Derrida, but alliteration won out over accuracy, and the mission statement was quickly adopted.

The approval of that departmental mission occurred in a blindingly swift fashion for faculty decisions at Mersley College: only eleven weeks or precisely one week per word. It was thus already the beginning of August before the scholars even took up the question of what each of them would be teaching. Since classes would begin in little more than two weeks, Sabrina Pope suggested an expedient compromise: Each faculty member should simply prepare a list of whatever it was he or she *wanted* to teach and, once the lists were collated, the result would be the department's curriculum.

"Ah," Briggs objected, ever the philosopher, "but which courses will be required and which will be electives?"

"Why not make them *all* required courses? In that way, we'll have the most intellectually rich program on campus."

"Agreed!" Garner said. "And I want some rigorous prerequisites, too. I don't want to waste my time teaching the basics that any student worth his salt should've learned in high school."

"Hear, hear!" Dittman chimed in. "It'll send the administration a statement that standards must be upheld."

"All right then," Briggs said, eager for the meeting to end because it was time for his afternoon nap. "Let's all submit *two* lists: One of all the prerequisites a student must have fulfilled, and the other of all the required courses each student must complete. There will be no electives and no permission given to any student wishing to enroll in any course outside the department. Our curriculum will be completely self-sufficient right here in Chudwell Hall."

The following day when the president and dean received the collated list prepared by the eminent scholars (typewritten, of course, not printed from a word processor), they were almost gleeful at the result.

In order to be accepted as a major in the Department of Eminent Scholars, each student must be:

- proficient in French, German, and Latin,
- capable of identifying and assigning a randomly selected body of artworks and musical compositions to the appropriate historical period,
- familiar with the essential concepts introduced in the works of J. L. Austin, Ludwig Wittgenstein, and John Searle,
- able to explain why <u>Hamlet</u> and <u>Macbeth</u> are works of oppression, written to deprive women and members of minority groups of their human rights and thus maintain the rule of the patriarchy.

In order to graduate with a major in Eminent Scholarship, students must have passed each of the following courses with a grade of B or better:

There then appeared an alphabetized list of sixty-two courses, many of which had names that neither Woolridge nor McDaniel could pronounce.

"It's perfect," the dean said. "*No one* could possibly want to sign up for such a major. Not that anyone would ever meet the prerequisites or be willing to take all these required courses."

"What is that? A 180-hour major?"

"That's what it says. Until now, nuclear engineering had been our longest program, requiring 141 credit-hours. And I've been after them to pare it down to the more typical 120 hours for years."

"Well, don't try to get *this* major pared down. The more unwieldy and impossible, the better."

"I agree," Dean McDaniel said. "I'm just trying to imagine what sort of student this mass of gobbledygook would appeal to."

"Don't try too hard. I don't think such a student has been invented yet."

Fourteen days later, President Jefferson Woolridge was to learn just how wrong he was.

CHAPTER THREE

P. Bradford Townsant III

Peter Townsant was most decidedly neither Peter Townshend of The Who nor Peter Townsend who'd briefly had a romance with Princess Margaret, and he was getting rather weary of being asked about both of them. He arrived on the campus of Mersley College that August, eager to rebrand himself. Throughout high school he'd done none of the things that tended to make one popular. He was not athletic, indifferent to the politics of the Student Council, abysmal as a dancer, and, most damning of all, studious. When Bright River High allowed students to replace Physical Education with another course, he was the only member of his class to do so. Already enrolled in German since middle school—the region around the Great Lakes where he grew up was heavily populated by second- and third-generation German Americans—he elected to take French as well. When he declined the optional driver's education course, he replaced it with Latin. By the time he graduated, he was unable to drive and still unable to dance, but he had read great swaths of Goethe, Voltaire, Caesar, and Cicero, and had he lived in the nineteenth rather than the twenty-first century, he probably would have been considered reasonably well educated.

He had chosen to attend Mersley because it was the only school he applied to that hadn't required him to list his volunteer and extracurricular activities, of which he had none. As an added attraction, it was close enough to home that he could return there easily if he wanted, but far enough away that his mother and father (whom he insisted on calling "the mater and the pater") couldn't drop in on him too frequently. Peter hoped he could conduct his rebranding effort out of sight of anyone who'd known him earlier, the better to appear at Christmastime as an unrecognizable but wholly remade man.

Peter briefly toyed with having others call him Petey at college, but he rejected that idea because he thought it sounded too plebeian. He opted instead for using his middle name in its place and began signing his admission forms as "P. Bradford Townsant III." Neither his father nor his grandfather shared that name, so the suffix wasn't his to claim, but he justified it to himself by thinking that, if he could search through history thoroughly enough, surely there must have been two P. Bradford Townsants living *somewhere* at *some time*. And so, the young man's rebranding effort had officially begun.

It had long been the policy of Mersley College that all students chose a major upon matriculation. That system actually hadn't worked particularly well since few of the entering students had any idea what ninety percent of the disciplines entailed, having encountered almost none of them in high school. And so, when classes opened in the fall, there were several hundred pre-med and business majors, many of whom would drift off into other fields by the time of Thanksgiving Break. During the college's orientation week, P. Bradford Townsant III decided against all the popular majors for no other reason than that they seemed to be popular. Remade he may have been, but he was as intent on forging his own path in college as he had been in high school.

By 4:00 p.m. on Friday of orientation week, he had still not selected his major, a requirement that had to be completed at 5:00. Having wandered into every other building on campus (and wandering out again as soon as he saw the long lines outside of departmental offices), he eventually made his way to Chudwell Hall and stepped inside.

The aroma of stale antiquity that alienated so many other visitors quite appealed to the young man. It reminded him of what books smelled like when they'd been stored in damp basements and left unopened for several decades. The emptiness of the building was also, of course, a great attraction. And even though the inside of the building was a sweltering ninety-five degrees, he felt rather like Aeneas did when he first caught sight of Latium. This, he concluded, would be his new home.

It was thus that Townsant reached the door of Professor Garner, the only student to do so all week. A soft rap at the door resulted in a somewhat irritated "Well, don't just stand there. Come in!" and Townsant stepped inside, where the student and the professor proceeded to take one another's measure. Garner looked at the figure standing before him: medium height, thin almost to the point of being gaunt, dressed in a blue, broadcloth button-down shirt, dark khaki slacks, well-polished oxblood brogues, and (despite the heat of the day) a navy blue blazer. Garner was not impressed.

"If you're looking for the Sociology Department or the Department of Business Administration, young man, your compass has led you badly off-course."

"The sign outside said that this was the Department of Imminent Scholarship?" Unwittingly, Townsant had stumbled into one of Professor Garner's pet peeves: making a statement but intoning it as though it were a question. Garner's low opinion sank even lower.

He sniffed. "It's an error. Just an error. Here the faculty members are all eminent scholars."

"That sounds good. What is it that you teach?"

"Only that which is worth knowing. I'm sure none of it would interest you. Good day."

But Townsant was not so easily deterred. After having been recruited and wooed by nearly every tuition-dependent college or university in the Great Lakes region, he was intrigued by a program where the faculty seemed almost adamant about showing him the door.

"Like what?" he asked.

Garner sighed. Clearly the interloper was less easily dissuaded than the typical undergraduate. Ignoring Townsant's question, he replied with a question of his own. "What was the last thing you read in German? I mean, *entirely* in German."

Without a moment's hesitation, Townsant replied, "Goethe's *Die Wahlverwandtschaften*. That's the novel commonly known in English as *Elective Affinities*."

A barely suppressed grumble issued from the depths of Garner's soul. But whether he was more offended that the young man could actually answer his question or that it was assumed he wouldn't know the work by its original title, it's impossible to say.

"That's a bit unusual for a high school teacher to assign."

"Oh, Ms. Beckworth didn't assign it. The class was reading *Emil und die Detektive*. A kid's book, if you can believe it. Anyway, I finished that in a weekend, went to the library, and got the Goethe. *Much* more satisfying."

At this point, it's worth recalling that neither Garner nor the other professors in the new department knew what the president and dean were up to. They assumed that, if their curriculum didn't appeal to students, then their courses simply wouldn't "make," and they could devote the resulting free time to their research. So, rather than being pleased that this prospective major had, in fact, satisfied one of the program's prerequisites, he decided to stump him with another.

"And in Latin? Manage any of the *Aeneid* yet?"

"All of it, in fact. Ms. Brumfield only wanted the class to read the first six books, but that's ridiculous, isn't it? So, I read the rest on my own. I must admit that I preferred the *Georgics*, though. So reminiscent of Theocritus. Although I only know the *Idylls* in translation. My high school didn't offer Greek. I'd love to learn it, though."

By now, Garner was torn. Looking at the young man, he was

almost reminded of himself at the age of eighteen. And yet, if he accepted him into the major, he'd actually have to teach the courses he'd scheduled for the fall, albeit the enrollment would consist of only a single student.

"I don't believe I caught your name," Garner said as he was still mulling over his dilemma.

"P. Bradford Townsant III. My friends call me Bradford." It was the first lie he'd told the professor. He had no friends, and no one was yet aware of his rebranding.

"Then I shall call you Townsant."

From this moment forward, the young man who'd had every intention of rechristening himself as Bradford would henceforth be known simply as Townsant.

The professor continued, "My name is Garner."

"Pleased to meet you, Garner."

It was an unfortunate misstep. Just when the professor had been warming to the newcomer, the latter said something that made him realize why colleges would be wonderful places if only there weren't any students.

"That's *Professor* Garner. And I'm sorry to disappoint you, Townsant, but you're the only student who's expressed an interest in our department's major this year." Or any year, for that matter. "I really don't believe it would be an appropriate use of the college's resources, to borrow one of the dean's favorite phrases, for us to start a new cohort of fewer than five students. And, you see, it's nearly 5:00 p.m. now. As you know, all incoming students must declare their majors by that deadline. So ... "

Townsant eyed the professor for an uncomfortably long moment, and then said, "Wait here."

CHAPTER FOUR

The Scipionic Circle

A quarter to five had come and gone, leaving Garner to conclude that, despite all his apparent merits, Townsant was the typical incoming freshman: all ambition and big plans without the slightest idea of how to transform dreams into reality. He sniffed in dismissal—not that there was anyone around to witness his somewhat melodramatic reaction—and reopened his Teubner edition of Bacchylides, intending to immerse himself in Odes 13 and 15 before unwrapping the turkey sandwich and packet of sunflower seeds that would constitute his dinner.

"Good. You're still in," he heard a voice say from his doorway. "I was afraid you might have already left."

Garner looked up to see that Townsant had returned. "Not so easy to find students who actually want to do the work, is it?" the professor asked with a tone of calculated condescension. "Ah, well. At least you tried. I'd recommend scampering off to the English Department, where I'm sure they could use ... "

"This is Esmé Dawson," Townsant interrupted him, ushering into Garner's office an underfed girl wearing a crisply starched white top and a skirt with pleats so sharp you could use them to slice bread. Add only a tie that matched her skirt, and you would think Dawson had been abducted from one of the area's tonier Catholic schools for girls.

"Delighted, I'm sure," Garner replied, "but as I told you, it would take at least five ... "

"And this is Bastian Lewis. Behind him, you'll find the twins, Mallory and Prudence Warren-Whitehead. They all want to be imminent scholars, too."

Garner looked over the five students who now filled his office and felt almost as though he could see his plans for a teaching-free semester vanishing before his eyes.

There seemed only one way to save it.

"I don't think any of you realize just how challenging this major will be. 180 credit hours. That means eighteen credits a semester for the first three years—keeping in mind that most Mersley students struggle to pass their courses while taking only twelve or fifteen hours a term—with a one-course reduction during your last year while you're completing a mandatory undergraduate thesis. You'll earn six credits for defending a successful thesis, but that means you're still thirty-six credits short. So, you'll either have to stay on for an additional two terms or attend all three sessions of summer school each year until you're seniors, so I'm sure you see now that ... "

"Excuse me, Professor," Townsant again interrupted. "But it's getting very close to the five o'clock deadline. Perhaps you could sign us into the major now and continue the sales pitch afterward."

"But if I enroll you in the major and then you decide to change programs ... "

"We won't."

"But if you *did* ... "

"Is there some *other* professor who could enroll us as imminent scholars?"

"Fine!" Garner spit out, snapping shut the Bacchylides. "It's your funeral. Now, one at a time, spell your names for me—slowly, please!—and give me your student I.D. numbers."

* * *

The Diogenes Club, named after the fictional club to which Sherlock Holmes's brother, Mycroft, belonged, served a narrow but genuine need on the Mersley College campus. The Faculty Club did not permit students to dine there. The Mersley Student Union discouraged, but did not actually forbid, faculty members from entering. The rationale was, apparently, that each of the school's two major stakeholder groups needed a "safe space" where it could complain about the other. That policy both made sense and created a new problem: Where could faculty members and students meet together on campus for a relaxing meal and conversation?

Sutlinger Library didn't permit food within its hallowed halls. A classroom was always a possibility, but the school's policies also stated that any food served within a classroom building must be purchased through Mersley's own catering services (at exorbitant prices) and that an extra fee (also exorbitant) be charged for security, overhead, and cleaning services. The compromise solution was the Diogenes Club, a facility open to both students and faculty members that served as something of an additional dining hall as well as a convenient meeting place.

The four faculty members and five students of the new department thus gathered at the club at 8:00 that evening, after Garner had placed hasty calls to his colleagues. Their reaction was not quite what he'd expected. He'd assumed that, like himself, they'd be annoyed that the victory of a student-free semester had been snatched from their teeth at the very last moment and eager to persuade the students to change their majors to something easier like organic chemistry or theoretical physics first thing Monday morning. But Wilda Dittman seemed positively giddy—or at least as giddy as the often-morose Wilda Dittman ever became—that she'd actually have someone to teach her recent and somewhat arcane insights into post-modernist literary theory. Ralph Briggs had simply assumed that his classes in the philosophy of language would "make." And Sabrina Pope seemed positively disappointed that *only* five students had decided to pursue the new degree. As the only member of the Department of Eminent Scholars whose course enrollments had been close to the university average, she'd expected her classes to start out at ten times the number of students Garner had mentioned and to grow from there once word of her scintillating wit became well known.

It was, in short, a lost cause. Garner quickly realized that his goal of spending all his time that year in solitary contemplation would no longer be possible. He now had only the weekend to plan his first class, and it would need to be the sort of thing he could teach in his sleep, if necessary. As a result, the goal of the dinner at the Diogenes Club was to discuss with the students who would be teaching what during their first term and to draw up a schedule that could quickly be entered into the registrar's computer so that the five newcomers could be enrolled.

Garner arrived at the club with a stack full of printouts, listing the courses proposed by the faculty members, all of which existed only as titles with remarkably little thought given to what those courses would actually contain. With a good deal of give and take, fueled by numerous rounds of the club's Professorial Martinis, the faculty members agreed that the department's fall offerings would be as follows:

1. Introduction to Ancient Greek I (MTWThF 8:00-8:50 am): Garner

2. The Art, Literature, and Music of the Ancient Near East (MWF 9:00-9:50 am): Pope

3. Gottlob Frege's Theory of Sense and Reference (MWF 11:00-11:50 am): Briggs

4. Modernism and Post-modernism: An Introduction (MWF 4:00-4:50 pm): Dittman

5. Proseminar in Eminent Scholarship (TTh 10:00-11:20 am): Pope

6. Wittgenstein, Austin, and Searle (TTh 3:00-4:20 pm): Briggs

"It's an incredibly attractive schedule," Garner said, delighted that, from 9:00 am onward each day his time would be his own and that all he'd have to teach that year were the fundamentals of ancient Greek, a task that would require absolutely no preparation at all.

"I quite agree," the Warren-Whitehead twins said in unison, although for entirely different reasons than those that occurred to the professor. Like the other students in the room, they were genuinely excited by the courses they'd now be taking.

"You know," Sabrina Pope added, "this dinner has been lovely. In order to help us all stay 'on the same page,' as it were, and pull together the material from these six courses, we should continue to get together like this."

"A weekly departmental dinner. I like it," concluded Ralph Briggs, who would have liked any idea that included the promise of a free meal.

"*Weekly?*" asked Garner, appalled at the idea of sacrificing so much time on "frivolous social events." "No, no, no. Once or twice a semester will do."

"Not often enough," objected Wilda Dittman. "How about monthly?"

"Semi-weekly?" countered Pope.

"Let's just leave it as 'periodically,' concluded Briggs, who sought to establish himself as the department's mediator and (he hoped) chair. "We can work out the details later. But what we need right now is a name for our little group."

"A name?" grumbled Garner. "We already *have* a name: the Eminent Scholars."

"That's fine for us," Briggs said. "But we need something that also includes our five outstanding majors, what we've all been calling our *imminent scholars*."

"The Eminent and Imminent Scholars?" Dittman suggested.

"Too prosaic," Garner replied.

"The Algonquin Roundtable?" Briggs proposed.

"Too *New Yorker*ish," Garner said, shaking his head. "Besides, we're neither Algonquin nor seated about a round table."

"The Bloomsbury Group?"

"Too English. And I doubt that any of us relishes filling our pockets with stones and marching off into the river."

"The Salon?"

"Too French. And people will expect us to do their hair and nails."

"I've got it," Bastian Lewis said, after having been silent the entire evening until this very moment. "Since we'll all be studying classical languages, art, and literature, why don't we call ourselves the Scipionic Circle?"

Something approaching a smile appeared on Garner's lips. "Out of the mouths of babes," he said. "I like it."

CHAPTER FIVE

The Caretaker

The original Scipionic Circle, a group of intellectuals during the Roman Republic who all came under the patronage of Scipio Aemilianus, the Roman general who oversaw the final defeat of Carthage, had included such figures as the playwright Terence, the historian Polybius, and the satirist Gaius Lucilius. There was no guarantee that either the faculty members or the students would produce works that would still be read two thousand years after their time, but what one fails to dream one fails to attain. And so, the Scipionic Circle it was, and the Scipionic Circle it would remain.

The gathering broke up soon afterward, the students returning to their residence halls with souls stirred by the promise of the semester ahead, and the faculty members returning to their homes with plans that mostly included glasses of port or sherry, a good book, and (eventually) sleep. Only one member of the group deviated from this pattern. Garner realized that he had an unanticipated problem on his hands: Because he had never expected that he'd actually be teaching that fall, he'd neglected to order any textbooks. His colleagues might well be in the same situation, but their courses were more easily handled with online assignments, scans to the college's course information system, or simply no textbook at all until their orders could be filled either by Amazon or the campus bookstore.

But introducing students to the ancient Greek language required textbooks from the very first day. And so, Garner headed back to Chudwell Hall, where he hoped to find a solution in his office. Since the class was small, he thought he might have just enough "desk copies"—the term used for the free books sent to professors who adopted a text for their courses—on the shelves to serve the students' immediate needs. Morally, desk copies were not supposed to be resold (and many publishers indicated as much by stamping on each book's fore-edge a severe warning similar to those threatening dire consequences to anyone who dared to open a pharaoh's tomb or remove the tag from a throw pillow), but giving them away or at least letting the students borrow them until their own copies came in? That was a gray area so light that it was practically as pure as the driven snow.

As he walked down the corridor toward his office, Garner felt distinctly ill at ease in his stomach, not from the numerous Professorial Martinis he'd consumed at dinner, but by the fact that his office door was open, and the light was on. He was sure that he'd locked up tightly before heading off to the Diogenes Club. Otherwise, someone might sneak in and steal his Teubner Bacchylides, a volume that he was certain would fetch a healthy sum on eBay. His anxiety turned to fear as soon as he saw an emaciated old man in gray overalls emerge from the office, carrying the wastepaper basket he kept beside his desk.

Both men were startled by the presence of the other.

"Who be you?" the stranger said.

"Who are *you*?" Garner replied.

The rail-thin worker sighed deeply and informed Garner that his name was Sexton, and he was the building's caretaker.

"I didn't know Chudwell Hall *had* a caretaker," Garner said.

"Who d'ya think was emptyin' your trash every day?"

"I always just assumed that just happened automatically somehow."

"I see," Sexton remarked, although he somehow made the expression *I see* sound almost like a synonym for *idiot*.

"I don't recall seeing you before," Garner observed.

"I works nights."

"I'm here most nights."

"Leavin' by about 1:00 a.m., I notice. That's why I usually do this wing last."

"Then what're you doing here now? It's only a bit past ten."

"You went out for dinner with them others. I assumed you wasn't coming back."

"You're rather observant for a janitor."

"I prefers the term *maintenance engineer* or, as I was sayin', *caretaker*. Besides, the word *janitor* ain't never used properly in this country, anyways. Originally, the term meant ... "

"'Door keeper,' from the Latin *ianua*, meaning *door*. Yes, I know. I'm a classicist." Then Garner hastened to clarify what he meant because, nine times out of ten, when he told people that he taught the Classics, they assumed he meant Dickens and Brontë. "That is to say, I teach Greek and Latin."

"Then ya shoulda known better."

"Observant *and* insolent. You missed your calling. *You* should've been a French waiter."

"Can't abide snails mesef'."

"Well, I'd love to stand here all night, bantering with you about vocational roads not taken, but, if you'll step aside, I have work to do in my office. I'm sure you have urinal cakes to deliver or some other pressing engagement."

Sexton eyed Garner for an uncomfortably long time. "I don't know you personally, Professor Garner, but I do *know* you. For more n' forty year I've spent most of every day here in Chudwell Hall, and I've come to be familiar with the type of professor whose head's too big and whose world's too small. So, if you don't mind, I'll be emptyin' your garbage, but I won't be takin' it."

"If you're not actually going to take that garbage you're holding there, you might as well hand it back."

"Not big on what's called mettyfors for a classicist, are you, Professor Garner?"

Sexton dumped the contents of the wastebasket into a nearby cart and stepped aside.

* * *

Garner's exchange with the caretaker hadn't concluded more than five minutes earlier, but Garner had already removed Sexton from his mind. He had his textbook problem to solve, and he wondered whether his bookshelves contained enough copies of Chase and Phillips (the book from which he himself had learned Greek) or Crosby and Schaeffer (a book that students seemed to prefer but that he regarded as insufficiently challenging for college students) for the start of his class. But he discovered that he owned only four copies of the first book and three of the second, not enough for himself and all five students.

Then, out of the corner of his eye, he caught sight of a row of newer books. Nine brand new copies of Frank Beetham's *Learning Greek with Plato*, which had only come out in 2007, stood side by side. He'd never actually adopted the textbook, but the publisher dutifully sent him an examination copy nearly every year. Garner hefted the book in his hand. It felt weighty, significant, scholarly. It contained twenty-five chapters, followed by more than 150 pages of supplementary material.

With his class meeting five days a week, assigning a chapter a day would mean that the students would have been introduced to the fundamentals of grammar by the end of September.

The book and his plan were perfect. The students would either rise to the occasion and truly *become* imminent scholars or they'd give up, drop his course, and free up his day for his own scholarly pursuits.

CHAPTER SIX

"The Road Up and the Road Down Are the Same"

At precisely 8:00 a.m. the following Monday, Garner entered his classroom in Chudwell Hall, closed the door, and locked it. The last of these actions was unnecessary. He'd made it his habit for years to lock the door at the start of class as a way of preventing any late-arriving students from entering. He saw this tactic as having a dual purpose: It prevented his lesson from being disrupted, and it made it far less likely that any student who was excluded from the class would ever commit that offense a second time. On this particular Monday, however, all five students enrolled in the new program were already in place, and there was thus no one left who might arrive late.

Nearly all the buildings at Mersley College had replaced chalkboards with marker boards or so-called "smart boards" ages ago. But Chudwell Hall, having been shuttered and virtually abandoned, still had old-fashioned blackboards on all the walls except the one that had windows to the outside. Garner stepped to the front of the room and wrote the following sentence with his typically neat and elegant handwriting:

ὁδὸς ἄνω κάτω μία καὶ ὠυτή.

Then he proceeded to read the sentence, using the Erasmian pronunciation of ancient Greek. "hah-DOSS AH-noh KAH-toh MEE-ya kye hoh-oo-TAY. Can anyone tell me what this means? No? Of course, you can't. If you could, you wouldn't need this course. So, let me translate it for you. 'The road up and the road down are the same.' It's an observation by the philosopher Heraclitus, and what *he* meant by it is likely to consume many of our discussions throughout your time here at Mersley. Some of you may think I chose to begin our course with this particular observation as a warning: The road up to success in this major and down to failure in this major are one and the same. Both consist of wholehearted dedication and constant study. Engage in them, and you'll succeed. Ignore them, even for a moment, and you'll surely fail. That would be an appropriate lesson for me to convey to you, but it wasn't exactly why I chose to begin our course with Heraclitus. My meaning will, I hope, become clear to you by the end of our hour together. For now, however, let me simply leave you to ponder my possible intention and to ask you a different question: 'Why, in this modern age, would anyone want to study a language no one speaks?' Behind that question is, of course, the first thing all of you must understand. Socrates spoke a language that we call Greek, and Yiorgos down at the Parthenon Grill speaks a language that we call Greek, but they're not entirely the same language. Cicero spoke a language we call Latin, but Marco down at Basta di Pasta speaks a language we call Italian, and yet ancient Greek bears to modern Greek a somewhat similar relationship that Latin bears to Italian. If you think that, at the end of this course, you'll be able to order a dish of moussaka on the island of Santorini, you're sorely mistaken. The grammatical rules we shall learn are somewhat different. The vocabulary is somewhat different. And the pronunciation is *entirely* different.

"You're about, in other words, to embark on a study of *classical* Greek. And that leads me to yet another question. Greek and Latin are together considered the 'classical' languages. My degrees are in a field called 'Classics.' You all know a good bit of Latin. Otherwise, you wouldn't have been admitted to this program. So, what makes Greek and Latin 'classical'? Why, for centuries, did those who wished to become 'classically educated' study works in these two languages?"

Garner paused for a moment and then said. "I know it can be confusing sometimes, but that *wasn't* a rhetorical question. I'd actually like you to answer it."

Immediately, Esmé Dawson raised her hand. "Because they were the languages of the church, and Western universities were created primarily to produce members of the clergy."

Garner pursed his lips and replied, "Not a bad answer ... as far as it goes. And, in fact, it's a better answer than I might have expected. But it can't be the *entire* answer. After all, the Christian scriptures are written primarily in *Hebrew* and Greek, with a little bit of Aramaic tossed in for seasoning, I suppose." He chuckled at his own joke. "Latin was indeed the language of the Western church, so it made sense for clergymen to know it, but why stop two-thirds of the way toward the goal? Why not also include *Hebrew* in a classical education? Does anyone else know of any *other* reason why Greek and Latin may have been singled out as *the* classical languages? You there, for instance."

He was pointing at Bastian Lewis, who'd also raised his hand. "Global power was achieved by building a navy and forging an empire," Lewis suggested. "Athens and Rome both had empires defended primarily by their navies, so for members of the elite to study them simply made sense and, in order to study Athens and Rome, one had to learn Greek and Latin."

Garner seemed pleasantly surprised. "Another intriguing possibility, and one that I might even acknowledge as the *complete* answer if we were living in the United Kingdom. Britain was, of course, the great empire and naval power throughout the nineteenth century, and I suspect that many members of the aristocracy *did* develop an interest in the classical languages for the very reasons you mentioned. But again, I believe there are more factors at work here. Shall I tell you? And, in case you're wondering, that *was* a rhetorical question. I'm going to tell you anyway. Greek and Latin became the classical languages because, in their grammar and hence in their reflection of the world, they are utterly and completely dissimilar. In fact, I'd go so far as to say that Latin stands at one pole when it comes to the way in which languages work, and Greek stands at the other.

"That answer surprises many people. The common assumption is that Greek and Latin are very *similar* languages. To hear some people speak, they're even the *same* language, and Greece and Rome were the *same* culture. They'll tell you that *democracy* and *philosophy* are derived from Latin roots. They're not; those words are purely Greek. They'll form what they call a 'Greek' fraternity and then throw a 'toga party,' adopting a term for a traditionally Roman style of dress and confusing tunics and togas in the process. But the very first thing you have to know in this course is that, for whatever you've learned about Latin, the opposite will be true for Greek.

"Latin is an astoundingly regular language. Depending on your perspective, I think it's possible to say that there are only six irregular verbs in Latin—*sum, possum, volo, nolo, mallo,* and *eo*—and several of those verbs are irregular *in the same way*. So, you could even claim that Latin has *no* irregular verbs, just six verbs that form their conjugations one way, and all the rest that form their conjugations a different way.

"Now, I can guess what you're thinking: 'That's not really true. There are four different conjugations in Latin, five if you treat third conjugation verbs ending in *-o* as different from third conjugation verbs ending in *-io*. But that distinction is minimal. Most Latin verbs really work by having a stem, following it with the characteristic vowel of the conjugation (*a*, long *e*, short *e*, or *i*), followed by a personal ending. What makes those six verbs I mentioned 'irregular' is that they don't have an easily recognizable characteristic vowel. There are other differences, too, but that's the main one.

"Greek is entirely different. It's hyperbole to say that there's no such thing as a 'regular' verb in Greek, but it's also not that far from the truth. Oh, I mean we'll learn the so-called 'regular' conjugations, but you'll notice that, once we get into actual texts, almost every verb you encounter has some peculiar form or another, at least in some tense or mood. And then there are *dialect* forms, which make the whole thing even more complicated.

"Once you begin to realize that, as a language, Latin is regular and systematic while Greek is irregular and unsystematic, you start seeing evidence of that everywhere. In fact, I have a little rule of thumb I use that refers to that very idea: Greek either has one more or one less of anything that Latin has ... whichever makes it harder. Latin has singulars and plurals; Greek has singulars, plurals, and *duals*, a special number used only for pairs of things. Latin has indicative and subjunctive moods; Greek has indicative, subjunctive, and *optative* moods, the last of these being one step further away from reality than the subjunctive. Latin has present, future, perfect, imperfect, pluperfect, and future perfect tenses; Greek has all these plus an *aorist* tense so that it can divide the Latin perfect in two: actions that were completed in the past and are now not really relevant versus actions that were completed in the past and are now still relevant. If that doesn't seem to make any sense, think about the ambiguity of the English sentence *Yesterday, I filled my car's gas tank*. In ancient Greek, if you filled the tank yesterday but then drove the car around so that the tank is no longer full, you would use the aorist. If you filled the tank yesterday but then put the car immediately into the garage with the result that the tank is still full, you would use the perfect. In fact, we'll learn later in the course that, technically, the aorist, perfect, and imperfect aren't even tenses. They're as*pects*, but that's a lesson for another day.

"Now, I said that Greek either has one more or one *less* of anything that Latin has, whichever makes it harder, so how can lacking something that Latin has create more challenges for new students of Greek? Well, think about declensions, for example. Latin has the nominative, genitive, dative, accusative, and ablative cases. You're all used to those. But Greek has no ablative case. That means that all those uses of the ablative you learn about in Latin class—place where, place from which, agent, means, and so on—are now distributed among the other cases. Which use then goes with which case? Well, you have to learn each one of those individually, and yes, there are exceptions. Loads of them.

"So, my view is that Greek and Latin are the bedrock of a classical education because they are utterly different ways of conveying meaning. Greek is an irrational, bear-hugging, frequently drunken uncle; Latin is a strict, teetotaling, church-going spinster. Which is better? Certainly, some students *prefer* one language over the other, but to me, that means they're not true classicists. It is my perspective—and since you're in my class, you'll be forced to share my perspective until you've become expert enough in the subject matter to earn a perspective of your own—is that the whole purpose of a classical education is to learn that life isn't about the either/or; it's about the both/and.

"Think about it for a moment. A classical education constantly confronts you with an entire series of contrasts: Greek versus Latin, Athens versus Sparta, Apollo versus Dionysus, Plato versus Aristotle, Stoicism versus Epicureanism, the Roman Republic versus the Roman Empire, Caesar versus Cicero ... we really could go on all day. The point is that, for all the temptation we have to say things like, 'I love Sophocles, can't stand Euripides' or 'Catullus is wonderful; Vergil is wretched,' we'd be missing the point. Life doesn't let you choose just one, and none of us should want to. There are times when we need the complexity of Greek and times when we need the rigid regularity of Latin, times when we need the simple style of Caesar and times when we need the robust style of Cicero. You could say something similar for any of the pairs I mentioned, as well as many others.

"It's also true that there are times when these contrasts are meaningless or when they collapse upon close examination. For example, a statement can be so simple that it becomes infinitely complex, as in haiku, and a mathematical formula can be so complex that it reveals something very simple and fundamental about the world. All of which leads us back to our starting point, Heraclitus here. 'The road up and the road down are the same.' There are times when a contrast is merely a matter of perspective. Person A says, 'Main Street is a road leading into Mersley,' while Person B says 'Main Street is a road leading out of Mersley,' and both of them are completely right. Those opposites are meaningful (when considering perspective) and meaningless (when considering identity) at the same time.

"I suspect you'll encounter Heraclitus quite a bit in this program. He was fascinated by opposites and by their ultimate unity. In one place, he says, 'The immortal are mortal, and the mortal are immortal, living their death and dying their lives.' I suppose what he means by this is ... no, it's better if I leave you to discover that for yourselves. But I will explain this saying of his: 'God is day/night, winter/summer, war/peace, satisfaction/hunger.' What I believe he's saying here is that if you investigate anything at its highest level—what he calls God or 'the divine,' and what we might call 'ultimate reality'—you discover that the pigeonholes we invent to place things in ultimately don't matter. The beginning and the end are always the same. Life itself isn't about the either/or. It's always about the both/and.

"So, I hope you'll contemplate the significance of these ideas as you begin your study of ancient Greek. And make no mistake about it: Even at the end of the year, even at the end of your entire program, you'll still only be at the *beginning* of your study of Greek. You won't master it until someday you teach a class like this yourself ... and perhaps not even then. Greek is the sort of pursuit that you need to steep yourself in for thirty or forty years, and only then might certain things begin to make sense.

"But if you're still keen to start, here's your assignment for tomorrow. Learn the Greek alphabet. It'll seem clumsy at first, but trust me: If you stick with this course, by the time six weeks have passed, you'll be reading it as easily as you can read the English alphabet now. For the moment, ignore the accents and breathing marks. I'll explain those later this week. But I want everyone who shows up here at 8:00 a.m. tomorrow to know all twenty-four letters by heart. Any questions? No? Good. Dismissed."

As the students filed out of the room, Garner handed each of them a textbook, informing them that it was only "on loan" until their own copies arrived and that they were to treat it with the utmost respect.

Once they turned the corner of the hallway and were en route to their class with Sabrina Pope, Mallory Warren-Whitehead asked her sister, "Well, what did you think?"

Rather breathlessly, Prudence replied, "I think I just learned more in the last hour than I did in all of high school."

CHAPTER SEVEN

The War on Whiteheads

Prudence Warren-Whitehead was ninety-three minutes older than her identical twin, Mallory, but few people would have guessed that. The two were so alike that they could trade places at will and go completely undetected. Even Hector and Julia Warren-Whitehead, the twins' parents, often could not tell them apart. There was only one subtle difference.

Mallory was the leader, Prudence the follower. As had occurred during their conversation in the hallway, Mallory was usually the one who asked the questions; Prudence was the one who answered. But that distinguishing trait was not as obvious as one might assume. The Warren-Whitehead girls thought so similarly about most things that it was rarely necessary for any questions to be asked. Nine times out of ten, Mallory knew precisely what Prudence was thinking, and vice versa. The inquiry about Garner's course thus arose, not so much from a desire for knowledge, as from a need for confirmation.

Hector Warren had married Julia Whitehead in an age when the surrender of a woman's identity by taking her husband's name was regarded as no less out-of-date than corsets and spittoons. If Julia had followed the custom subscribed to by most of her friends, she would have become Julia Warren-Whitehead while Hector's name would have remained unchanged. But Hector told Julia that, if she was willing to change her last name, then so would he. And so, the pair jointly became the Warren-Whiteheads the moment they filed their marriage license. Nevertheless, Hector was not as progressive as he claimed to be. He actually regarded the family name Warren-Whitehead as sounding a bit more impressive than the name Warren alone, and with his pretensions of not merely being employed by the New National Financial Group, but of someday *heading* it, a hyphenated name that bore a whiff of aristocracy seemed a highly desirable possession.

That decision did not, however, do any favors to Hector and Julia's offspring. Prudence and Mallory were the couple's only children, and they were, if one may be so tactless as to mention it, far from beautiful. They were the sort of girls that one describes as "sweet" or "having a good personality," largely as a means of avoiding references to their physical appearance altogether. On the best of days, the twins might be generously regarded as "plain." On the worst of days (and there were plenty enough of those), they were the sort of people who soon learned never to ask, "What do you think of my new haircut?" because the frozen look on their interlocutors' faces told a tale they rarely wished to hear.

By the time they reached high-school age, problematic complexions complicated their already-troubled appearance. Thus, saddled with the patronymic "Warren-Whitehead," their attempts to ameliorate this situation quickly caused them to be dubbed "The War on Whiteheads" by those students at Middleton Country Day School who considered themselves the Oscar Wildes and Dorothy Parkers of their generation.

The girls, who had from birth felt more at ease in one another's company than in anyone else's, thus turned more and more inward as the days went by. Some twins invent their own language; the Warren-Whiteheads invented their own universe. While their contemporaries spent their free afternoons at field hockey and impromptu parties, the twins spent theirs in libraries and dusty bookshops. While their contemporaries were reading Harry Potter and immersing themselves in *The Lord of The Rings*, Prudence and Mallory were reading Harold Bloom and immersing themselves in *Lord of the Flies*. Students at their school were allotted two free periods a day in order to study, attend meetings of clubs, or engage in team sports. The twins were having none of that nonsense. Already enrolled in Latin, they had their parents petition the school for permission to replace their first free period with French and their second free period with German. In their final year, when other Country Day students eagerly enrolled in a newly-created physical education course, Prudence and Mallory chose instead to add Mandarin Chinese to their schedules. Such decisions meant that "The War on Whiteheads" soon became the *least* offensive sobriquet applied to the girls.

But the Warren-Whiteheads were blithely indifferent to peer pressure, popular taste, and the sort of groupthink that commonly afflicts youths of their age. Their contemporaries applied to flagship universities and tony private colleges in their senior year. Prudence and Mallory resolved to attend Mersley College, and no other, largely because *none* of the other students at Middleton Country Day would deign to set foot there. Although private, Mersley could hardly be called "tony." Its tuition was regarded as reasonable by the sheer fact that it offered no scholarships and never engaged in "tuition discounting." The price listed online was, to the dollar, the price one paid to attend the school ... unless, like their new companion Esmé Dawson, their tuition was subsidized by one of the so-called Mersley Angels, private citizens who underwrote the cost for a student with limited financial resources. For an up-and-coming employee of the New National Financial Group, Mersley college's tuition was still quite reasonable, even when two children were enrolled at once.

As much as the two girls had been looking forward to their transition from high school to college, they were disappointed during the school's new student orientation, an event that the admissions staff had dubbed WOW! for "Week of Welcome!" The dark earth tones of their tweed skirts, the chunkiness of their loafers, and the old-fashioned look of their button-up tops set them apart from the bright colors and political-button-burdened backpacks of the other women in their cohort. When the simplest activity made other first-year women squeal with delight, "The War on Whiteheads" (yes, the name had already been reinvented at Mersley) engaged in the numerous icebreakers with the same grit that severely injured patients use when struggling through physical therapy. "Perhaps if we just get through this," they seemed to be thinking, "it will pay off somehow."

By the second day of WOW!, the twins were the last to be selected by any team for group activities. By the third day, they weren't selected at all. They ate alone. They completed their paperwork alone. At the end of each day, they returned to their residence hall alone.

It was the very isolation of the girls that caused Townsant to notice them. Although he never exchanged a word with them, he sensed that the three of them were somehow kindred spirits. Thus, when Professor Garner insisted that he find four other students to enroll with him in the new major, he began to walk along the quad like Jesus strolling along the shore of the Sea of Galilee, and summoned them to be his Peter and Andrew, leaving Esmé and Bastian to become his James and John.

CHAPTER EIGHT

The Department Chair

The first week of classes continued uneventfully, and Garner felt a combination of surprise, disappointment, and satisfaction that none of the five students dropped any of their courses. He was surprised because he knew that the homework he assigned each night required at least an hour to complete; Briggs and Dittman were notorious for their lengthy assignments, often requiring more than a hundred pages of reading *per class session*. He was disappointed because the add-drop period at Mersley lasted only a week and, if his course was not canceled for low enrollment by the following Monday, his dreams of a full semester devoted to nothing but research were well and truly dead. But he was also satisfied because, for the moment, all five imminent scholars were keeping up with their work and actually seemed capable of fulfilling his plan of reading Plato in Greek after only five weeks of language instruction.

Thursday afternoon, just as Professor Briggs' course on Wittgenstein, Austin, and Searle was about to conclude, Garner heard a "ping" on his computer. He glanced up from his Bacchylides to see the following email.

> TO: rbriggs@mersley.edu; wdittman@mersley.edu; wgarner@mersley.edu; spope@mersley.edu
>
> FROM: dmcdaniel@mersley.edu
>
> RE: Department Chair
>
> The Department of Eminent Scholars was not represented at this week's meeting of the Dean's Council. After checking my records, I have discovered that your program never elected a department chair or, if it did, never reported the result to my office.

> Please elect your chair as soon as possible, submit the chair's name to my office, and have the chair present at next week's meeting of the Dean's Council, 8:00 am Thursday, in Old Main 104.

"Administrivia," Garner muttered to himself. He clicked REPLY ALL and tapped out the following message.

> TO: dmcdaniel@mersley.edu
>
> CC: rbriggs@mersley.edu; wdittman@mersley.edu; spope@mersley.edu
>
> FROM: wgarner@mersley.edu
>
> RE: Re: Department Chair
>
> As a small department that consists of nothing but dedicated and conscientious professionals, the Department of Eminent Scholars makes all its decisions in camera and in plenary. (Feel free to ask if either term is unfamiliar to you.) Therefore, the department has no need for a department chair.
>
> Moreover, given that most sessions of the Dean's Council are devoted to such scintillating topics as "learning outcomes assessment" and "inclusivity initiatives," which have no relevance to our program, we respectfully (?) decline your invitation to be represented at these meetings.

Fewer than five minutes had elapsed before another "ping" was heard on Garner's computer. What the Mersley faculty would later refer to as "the email wars" had begun.

> TO: rbriggs@mersley.edu; wdittman@mersley.edu; wgarner@mersley.edu; spope@mersley.edu
>
> FROM: dmcdaniel@mersley.edu
>
> RE: Re: Re: Department Chair

Please consult Section 45.A.1 on page 412 of the Mersley College Faculty Handbook where it states that each department MUST elect or have appointed a department chair and be represented at the weekly meetings of the Dean's Council.

Furthermore, I am alarmed to discover that you claim learning outcomes assessment and inclusivity initiatives have no relevance to your program. Might I remind you that quality assurance and our multiculturalism, diversity, and inclusivity initiative are taken very seriously by our governing board, accreditors, and donors? Please rectify these oversights and notify my office when you have done so.

By the way, I will remind you as well that I am a classicist myself and, like you, a recipient of the Covington Prize. I am perfectly aware of what "in camera" and "in plenary" mean.

Moments before sending this message, Dean McDaniel had used the DELETE key to remove the words *damn well* and replace them with *perfectly*. These messages might serve as evidence in a hearing someday, and the dean wanted to avoid any appearance of personal rancor in her dealings with the department.

Warming to his task, Garner then submitted the following reply immediately upon receipt of the new message.

> TO: dmcdaniel@mersley.edu
>
> CC: rbriggs@mersley.edu; wdittman@mersley.edu; spope@mersley.edu
>
> FROM: wgarner@mersley.edu
>
> RE: Re: Re: Re: Department Chair
>
> I note that, while the aforementioned Section 45.A.1 on page 412 of the Mersley College Faculty Handbook

> does indeed state that each department must have a chair who attends meetings of the Dean's Council, it provides absolutely no sanctions for failure to do so. Confronted by what is no more than a toothless lion, I reiterate that we waive our rights to have a department chair and to ~~waste~~ spend our time in meetings of yet another committee.
>
> Moreover, if the goal of Mersley College is quality assurance, then I can assure you that the quality of teaching, research, and service in the Department of Eminent Scholars is already excellent. If the goal of Mersley College is multiculturalism, then I can assure you we have attained that goal as well: In my own courses, students will study both Latin and Greek, two cultures that thus make my courses, by definition, multicultural. Other members of the department will be assigning works in English, French, and German, making our program perhaps the MOST multicultural on campus.

If Garner had followed McDaniel's lead and actually *replaced* the word *waste* with *spend*, no trace of that substitution would have remained in the message. The fact that he lined out the word *waste* meant that he had needed to consult the email system's online manual for instructions on alternate character styles in an effort to insert an unmistakable barb into his reply.

This time, barely a minute elapsed before the next "ping" was heard.

> TO: rbriggs@mersley.edu; wdittman@mersley.edu; wgarner@mersley.edu; spope@mersley.edu
>
> FROM: dmcdaniel@mersley.edu
>
> RE: Re: Re: Re: Re: Department Chair
>
> Isn't there anyone ELSE in the department I can talk to?

Apparently, interactions with Professor Garner had made the dean feel precisely the way that Townsant had felt on their first meeting. Moments later, McDaniel's message elicited the following response.

> TO: dmcdaniel@mersley.edu
>
> CC: rbriggs@mersley.edu; wdittman@mersley.edu; spope@mersley.edu
>
> FROM: wgarner@mersley.edu
>
> RE: Re: Re: Re: Re: Re: Department Chair
>
> Regrettably, Professor Briggs has not yet returned from class, and my other colleagues have already left for the day. By default, therefore, I speak for all of us.

Dean McDaniel must have been typing her answer even before she received Garner's email because it arrived while his finger was still on the SEND key.

> TO: rbriggs@mersley.edu; wdittman@mersley.edu; wgarner@mersley.edu; spope@mersley.edu
>
> FROM: dmcdaniel@mersley.edu
>
> RE: Re: Re: Re: Re: Re: Re: Department Chair
>
> Although it goes against my grain to issue a direct order to a faculty member, I am empowered to do so and shall do so now.
>
> 1. The Department of Eminent Scholars is hereby ORDERED to elect a department chair before next week's meeting of the Dean's Council.
>
> 2. That chair is hereby ORDERED to attend all meetings of the Dean's Council from this date forward.
>
> 3. The Department of Eminent Scholars is hereby ORDERED to submit a plan for the assessment of student learning outcomes that meets with my approval

and the approval of the college-wide curriculum committee. This plan must have received all approvals by the end of the fall semester.

4. The Department of Eminent Scholars is hereby ORDERED to submit a plan for diversity, equity, and inclusivity that meets with my approval and the approval of the college-wide diversity committee. This plan must have received all approvals by the end of the fall semester.

Failure to comply with ANY of these requirements will be regarded as insubordination and grounds for the dissolution of the Department of Eminent Scholars, along with the termination of all faculty members as permitted in Section 91.E.7 on page 981 of the Mersley College Faculty Handbook.

Garner stared at the new message, aware that his own petulant reference to outcomes assessment and multiculturalism had now made the matter much, much worse. He hadn't quite decided how to deal with the situation when another reply arrived from the dean, this one addressed to Garner alone.

TO: wgarner@mersley.edu

FROM: dmcdaniel@mersley.edu

RE: Re: Re: Re: Re: Re: Re: Department Chair

CHECK and MATE.

* * *

It was Monday afternoon, in the scheduling gap that occurred between Briggs's Theory of Sense and Reference course and Dittman's Modernism and Post-modernism course, that the eminent scholars finally met in order to deal with the dean's directives.

"Well, obviously, the chair issue is the most pressing," Sabrina Pope said. "These other two issues could wait. We've got the whole semester."

"A semester that'll be over before we know it," Ralph Briggs replied. "No, I say, we jump on all of this and get it off our agendas."

"Agenda," Garner corrected him. "The word is already plural. The singular is *agendum*."

Now, until this point, Briggs had coveted the chair's position like he had never coveted anything before. He believed it would be a sinecure that would both raise his salary and significantly improve his retirement fund. But suddenly it became very clear to him what serving as Winton Garner's supervisor on a daily basis would be like, and his passion for college administration left him as swiftly as the air escaping from a punctured balloon.

"Noted," he said tersely.

"Anyway, how do you propose we resolve these matters quickly?" Garner asked. "We just created a 180-hour major. That's fifty-four different courses, not including the thesis. If each course requires five to ten learning outcomes plus a policy statement on diversity, equity and 'inclusivity,' we'll be at this for *weeks*."

"Nonsense," Briggs contradicted him. "We can wrap up this nonsense even before lunch."

"Tell me, Obi-Wan Kenobi," Wilda Dittman asked, "just how do you propose we accomplish this miracle?"

"I'm so glad you asked," Briggs replied. He opened up a weather-beaten leather portfolio and extracted a stack of papers. He handed part of the stack to each of the others and kept an equal portion for himself. "These are the assessment and diversity plans of all the other programs at Mersley. I took the liberty of sending electronic copies to your faculty drives. Here's what I propose: For each course, take one assessment plan and one diversity plan from another department's course, open it in your word processor, and do a global search-and-replace on the name of the original course with the name of your course. I've already tried it with five courses of my own. Literally, it takes seconds."

"But that's plagiarism, isn't it?" Sabrina Pope asked.

"If you read what other departments have submitted," Briggs explained, "you'll find that, except for a word or two, most of these plans are identical, anyway. Don't call it plagiarism; call it research."

"But then, after we submit the assessments," Dittman asked, "won't it look strange that we haven't actually *done* any of these things?"

"You don't seriously believe that anyone *reads* assessment reports, do you?" Briggs countered. "It's just a matter of ticking off a few boxes. As long as you turn something in, no one will care."

"Great," Garner said, "we can ship all this stuff to the dean's office this afternoon, then."

"Oh, I wouldn't do that," Briggs replied. "I'd say we do the work this afternoon, but then hold on to it. In maybe three weeks, one of us sends in his or her submissions. A week or two later, a second person does, and so on. That way, it looks as though we're really giving our full attention to this nonsense."

"Brilliant!" Garner replied. "But it still doesn't solve the chair issue."

"I've been thinking about that, too," Briggs said. And that was true. He'd been thinking about it for much of the last thirty seconds. "I think it best that we all 'spread the wealth,' as it were."

"You mean spread the manure," Garner corrected him.

"Same principle. Each of us serves as department chair for one year, and then the baton is passed to the next person. Whoever is chair should be one of the people who's only teaching a single course that year. Now, Sabrina and I are both teaching two courses this term, so that means we need to elect either Winton or Wilda as our founding chair."

"Can't be me," Garner informed the others. "Dean's Council meets at 8:00 each Thursday. That conflicts with my Greek class."

All eyes turned to Wilda Dittman. Her only course met at four o'clock three days a week, none of which was Thursday.

Seeing the inevitable, she said. "All right. But here's my first decree as chair of the Department of Eminent Scholars." She divided her packet of papers into three and distributed them among the others. "You all do my outcomes and diversity policies *for* me. I'm off to prepare for class."

CHAPTER NINE

A Theory on Theories

Unlike Winton Garner, Wilda Dittman never closed her door at the start of class. She simply strode in, usually with a thick book under her arm, and started to speak. She gave the impression that she was merely repeating thoughts that had only entered her head moments before, but in fact, each of her class sessions was carefully planned, almost scripted in terms of how it would progress.

"Last week, as you'll recall," she began, "we discussed Charles Darwin's *On the Origin of Species* and *The Descent of Man*. This week we'll devote our attention to Karl Marx's *The Communist Manifesto* and *Das Kapital*. I wanted to start our course in this way because, to my mind and in the opinion of many other scholars, those four works represent the beginning of what we now call 'modernism' in intellectual history. Can anyone tell me why?"

Esmé Dawson, who'd answered Garner's first question with a reference to the church, thought it best to attempt the same strategy in this course as well. "Because they were some of the last nails in the coffin of the Christian church's domination of ideas in the West. Darwin challenged the Adam and Eve story, and Marx challenged the divine right of kings."

"Excellent, Esmé. Bravo." Then Dittman pursed her lips as though a new thought had just occurred to her, even though she was virtually certain at least one of the five students would make this point. "Although it strikes me that it may be a bit much to say that Darwin and Marx put the *last* nails in the coffin of the Christian church's domination of intellectual criticism. In your proseminar with Professor Pope, I'm sure that you'll be discussing such concepts as source criticism, redaction criticism, and form criticism. Early advocates of those intellectual approaches, like Jean Astruc in the eighteenth century or Hermann Gunkel in the nineteenth, did at least as much damage to the Bible's claims of literal accuracy as did Darwin and Marx. Does anyone else care to make a suggestion?"

Even in their first week of college, the five students had learned that success in coursework required two fundamental skills: mastery of the material and mastery of how to *be* a college student. They'd already experienced enough of the pseudo-Socratic method Dittman was using to realize that none of their answers would satisfy her any more than did their answers to Professor Garner on the first day of Greek class. Sooner or later, she would simply answer her own question and, for the sake of efficiency, it may as well be sooner.

"No one? All right. I'll tell you, then. Darwin and Marx began the first widespread use of *theory* by scholars, and it's theory, more than anything else, that defines the Modern Period in the history of ideas. Now, I don't mean to overstate my case. There had been theories long before Darwin and Marx. It's simply that those theories rarely shook society to its core. Galileo and Copernicus did have that kind of effect, of course, and there are others we could name. But after Darwin and Marx, it seemed that, for a time, *every* intellectual discipline became fixated on theory.

"At this point, I should clarify that, unlike its use in everyday speech, an intellectual theory is not the same as an intellectual hypothesis. A hypothesis is a proposed solution that is to be tested by further investigation. To academics, a theory is much larger than that. It's a system of hypotheses, assumptions, and evidence that serves to explain a wide range of phenomena. Darwin's theory of evolution wasn't a mere hypothesis or guess. It was based on qualitative evidence—an impressively large *body* of qualitative evidence at that—as well as certain hypotheses and assumptions. Marx's economic theory wasn't, despite the claim of some politicians, a mere conviction that communism is the best form of government. It wasn't really about government at all. It was a combination of evidence, hypotheses, and assumptions that used economic motivation as an explanation for personal decisions, social trends, history, political movements ... in fact, everything.

"And the theories of Darwin and Marx so took the world by storm that pretty much *every* discipline sought to redesign itself in terms of one or more grand theories. Those are the theories you'll be studying in proseminar. I've already mentioned source criticism, redaction criticism, and form criticism, but there are also Freudian theory, Structuralism, and Reader Response Theory, not to mention literally dozens and dozens of others. Theory is the basis for modernism.

"So, what then is *post*-modernism? Post-modernism is nothing more than throwing theory out the window and seeking other ways of understanding the world. Different scholars will define it in different ways, but, to me, post-modernism is derived from two primary approaches: It is hypothetical rather than foundational, and it is model-based rather than theory-based.

"Now, what do I mean by that distinction? A foundation, as we use the term in intellectual history, is the ultimate, unchallenged basis for any system of thought. If you believe that the Bible is the source of all truth and cannot be challenged, then that's your foundation. In Euclidean geometry, students learn three definitions and five axioms or postulates; those are Euclidean geometry's foundation. In Cartesian philosophy, "*Cogito, ergo sum*" is the foundation. A foundation is whatever we take for granted and then build the rest of our intellectual construct on top of that.

"The post-modernists said, 'Let's have no foundation whatsoever.' How do you do that? You base everything on hypotheses. You develop an idea that you believe may explain a phenomenon or some select group of phenomena, and then you test it. As long as the hypothesis remains undisproved (a horrible word, I must admit, but a useful one), the hypothesis is considered valid. But even a single piece of contrary evidence would be enough to disprove the hypothesis and, once the hypothesis is disproven, it must be cast aside and a new hypothesis formed. That's what it means to be hypothetical rather than foundational.

"But what does it mean to be model-based rather than theory-based? Theories, as we've seen, are rather huge constructs. They consist of evidence, hypotheses, and assumptions. But an assumption is a foundation and, remember, the post-modernists reject all foundations. So, they use models instead of theories. A model is simply a collection of evidence and hypotheses that explains a broad range of phenomena and, because it contains hypotheses, a single contrary piece of evidence is all it takes to disprove a model.

"So, there we have it: Modernism equals theory; post-modernism equals hypotheses and models. You can make the distinction as complicated as you like but, once you clear away all the smoke and mirrors, that's what you have left. The whole idea of post-modernism began by coalescing around resistance to one particular literary theory: structuralism. Structuralism arose out of linguistics and, in its original form, is actually quite interesting. It dealt with examining languages in terms of their structures, distinguishing what the linguist Ferdinand de Saussure called *parole* (which you might think of as the grammar or "rules" of a language) and *langue* (actual examples of speech). A further distinction was between the *signifier* (a word or image that represented a person, thing, or idea) and the *signified* (what was represented).

"Theories, however, tend to grow and evolve over time. From Darwinism arose the now-discredited idea of 'social Darwinism,' the concept that societies also 'evolve' and 'become better' over time since only the 'fit' societies survive. From Marxism arose such variants as structural Marxism, neo-Marxism, and a host of others. Structuralism, too, came to be viewed as applicable to anthropology, literary criticism, and other academic pursuits. One branch of structuralism, led by the anthropologist Claude Lévi-Strauss, analyzed a great deal of human experience in terms of contrasting pairs: the raw and the cooked, the fresh and the decayed, the wet and the dry, and so on. Structural literary critics believed that nearly all works of fiction could be examined in terms of a tension between various pairs of opposites.

"But then, a group of literary scholars began to ask: Does anyone really write that way? Can works like *Oedipus* and *Hamlet* and *Jane Eyre* really have originated out of a tension between opposite qualities? Maybe the structuralists are just reading into the works what they *want* to see, like someone seeing a shape image in the clouds, because structuralism is their *foundation*. Let's ignore that foundation and start over. This school of thought is what we know as post-structuralism, and post-structuralists are simply the people who thought they'd developed an approach that superseded structuralism. In time, however, others began to ask 'What's so special about structuralism? Let's throw out *all* foundations and theories and adopt an approach based on hypotheses and models, an approach in which evidence can be used to disprove any inadequate theory. Post-structuralism thus expanded into post-modernism and writers like Darwin, Marx, and Freud were essentially 'shown the door.'

"Okay, then. Let's get back to what we were talking about last week: Darwin's theory is that natural selection results in evolution. If we look at *The Communist Manifesto* and *Das Kapital*, what could we say constituted Marx's theory, and why did so many people find it compelling? I've been talking way too long, so feel free to jump in here. You all did some reading over the weekend. Who can describe for me the Marxist theory in a nutshell? And don't be afraid of oversimplifying. That's what I just did with structuralism and post-structuralism, so a precedent has been set. Yes, Bastian?"

"I think you said it earlier, didn't you?" he asked with an informality that he probably wouldn't have used in his class with

Garner. "All decisions are ultimately economic decisions. People and society may try to veil those decisions with a claim of 'higher motives,' but ultimately they're always just acting in their own economic self-interest."

"Good, Bastian. That shows that you've been paying attention. But your answer could have been given even by a person who was in class today but had done none of the reading assigned over the weekend. Let's probe a little deeper. Why might a classic Marxist say that all decisions are economic decisions? Yes? How would you answer that question?"

Dittman called on a student with a nod of her head. The Warren-Whiteheads had, as they often did, raised their hands simultaneously, and Dittman couldn't tell them apart. The safest solution, the professors had found, was either to gesture namelessly toward one of the twins or say one of their names while not looking at either one of them. In this case, it was Mallory who had, quite literally, gotten the nod.

"All decisions *have* to be economic decisions because Marxism is based on materialism. There is nothing that exists except for the material universe, and so people protect their economic interests even though they may try to glamorize those decisions in terms of religion, ethics, patriotism, or anything else."

"And the result is what? Perhaps your sister might like to have a go at this one."

"I would say that everything that Marx believed about the materialistic nature of the universe and the economic basis of decision-making resulted in the political structures that were in place during his lifetime, social classes, religious values ... "

"And alienation. Don't forget alienation," Bastian interrupted in an attempt to prove that he actually had read the assignment.

Dittman stared over her reading glasses at him. "Perhaps male domination, too, Mr. Lewis. I've noticed in my years of teaching that, when one student does not let another finish a thought, it is usually a male student who breaks in and usually a female student who is interrupted. Go on, Ms. Warren-Whitehead. You were saying?"

Somewhat flustered, Prudence continued, "Yes, well, alienation, too. Capitalism results as a means of protecting the economic interests of those in power, and workers feel alienated and disenfranchised because they don't share equally in the products of their labor. Ultimately, many people stop *trying* to make a difference because they don't believe they *can* make a difference."

"Fine. So, we've laid out at least some of the main concerns of classical Marxist theory: materialism, economic motivation, capitalism, class structure, imbalance of political power, alienation ... there are plenty more, but that's a good start. Let me ask everyone for an opinion then. Do you believe Marx was right? Are all decisions made, both by individuals and by societies, largely for economic reasons?"

The students were reluctant to answer. Either they didn't yet have an opinion on this issue, or they thought Dittman might be asking a trick question.

Assuming the latter, she decided to explain. "It's really only an opinion I want. No right or wrong answers here. Are all decisions ultimately economic in nature. Bradford?"

It took Townsant a moment to realize that he was the person being called on. Although Professor Dittman was addressing him by the name he had originally wanted to adopt in college, he was so used to people simply using his last name that he thought she must be speaking to someone else. His new identity was something he wore like a pair of shoes that hadn't yet become quite comfortable.

Finally, he replied, "Um. I'd say yes."

His answer was quite tentative. It was as though he was holding it out in such a way that it could be retracted immediately if necessary. "I mean, I can't think at the moment of a decision that ultimately isn't. Wait. What about monks and nuns? They give up everything for religious motives. There doesn't seem to be anything economic about that."

"I disagree," Bastian said, still eager to make up for his initial gaffe ... which no one except himself remembered.

"Go on, Bastian," Dittman nudged him.

"They're doing so because they believe it'll gain them access to heaven. If I acted in a way that I thought would get me into some kind of fraternity, Marx would say that *is* an economic motivation because of the contacts and prestige the fraternity would give me. If you strip away the religious façade, aren't monks and nuns simply trying to gain entry into the 'fraternity' of heaven for the presumed benefits they'd receive? Sounds pretty economically-based to me."

"Perhaps." Dittman reverted to one of her calculated moments of reflection, even though she had her next thought already in mind. "But wait a minute. What about starving artists? Don't they give up a great deal of material comfort for the sheer satisfaction of producing art? Esmé, we haven't heard from you for a while. What do you think?"

"Well, I mean, it depends, doesn't it? Just because someone's a starving artist, that doesn't mean that they want to starve forever. Maybe they think, 'If I suffer now, it'll all be worth it in the end because some gallery will display my art, and then I'll become wealthy.'"

"We call that a 'net benefits case,' and I imagine that there are artists who do indeed believe that. But you said, 'It depends.' Depends on what?"

"If an artist produces art for the sheer pleasure of it without any hope of material gain—and people like that must exist—then I fail to see what's 'economic' about that decision."

"You've answered it yourself." Bastian was regaining his confidence. "They do it for *pleasure*. Pleasure is part of an economic motive. Why else do people want money, power, fame, and all the rest? They think these things will give them pleasure. So, beyond Marx's materialism, there's another motive people have for doing things: They want to be happy."

"Ah, I see we have a hedonist in our midst, someone who equates happiness with pleasure," Dittman said. "We could engage in a long debate on whether pleasure and happiness are indeed identical, but it would take us rather far afield, I'm afraid. For now, though, let me just ask you this, Bastian: Would you ever willingly run out in front of a fast-moving car if you knew without a doubt that it would hit you? Would you do that for pleasure?"

"Certainly not."

"Suppose you were a parent, and your infant child had wandered out into the road. The only way you could save it is to run out in front of that charging automobile and push your beloved child out of the way, sacrificing your own life or, at least, spending months in the hospital and the rest of your life in pain. Would you do it then?"

Bastian felt he was increasingly being backed into a corner. "I suppose so," he said quietly.

"And you'd do that for pleasure?"

Bastian saw a way out of his predicament. "Yes, indeed. The pleasure of saving my child."

"And you really believe that, at some level, your brain would be performing that type of syllogism: Saving my child is pleasurable. Running out in front of traffic means saving my child. Thus, running out in front of traffic is pleasurable. Is that how it works?"

The room grew silent.

Dittman finally decided to bring the lesson to a close.

"You might have another motivation, of course. In evolutionary terms, you might be programmed to sacrifice yourself to save your child so that your genes have a chance of being passed on to future generations. That's Richard Dawkins's Selfish Gene Theory, which he believes can be used to explain any instance of altruism we can imagine. And the Selfish Gene Theory is a direct descendent of Darwin's evolutionary theory, which we discussed last week.

"And that is the point I'm trying to make today: Any theory, the distinguishing feature of modernism, tends to expand so that it can explain as much as possible. And some theories, like Marxist theory, end up trying to explain *everything*. And it's that very tendency that the post-modernists rejected. That's where this course is heading. But in the meantime, I'd like you to read the sections of *Das Kapital* that I've noted on the syllabus in the section marked 'Absolute and Relative Surplus Value.' *That* will be our topic for Wednesday. I'll see you all then."

The students filed out of the classroom, some heading for an early dinner, some heading to the residence hall in order to get a jump on their new assignments, and one to sit alone under a huge fig tree that stood near a corner of the South Quad. That one student was Bastian Lewis, licking his wounds because he felt humiliated by Dittman's treatment of him in class.

It was that Monday afternoon that Bastian Lewis became, at least in his own mind, the Bad Boy of the Scipionic Circle.

CHAPTER TEN

"Cold ... Soooooo Cold"

The conversation was getting heated. "No, no. That's not it at all. I'm not saying that what Professor Dittman told us today *disproves* what we learned on the first day of Greek class. I'm just saying that it *contradicts* it."

"Well, if it contradicts it, then one of them has to be right, and one of them has to be wrong. Which is it?"

"Just because they contradict one another doesn't mean they can't *both* be right. This isn't algebra. You can't just say, 'If A is not equal to B, A can't also be equal to B.'"

"What about Heraclitus? Let A be the road up and B be the road down. That's a contradiction that's also an identity."

"You're just logic chopping. That was a matter of perspective. I'm talking about *essence* here."

"So was Heraclitus."

"You're saying that Professor Garner's right and Professor Dittman's wrong then?"

"I'm not saying anything of the sort. I'm just saying they were talking about two completely different things."

"And don't forget: They weren't really voicing their own opinions. Professor Garner was merely explaining Heraclitus' view that, at the ultimate level of reality, opposite qualities don't matter or don't exist. Professor Dittman was saying that, for the post-structuralists, all the literary criticism made by the structuralists about contrasting pairs being a useful way of examining literature was ridiculous. They weren't saying that contrasting pairs didn't matter at all or that they didn't exist. They were just claiming that structural theory wasn't a useful way of interpreting literature."

This debate, typical of a sort of discussion you might find among at least a certain category of undergraduates at 2:00 a.m. on nearly any university campus, was being conducted in Room 2B of Chudwell Hall in the early morning hours after Wilda Dittman's class on modernism and post-modernism. An outside observer might assume that, because the temperature of the conversation had risen to such a fever pitch, friendships were on the verge of being lost, and the participants in the argument cared deeply about each word that left their mouths.

Nothing could be further from the truth.

The students cared about the cases they were putting forth; they simply didn't care about them *deeply*. They played their propositions as though they were cards in a casual game of bridge in which the only thing that mattered was taking that particular trick, not winning the entire tournament. None of them staked their identities on being "right," and none of them would remember who said what by lunchtime the next day.

During the first week of classes, the students had been scouting for somewhere they could study—and let it be said: engage in intellectual posturing like that characterized above—away from the loud music and slamming doors of their residence halls. The vast majority of Mersley students were at the college as sort of a rite of passage between playing by their parents' rules at home and playing by their employers' rules after graduation. They were letting off steam in a manner similar to the way in which some Amish youths did during that period they called their "rumspringa," with the exception that rumspringa usually lasted about two years whereas the typical Mersley College student spent four (and, as increasingly became common, five or six) years in the collective bacchanal that led to a baccalaureate degree.

The search for a quiet study area drew the five students back to Chudwell Hall where they discovered an unused room down one dark hallway in the building's basement. The room had no name, but simply bore the designation 2B, under which one of the students couldn't help writing:

> or not 2B. That is the question.
> Scipionic Circle Meeting Room: Student Division
> Imminent Scholars only!!!

Once claimed by these squatters, Room 2B began to be used each night for a few hours of individual study, followed by an additional hour or two of intellectual debate about various issues they'd encountered in their coursework. Finally, at about 3:00 or 3:30, they'd return to their residence halls for sleep, somehow managing to be in their seats before Garner locked the door and began Introduction to Ancient Greek I.

On the night of the discussion about whether Heraclitus and the post-structuralists contradicted or confirmed one another, Bastian Lewis, still neck-deep in self-pity after his perceived mistreatment in Professor Dittman's class, remained in his room. He decided that his roommate's taunts about his clothing and general neatness were infinitely preferable to the fact that none of the other students in the course rose to his defense. After all, he didn't care about his *roommate's* opinion of him.

As a result, only four students were present in the recently-named Scipionic Circle Meeting Room: Student Division when their debate was punctuated by what sounded like several loud raps on the building's pipes. The heating system in Chudwell Hall being "positively antediluvian" (in Townsant's words), the students weren't disturbed at all by the occasional creaks, bangs, and groans they heard during their nightly sessions. But that particular night, the noises seemed louder and more frequent than usual. And what seemed most troubling of all were the sounds of muffled curses that occasionally drifted into the room through what appeared to be the walls themselves. Naturally, the students had met Sexton engaged in his various caretaker duties since he, like they, was a common presence late at night in the basement of Chudwell Hall. So, they comforted themselves by concluding that the old man must be repairing yet another part of the building's decaying infrastructure and cursing when the task proved more difficult than it should.

But that explanation collapsed when the muttering grew louder and louder until the speaker's words could be clearly heard. "Cold ... soooooo cold." The phrase was repeated over and over, bringing the study session to a premature halt.

"Do you think Sexton hurt himself or is in some kind of danger?" Esmé asked.

None of the four was what might be considered "heroic" in any traditional sense, but Chudwell Hall and its denizens were, in their opinion, all part of a great academic movement of "Us versus the Rest of the World," and so, tentatively at first but then with greater courage, they emerged from Room 2B and ventured down the narrow, unlit hallway toward the alcove that Sexton had told them was his "office."

The caretaker wasn't there, and the area looked as though no one had been there for quite some time.

CHAPTER ELEVEN

An Advocate for Mersley College Students

Depending on whether you were speaking to a student or a faculty member, you would receive entirely different impressions of what it was like to be in the presence of Professor Sabrina Pope. The students universally loved her and flocked to her courses in the history of art, music, and literature in great numbers. Indeed, there was a general outcry among members of the Mersley Student Council when Pope was moved from the Department of Humanities to the Department of Eminent Scholars because all courses in the new program were labeled, at Garner's insistence, as "Restricted to departmental majors only." Regarded as something of a substitute mother and a tireless warrior for student rights, Sabrina Pope regularly was chosen by the graduating class as its favorite professor.

The faculty and administration of Mersley College would, however, paint for you an entirely different portrait of Sabrina Pope. At meetings of the Faculty Senate, she could easily delay approval of the previous meeting's minutes by forty or fifty minutes. She challenged every statement, asked for clarification on matters that were perfectly clear to everyone else, and insisted on the insertion of the Oxford comma and two spaces after each period even though Sydney Mills, the only person who ever agreed to serve as faculty secretary, resolutely refused to adopt this style when the initial drafts of the minutes were prepared. Once this arduous task was finally completed, Pope then proceeded to ask for revision of the meeting agenda, a task that delayed the start of the meeting even further.

Since the Mersley College Faculty Handbook stated that meetings of the Senate could never run longer than an hour, the result was that fewer than five minutes often remained for the president's remarks, the dean's remarks, Old Business, New Business, and motions from the floor. On more than one occasion, the Faculty Senate accomplished only three objectives within its allotted hour: approval of the minutes, approval of the agenda, and adjournment. Pope's election to this once-august body thus became part of a vicious circle: She was so awful to serve with that few other members of the faculty were willing to run; since there were only a handful of names on the ballot, Pope continually won re-election despite her lack of popularity; she would then resume her irritating behavior, and the cycle would continue. Several times, some other senator would try to short-circuit this process by proposing term limits. But because there was never any time to conduct actual business at meetings of the Senate, that idea never came to a vote.

On the day following the study session in which the strange voice was heard, Pope's course, the Proseminar in Eminent Scholarship, was just completed when the five students approached her desk. "Something I can help you with?" she asked.

"Yes, ma'am," Esmé Dawson replied. "But it doesn't really have to do with your course, so if you'd rather we ... "

"Nonsense," Pope told the group. "If a matter concerns the students of Mersley College, then the matter concerns me. I am, above all things, an advocate for Mersley College students. What is the issue?"

Esmé informed the professor of the sounds that had been heard the previous night in Room 2B and the voice that seemed to be moaning "Cold ... soooooo cold."

"Ordinarily, we wouldn't bother you with something like this," Esmé explained. "It's just that ... well ... four of us were in the building late at night—we use that room most nights—and we just feel ... "

"Say no more!" Pope held up a hand. "This kind of practical joke is endemic here at Mersley, and I'm appalled that it's happening in our program as well. Probably some student's trying to scare you or have a laugh at your expense. I'd recommend speaking to the caretaker about it. He's here at night, and it's his job to handle matters of this sort."

"We did *try* to speak to Mr. Sexton," Townsant said. "He wasn't around."

"Wasn't around? What time was this?"

"Sometime after 2:00 a.m. 2:30 or 3:00 more likely."

"Well, he has no business leaving the building when he's supposed to be on duty. The caretaker works at night so as not to be in our way when classes are in session. But he certainly should have been there at *that* time of night. This is dereliction of duty. I'll talk to him and get things sorted. You can all go and put this annoying incident out of your minds. And have a good lunch!" Pope wagged her finger at the group during this last remark. "You can't master Reader Response Theory on an empty stomach."

* * *

Unlike Garner, Sabrina Pope tended not to linger in her office any longer than necessary. As a result, she had to return to campus after 11:00 that night in order to find Sexton when he was on duty. She entered Chudwell Hall just in time to see the caretaker removing the trash from the office of Ralph Briggs and head into the adjacent classroom to erase the blackboard. Like professors everywhere, the eminent scholars regarded it as their job to fill the boards with writing, leaving it for others to remove it.

"Sexton, a word!" she called out in the same imperious voice that caused her colleagues in the Faculty Senate to have flashbacks to the reprimands they'd received from their first-grade teachers for peeling glue from the palms of their hands.

The caretaker was, however, blithely indifferent to the tone of Pope's voice. While he did turn to face her, his expression betrayed no fear, discomfort, or surprise. Still working at an age when most of his contemporaries were either retired or mourned by those who loved them, Sexton was, it seemed, a hard man to "rattle."

Without waiting for him to say anything, Sabrina Pope continued with her "word." "It has come to my attention that a group of our students were in the study lounge last night ... "

"S'not a study lounge. It's a storage room—*my* storage room, in fact—and the five of 'em just took it over. Didn't even ask permission."

"Permission from *whom*? You? I might remind you that you don't own Chudwell Hall. It belongs to the college and has been assigned to the Department of Eminent Scholars for our exclusive use. If we want our students to study in Room 2B, then our students shall study in Room 2B. It's a big enough building. You can just find somewhere else to store your ... whatever it is that janitors store these days."

"Z'at so, ma'am?" Sexton turned back to the blackboard and resumed cleaning it.

"I'm not done talking to you yet."

"Oh? Thoughtcha was."

"As I started to say before you so rudely interrupted me, our students were studying here last night when they started to hear strange noises."

"It's an old building, ma'am. They's strange noises all the time."

"Not like these, as I understand it. Loud banging on the pipes and a voice moaning about it being cold."

"Probably one of them fraternity boys having a joke."

"Exactly. But I expect you to put an end to it. I want you to start patrolling the building at night when the students are studying here."

"I ain't Security."

"Well, if you'd rather I *called* Security ... "

"No. Last thing we needs is more people tromping through here at night when I'm trying to do me work. I'll do it. I'm just saying it ain't my real job."

"Speaking of your 'real job,' you were negligent in doing it last night. My students needed you at 2:00 or 2:30 a.m., and they say you were nowhere to be found."

"Remind me again what day it is today, ma'am. I gets forgetful sometimes."

"Tuesday. I know it's Tuesday because today my proseminar met."

"Well, that's just it, ma'am, ain't it? Even us 'janitors' gets two days off a week. Mine are Sunday and Monday. I ain't *supposed* to be here Monday nights."

"Oh. I see. Can't you switch your days off to the standard weekend? I mean, Saturday and Sunday. It'd make the building safer for the students if some adult's here when they're studying."

"Professor Garner's here most nights 'til at least 1:00."

"I hardly think it's Professor Garner's job to serve as bodyguard for our undergraduates."

"But it's *my* job. Z'at whatcher sayin'?"

"I just mean ... "

"Yeah, I know what you means. Okay, tells ya what. I'll switch me days off to the standard weekend like ya wants. But then tell yer students they can't use that there room on weekend nights. I won't be here to protect them ... " The next few words were muttered under Sexton's breath. " ... s'much as a seventy-eight-year-old man *can* protect 'em."

"That seems to me to be a good compromise. Do you need me to notify the HR office about the change in your assigned days?"

"Nah, I'll do it mesef'. Now, if it's all the same to ya, this here blackboard ain't gonna clean its own sef'."

CHAPTER TWELVE

The Bad Boy of the Scipionic Circle

It would be a distressing thing indeed to go on strike only to have not a single member of management realize you were missing. Such was very nearly the experience of Bastian Lewis in the days after he became the self-appointed Bad Boy of the Scipionic Circle. He abandoned his former style of dress, not adopting that of most other male students at Mersley (jeans, plaid shirts unbuttoned with colored t-shirts beneath, and running shoes so large and brightly colored they might have been hand-me-downs from one of the less successful clowns at the local circus), but wearing sweaters that did vary at least a shade or two from what might be called earth tones and selecting sports coats that, somewhat alarmingly, had no patches on their elbows. If he thought this deviation in his apparel would elicit cries of "Good God, man! What's the matter?" from his peers, he was sorely mistaken. He even absented himself from the nightly study sessions *for an entire week* without anyone asking him where he was. If treated this way, most people might conclude that their childish snit had been little more than a stunt and resume their "normal" behavior with neither explanation nor apology. But not Bastian Lewis. He doubled-down on his new role as an outcast.

Nevertheless, Bastian also yearned to be *seen* as an outcast. And so, the following Monday he returned to Room 2B and hoped that his disdain for the opinions of the others in the Scipionic Circle could be noticed in the slightly contemptuous curl of his lip and the merest hint of a slouch he adopted as he sat in his chair. In this hope, too, Bastian was to be disappointed. He hadn't yet learned the important lesson that was true of both student and faculty members of the Scipionic Circle: They were never really thinking about *you*; they were always thinking only of themselves.

The first set of exams was coming up in several of the program's courses. Ancient Greek had daily assignments, so the first exam wouldn't occur until roughly a third of the term had elapsed. Professor Briggs preferred to assign research papers rather than administer exams, so that meant that there would be tests in only the three courses taught by Professors Pope and Dittman. And Professor Pope had thrown the students a curve. In Friday's course on the Art, Literature, and Music of the Ancient Near East, she had announced that, because the same five students were enrolled in both that course and in the proseminar, she'd be conducting a single exam that covered the material of the two classes. In short, the students would need to apply the techniques they'd learned in the proseminar to the content they'd studied in the Ancient Near East course.

The term *proseminar* wasn't one that the five students had encountered before. Like *Gestalt*, *Weltanschauung*, and *signposting*, it was a word that most people encountered only when they were in college and that only college graduates tended to use once they re-entered "the real world." As such, these words were a kind of *shibboleth*—another term that fell into this same category—that the college-educated used to recognize one another. It was their secret handshake, their token of having been initiated into an elite fraternity that set them apart from the majority of people they would meet in their daily lives.

As Professor Pope had announced on the first day of the course, a proseminar was itself a kind of initiation. It introduced students to the fundamental techniques used in a given discipline, as well as its vocabulary, most important resources, and scholars of note. Originally signifying a graduate seminar that was also open to advanced undergraduates, a proseminar at Mersley College had evolved into a type of "methods" course that sought to give students a head start on how to succeed in their chosen fields.

The problem was that the Department of Eminent Scholars was

a hybrid program, consisting of professors who'd originally served in several different departments. Their fields were all related to the liberal arts and humanities, areas of study that were then in decline at Mersley as at many other colleges and universities, but there already were a Division of Liberal Arts and a Department of Humanities at the school, so Professor Pope could not simply duplicate the existing proseminars that already existed in those units. Her solution was to conclude that, since all four professors were conducting research that focused on texts, the new department's proseminar would be a "baptism by fire" (to quote her exact words) into the techniques, vocabulary, and principal figures of textual criticism.

That solution, of course, simply led to another problem. Her own discipline included the history, not only of literature, but also art and music. Was she then to limit her future courses only to articles and books written by art historians and musicologists, or was there some way in which she could include even transient creations like a piece of performance art or a bit of music that was improvised and never recorded or written down as *texts*? She decided that the latter approach gave her the greatest amount of flexibility, and so, rather than distributing a printed syllabus on the first day of class as the Mersley College Faculty Handbook required, she simply entered the room, walked to the blackboard, and wrote on it the question, "What is a text?" Then she announced to the class, "Those four words *are* the syllabus for this course. It's a deceptively simple question and one that will take us the entire semester even to begin answering, but it is also a question that will cause us to examine which techniques literary critics, art critics, musicologists, philosophers, historians, and other eminent scholars used to determine what constitutes evidence and what does not. We shall also learn who many of those eminent scholars were and how they advanced the discipline that is to be your major field of study. So, as Aristotle says at the end of the *Nicomachean Ethics*, 'Now let us begin.'"

On that first day, the five students had proposed all the standard definitions of the word *text* that one could think of. They noted that texts are written works and, since they'd all studied Latin, eventually traced the term etymologically to the verb *texere*, meaning "to weave." A text, they decided that day, was a group of words "woven together" into a meaningful whole, just as a *textile* was a group of fibers woven together into a meaningful whole. Words were, the students posited, the ultimate building blocks of a text. If you had no words, you had no text.

"Excellent," Pope concluded at the end of that first class. "So, in view of today's discussion, I want each of you in Thursday's class to bring me at least one example of a text that has no words. And no duplication, please. I want each of your examples to be different. If we're going to spend this semester learning how to analyze texts, we'd better know more about what one is. And believe me: We're not there yet."

That first class left the students confused, which was exactly the effect that Pope had wanted to produce. Nevertheless, by the time of Thursday's class, they had risen to the occasion. Prudence brought in a child's picture book that could be "read" even though it contained no words at all. Townsant cited the example of Picasso's *Guernica* as a painting that "speaks" to viewers and conveys a relatively consistent "message" even though it is devoid of words. Esmé mentioned Vivaldi's *Four Seasons* and other types of "program music" that, in her opinion, could be "read." Bastian described how archaeologists examine material culture and "read" the strata and the artifacts found in each stratum as a way of understanding a settlement. And Mallory noted that detectives "read" and interpret evidence as clues to a crime that has been committed.

"Now we're getting somewhere," Pope had concluded after hearing these examples. "So, you see? Despite everything we discussed last time, it's perfectly possible for there to be a 'text' in which no 'words' have been 'woven together.' Which leads us back to our central question: What *is* a text? And now I'll add a second question: How do we know when we're reading a text *correctly*? Or, to put it another way, *is* there such a thing as reading a text correctly?"

Since Townsant had mentioned *Guernica*, Professor Pope did a quick Internet search and found a high-definition image of the painting, which she then proceeded to project onto a screen. All the other classroom buildings on campus were equipped with digital projectors and screens that lowered at the touch of a button. Chudwell Hall, having sat abandoned for over two decades, lacked all equipment of this sort. Its screen was a tattered white monstrosity that was pulled down in front of one of the blackboards (usually several times before it would eventually lock in place), and the projector Pope used was wheeled into the room on a cart she kept in her office. She had salvaged both cart and projector when newer equipment was being installed in Old Main, and she connected her own personal laptop to the projector in order to cast the image onto the screen. Fortunately, the campus Wi-Fi system was strong enough that it reached Chudwell Hall but, if it hadn't, Pope was perfectly prepared to link the laptop to her phone and use her personal data plan in the interests of furthering her students' education.

"Now, Mr. Townsant, since you were the one who mentioned this particular example, how do we go about 'reading' this text? What does it 'say'"? The resulting discussion led the class into considering the difference between Authorial Intent Theory (the approach that seeks to understand what the creator of a work meant by his or her text) and Reader Response Theory (the approach that claimed 'meaning' was only created when someone 'read' the text and that this meaning could be different, not only from that of the work's creator, but also from reader to reader).

It was the second of these two approaches that Bastian wanted to bring up again at that Friday's study session. "I've got to tell you," he said in a voice he regarded as appropriate for a Bad Boy, "I'm not wild about this whole Reader Response thing. If I'm free to interpret any text as I like, and you're free to do the same, does the text have any meaning at all? Doesn't it just mean that anything we study is basically a Rorschach inkblot into which we read whatever we like? How can Pope test us on *that*? It just means I'm right, no matter what I say."

"Perhaps," Mallory suggested, "the test isn't about parroting back the 'right' answer. It's about seeing if we can use the *method* correctly. As long as our answers are consistent and legitimately based on evidence, they should be fine."

"I don't like that," Bastian objected. "Ultimately, where does that get you? It's just the legitimization of opinion, and that's not what I came to college for. When I read a novel, hear a piece of music, or view a piece of art, I want to understand the *noumenon*, the *Ding an sich*, the text-*qua*-text, not just look into it as though it were a mirror where all I see is a reflection of myself."

"Kudos for paying attention in Professor Briggs's courses," Townsant said sarcastically. "You managed to use *legitimization*, *noumenon*, *Ding an sich*, and text-*qua*-text, all in a single sentence. You've really mastered the vocab."

"Technically, it wasn't a single sentence," Bastian countered.

"And pedantic, too," Townsant continued. "I'd say we've all come a long way in only two weeks."

Townsant believed he was being humorous, using the kind of repartee that he thought was common among intellectual equals. But Bastian wasn't minded to interpret matters that way. "How do you of all people ... ?"

"I think we're getting a bit off-topic here," Esmé interjected. "What we ought to be doing is trying to anticipate what Professor Pope's combined exam next week might be like. How does her course on the Near East overlap with the proseminar?"

"You mean draw a Venn diagram and see where the two classes intersect?" Bastian asked derisively.

But Esmé took the question seriously. "If you like."

"Okay," Mallory said as she got up and walked over to a chalkboard. "Let's list the most important works we've discussed in Near Eastern class in one column and the analytical techniques we covered in proseminar in another and then use each technique to imagine a question Professor Pope could invent about applying that technique to each work."

"Sounds like a plan," Prudence replied, following in her sister's footsteps, as usual.

"Okay. So, what've we looked at so far in the Ancient Near East?"

Together, the five students came up with a list that they thought was exhaustive. Even Bastian participated, although he tried to give the impression he was doing so under duress. In fewer than ten minutes, the students had drawn up the following two lists:

WORKS

1. The Standard of Ur
2. The Worshippers Statues From Tell Asmar
3. The Head of "Sargon"
4. The Statues of Gudea
5. The Palette of Narmer
6. The Statuette of Pepy I
7. Rahotep and Nofret
8. The Story of Si-Nuhe
9. The Epic of Gilgamesh
10. The Story of Sargon

TECHNIQUES

1. Form Criticism
2. Source Criticism
3. Philological Criticism
4. Authorial Intent Theory
5. Reader Response Theory

"Ten major works, plus probably just as many minor ones that we haven't talked about yet," Bastian observed, "and five critical methods. That makes fifty different analyses. If we get started now, we should be nearly finished by the time we graduate."

"Nonsense," Townsant replied. "We'll just split them up. There are five methods and five of us. If each of us takes a method and sketches out a general outline of how that method applies to each work, it shouldn't take that long."

"Don't forget we also have Greek homework," Prudence prudently reminded the others. "Imperatives and prohibitions."

"Pffft. That'll be easy," Townsant replied. "We've got Sunday."

"And we've also got more Frege and Austin to read," Bastian said. "Plus that essay by Hulme. Can't forget Hulme."

"Well, we can sit here worrying about it, or we can get started," Townsant concluded. "I, for one, would prefer to get started. Tomorrow's Saturday. I'll bet, if we put our minds to it, we're all finished when we get back here tomorrow night."

"Can't," Mallory said.

"Why?" Bastian asked. "Hot date?"

Mallory blushed. "*No.* I just mean we can't meet back *here* tomorrow night. Remember what Professor Pope told us? From now on, we can't use this room or anywhere else in Chudwell

Hall on the weekends. 'Closed for maintenance,' she said."

"Great," Bastian complained. "And just when we need a quiet study space the most."

"What about the library?" Esmé suggested. "Nobody uses Sutlinger Library on a Saturday night."

"Brilliant!" Townsant exclaimed.

"Still leaves Sunday," Bastian said. "Library's *packed* on Sunday night. Everyone rushing to get done what they didn't get done over the weekend."

"Well, we'll just *find* something then," Townsant said, tired of the whole debate. "Now, let's get started. Who's up for taking on form criticism?"

As the topics were parceled out, Bastian once again felt like an outsider. He'd been used to being chosen last for teams in his high school physical education class. But he'd also been used to being the smartest one in class everywhere else. His first two weeks at Mersley had taught him that that was no longer true, and he didn't like it.

He didn't like it one bit.

CHAPTER THIRTEEN

Barbara the Barbarian Librarian

Unlike Sabrina Pope, Barbara Winchester, the head librarian at Mersley College, did *not* see herself as an advocate for students. Instead, she regarded herself as a bulwark that protected the peaceful domain of the West Quad from the chaos of overly hormonal undergraduates who had no higher purpose in life than to destroy the roughly half a million volumes she'd devoted her life to preserving. And *preserving* was central to Barbara Winchester's mission in life. There are those librarians who view the facilities where they work as portals through which the public can gain access to a universe of information, and there are librarians who view their facilities as museums where outsiders may view, but only occasionally touch, their precious contents. Winchester was in a third category all her own. To her, the library was a prison in which each book was serving an unappealable life sentence and where students and faculty members alike were disruptive visitors whose presence had to be tolerated but should never be encouraged. If it were up to Barbara Winchester, Sutlinger Library would *have* no opening hours. She would merely spend her days adding to its collection and strolling through the stacks, admiring her fruits of a life well led.

Students who entered Sutlinger were thus regularly greeted with something between a snarl and a growl. Backpacks were thoroughly searched for such contraband as gum, soft drinks, and indelible markers. If you were a Mersley student, Winchester automatically assumed that you preferred destroying books to reading them and that you came to the library solely to find a location for what she quaintly called "canoodling." The students mocked her by calling her "Barbara the Barbarian Librarian" and declaring that, if she had her way, there would be an eleventh commandment, reading "Thou shalt not canoodle within the confines of Sutlinger Library."

The advent of computers and other devices of modern technology has meant that the old-fashioned librarian who shushed patrons and wore her hair in a bun is more a denizen of fiction than of the real world. Barbara Winchester did not, however, receive this memo. Bun-adorned and looking like no one as much as Almira Gulch from *The Wizard of Oz*, she insisted that all sections of the library be kept in absolute silence. Were even a pin to drop, she would probably ban the pin from the premises for up to six weeks and insist that a scathing report be placed in the pin's "permanent file."

The use of Sutlinger Library as a Saturday-night substitute for Chudwell 2B was thus unlikely to be met by jetés and pirouettes of rapture. As soon as the imminent scholars sat down at one of the tables in the reference section and began to discuss the relevance of form criticism to *The Epic of Gilgamesh*, Barbara the Barbarian Librarian was on them like a voracious leopard. She reminded them in a whisper that could itself be heard as far away as the East Quad that libraries are places for *silent* study, not "frolicking, cavorting, or engaging in typical undergraduate hijinks."

Prudence Warren-Whitehead, who of the five was most able to open her eyes so wide she looked like a figure in a Margaret Keane painting, complimented "Miss Winchester" on her "frock" (choosing each of those words as carefully as a jeweler might select precious stones) and noted that the group was there because they needed a quiet place to study and "Everyone knows that there's no place on campus as quiet as Sutlinger Library." Opening her books to show the librarian that she was truly there for "serious intellectual purposes," Prudence appealed to Winchester's good nature to allow them to stay.

It cannot be claimed that the heart of Barbara Winchester actually melted at the sights and sounds before her. It remained at zero, even if not at *absolute* zero, and she grudgingly admitted that, if the group did indeed wish to study—and could *do so quietly*—she did know of a place in the library where that may be possible. Beckoning the five to follow her like the ghostly figure of Charon as spirits approached the river Styx, Winchester led them down a long corridor to a locked room that, in all probability, had not been used in all the years that Chudwell Hall had been abandoned.

She opened the doors, flicked a switch that caused several fluorescent lights to click, pop, and spring to life, and ushered them into a room equipped with a large oak table that sat in the midst of a U formed by three multi-drawered cabinets. Each drawer was approximately five inches high and not quite seven inches wide. Twelve drawers were stacked vertically in twenty columns, each made of the same heavy and highly varnished oak as the table in the middle of the room.

"What *are* they?" Bastian asked.

"Don't tell me you've never seen a card catalog before," the librarian replied.

The students' blank looks informed her that the expression was unknown to them.

She sighed. "Before computerized databases, these were the way you found books stored in the library. There are three types of catalog—title, subject, and author—thus providing three ways of locating any specific item. If you knew the title of the book you were looking for was *The Meaning of Relativity*, you'd search for the card here. If you didn't know the title but recalled that it was written by Albert Einstein, you'd use the author catalog over there. And if you couldn't remember either one, you might search through cards labeled 'Relativity, Theory of' in the subject catalog over there."

"And what did you do if you found the card you were looking for?" Esmé asked.

Miss Winchester gave her a look that basically said, "These kids today! What *do* they learn in schools?" and led the group over to the title cabinet. Scanning the labels at the front, she finally found the drawer she wanted, opened it, and flipped through the cards, leaving the drawer open in order for the students to see the following:

```
530.11      The Meaning of Relativity
Ein
            AU: Einstein, Albert (1979-1955)
            The Meaning of Relativity: Including the
            Relativistic Theory of the Non-Symmetric
            Field. Methuen. London, 1922.

            129 pp. Illustrations. Tan cloth binding.
            20 x 11 cm.



SU: Natural sciences and mathematics > Physics > Theoretical
Physics > Relativity
```

"The main title of the book is across the top right of the card. The line labeled 'AU:' tells you where you'd find a corresponding card in the 'Author' cabinet. The line at the bottom, beginning with 'SU:' does the same for the 'Subject' cabinet: You'd first find the section on natural sciences and mathematics, within that the subsection on physics, then within that the subsubsection on theoretical physics, and on until you come to the group of cards dealing with relativity."

"What're those numbers at the upper left?" Mallory asked.

"Ah. Now, *that's* how you find the book. Here at the Sutlinger Library, we still use the time-honored Dewey Decimal System. We never bothered with that Library of Congress monstrosity you probably learned in high school with all its letters and numbers and dates just jumbled together. No, the Dewey Decimal System is traditional. It's intuitive. And as long as I'm head librarian, it's the way we do things here at the college. Books on the natural sciences and mathematics have a number beginning with a 5. Those on physics begin with a 53. Those on theoretical physics begin with 530.1, all of which leads you to books on relativity, which are grouped under 530.11. Within that category, books are alphabetized by the author's last name. See how 'Ein,' the first three letters of Einstein's name are typed below the call number? That tells you to go to the 530.11 section, search alphabetically by author until you come to 'Ein' or 'Einstein,' and then look for the title of the book you want. Easy."

"Doesn't *sound* easy," Bastian grumbled.

The "barbarian" part of the librarian's nickname then returned to the fore. Her eyes flashed as she said, "Look. Do you want to use this room or not? I can't stand here all night, teaching you things you should've learned in middle school. Heaven only knows the pandemonium I'll find when I return to my desk."

"Absolutely we want it," Esmé said. "Do you think we could come here and study every Saturday night?"

Miss Winchester was about to tell the students that she was making a one-time-only exception to her general policies under the current circumstances, but then she caught sight of Prudence's eyes, which, if it is possible, had grown even larger and more puppy-like in the interim.

"Let's just see how it goes, shall we?" Then, as she was about to close the door behind her, she added, "Mind you, I'm making no promises. And whatever you do, *don't* touch anything in the card catalog. These drawers have historical significance now."

CHAPTER FOURTEEN

Esmé

Promises or not, use of the old card catalog room for Saturday-night study sessions became the general rule for the five students. Their regular custom became: Monday through Friday: study in Chudwell 2B; Saturday: study in the library; and Sunday: study in Banworth Chapel, a small building accessible only by a long flight of stone steps that was located just beside the Alumni Building on the North Quad.

The reason for the chapel's location is easily explained. Elisabeth Banworth had graduated from Mersley College in 1922 and, by the 1950s, reached the pinnacle of her career as chair of the school's alumni board. Miss Banworth ran that board with an iron hand and, depending on your perspective, was either far ahead of her time or somewhat behind it. When the cultural shift of the 1960s began to roil the campuses of colleges and universities all across the United States, Miss Banworth was already in possession of her Social Security card and about to be among the first wave to receive their Medicare cards. She attended meetings of Mersley's governing board with a nameplate reading "Elisabeth Banworth, Chair Emerita" propped conspicuously in front of her but with the power only of moral suasion now that her official terms as chair had elapsed. Nevertheless, she felt free to speak her mind at meetings and to do so regardless of whether her observations had any relevance to the topic at hand.

As the counterculture took an ever-stronger hold on American college education, and as female students stopped wearing strings of pearls and being referred to as "coeds," Elisabeth Banworth was determined to take a stand against what she called "the cheapening of Mersley College." A decade earlier she had applauded the introduction of the phrase "under God" into the Pledge of Allegiance and actually wrote fan mail to

President Dwight D. Eisenhower when he signed the bill proclaiming "In God We Trust" to be the nation's *official* motto. Miss Banworth might feel some esteem for the older, traditional motto of *E pluribus unum* for being in Latin, which was a required subject for all Mersley students when she was enrolled, but she otherwise felt about it roughly in the same way that Barbara Winchester felt about the Library of Congress classification system. The nation, she believed, was placing far too much emphasis on the *pluribus* and far too little on the *unum*, and it needed to have a literal "come to Jesus" moment. And so, when the old North Dormitory building was at last torn down, her cries "What Mersley needs is a chapel!" became the Mersley College equivalent of Cato's "*Carthago delenda est!*"

In the end, she got her way, as squeaky wheels often do. A chapel was built and named in her honor. Ironically, the opening ribbon was cut at roughly the same time that fewer and fewer of the college's students felt any inclination to attend religious services, and well more than fifty years before politicians would try to seize control of higher education and make it stop indoctrinating students in socialism and start indoctrinating them in evangelical Christianity. Thus, she was, as previously noted, either far ahead of her time or somewhat behind it.

For most of its existence, Banworth Chapel sat empty except for a single non-denominational service held there each Sunday at 11:00 and for the occasional student who, having neglected to study for an exam, thought that divine intervention might be the only remaining avenue to a passing grade.

One of the few students who attended the weekly chapel services religiously (in all senses of that word) was Esmé Dawson, the only member of the Scipionic Circle who was what is called "a true believer." Winton Garner and Sabrina Pope could, it is true, occasionally be seen among the pews of St. Mark's Episcopal Church in downtown Mersley, but they were "cultural Anglicans" of the type often dismissed as "the Smells and Bells

Coalition." They enjoyed the incense, the vestments, the stained glass windows, and the swelling organ music, particularly if the organist had selected something by Bach or Franck, but, as for theology, they were having none of it. As Garner once said to one of the priests at St. Mark's who insisted that Jesus was indeed God and a loving God at that, "So, let me get this straight. You're asking me to believe in a God who incarnated Himself so that he could sacrifice Himself ... to Himself ... in order to save the world from ... Himself? *That's* the essence of your faith?"

Needless to say, Winton Garner was *never* asked to serve on the vestry.

But, unless her path in life changed substantially, someday Esmé Dawson *would* be so invited. She felt that she had a personal relationship with Jesus that was far more intimate and satisfying than any relationship she'd ever had with a living, breathing boy. And there were few enough of those. She quickly learned to keep her beliefs to herself since her one attempt to witness to her four colleagues ended badly. She had wanted to thrill them with the beauty of Paul's first letter to the Corinthians. They wanted to argue about the unsolvable question of theodicy. It was almost as though she and the others were speaking entirely different languages.

Esmé's devotion to her faith did have one advantage for the Scipionic Circle, however. Her regular attendance at services brought her the right of possessing a key to Banworth Chapel, a key that was happily surrendered to her by the chapel's faculty advisor, who was delighted no longer to have to drive into campus on Sunday mornings. Her task was to arrive each Sunday by 10:00 and serve as a one-person altar guild, making sure that all was ready by the time the six or seven students who would participate in the services arrived by 10:45 and the chaplain, who would conduct the actual service, would come dashing through the door a minute or two before 11:00.

So, when the students of the Scipionic Circle were looking for a quiet area in which to study on Sunday nights, Esmé's chain of thought progressed something like this:

1. Sunday reminds me of Banworth Chapel.

2. Banworth Chapel reminds me that I have a key.

3. The key reminds me that I'm supposed to lock up immediately after Sunday services have concluded.

4. The conclusion of Sunday services reminds me that the chapel is standing empty 166 hours per week.

5. The emptiness of the chapel and my possession of a key remind me that I have a solution to our group's need for a Sunday-night study area. QED.

After the first study session in the chapel, the other students were so pleased with the space that they suggested it be used in lieu of Chudwell 2B and the library's catalog room *every* night, but Esmé demurred. She felt that, if anyone saw lights on in the chapel late on a Sunday evening, she could always explain the group's presence as a new Bible study group she'd formed. But, even as pious as Esmé was, few would believe her Bible study group would meet *every* night. And so, the weekly rotation of the three study spaces continued throughout the rest of the five students' first semester at Mersley.

CHAPTER FIFTEEN

Professor Fitzgerald

Winton Garner was as good as his word. He raced the students through the basic vocabulary and grammar of ancient Greek in record time and, by the beginning of October, moved them from what he called "pablum Greek" to "the real meat of the language": reading actual passages of Plato.

Plato is an unusual figure in the history of ideas. His concepts can be difficult, but his grammar is relatively easy. As such, by using such resources as Smyth's *Greek Grammar*, Liddell and Scott's *Intermediate Greek Lexicon*, Marinone and Guala's *Tutti I Verbi Greci*, and Professor Garner's own copious notes (which he prepared each afternoon on a mimeograph machine that he was delighted to find in a cabinet full of supplies deep in the bowels of Chudwell Hall), the students slowly began making their way through some of the dialogues. Since Beetham's textbook had been based on the *Meno*, Garner's plan was to begin with healthy "chunks" of that work, introducing students to Plato's Theory of Forms and his Doctrine of Recollection, and then move on to the *Apology* and *Crito*, which the class would read in their entirety before the end of the academic year.

Since Elementary Greek was competing for study time with five other courses, the students' nightly study sessions became even more intense than before. Four of the students were there without fail every single night. Bastian would drift in and out, becoming a bit more regular in his attendance when an exam was imminent, a little less regular at other times.

One Wednesday, a week before Halloween, Bastian arrived at the study session (let it be noted: more than an hour late) even though only minor assignments were due in the immediate future.

"Guess what I just heard," he stated as he walked through the door of Chudwell 2B, interrupting an otherwise scintillating discussion about *oratio obliqua* in Greek and Latin.

"You know that's a meaningless request," Townsant pointed out.

"Yes. Care to give us any context for our guessing?" Mallory asked.

"Never mind," Bastian replied. "It's just something people say. I was at the Dugout," he continued, referring to one of the most popular snack bars on campus, "and I overheard a group of seniors talking about why they closed Chudwell Hall decades ago."

"Seniors as in senior citizens, or seniors as in fourth-year students?" Esmé asked.

"What do *you* think?" Bastian asked sarcastically.

"Doesn't matter," Townsant said. "We already *know* why they closed Chudwell Hall: It was too expensive to either renovate or tear down."

"That's just the cover story," Bastian told the group. "The real story's far more interesting. Here's what I learned."

Bastian then proceeded to recount the tale of Tolbert Fitzgerald and his missing manuscript.

According to legend retold to each incoming class at Mersley, Tolbert Fitzgerald had been a young Classics professor at the college nearly half a century earlier. Fitzgerald, it was said, was brilliant, egotistical, and the sort of professor that female students—who, to Elisabeth Banworth's dismay, no longer kept a drawer full of gloves that matched their handbags—tended to fantasize about marrying. His very popularity made him suspect to other professors who felt it was their job to serve as gatekeepers to the world of higher learning, admitting the worthy and driving out the unworthy who, it was presumed, would spend the rest of their lives wailing and gnashing their teeth. For a professor to be "popular," it must mean that he or she had low academic standards, coddling students and holding classes that may be long on wit but inevitably short on wisdom.

Senior members of the Department of Classics disagreed on most things, but there was one subject about which there was absolute unanimity: When Professor Fitzgerald applied for tenure the following year, he would be voted down decisively. "Mersley College has no place for lightweights," one faculty member is reported to have said. "If we reduce our standards to the level of his," another agreed, "we'd be merely pandering to popularity. No, Fitzgerald's just not one of us. Some junior college can snap him up if they see fit. But a future at Mersley? The very idea gives me dyspepsia."

The forces of academia seemed aligned against Professor Fitzgerald, but then an unexpected thing happened. Late one night, he visited one of his colleagues, a recently-tenured associate professor, looking for advice. He said he had a manuscript for a book, a book that, in his own humble opinion, he thought might be rather good. But with his tenure review coming up in a year, he faced a dilemma. The major university presses, such as those at Harvard or Oxford, sometimes took as long as two full years to review a manuscript before deciding whether it was worthy of publication. Even then, due to requests for revisions, it might be as long as three more years before such a book ever saw the light of day. On the other hand, there was a university press at one of the regional campuses in another state—"Southeastern Something-or-Other University," was how Bastian described it—that assured Fitzgerald it would accept the manuscript, sight unseen, and have it in campus bookstores within three months.

"So, I don't know what to do," Fitzgerald is reported to have said. "I mean, I think this work is my best so far, and one of the big presses might eventually accept it. If they do, my career would be made. But that would come far too late for my tenure hearing and, given my publication record so far, I think a positive vote is far from certain. If I have the small university press publish it, I'd at least have a book out by the time I apply for tenure, but I'm not sure that would mean anything because the publisher doesn't have much of a reputation. What should I do?"

The colleague, who was one of those who had already decided to vote against Fitzgerald's tenure application, encouraged him to give Harvard University Press the right of first refusal. "Better late than never," is the advice the young professor was given. "But you really only want to submit the book if it's as good as you say it is. Why don't you leave the manuscript with me, and I'll read it over? That way I can tell you candidly whether it's worth sending out to one of the big presses. And since their review time is so long, I'll at least be able to speak about the manuscript when we meet to consider your tenure application."

Fitzgerald agreed. And there the matter stayed for one month, two months, three months. Finally, the young professor could wait no longer and asked the colleague about the manuscript. "Still working my way through it," he was told. "It's rather dense, isn't it?"

More months went by, and still Fitzgerald never heard anything more from his colleague. The date for tenure applications came and went, Fitzgerald applied, and, as the rest of the department had planned, his case was denied. "I did everything I could for you," the colleague lied. "I told them what a marvelous book you'd written. Why, it isn't just publishable; it's likely to change the whole field!"

"Well, that's some good news, anyway," Fitzgerald replied. "Speaking of which, may I have the manuscript back? If I'm going to have to look for a new job, I might as well start searching for a publisher."

"My dear boy," the answer came, "I felt so badly about how the whole tenure business went that I sent in the manuscript to Harvard *for* you. Included a letter of strong endorsement and everything. Even called in a favor from a friend of mine who's on the editorial board. They agreed to put a rush on it. Your book's going to be published, all right, and by one of the most prestigious university presses in the world. Mersley College may be losing you, but your career's made. You just wait and see."

Tolbert Fitzgerald did wait and see. At the end of his contract at Mersley, he took a job at a nearby junior college, just to make ends meet until his book came out. Then he intended to search for another job at the type of school that regularly hired classicists who'd been published by Harvard. Why, he thought, he might even get a job at Harvard itself.

More months went by and, one day, he happened to be walking through town and passed one of those dank, dusty bookshops that cater to clients interested in books too abstruse and intellectual for what is commonly called "the average reader." There he saw his book, featured prominently in the window, which had indeed been published by Harvard University Press:

The Deleuzian Rhizomatics of Ontological Temporality:
A Deconstructionist Approach

There was only one problem. It was not Fitzgerald's own name that appeared on the cover; it was the name of the colleague to whom he'd shown the manuscript.

Irate, Fitzgerald drove back to Mersley College at speeds that would likely have been frowned upon by any state patrol officer who happened to be in the area. He arrived on campus just in time to find the members of the Classics Department in a meeting, discussing which works of Sallust would be considered mandatory reading and which would be optional for students majoring in the field the following year. Fitzgerald stormed into the meeting, accused his former colleague of the most egregious form of plagiarism, and demanded that he be reinstated into his faculty position immediately.

"Manuscript? What manuscript, dear boy?" the colleague asked. "You never showed me a manuscript. I do recall you're talking about some vague plan you had for potentially writing a monograph on something or other *someday*. But you had no manuscript already prepared, and you certainly never showed it to me."

"I most certainly did. You even said it would revolutionize the field: *The Deleuzian Rhizomatics of* ... "

But Fitzgerald got no further. "Do you mean the manuscript *I* was working on at the time and was gracious enough to share with you? You'll be delighted to know that it's been published. By Harvard University Press, no less."

The former colleague's smile made it clear to Fitzgerald what had happened. There had been no positive report about the forthcoming book to the tenure committee, no letter of endorsement when the manuscript was submitted, no hope that he'd get a job anywhere other than at a small, obscure junior college ever again.

One of the other faculty members threatened to call Security and have Fitzgerald removed from the building, but Fitzgerald agreed to leave of his own free will. That is to say, he left the meeting, but he did not leave the building.

He went downstairs, entered a rear corridor, and found a piece of rope that he tossed over one of the building's old heating pipes. There he hung himself, his body not being found for nearly a week.

"They say that, on moonless nights, the spirit of this professor still wanders the halls of that building, searching for his lost manuscript, hoping to prove that *he* is the book's true author. And do you know in what building Tolbert Fitzgerald hung himself?"

The other four students would have to have been fools not to know the name of the building in question, but Bastian went ahead and told them, anyway.

"Chudwell Hall!"

CHAPTER SIXTEEN

The Dean's Den

Bastian had a strange gleam in his eye as he asked the others, "Didn't you tell me that you once heard voices and banging one night when you were studying in the lounge? That must have been Professor Fitzgerald, still searching for his lost manuscript."

"That's nonsense," Townsant replied. "The bangs and pops we hear in the study lounge are simply due to the fact that the building's old."

"And the mysterious voice?"

"Some frat boy's idea of a prank. Ever since Sexton's been patrolling the building at night, we've never heard them again."

"And the stench that seems to be everywhere in the building? Remember: The body went undiscovered for days."

"Old, decaying buildings smell bad. That just goes with the territory."

"Why don't we ask someone who can tell us what really happened?" Esmé suggested, ever the peacemaker.

"We can't ask Professor Garner," Mallory replied. "He's old, but he's not *that* old."

"Yes, but we all know someone who *is*," Esmé said. "Dean McDaniel."

* * *

Dean McDaniel wasn't surprised when the five majors in the Department of Eminent Scholars appeared in her office. She'd been expecting them. In fact, she already had her speech ready. "Yes, yes. Terrible business, I know. And I'm so sorry you haven't been satisfied with your courses. Let's transfer you into a new program and get you back on track as quickly as possible, shall we?"

Dawn McDaniel hadn't survived at Mersley College as long as she had by not knowing which way the wind was blowing. Nearly anyone else in her position would have retired years ago but, like Barbara Winchester and the dean's slightly younger colleague, Winton Garner, the dean wasn't sure what she'd do if she did leave the college. Indeed, ever since she'd turned eighteen, she'd been at Mersley, either as a student, teacher, or administrator, all her life. Now in her eighties, the academic year set the rhythm of her days far more than did the calendar year. And if she were no longer *Dean* McDaniel or *Professor* McDaniel, she wasn't quite sure who she *would* be.

On that particular day, however, her sense of judging the wind's direction seemed to have failed her. The students hadn't come to her office to complain about their professors. They were happy with their classes and eagerly looking forward to future terms. No, they wanted to meet with her to discuss another matter: Was it true that there had once been a Classics professor by the name of Fitzgerald who had hung himself in Chudwell Hall because another faculty member had stolen his work?

For an uncomfortably long time, Dean McDaniel simply looked from one student to another in disbelief. Then, concluding that she was not on the receiving end of some undergraduate prank, she suddenly burst into laughter. "Who in the world told you that?"

The students all turned their eyes toward Bastian.

"Well, some students were talking in the Dugout and ... "

"Let me guess," the dean interrupted. "They told you that Professor Fitzgerald went crazy because some other faculty member had stolen and published his 'secret' manuscript."

"Yes, and ... "

"Then Fitzgerald hung himself in the basement of Chudwell Hall, and that's why the building had been closed up for so many years. Is that about it?"

"Yes," Bastian confirmed, his voice now much less confident.

"Listen," the dean explained, "do you know what an urban legend is?"

"That's one of those tall tales," Townsant answered, "that a lot of people think are true but are really nothing more than nonsense."

"Exactly," Dean McDaniel confirmed. "And colleges are *hotbeds* of urban legends. The professor-who-hung-himself-in-the-basement-because-his-research-was-stolen trope is just one of a thousand. They cycle around every few years. Must be time for that one again."

"So, there was no Professor Fitzgerald?" Esmé asked.

"Oh, there most certainly was. He was in my department. But no one stole his research, and he certainly never hung himself. He was just a third-rate scholar like a lot of other third-rate scholars, and he was denied tenure for perfectly logical reasons. He wasn't outraged. He didn't go crazy. He just left the college and went somewhere else. I'll bet if you hunted him down on the Internet, you'd find that he became a high school teacher somewhere. Or perhaps he left academia entirely."

"We'd never find him," Bastian protested. "There must be millions of people with the last name Fitzgerald."

"Maybe not millions," the dean corrected him, "but lots anyway. I'd wager, though, there aren't very many *Tolbert* Fitzgeralds."

"So, none of that story is true?" Mallory asked, disappointed.

"Well, as I say, like a lot of urban legends, this one attached itself to the name of a real person and a real place. But if you know someone at another college or university, ask that person if they heard about the professor who hung himself in a now-abandoned building. They'll probably tell you it happened right there on his or her campus, and they know it's true because 'a friend of a friend' knew the professor."

The students were embarrassed and didn't quite know how to bring the conversation to a close.

"Look," Dean McDaniel said, taking pity on them, "urban legends are just modern myths, and every age has its own myths. The Greeks had Perseus, the Romans had Romulus and Remus, mediaeval Christians had Sir Gawain, and we've got the Killer in the Backseat and whatever. Consider this a learning opportunity. Next time you hear one of these ludicrous stories, don't believe it."

"You said there were lots of other urban legends that take place at college. What are some of them?" Esmé asked.

"Oh, let me see now," Dean McDaniel said, leaning back in her chair. Despite her initial irritation at being disturbed, she was beginning to enjoy this opportunity to tell stories she herself had once heard as a student. "There's the library that's sinking because, when the architects designed it, they forgot to account for the weight of the books. There's the seated statue of Uriah Chudwell that's supposed to stand up and bow whenever a virgin walks by."

"There's a statue of General Chudwell on campus?" Prudence asked, clearly focusing on the least surprising aspect of the legend.

"Well, if you see one," the dean told her, "let me know because *I* never have ... standing, seated, or otherwise. Oh, and there's supposed to be a staircase that goes nowhere here in Old Main." She slapped her hand down on the desk, startling the five students. "I almost forgot the best one: the tunnels!"

"Tunnels?" Mallory asked.

"Yes, tunnels." The dean's voice dropped low. She leaned forward, almost as though she were telling a story by a campfire. "Apparently, the founders of the college, back in the early nineteenth century, were all members of a secret society, the Fraternity of the Broken Omen. I'm surprised you haven't heard this before. That's really why Mersley College was created: to identify potential members of this fraternity and then induct them into the order. The rituals performed by this group were so vile and so secret that, as the campus was being constructed, a vast underground set of tunnels known as the Catacombs was built with all the passageways leading to the Chamber of the Broken Omen. In that way, members could go to the chamber without anyone seeing them and then conduct their savage rites in secret. The entrances to the tunnels are still there, I'm told, but heavily concealed. Some are behind paintings. Others are behind panels that can only be opened by flipping a hidden switch."

The students were hanging onto every word. Dean McDaniel took a sip of water and then continued. "Somewhere around the end of the nineteenth century, something happened—nobody quite knows what; maybe an innocent student discovered the tunnels and witnessed the secret rites; maybe a member of the order betrayed the others; we just don't know—but, whatever it was, it caused the fraternity to die out within the span of a few months. In time, the tunnels and the cult's hidden chamber were forgotten. But, even today, you might occasionally see shadowy figures darting in and out of various doorways, the ghosts of the original members on their way to their next ritual. When that happens, eerie sounds can be heard, echoing through the halls. You might even enter a darkened room only to see glowing eyes staring back at you, eyes that vanish the moment you switch on the light. Those spirits are harmless ... except in the hall where the secret rituals occurred. So, if you see an entrance to a tunnel behind a painting or after accidentally pressing a hidden switch, don't go in. No student who has ever done so survived."

The room was silent for several minutes. Finally, Esmé whispered, "Really?"

"*Nooooooooooooooo!*" the dean shouted, startling all of them. "Haven't you been listening? These are urban legends. Not a word of them is true. I've no more seen a secret tunnel beneath campus than I've seen a statue of Uriah Chudwell. Listen. College is about developing your critical thinking skills, not giving in to your credulity. I'm surprised you haven't learned that already. Maybe this new program of yours isn't quite up to the standards we expect here at Mersley College, so if you'd like to switch majors ... "

The students thanked the dean politely for her offer and for sharing the stories with her, but they said that, for the moment at least, they'd rather continue their course of study with the eminent scholars.

"Well, it's your funeral if you can't find a job after you graduate." The dean shrugged them off, and they left.

As they walked down the steps of Old Main, Townsant asked Bastian, "What're you going to do now?" He expected the answer "Heading back to the dorm." or "Gonna study in the library for a bit." or even "Think I'll go back to the Dugout and see if I can find those guys again." The one answer he *didn't* expect was the one Bastian gave him.

"I'm going to start hunting for those Catacombs."

CHAPTER SEVENTEEN

The Catacombs

Townsant chased after him. "You can't be serious," he said when he'd caught up to Bastian. "Didn't you hear the dean? There *are* no Catacombs."

"And didn't you hear Professor Garner?" Bastian asked. "'Life isn't about the either/or. It's about the both/and.' Just because something's a legend, that doesn't mean it's not true."

"That's *exactly* what it means."

"For centuries, people thought that the city of Troy was a legend. But Heinrich Schliemann found it. Plato talks about a strange metal called *orichalcum* that scholars assumed was just one of his myths. But a few years ago, ingots of something that perfectly matched Plato's description of *orichalcum* began turning up in Sicily. People thought the stories about tunnels carved beneath Puebla City in Mexico were legends. But construction workers found them while building an underpass. If Puebla City can have hidden tunnels, why can't Mersley College?"

Townsant smiled. "Well, if you *do* find these hidden tunnels, don't go down into them. Remember: None of the students who did so ever lived to tell the tale."

"Oh, that's the part of the story that's just a myth."

"So, now you're cherrypicking which parts of the story to believe and which not to?"

"Why not? People do it all the time. And besides, you're the one who heard the banging and weird voices, not me."

"*Once*. We heard the loud banging *once*. And it was a *single* strange voice, not a bunch of strange voices. I *told* you: It was probably a fraternity prank."

"Why not the Fraternity of the Broken Omen then? Look, I know what *I* believe, and you know what *you* believe. I'm going to start searching for the Catacombs. You can help me or not, just as you like. Go to the cafeteria. Go study some more. Or go make eyes at Esmé like I've seen in class. You know you do."

"I? What?" Townsant was clearly flustered by Bastian's accusation. "I do *not*. If anyone does, *you* ... "

"And *that* is what Professor Briggs referred to as *projection*. Now, if you'll excuse me, I've got a mystery to solve."

* * *

Bastian's search for the Catacombs continued far into the night. He missed Professor Dittman's Modernism and Post-modernism class, the first time any of the five students had missed any of their classes. And he didn't appear in Chudwell 2B when that night's study session began.

Not that Bastian was all that far away from the others. He, too, was in the basement of Chudwell Hall, simply on a different corridor, tapping bricks and running his hand over crevices, searching for some type of button or lever that would gain him entry into the Catacombs.

The light switch in that corridor wasn't working. Either the power had been turned off or the bulbs had burned out before the building had been abandoned and never replaced. He held his phone in one hand, using the flashlight app to see a few feet in front of him, while he explored the drab yellow wall with his other hand.

At some point after midnight, Bastian suddenly stopped his tapping and froze in place. A low, guttural sound came out of the darkness. What was it? Another student? Some animal that had taken up residence in the building? A spirit of some sort? Bastian listened carefully as the growling subsided and was replaced by a hollow, rasping, almost asthmatic sort of breathing. The regularity of the breaths made Bastian feel that he was being watched.

In fact, he *was* being watched.

"And just what d'ya think you're doin' down here at this time of night?" a voice said in the darkness.

Bastian thought his heart would leap out of his chest, but the shock made him turn involuntarily toward the sound, and he caught the source of the voice in the beam of his phone.

"Oh, sorry, Mr. Sexton," Bastian replied as soon as he recognized the caretaker. "I was just looking for something."

"Lookin' for what?"

"Um ... just something I'd lost."

"What was it? Mebbe I seen it on my rounds."

Bastian flushed a deep red that he was glad Sexton couldn't see in the darkened hallway. Running out of excuses, he decided to come clean and told the caretaker the story of the secret tunnels, just as the dean had told it earlier that day.

The old man's face showed no expression as he stood there, simply watching Bastian. Finally, he said, "And ya believe that, do ya?"

"Well, *believe* ... um, no, not really ... *believe* is such a strong word. Let's just say I'm doing research. I'm investigating a hypothesis that these Catacombs do actually exist, and I'm searching for evidence to prove it."

"And ya found it, didja?"

"Um, no. Not yet. But this is my first night exploring, so ... "

Sexton sighed deeply, the same low, distressed sigh that Bastian had earlier mistaken for a growl. "So, I've got *this* to deal with from now on, do I? Every night?"

"I'm not sure about *every* night."

"First, I've got to change my nights off from Sunday and Monday to Saturday and Sunday, just to accommodate you lot. Then I've got to patrol the buildin' like some sort of night watchman just 'cause one of yer professors thinks I oughta be protectin' ya. Now, I've got to work around ya so thatcha c'n 'feel the walls' to yer heart's content. What's next? Ya want me to hep' ya with yer homework as well?"

"Homework? No, well, that's really not ... "

"Look, ya can't believe whatever ya hear. Ya prolly b'lieve that professor hung hissef' down here, too. What was his name? Fitzroy?"

"Fitzgerald."

"Yeah, him. Or thatcha automatically get all A's if your roommate tops hissef'. Or ... "

"Don't you?"

"Or that the faculty built a still b'neath Old Main back when Prohibition started just so's they could continue their sherry parties."

"I hadn't actually heard that one."

In the light of his phone, Bastian could see that Sexton was shaking his head. "Look," the caretaker said. "Whatcher name?"

"Bastian. Bastian Lewis."

"Look, Mr. Bastian Lewis, there ain't no secret Catacombs and there ain't no hall for rituals and there ain't no passageways that open up if ya press the right place in the wall. If there were, I'da found 'em in all the years I been cleanin' up down here after you lot. So, ya seem like a nice kid 'n all. Why doncha just go study yer Play-Doh ... "

"It's Plato, actually. Unvoiced dental. Not a voiced stop."

" ... or whatever it is yer wastin' your time on and lemme do my work."

"Well, I'm sorry if I interfered, but ... "

Something about the old man's gaze in the light from his phone told Bastian that the conversation, such as it was, was now over.

"Um, yes, sir. I'll just head back to my dorm now, sir."

He started to walk away and then turned to speak to the caretaker, who was now once again hidden by darkness.

"But if you *do* find something, sir ... "

"Y'll be the first t'know," the voice of the unseen old man echoed around him.

CHAPTER EIGHTEEN

The Golden Mean

Professor Garner passed back the exams. "Not *too* bad. One or two of you might even make decent classical scholars someday. Vocabulary's weak, though. You should know by now that ὅτι, written all together, means *that* or *because*; ὅ τι, with a space between the first two letters, or ὅ, τι, with both a comma and a space between them, means *anything which* or *anything that*. So, that sentence in the fourth paragraph on the second page means 'I didn't understand anything that you'd said,' not 'I didn't understand that you were speaking.' I'm not sure what sense that would make in that context, anyway, not to mention that you'd be translating a pluperfect as though it were an imperfect. Anyway, lots to work on before we start the *Apology*. Lewis, I know it's early, but I do expect you to be awake in my class, you know."

"Sorry, sir."

"What's the problem, anyway? You don't have any more tests this week. I know that for a fact. So, you weren't up late last night *studying*."

The Warren-Whitehead twins stifled a laugh.

"And now what's this? Has all decorum been cast aside even before the end of your first term here at the college? I *expect* other Mersley students to giggle, but not this group. What's going on? Lewis, I can tell from the expression of the others that it involves you. So, out with it."

Sheepishly, Bastian provided a somewhat-edited account of what the group had heard from Dean McDaniel and what he'd been trying to do during the night.

"I see," Garner replied, his voice utterly emotionless. "Apparently, the analytical skills I've been teaching you on how to parse Greek words have not yet transferred to other aspects of your life."

Immediately, Bastian became defensive. "But I did it because of *you*."

"Oh, for heaven's sake. Pray don't drag *me* into this sordid tale of time wasted and gullibility demonstrated. Absolutely nothing we've done either in my classroom or outside of it should have prompted you to believe such an idiotic tale."

"If I may," Townsant began either helpfully or as a way of distancing himself from Bastian, "I think it's likely he's referring to your observation that life isn't about the either/or. It's always about the both/and."

Bastian clung to this statement as though it were a life preserver. "That's right. Not everything that's true has to be logical. Life can't be *either* rational deduction *or* emotional intuition. It has to be both of them. You said so yourself in one of your examples. It's Apollo *and* Dionysus. I was just trusting my intuition for a bit. Something about that story of hidden tunnels resonated with me."

"I see," Garner repeated. He paused for a few moments, reflecting on what he's just heard. Then he said, "You know, I've come to hate that modern use of the expression *to resonate with* to mean little more than *to interest, fascinate,* or *intrigue*. And as you say, part of this may be my fault for drawing the whole Apollo versus Dionysus distinction from Nietzsche but not providing the proper context for it."

He walked to the blackboard and wrote μέτρον ἄριστον. "MEH-tron AHR-iss-tawn," he said, pronouncing the words he had written. "You recently encountered the second word in one of your exercises, but not the first. Even so, it shouldn't be too hard to figure out if you think of how it's been borrowed by English. Anyone care to hazard a guess as to what this sentence means?"

Esmé's hand shot into the air almost before Garner had finished his question. He nodded at her, and she confidently replied, "Moderation is best."

"Precisely. Moderation is best. It could also mean 'Moderation is breakfast,' of course, but that's just a little classicist joke that you probably won't understand until later. Anyway, yes, moderation is best. That was a key concept to Greeks, at least during the Classical Period. Μηδὲν ἄγαν. may-DEN AH-gahn. 'Nothing too much.' Γνῶθι σαυτόν. GNOH-thee sow-TAHN. 'Know thyself.' Thanks to Socrates, we assume the last of these means something like 'Be introspective.' But when it was originally said, reportedly by the philosopher Thales of Miletus, it meant something more like 'Know your *place*. Don't get too uppity.'"

"'Uppity'?" asked Mallory, although it wasn't clear whether the word was unfamiliar to her or just one that sounded odd coming from Professor Garner.

"Yes, it's a perfectly good English word that's, regrettably, fallen into disuse. It means *arrogant, conceited,* 'too big for your britches.' I happen to like it because that concept of *up* seems to imply social climbing, although to the Greeks the idea would have been more about assuming you're better than other *mortals*, not just better than your peers. 'Know thyself' meant that there was a certain order to things. Animals were down here. The gods were up here. And human beings were in the middle. If you were immoderate, say, in eating or drinking, you were at fault because you were acting like an animal. No manners or breeding. But if you thought you were perfect, that meant you were guilty of *hubris*, of trying to rise above your station and assuming you were more like the gods than other men and women."

If the word *uppity* appeared strange in Garner's mouth, so did the last sentence. If anyone ever gave the impression that he thought he was better than anyone else, it was Professor Winton Garner.

But then he went on to explain. "We hear these truisms uttered by the Greeks, and we nod politely when we hear them, call the ancients wise for uttering such profound insights, while inwardly ... we absolutely *hate* the very idea that moderation might possibly be a virtue. There is nothing more modern, more American, or more modern American than a belief that moderation is most definitely *not* what's best. We prefer sentiments like 'It doesn't matter what you believe as long as you care about it deeply' or 'You can't be too thin or too rich.' We care about *passion, commitment*, things that '*resonate with*' us. We don't care about moderation. We even write songs *condemning* moderation: 'If somebody loves you, it's no good unless they love you *all the way*' and 'Accentuate the positive, eliminate the negative, and don't mess with Mr. In-Between.' But the ancient Greeks were all *about* Mr. In-Between."

"So, why?" Bastian asked. "Why did this change?"

"An excellent question," Garner answered him. "Two things changed our commitment to moderation: Christianity and the Romantic Movement. Think of Revelations 3.16: 'So, because you are lukewarm, and neither hot nor cold, I will spit you out of my mouth.' Revelations 3.16 is decidedly less 'warm and fuzzy' than John 3.16."

Garner made the last remark while looking directly at Esmé. Apparently, rumors of her attendance at weekly chapel had made their way to the eminent scholars and, as a "cultural" rather than a "pious" Anglican, the professor wanted her to understand that his *Weltanschauung* was decidedly different from hers. Esmé blushed at this realization.

Professor Garner continued. "That attitude was only exacerbated by the Romantics who suggested that artists should 'throw themselves' entirely into their art and who elevated passion from a classical vice into the principal virtue of their age.

And we're still *in* the Romantic Age in many ways. Barry Goldwater certainly wouldn't have seen himself as a Romantic, but he captured the essence of their beliefs when he said. 'I would remind you that extremism in the defense of liberty is no vice! And let me remind you also that moderation in the pursuit of justice is no virtue!' The ancient Greeks would have recoiled at such an idea. When Aristotle set out to define virtue, he explained it as a point of moderation between two vices. Courage is neither cowardice nor rashness, but a point somewhere in between. Temperance comes from neither gluttony nor starvation, but a point somewhere in between. Generosity means being neither a miser nor an 'easy mark.' And so on. This idea of the so-called 'Golden Mean' can be seen everywhere in ancient Greek art and architecture, from the symmetry and harmony of their temples to the carefully balanced, *contrapposto* pose of their statues. In tragedy, the Sophoclean hero is frequently brought down by the very quality that made him great when he starts to demonstrate a bit too much of that quality, and Euripides even wrote an entire play about this idea. One way of reading *The Bacchae*, for instance, is to see it as an illustration that too much rationality is just as dangerous as too much passion. Despite what the Romantics may have claimed, Euripides believed that if you yield to your passions, they'll destroy you in the end."

The class period was almost up, and not a line of Plato's *Meno* had been translated that day. "The point I'm trying to make is that understanding life to be not about the either/or but about the both/and doesn't mean that it's a good thing to be wise one day and foolish the next. It means tempering the tendency to be all one or all the other *every* day. What you did, Bastian, was precisely the *opposite* of the lesson I was trying to convey. Reason means giving in to neither cynicism nor gullibility, and I'm afraid that believing any myth, whether it's about Phaethon driving the chariot of the sun or about secret chambers beneath the campus of Mersley College, is yielding a bit too much to gullibility. Some may regard faith as a virtue," and here again

Garner looked directly at Esmé, "but at this school, or at least in my classes, we draw conclusions based on evidence, not faith. Because, regardless of how you glamorize it, what 'faith' involves is nothing more and nothing less than accepting a proposition as true despite lack of (or, in extreme cases, despite the *contradiction* of) actual evidence."

Garner closed his textbook. "It seems to me that, in light of today, I'm going to need to rethink my plan for the rest of the semester. There'll be no assignment for tomorrow. I'm going to abandon the remaining passages of the *Meno* we were going to read and reverse the order in which we study the remaining two works. Starting tomorrow, we'll work on the *Crito* even before we take on the *Apology*. In terms of the chronology of Socrates's life, that may appear to make no sense. But in terms of what I believe this class needs, I believe it's the preferable option. The question we'll need to consider is: Why is Socrates willing to die when he could so easily have lived? Class dismissed."

CHAPTER NINETEEN

The Transmundane Codex of Berossus

Having no Greek assignment for the next day greatly reduced the students' workload when they met that night for their study session. They devoted their attention instead to a question that had been coming up repeatedly in Professor Briggs's course on Wittgenstein, Austin, and Searle: What is the meaning of "meaning"?

For over an hour, they debated the linguistic theory of meaning versus the sense, social, and affective theories of meaning, until finally, Bastian entered Chudwell 2B, arriving late as had increasingly become his custom. Ignoring the topic at hand, he walked into the room asking, "Why was Garner so intent on picking on me today?"

"Never mind that," Mallory said, glad for the change of subject. "Why was he picking on *Esmé*?"

"Esmé?" Townsant asked, oblivious to the rather pointed remarks that Garner had made.

"Yes," Mallory continued. "Don't tell me *I* was the only one who noticed it."

"No, I noticed it, too," Prudence said, taking up her sister's cause as she so often did.

"What are you *talking* about?" Bastian asked, annoyed that the focus of everyone's attention had shifted so quickly from him to Esmé.

"Weren't you paying attention ... again?" Mallory replied. "All those barbs about Revelations being less 'warm and fuzzy' than the Gospel of John and about faith being incompatible with evidence-based reasoning?"

"Well, it *is*, isn't it?" Townsant said. "I mean, you can either accept that something is true because you have evidence that it's true or because you *believe* it to be true. You can't have it both ways."

"Of course, you can," Mallory contradicted him. "Because a certain chain of evidence suggests that such-and-such is the case, I can *believe* that such-and-such is the case. I've seen evidence that antibiotics work, and that makes me *believe* they work, but I can't say I have enough medical knowledge to know *why* they work."

"You're talking about two completely different things," Townsant countered, warming to his subject. "It's like what we're talking about in Greek class. There's γνῶσις, which is knowledge that could well be empirical in origin, ἐπιστήμη, which is knowledge derived from logical deduction, and δόξα, which is mere opinion."

"Oh, Lord," Esmé interjected, "let's not drag Plato into this whole discussion. I've had more than enough Plato for one day."

"The point *is*," Townsant insisted, "that *knowing* something and *believing* something are two different things, and religious claims—faith, if you will—can never arise above the level of belief. Garner wasn't picking on you, Esmé. He was simply alerting you not to mistake δόξα for ἐπιστήμη."

"Oh, Garner doesn't bother me," Esmé insisted. "You don't get to be my age without encountering a few Doubting Thomases. 'Blessed are they who believe and have *not* seen.'"

"'*Your* age'?" Mallory challenged her. "You make it sound as though you're on Social Security. What are you? Eighteen?"

"Nineteen, actually," Esmé corrected her.

"Well, excuse *me*," Mallory responded sarcastically. "I didn't realize we had someone so elderly in our midst."

"Um, I hate to interrupt this lovely conversation," Bastian said. "But which one of you stole this from the library?"

He held up one of the cards from the catalog room.

"What *is* that?" Townsant asked. "Pass it here so we can see it."

Bastian handed a yellowed card to Prudence, who passed it down the table. Each student in turn saw the following:

```
182           The Transmundane Codex of
Fit           Berossus

              AU: Berossus (Bel-Usur? or Bēl-rē' Ušunu?)
              ca. 330-250 B.C.
              The Transmundane Codex of Berossus.
              Harvard U. Pr. Cambridge, Mass., 1979.

              395 pp. Maroon leather binding. 21.5 x 28
              cm.


SU: Religions > Classical/Hellenistic Religions > Theological
Orientation and Doctrines > Heroes, Rulers, & Other Personages
```

"*The Transmundane Codex of Berossus*," Townsant read off the card. "Can't say I've heard of it."

"I'm surprised you're willing to admit there's something you don't know," Bastian muttered.

"Where'd you find this?" Esmé asked. "And who's this Berossus, anyway?"

"It was just lying here on the table when I came in," Bastian answered. "Why didn't any of *you* notice it?"

"We were *studying*," Esmé explained. "You should try it sometime."

Meanwhile, Mallory had been using her phone to search the Internet for this mysterious author. "Berossus," she finally reported, "a Hellenistic author, reputedly from Babylon. Josephus says that he was a priest of Ba'al."

"I wonder if he followed Ba'al by faith or by knowledge," Townsant interrupted.

Mallory ignored him and kept reading. "His *History of Babylon* consists of three books and was commissioned by Antiochus I Soter. Aratus attributes a second work to Berossus, the *Procreatio*, but some scholars think that's just an alternate name for the first book of his *History of Babylon*."

"What does it say about this 'transmundane' thing?" Bastian asked.

"It doesn't," Mallory replied. "The *History* and the *Procreatio* are the only works that it mentions. Oh, wait. It also says that several other ancient authors attribute some astrological observations to Berossus. Maybe they're from this work?"

"What does it mean to be 'transmundane' anyway?" Prudence asked.

"And what's a 'codex'?" Townsant added.

"Well, the second one I can answer," Esmé said. "A codex is a book in the form that *we* know books: bound together with pages that have writing on both sides. They come in rather late. Most of what the Greeks and Romans call 'books' are actually scrolls: long strips of material with writing only on one side."

"Interesting," Townsant noted.

"But if codexes ... " Mallory began.

"Codices," Esmé corrected her.

"Excuse me. *Codices*," Mallory said in a tone that suggested "Are you happy now?" Then she went on. "If codices only start appearing late, as you suggest, what was Berossus doing writing one in the fourth or fifth century B.C.E.?"

"I don't know," Esmé replied. "Maybe that's late enough. I don't recall exactly."

"Or maybe he was just ahead of his time," Bastian suggested.

"More likely that wasn't the name he gave the work," Townsant speculated. "Perhaps he wrote it on scrolls, and some later monk made a codex out of it when it was transcribed. Maybe it's just another name for this *Procreatio*."

"Speaking of *transcribed*," Prudence said, "we still haven't figured out what *transmundane* means."

"Well, the Latin's fairly simple," Townsant said, doing his best to sound like Professor Garner. "*Trans*, of course, mean *across* or *beyond*. *Mundus* is *the world*. So, a *transmundane codex* would be something like an *otherworldly book*. That would make sense if it was astrological, I suppose."

"That's assuming it's the same thing as the *Procreatio*," Bastian argued, wanting to contradict Townsant just for the sake of contradicting him. "Maybe it means something more like 'a book written *across* the world,' something like a geography of some sort."

"I don't believe so," Townsant said.

"You don't *believe*, or you don't *know*?" Bastian asked. "You're the one who was making a big deal of the difference between them."

"Not me. Plato," Townsant said.

While the men were arguing in this way, trying to score points off one another, the women were engaged in a different conversation entirely.

"What intrigues me," Mallory was saying, "is how the card ended up here."

"Barbara the Barbarian'll kill whoever did it," Esmé pointed out.

"What? You think she actually goes through the old card catalog every night," Townsant scoffed, "checking to see if any cards are missing?"

"I wouldn't put it past her," Esmé said. "She doesn't have a life."

"*No one* on the Mersley College faculty or staff seems to have much of a life," Mallory noted.

"Even so, I'm not saying that Winchester *will* find out the card is gone," Esmé insisted. "I'm just saying that, *if* she learns it's here, she'll kill one of us."

"Correction," Mallory said. "She'll kill *all* of us for no better reason than that she'll assume a student took the card, and we happen to be students."

"It *has* to be one of us who took it," Esmé continued. "We're the only ones who use this room."

"But which of us, though?" Mallory asked.

"We'll probably lose access to the catalog room on Saturday nights," Esmé complained.

Prudence, who'd been silent throughout this exchange, then spoke up. "That's our answer. We take the card with us this Saturday and simply put it back."

CHAPTER TWENTY

"Problem Solved"

The following Saturday, the imminent scholars got to the library even earlier than usual. For one thing, they were eager to return the purloined card to the catalog before, somehow or other, the head librarian figured out it was missing. For another thing, the residence halls were particularly noisy that weekend. Fall Break was coming up, and many of the undergraduates at Mersley College were eager to get a head start. As a result, Sutlinger Library was even emptier than usual for a Saturday night when the study group gathered.

Prudence, who'd perfected the art of sweet-talking Barbara Winchester, was stationed just outside the door of the catalog room in case the librarian should happen by. Meanwhile, Mallory and Esmé flipped through the title catalog, looking for the spot where the Berossus card had originally been.

Mallory read off the titles as each card went by. "*Transmitting Antennas and Couplers, Transmitting World News, Transmountain Diversions, Transnational Taxation ... *"

"Stop," Esmé said. "That's where it goes. Just before the last one."

"The problem is, though: How did the card come out of there, and how does it go back in?"

Mallory's question arose because all the cards seemed attached to metal hinges on the bottom that allowed the cards to be easily flipped without damaging them. Inserting or removing a single card from most card catalogs is a big enough challenge—a rod extending from the front of the drawer to the back is passed through a hole near the bottom of each card; in order to add or extract a card, the rod needed to be pulled out and then, when the change had been made, reinserted through the hole in each of the hundreds of cards in the drawer—but, with this particular design, it seemed impossible. In the space where the card needed to go, there were no hinges at the bottom to which the card could be attached. Even if spare hinges could be found elsewhere in the room, none of the students knew how to remove the cards already in the drawer, add the missing card, and then replace all the others.

"Maybe we should just forget about it," Esmé suggested. "After all, what're the odds anyone'll even look through this old card catalog again? And even if they do, what're the odds they'll look through this particular drawer for this particular card?"

"Barbara the Barbarian'll know," Bastian objected. "She's got almost a sixth sense about what goes on here at the library."

"Well, she didn't realize the card was stolen in the first place, did she? Townsant, what do you … wait. What're you doing over there?"

Townsant was standing on the other side of the room at an open drawer of the author catalog. "Hmmm? Oh, I'm just trying to track down other references to Berossus. It's odd, but the library doesn't seem to have a copy of *The History of Babylon*."

"Why's that odd?" Bastian replied. "I'd never heard of it until this week, and I'll bet you hadn't either."

"No, but that's not the point, is it?"

"Then what *is* the point?"

"Doesn't it seem odd that the library would have a copy of this really obscure work of Berossus but not a copy of what's supposed to be his best-known work?"

Bastian shrugged. "Maybe some professor was just doing research on the *Transmundane Codex* and didn't care about *The History of Babylon*. Or maybe that card's missing, too."

"That's an idea," Mallory said. She took the card over to the third set of drawers. "Let's see if there's a subject card. It *should* be there, what with all the breadcrumbs spelled out here at the bottom."

Mallory was referring to the ordered listing of subject, sub-subject, and sub-sub-subject that were separated by a series of angle brackets on Berossus's author card.

"Let's see."

She found the subject cards on religions easily enough; they occupied nearly an entire drawer. The sections on Classical/Hellenistic Religions and Theological Orientation and Doctrines were progressively smaller, while the final section—Heroes, Rulers, & Other Personages—held fewer than thirty cards. There were references to works about Heracles, the worship of Alexander the Great's successors as gods, and even a card devoted to the relatively obscure Greek hero Cleomedes of Astypalaea, but no reference to Berossus's *Transmundane Codex*.

"They're *all* missing," Mallory concluded.

"It's like someone didn't want that book to be found," Esmé added.

"But then, how did the author card show up in the study room?" Townsant asked.

The door opened, and the students were all startled. They were certain that the head librarian had found them and they were about to be expelled or at least lose access to the catalog room.

But instead of Barbara Winchester, it was just Prudence who stuck her head into the room. "Is it safe to come in yet?"

"Give us a moment," Mallory replied. "We still haven't figured out what to do with the card."

"We don't have to do *anything*," Bastian said. "Look, it's like what Esmé said earlier: The odds of anyone using this card catalog again are minimal, and the odds that anyone's going to be going through an outdated card catalog looking for a Hellenistic author no one's ever heard of are even more remote. Let's just keep the card and get back to studying Frege."

"That makes me nervous," Esmé said.

"Nervous? Why?" Bastian asked in exasperation.

"What if one of us is found with the card? It'd be theft."

"Good grief." Bastian shook his head. "Fine. We'll *burn* the damn thing."

Prudence's eyes opened in shock. "No! That's worse! That's intentional destruction of school property. That card may have some historical value someday."

Bastian walked up to Mallory, snatched the card from her hand, and returned to the open drawer of author cards. He fit the card in the spot that had been left open for it and flipped all the other cards back. Since Berossus's card wouldn't fit into the hinges at the bottom, it still extended a few millimeters above the others but, by this point, Bastian had lost interest in the whole issue.

He slammed the drawer closed and announced, "Problem solved. Now let's get back to Basic Law V. I guess I understand the central point, but I'd really like to know if I'm missing any of the nuances."

CHAPTER TWENTY-ONE

Fall Break

It is sometimes said that, although there's a valid pedagogical reason for colleges and universities to schedule a weeklong vacation period in the spring, no equivalent justification exists for a parallel vacation in the autumn. By springtime, many argue, students have been so immersed in their studies that, unless they're given a brief opportunity to refocus, their performance will diminish well before final exams. Besides, after being cooped up in stuffy classrooms all winter, the arrival of spring is bound to be a distraction, anyway. It's better for the students to be distracted on a beach somewhere than in a lecture on the commercial activity of the Hanseatic League.

But neither of those conditions applies to the autumn. And so, schools in the United States generally fall into one of two categories: those that create a short break by canceling classes on the day before Thanksgiving and resuming them the following Monday, and those that shut down for an entire week every fall just as they do each spring. Mersley College was decidedly in the latter category.

It may seem surprising that this policy was not of recent origin. As early as the 1880s, when Mersley was more often referred to as a "pressure cooker" than a "diploma mill," President Silas Mason observed that the school's students, who generally started each academic year as friends or at least as amiable colleagues, had largely had enough of one another by the second or third week of October. In Mason's day, the Ratskeller, the ancestor of the present-day Dugout, frequently erupted in fights by the time of the first November chill, and so, more out of an interest in reducing damages to the facilities than out of any lofty academic motivation, he instituted Mersley's first Fall Break.

These days, however, with videogames and cell phones, Mersley students generally don't get on one another's nerves until the last week of February or the first week of March, so the original justification for Fall Break had somewhat vanished. But that was not true for the Scipionic Circle. Originally united in common cause—the faculty members to pursue their own academic interests and the students not to be bored by an endless series of courses with titles starting with "Introduction to … " or "Survey of … "—those bonds had frayed somewhat with the passing weeks. As witnessed in the preceding few chapters, they'd begun to bicker more and come to consensus less. Thus, if anyone still needed a fall break at Mersley College, it was the members of the Scipionic Circle.

Not that their day-to-day routines changed substantially even though they were technically "on holiday." Professor Briggs had assigned a term paper that was due the week after Thanksgiving. Townsant, being the sort of person he was, had begun drafting the paper several weeks earlier; he spent much of Fall Break polishing his draft, adding new references he'd found, and trying to draw what he thought were novel connections between Gottlob Frege's principle of compositionality and Wittgenstein's concept of language games. Nothing that he said could not already be accounted for in dozens of other articles, but Townsant was, of course, an undergraduate, and all these ideas were new to him.

Esmé Dawson worked on her term paper, too, but she also devoted equal attention to a project she was assigned by Professor Pope. Pope had informed the class that there was no such thing in her courses as "extra credit," and Esmé's 99.5 average in The Art, Literature, and Music of the Ancient Near East certainly proved that she needed no extra credit, but she was so interested in the course that she had pleaded for an opportunity to complete some, anyway. Her rationale was this: Now that they were more than two-thirds of the way into the course, they'd had plenty of opportunities to discuss art and literature. But references to the music of the ancient Near East had been almost non-existent. They'd looked at photographs of the golden bull's head lyre from Ur, the images of musicians on seals and the walls of Egyptian tombs, and bas-reliefs of the musical instruments that accompanied the Assyrian army into war. But they hadn't *heard* any music from Mesopotamia, Egypt, or Israel.

"Well, it's not as if they made recordings back then, Miss Dawson," Professor Pope had told her.

"I know that. But didn't you say that there were a few Ugaritic tablets with cuneiform characters that appear to be some kind of musical notation?"

"Yes, but," Professor Pope replied in a tone that wasn't at all encouraging, "all the interpretations of those characters are based on speculation. We can't possibly *know* what the music sounded like, and even where we might have some idea of pitch, we don't necessarily have any indication of rhythm, dynamics, or anything else. People have tried, but ... "

"So, there *have* been attempted reconstructions?"

"Attempts, yes, but still highly speculative attempts."

"Let me start there, then. Let me see what the various reconstructions have been and determine whether I can find any commonalities among them."

"To what end, Miss Dawson?"

Esmé removed from a large satchel the framework of a lyre she'd made during her afternoon breaks on Tuesdays and Thursdays, based on images from the artwork they'd discussed in the course.

"We can tell the relative size of the lyres they used, and we can tell the lengths of the strings. What we *can't* tell is how they were tuned. I'm hoping that I might gain some clues to that from the scholarly reconstructions you mentioned. In that way, I could tune this lyre."

"Again I ask: To what end, Miss Dawson?"

"Why, to the end of a brief concert on the last day of class. Even five minutes. Aren't you curious as to what these ancient instruments may have *sounded* like?"

"I do think you're taking on an impossible task."

"I like impossible tasks, Professor Pope. Why settle for something that's merely possible?"

Sabrina Pope had eventually and reluctantly agreed to Esmé's request, allotting her no more than the requested five minutes on the last day of class for her "performance" and not making any promises of actual extra credit.

Meanwhile, the Warren-Whitehead twins devoted much of the week to reviewing their Greek. They were struggling more with that class than were either Townsant or Esmé, in particular finding it difficult to wrap their head around the grammatical concept known as the "sequence of moods" and constantly confusing "final" clauses with "consecutive" clauses.

And as for Bastian, the Bad Boy of the Scipionic Circle spent much of his days in the basement of Chudwell Hall, still searching for the hidden Catacombs, despite all the assurances he'd received that the tunnels did not actually exist. In truth, he'd been biding his time for several weeks. In most weeks, his investigations could easily be interrupted by one of the other students or a professor during the day, and they almost certainly would have been interrupted by Sexton at night. But Chudwell was virtually abandoned during daylight hours over Fall Break, and the caretaker worked only at night. So, Bastian Lewis was free to search and to dream as much as his heart desired.

Then, in the evenings, when he should have been working on his paper for Professor Briggs or studying his Greek for Professor Garner, he spent his time rereading Donna Tartt's novel *The Secret History* for perhaps the tenth or twelfth time. It was this novel, more than anything else, that led him to accept Townsant's invitation to become one of the five students needed for the new program to be launched. In his mind, each of his colleagues among the imminent scholars had parallels to characters from the novel. He saw himself as Richard, Townsant as "Bunny," Esmé as Francis, and the twins as Charles and Camilla Macaulay. (The gender of the latter pair didn't fit Bastian's mental model, but Professor Dittman's class had taught him that gender identity was a social construct and fluid anyway.) Mersley College was, of course, a mere stand-in for Hampden College, never mind that Hampden was supposedly in Vermont while Mersley was in the Midwest.

"You know, what this group needs are a few good murders," he thought as he removed picture after picture from the hallways of Chudwell and slid his hands along the walls, searching for hidden levers.

* * *

If the students needed Fall Break to repair their increasingly frayed relations, so did the faculty. Their initial meetings over the summer had been surprisingly amicable for a group of professors who had developed reputations for their lack of amicability. But, like academic departments everywhere, conflicting egos and demands for limited resources soon changed the tenor of the program. When students were present, these tensions were hidden. It was all "Good day, Professor Briggs. I've been hearing great things about your course this semester." and "I hope my classroom wasn't too noisy today, Professor Dittman. Our discussion, I'm afraid, became rather ... um ... 'spirited.'"

In private, however, the professors were not quite so collegial. When Professor Pope learned that the room assigned to Professor Garner's class received more light than hers did, she demanded that they switch.

"What do you need light for?" he asked her. "All you do all day is show slides with the lights off, anyway."

"That is a gross distortion of what we do in the study of art, literature, and music," she protested. "It seems to me that any place with a blackboard is good enough for teaching Greek."

"It's the poor workman who blames his tools," he replied.

And so it went until department meetings, which once had been almost bearable, degenerated into the trials of endurance that academic department meetings are everywhere.

Things came to a head just before Fall Break, when the registrar notified Professor Dittman as the program's chair that the Department of Eminent Scholars was the only unit on campus that had not yet submitted its spring schedule.

"When was it due?" she asked.

"More than three weeks ago."

"Oh, all right. We'll get you a schedule by Friday."

"I really need it soo- ... "

"Friday it is, then," and she hung up the phone.

Foolishly, perhaps, the faculty members of the Scipionic Circle thought that planning each term's courses would be easy since they'd already decided which courses the program would offer and that it would merely be a matter of choosing "the next six" in succession. But matters were far from that easy.

Certain choices were obvious. Introduction to Ancient Greek I would need to be followed by Introduction to Ancient Greek II, and The Art, Literature, and Music of the Ancient Near East would logically become The Art, Literature, and Music of Ancient Greece. But everything after that was a battle. Sabrina Pope insisted that, since she and Ralph Briggs had each taught two courses in the fall, their loads should be reduced to one course in the spring. Wilda Dittman argued that she'd agreed to become department chair with the assumption that she'd have a one-course teaching load all year, so all eyes turned to Winton Garner. "Like hell I'm teaching three courses in the spring!" he protested. "I'm an eminent scholar, not some assistant professor just out of graduate school. That has to count for something."

"We're *all* eminent scholars," Professor Briggs pointed out. "I'd say the whole status issue is a wash."

"But three classes!" Garner said, as though such a load was unheard of. "I have a life, too, you know."

"Do you?" Professor Dittman asked. "Rumor is that you hardly leave the building."

"But my Bacchylides!"

"Fine. Teach a course on Bacchylides then," Professor Briggs replied.

"The students have only had a single semester of Greek. Bacchylides would be far too difficult for them."

"Well, then, teach it in translation," Professor Pope proposed. "I certainly didn't expect my students to read literature in Sumerian, Akkadian, and Egyptian this semester."

"I'd rather die first," Garner moaned. "Besides, a translation course on Bacchylides isn't on our list of approved courses. It's just not possible."

Professor Dittman decided that she needed to use her authority as chair to reach some sort of settlement. "Look, Winton, Ralph and Sabrina have a point: They *did* their bit this semester. It's time for you to step up." She went to her desk and removed the list of courses that had been approved for the department. "Go through the list and pick out the three easiest courses for you to teach next semester. You already said you need to offer Introduction to Ancient Greek II, so choose two others. And to make sure it's fair, how about this? When we select who'll be chair next year, we'll remove your name from the list. Is that okay with you, Sabrina and Ralph? One of you will be chair next year?"

The bird of a lighter spring load in the hand seeming better than the two birds of not serving as next year's chair in the bush, they agreed. "Who knows?" Professor Briggs thought. "Maybe Mersley will go bankrupt or the world will end before then, anyway."

So, after much debate and resistance, the Department of Eminent Scholars submitted to the register the following as their spring schedule:

1. Introduction to Ancient Greek II (MTWThF 8:00-8:50 am): Garner

2. The Art, Literature, and Music of Ancient Greece (MWF 9:00-9:50 am): Pope

3. Classical Mythology (MWF 11:00-11:50 am): Garner

4. Queer Theory and Feminist Theory (MWF 4:00-4:50 pm): Dittman

5. Roman Satire (TTh 10:00-11:20 am): Garner

6. Semantics, Semiology, and Semiotics (TTh 3:00-4:20 pm): Briggs

CHAPTER TWENTY-TWO

Final Exams

At Mersley College, as at many other American colleges and universities, it was not uncommon for students to show up in pajamas for any class that began before noon. During Final Exam Week, this practice became almost universal. The typical Mersley student only began studying for the exam at 10:00 or 11:00 p.m. on the night before, tried to fit a semester's worth of learning into a few short hours, and eventually succumbed to sleep as the sun was rising. Dashing off to the test often meant waking up only ten or fifteen minutes before it began. The result was that most students didn't have enough time to shower and dress before the test began, even if they had wanted to. Which they didn't.

Peer pressure meant that even that minority of students who had gone to sleep at a reasonable hour still came to their exams dressed only in pajamas. This act of rebellion meant that Mersley students demonstrated their individuality by engaging in a practice that somehow made them even more alike. For whatever reason, the irony of this situation never occurred to them.

The sole exceptions to this practice that semester were, as one might expect, the students from the Department of Eminent Scholars. The cold December weather meant that clothing chosen in August, more as a statement than for comfort, now had some practical purpose. Esmé appeared for her Greek exam, the first test the students had, in a beret, turtleneck, and socks that were all black, a plaid suspenders skirt, and chunky heel loafers. The twins opted for the more "professorial" look of tan argyle sweater vests, collarless white linen blouses, surprisingly short brown skirts, off-white ankle socks, and brown loafers. Townsant seemed to have selected an outfit especially for final exams. Everyone could recall each element of the women's clothing combined with different accessories so as to create a variety of ensembles throughout the fall. Townsant, however, wore clothing no one had ever seen before. It strove to look vintage but was, in fact, brand new: a tweed vest with lapels and flap pockets, a gold watch chain (that remained unattached to any watch) extended between two of these vest pockets, houndstooth slacks, and penny loafers (that, of course, bore no pennies).

As had become his wont, Bastian was the outsider. He wore a white collared shirt that protruded from a dark gray shawl-neck cardigan, black corduroy pants, and black, highly polished oxfords. His act of apostasy? He intentionally allowed his shirt to remain slightly untucked in the back. The other students were, despite their differences in other ways, always consistently "tucked."

More than one pajama-clad Mersley student could be seen shaking her head as the quintet passed by on the quad, and one or two of them may even have muttered expressions like "Weirdo" or "Spaz" under their breaths. Obviously, not every term they chose was anything close to being politically correct, but even the students who might object most vocally in class if a professor slipped into language that was no longer deemed acceptable—despite the fact that some of that language may have been perfectly acceptable only the day before—tended to waive this rule for themselves when it came to the imminent scholars.

The weeklong break seemed to have restored at least a modicum of collegiality to the faculty members of the department. Since all their students would only be taking exams from other eminent scholars, they agreed to ignore the registrar's cumbersome final exam schedule and adopt their own. Professor Pope had already declared that, because her proseminar was a course on methods without content of its own, she would continue to do what she had been doing throughout the semester: combining her two courses into a test that required the students to apply the methods they'd learned in the proseminar to the material they'd encountered in The Art, Literature, and Music of the Ancient Near East. She also announced that, since administering the college's mandatory student course evaluations had cut into her teaching time on the last day of class, the five minutes she'd promised Esmé for what she called "Esmé's little concert" and what Esmé called "An Inquiry into the Tonal Qualities of Near Eastern Lyres: A Meta-Analysis of the Research" would occur at the start of the exam.

With five days in the exam period and five exams (plus one meta-analysis or little concert as you please), the faculty decreed that each exam would take place from 8:00 until 10:00 am Monday through Friday. Since Greek had been the first class that the students took at Mersley, it had the honor of being Monday's exam. The days for the remaining four tests were chosen by lot.

It wasn't hard for the students to imagine what Professor Garner's final would be like. Since beginning Plato's *Crito*, they had devoted class time to nothing else. Each class period had consisted of reading the day's assigned passage aloud in Greek, translating it, explaining any confusing points of grammar the passage may have contained, and then discussing the philosophical, historical, or cultural ramifications of that day's reading. The final exam was likely to be similar: several passages that had already been discussed in class (plus perhaps one or two that the students hadn't seen before) with the expectation that each passage would be translated and its grammar explained. The familiar passages were likely to be the most complex sections they'd encountered; the previously unseen passages would, of necessity, be far easier. There would also be one passage that was not covered in class but that the students would have a chance to prepare independently before the exam: the section of Xenophon's *Anabasis* where the Greek army shouted for joy when they finally saw the sea after a desperate march across Asia Minor. After all these translations, Garner would undoubtedly ask a number of essay questions, any one of which could probably occupy the entire two hours of the exam if the students were able to answer it in the depth it deserved.

Professor Pope's combined exam wasn't until Friday, which enabled Esmé to come down with a thorough case of stage fright throughout the week. The test itself didn't worry her. Like the other students in the program, she wouldn't have reached the level she had in school if she hadn't mastered the art of figuring out what each professor expected and then handing it back to them, using the keywords and other bits of jargon that each professor particularly liked. No, it was that five minutes *before* the test that had begun giving her palpitations. What had sounded like a wonderful idea before Fall Break now began to seem to her like a ridiculous suggestion she never should have made. It was, however, too late to back out now.

When Friday came, Professor Pope entered the classroom and began talking about the exam. For a brief moment, Esmé was filled with hope that her "little concert" had been forgotten. But she had no such luck. Professor Pope concluded her initial remarks by saying, "And now, before we begin, Esmé Dawson has agreed to demonstrate for us her reconstruction of a Near Eastern lyre. Esmé?"

Professor Pope sat down, and Esmé went up to the lectern. Suddenly the room looked from that perspective very different from its appearance when she sat among the other students. She felt her knees shake and hoped that no one else could sense her nervousness. In a voice so soft that Professor Pope had to call out "Louder, please!" Esmé began to explain the challenges involved in reconstructing what ancient music actually sounded like. She passed around images of the Standard of Ur and other artwork depicting lyres, as well as photos of several other modern attempts to reconstruct Sumerian and Assyrian instruments. She gave a brief summary of how other scholars had interpreted the few remaining texts that contained or even appeared to contain some type of musical notation and informed the others why she chose to base her own reconstruction and tuning on specific scholarly works while ignoring others.

Finally, she said that she would demonstrate to the class how she believed an ancient cult hymn annotated in a Ugarit text may have sounded. The tune she played wasn't more than a minute in length and sounded vaguely like the music that a traveling mediaeval and renaissance reenactment group had performed on campus earlier that semester. At the end of the piece, Esmé looked up at the group, not quite knowing what to expect and having prepared no way of bringing her demonstration to a close.

So, she stood there, staring at the students and professor who simply stared back at her, until finally Townsant rose from his seat and started to applaud. Professor Pope then followed his example. Thus given permission, the twins did the same, followed at last by Bastian.

The applause continued for several minutes as Esmé gathered up her materials and, feeling both proud and embarrassed, returned to her seat. It was only once she'd sat down again that she glanced at the clock: Far from the five minutes she's been allotted, her demonstration had consumed a full fifty-two minutes of the two-hour exam period.

Professor Pope returned to the front of the room, an inscrutable look on her face. Then she said, "You know, the whole purpose of *having* a final exam is to give you all a chance to review the material we covered throughout the entire course. And from what we just heard, I see that at least one of you has done that. Based on the discussions we had throughout this term, I strongly suspect that the rest of you have done so, too. After Ms. Dawson's very polished presentation, it seems almost blasphemous to ruin the atmosphere we're now experiencing with something as mundane as these exams." She tapped the leather portfolio she'd brought with her into the classroom.

"So—and I've never done this before—I'm simply going to waive the final exam this semester and grant you all a grade of A. I hope that's all right with you. None of you too disappointed not to take the final? I mean, you all still could. No? Well, fine, then. Let's just go, get ready for this afternoon's end-of-term party, and carry this mood with us."

It was a moment that the five students would cherish throughout their lives.

It was not, however, a moment that was based on perfect honesty.

The leather portfolio that Professor Pope tapped actually contained no exams. She had never intended to give one. As much as students hate taking finals, professors hate grading them even more, and so Professor Pope would periodically decide in advance to forego an exam and trot out her well-worn "the whole purpose of *having* a final exam" speech. It was not, despite her words, something she'd never done before.

That was only one of the reasons why, unique among the eminent scholars, her courses had once received record enrollments.

CHAPTER TWENTY-THREE

"The First Annual Hallothankmas Party"

The eminent scholars decided that they would hold a celebration of the successful launch of their new program on the last day of final exams. The timing turned out to be fortuitous since, having only five exam papers each to mark, Professors Garner, Briggs, and Dettmer had all finished their grading and submitted those grades to the registrar by noon that Friday. Professor Pope wasn't that far behind. Having no exams at all to grade, she waited what she thought was a suitable interval after her exam period was over, and then, by 2:30 that afternoon, submitted five A's for the students in her two courses.

By 5:00 p.m. all nine members of the Scipionic Circle were thus once again ensconced in the Diogenes Club. In fact, they were the sole patrons that day, the other students being already on their way home and the other faculty members cursing themselves for having assigned end-of-term papers that they now had to read.

Mersley College may have been traditional to the point of being stodgy in some ways but, in others, it strove to keep up with current trends in higher education. It had developed extensive policies for the assessment of student learning outcomes. It had replaced now-archaic terms such as *freshman*, *sophomore*, and the like with the currently-more-acceptable expressions *first-year student*, *second-year student*, and so on. This second change proved exceedingly useful because Mersley, like many other colleges and universities, increasingly had on campus *sixth-year students*, *seventh-year students*, and even the occasional *eighth-

year student, while fewer than twenty percent of the student body graduated before the fifth year. And it had long ago retired such religiously-based terms as *Christmas Vacation* and *Easter Vacation* in favor of *Winter Break* and *Spring Break*.

We've already seen that the eminent scholars had made a mockery of learning outcomes assessment from the very start of the term and, on the day of final exams, they would make a mockery of the other two conventions as well.

The last of the three was, ironically, the first to go. As soon as the students arrived at the club, Garner started the event by welcoming them to "our Christmas party." Pope, who had at least some understanding of political correctness, immediately corrected him by welcoming the students to "our Hanukkah, Christmas, and Kwanzaa party. And, if you're not religious at all, our 'holiday' party. Oh, wait. Are there any Muslim or Hindu holidays going on right now? I meant to look that up. It's so embarrassing."

"Never mind *that*," Briggs said. "What annoys *me* is that the stores in town start putting up their Christmas decorations as soon as Labor Day is over."

"What? You mean there *are* such things as Labor Day decorations?" Dittman asked. "*I've* not seen any."

"I didn't mean that they took *down* Labor Day decorations in order to put up Christmas decorations," Briggs explained. "I just meant that's when the red and green bows start appearing in stores. *And* the stars. *And* all the shiny wrapped boxes."

"In my day," Garner reminisced, "Halloween decorations never went up until the first of October *at the earliest*. Then they came down and the Thanksgiving decorations went up on November 1. The second the turkey'd been carved, those came down and were replaced by Christmas decorations that stayed up until New Year."

"It's all muddled now," Briggs complained. "One big, long, indistinguishable holiday season from the start of October through the end of the year. Its signature color should be beige."

"Hallothankmas," Esmé said, the first student to interject anything into this faculty-dominated conversation.

"Say what?" Garner asked, his brows furrowed.

"Hallothankmas," she repeated. "That's what they call it: Halloween, Thanksgiving, and Christmas, all jumbled into a single three-month holiday."

"Hallothankmas! Ha!" Briggs said. "I love it. That's it. That's exactly what it's become."

"Well, then," Dittman said, raising a glass, "I hereby declare this to be the Department of Eminent Scholars's First Annual Hallothankmas Party."

The others all joined in the toast, the faculty members with the first of what would eventually be far too many Professorial Martinis, and the students with water or soft drinks.

There then followed a forty-five-minute discussion on whether something may truly be called "annual," if it is indeed the first of its kind. If anyone except the wait staff—who'd learned simply to ignore the eminent scholars—had been present, their experience would have been something of a miniature version of what *any* class, faculty meeting, or other event held by the new program had been since the department's inception.

The featured entrée that evening was duck a l'orange, which most of them ordered, except for two who preferred the chef salad and one (Bastian, of course) who insisted on ordering a well-done steak to the barely suppressed horror of Professor Garner.

The conversation covered such topics as whether there was life after death, the meaning of *King Lear*, the best place to get bagels in the town of Mersley, the comparative merits of

Mozart and Wagner, the cause of civilization's downfall (with Dittman surprisingly and rather vocally tracing the majority of the ills in society to professional athletics), the ultimate purpose of a college education, the country each of them would visit if money were no object, and the specific differences between a crumpet and an English muffin.

As more and more alcoholic beverages were brought to the table, the conversation grew more boisterous but less coherent. Finally, near 11:00 p.m., when it had become apparent that the department's First Annual Hallothankmas Party had lasted far longer than anyone had expected, Professor Briggs attempted to make a few closing remarks to the students. His eyes were, by then, mere slits, and his voice was slurred, but the gist of his remarks was as follows:

"You know, you five students are the lucky ones. *God*, I wish there'd been a program like this back when I went to college. Even tonight, the level of discourse we've had has been admirable." He actually pronounced the last word as *admiral*, but none of the other faculty members seemed to notice. "You probably don't realize it yet, 'cause of that old saying. What is it? 'Freshmen don't know, and they don't know that they don't know. Sophomores don't know, but they know that they don't know. Juniors know, but they don't know that they know. And seniors know, and they know that they know.'"

With these words of wisdom, the party broke up, and all three of the current trends in higher education that were mentioned earlier had thoroughly and convincingly been broken.

CHAPTER TWENTY-FOUR

"The Flowers That Bloom in the Spring, Tra la!"

For three weeks, the students' minds were blissfully free of Gottlob Frege, *The Epic of Gilgamesh*, the Catacombs beneath Mersley College, *The Transmundane Codex of Berossus*, and the Fraternity of the Broken Omen. Their parents, like parents of all first-year college students who had not returned home for a semester, found them changed by the experience. The students had a tendency to say things like, "Well, let's unpack that" when their parents made any rather general or overarching sort of statement, and to begin sentences with "*Actually*" when they were about to correct another person's observation that, six months earlier, they wouldn't have bothered to correct at all.

Eventually, however, all good things must come to an end, and so, in the second week of January, the five imminent scholars left their homes (admittedly to the utter relief of their parents) and returned to the bucolic environment of Mersley College, which had *not* changed in the interim. Any tensions among the five that had developed during the fall term had faded completely. Even Bastian seemed happy to see the others, and they were overjoyed at seeing him. Such a détente couldn't last, of course, but it provided a pleasant enough interlude for the moment.

The four professors in the program were determined to "hit the ground running this spring." In fact, three of the four of them used those very words on the first day of class. (Sabrina Pope was, as often occurred, the lone exception.) Garner assigned them twice as many lines of the *Crito* to translate as he'd been assigning in the fall. Pope had them read the entire *Iliad* in Robert Fagles's translation, an almost unimaginable feat that encompassed more than six hundred pages, between Monday and Wednesday. And Dittman assigned an article relating queer theory to feminist theory that, although it was only thirty pages long, was so convoluted and jargon-laden that reading it felt like wading one's way across a swamp of rapidly solidifying epoxy.

When Garner added further long assignments in both his mythology and satire courses, the students were at their wits' end. They were complaining about these assignments, vociferously, when Professor Briggs entered the classroom for his course late on Tuesday afternoon. "What's all this brouhaha?" he asked with a tone that expressed his belief that, no matter what the cause might be, it couldn't be particularly serious.

The question uncorked the bottle, as it were. The students' complaints about the new, unreasonable workload spilled out, forcing Briggs to interject, "One at a time, please. One at a time." They thus began to voice their complaints in Whac-A-Mole fashion. Whenever one student paused for breath, another student began a fresh catalog of perceived injuries.

"Ah, well," Briggs concluded when he'd caught the gist of their concerns. "You were babes in the woods in the fall, as it were, but now it's spring, and 'The flowers that bloom in the spring, Tra la!' and all that. Time to remove the training wheels and fight the good fight, as it were."

"You're mixing metaphors," Townsant pointed out.

"You see?" Briggs concluded. "None of you would've said something like that to a faculty member back when you first joined this program. You sat there like quivering lumps of jelly—which is yet another simile, Mr. Townsant, as I'm sure you were just about to mention—and acted as though you were afraid we were going to slaughter the lot of you. That 'freshman terror' has, it seems, now worn off, and I, for one, shall miss it. But the point is that the program into which you've enrolled is intended to be challenging. I mean, the department is staffed solely by eminent scholars, for heaven's sake. We expect a lot of ourselves, and we expect a lot of you as well. I'm reminded of this every time I enter campus, passing that sign out front that reads Mersley ... oh, stale coconuts ... I've forgotten. I never can remember the word that comes after that. Can anyone help me? It's Mersley ... ?"

"College?" Esmé suggested helpfully, blithely unaware of Briggs's strategy at the moment.

"That's right. *College*. This is *college*, ladies and gentlemen, not elementary school, middle school, or even high school. The purpose of college is—not to find you a job, despite what our governor and his cronies might believe—but to teach you how to think, to make you better citizens, to prepare you for life, which *includes* making you employable, but isn't limited to that. There's more to life than work, you know. There are social issues, opportunities to grow through cultural experiences, discoveries about yourself and others to make ... all these are among the reasons why a college exists. And, in order to do that during the short time when you're among us, it requires hard work and long hours. So, if you're asked to read the whole damn *Iliad* in two days, I suggest you *read* the whole damn *Iliad* in two days. In the time you just spent complaining about it, you could have already learned what made Achilles storm off from the assembly with Agamemnon and been better people for it. Keep in mind that, if you're going to be educated people, this isn't the only time you'll ever read the *Iliad* in your lifetime. In fact, if I know Professor Garner, he'll have you read most or all of it *in Greek* within a year or two. So, what I suggest is that, instead of devoting any more time to lamenting what you have to do, you simply redirect your attention toward *doing* it. And, with that in mind, I would now like to begin our class."

If Briggs's intention had been to restore the five students to the "quivering lumps of jelly" stage he had mentioned earlier, his speech was quite successful. The students were shocked into silence. Briggs had never spoken to them like this before, and so, they all took out notebooks, tablets, or laptop computers as was their custom so that they could begin preparing notes on that day's class.

Briggs began by distributing his syllabus and then defining the material of the course. Semantics, he noted, was nothing more and nothing less than the study of meaning. "When a linguist or philosopher asks not 'Is this proposition correct?' but 'What does this proposition *mean*?' it's clear that we've entered the field of study that is known as semantics. Semiotics and semiology both deal with *signs*. So, if I say, 'You need to stop complaining,' you understand me through the operation of semantics. But if I simply show you the palm of my hand like a traffic cop ... " Briggs proceeded to do so. " ... then we've entered the realm of semiotics and semiology. Now, many people use those last two words interchangeably, but, in my course, we'll be making a subtle distinction between them. We'll use the term *semiotics* when we're discussing the relationship of a sign to the physical world. To return to our discussions of Wittgenstein last semester, if I write the numeral 2 on the blackboard, and you correctly bring me two slabs ... you know, I never mentioned it, but I'm always amused by Wittgenstein's fixation with slabs; he preferred to write in German, so perhaps he just liked the word *Platte*. Anyway, if I write the numeral 2 on the blackboard, and you correctly bring me two slabs, we've had a successful transaction in semiotic terms. But if we were to explore how your mind perceives the concept of 'twoness,' anything from the Greek dual number to pairs of anything at all to the mathematical concept of 'two,' we'd have crossed over into semiology. As I say, the distinction is subtle, and the lines between semiotics and semiology are sometimes blurred, but I think my reasons for distinguishing these concepts will become clearer as the semester goes on."

He turned back to the blackboard and wrote the words σῆμα and σημαίνω. "SAY-ma and say-MY-noh," he said, reading what he'd written. "The first is the Greek word for a sign. Originally, it meant something like a distinguishing mark on a horse or a peg stuck in the ground that indicates how far a javelin was thrown in an athletic contest. And the second word is the verb 'to indicate' or 'point out.' Eventually it becomes the verb that means 'to signify' or, not to put too fine a point on it, 'to *mean*.' Those are the roots of all three English words that appear in the title of this course. And as an example of how everything you study in our program is ultimately related to everything else, you'll find both of those words in the *Iliad*."

He paused for a moment to let his point sink in. Then he continued, "Oh, and don't look so surprised. Professor Garner's not the only one on the faculty who's studied Greek. I dare say that everyone in our department has had at least *some* exposure to the classical languages. That's the thing about becoming an educated person: There's no impenetrable barrier between disciplines. I dare say that Professor Garner discusses philosophy in his courses, so why shouldn't I include a bit of Greek vocabulary in mine? Who knows? You may even find us touching on post-modernism and the history of art, music, and literature before this semester is over."

Briggs looked at the five students and thought that, just perhaps, he had been too negative with them. So, he shifted his approach. "Now, just to show you that we eminent scholars are not as heartless as you seem to believe, and also to build on what we covered last semester, your only assignment for Thursday will be to review your notes on C.S. Peirce and John Searle from last semester and be prepared to discuss how their work on signs and the philosophy of mind will provide us with a proper entrée into the material of this course. In the meantime, 'The flowers that bloom in the spring, Tra la!' and all that. Now, class dismissed. Go do all that work you feel has been weighing you down, and I trust you'll emerge lighter as a result."

CHAPTER TWENTY-FIVE

The Revenant

Professor Briggs' class had been scheduled to go until 4:20 but, in light of the unusual turn it took, all the students were back in their rooms by 4:00. The Warren-Whiteheads devoted themselves to their Greek assignment. Townsant and Esmé read as much of the *Iliad* as they could before dinner time. And Bastian lay on his bed, thinking.

He thought about how he himself might treat students someday if he were to become a professor in a program like the Department of Eminent Scholars. He thought about which of the many long assignments that were due within the next two days he ought to start on first (but he never actually started any of them). And he thought about the Fraternity of the Broken Omen and their ritual chamber located somewhere within the Catacombs beneath campus.

Bastian had a clear image in his mind of what that chamber would look like. He imagined a perfectly round room with polished stone walls and eight open archways leading into it from rock-cut tunnels. He envisioned an altar standing at the very center of the chamber and thirteen black-robed initiates gathered around the altar. Twelve of them formed a circle and sang a mysterious chant in voices so low they would be perfect for a Russian opera. The thirteenth member served as the priest. As the lugubrious prayer reached its critical moment, the priest would raise a sacrificial dagger and plunge it into ... what?

That final detail was never clear in Bastian's fantasy. When he was feeling particularly overshadowed by one of his fellow students, he would imagine that person, bound and gagged on the altar, as the gleaming blade sliced into his or her chest. When he was feeling less bloodthirsty, he would visualize some inanimate object on the altar. A crystal that somehow shattered into millions of glistening fragments as the blade came down. An offering of fruit and grain made to some nameless chthonic deity. But mostly he fancied that the object before the mysterious priest was a leather-bound book, specifically *The Transmundane Codex of Berossus*. The ritual would explain why there had been an effort to expunge every indication of the text from Sutlinger Library: Its contexts were too powerful to be left for mere mortals to chance upon. It had to be sacrificed again and again. Like the liver of Prometheus, it would be restored each night, only to be torn apart once more the next day. It would vanish only to return, the type of object known as a revenant.

Bastian knew about revenants from the books he read *between* his numerous re-readings of *The Secret History*. He favored works by H. P. Lovecraft, Algernon Blackwood, and Edgar Allan Poe. The more they made his skin crawl, the better he liked them. Best of all were old, musty copies of books he found in some secondhand bookstore, the kind with covers that cracked when you opened them and that exuded an aroma not unlike that which permeated Chudwell Hall.

Most of the revenants Bastian encountered in these books were once human, people long dead or thought to be dead who returned, like Banquo's ghost, to bring terror to the living. But at times what returned from the past was an object, such as a locket destroyed in the fire that had killed its owner or a letter that proved its author's guilt, and Bastian had a singular attraction to that type of story. He imagined that *The Transmundane Codex of Berossus* was that sort of book, forgotten for generations but now brought to the attention of the five students (and to himself most of all) because at last someone had arrived at Chudwell Hall who was worthy of learning its secrets. The library card had materialized as a token sent to beckon him to find the missing text, no doubt hidden somewhere in the sprawling Catacombs, and restore the once powerful Fraternity of the Broken Omen.

The more he dreamed as he lay upon his bed, the more certain he was that all the secrets they'd stumbled across were connected. The research that the mysterious Tolbert Fitzgerald had been conducting must have dealt with the obscure text of Berossus. He wasn't quite sure what that title *The Deleuzian Rhizomatics of Ontological Temporality: A Deconstructionist Approach* meant, but he was sure that, at its heart, it *must* have something to do with the book he and the others were being challenged to find. In Bastian's imagination, Fitzgerald's research must have brought him far too close to the occult knowledge protected by the Fraternity of the Broken Omen. That's why one of them stole his manuscript, redacted its most dangerous secrets, and then published the book under his own name, all in an elaborate plot to destroy Fitzgerald's reputation. Upon learning of this betrayal, Fitzgerald then must have sought out the Catacombs in order to confront the fraternity. But, unable to locate the hidden entrance, he had hanged himself in despair. Now the spirit of Tolbert Fitzgerald was beckoning Bastian Lewis to complete the quest that he himself could not complete.

It all made sense.

And to Bastian, it all seemed much more compelling than wading his way through the dense thickets of the article Dittman had assigned them.

He indulged in these thoughts for so long that he barely made it to dinner before the dining hall closed. Then, wolfing down a tepid plate of chicken parmesan, the only entrée left on offer, he grabbed his backpack and headed to Chudwell 2B to get in a few hours of quiet study before the others began arriving for that night's study session.

Perhaps it was his thoughts of that afternoon or perhaps it was because Chudwell Hall was indeed an outdated building badly in need of repair, but as he sat in the empty room while the lights flickered about him, he thought that the bangs and groans of the foundation settling seemed even louder than usual.

When the door opened a few minutes after 10:00, Bastian leapt from his chair. Struggling to recall the precise difference between Chryseis and Briseis in the *Iliad*, he had forgotten that the others would be joining him as soon as their own individual studies were complete.

It was Esmé who was the first to enter.

She stood in the doorway and seemed unwilling or unable to take the final step inside. Her eyes were fixed on the table where Bastian sat. But it wasn't Bastian who'd absorbed her attention.

There, at the far end of the table, a small, off-white object was the first thing she saw.

The missing catalog card had returned.

CHAPTER TWENTY-SIX

Interlibrary Loan

Despite the pressure of all their assignments, the students did surprisingly little work in their study session that night. Even Townsant, who wasn't easily spooked by seemingly supernatural events, felt that the reappearance of the card was spooky. Suddenly, Bastian's convictions about Professor Fitzgerald's death and the hidden tunnels that ran beneath campus didn't seem quite so outlandish. While still convinced that there had to be a logical explanation for the return of the card *somehow*, Townsant did not openly challenge Bastian who had begun using expressions like "forces beyond our control" and "secrets that remain to be discovered."

Where the two did part company, however, was in what to do about the new development. Bastian insisted that the group had a "calling," that it was being summoned to a "mission," perhaps by the ghost of Tolbert Fitzgerald who still haunted Chudwell Hall or perhaps by mysterious "emanations" that Bastian swore he could feel each time he entered Room 2B.

Townsant wanted no part in these "fantasies," as he called them. "Sure, we don't yet know how this card got here, why it's here, and why it came back after we returned it to the library, but, I mean, Occam's Razor, people: The simplest explanation is usually the best. Merely because we don't have an explanation, that doesn't mean we have to assume occult forces are at work."

"Okay," Bastian challenged him. "What other explanation can *you* come up with?"

"I don't know. Maybe one of the professors left it here."

"Really? The exact card that appeared here before, that we returned to the library, and that we placed back into a card catalog no one uses? One of the professors just happened to remove that particular card from the library and brought it here *twice? That's* your explanation?"

"I didn't say it was the *final* explanation. I just said that some completely natural explanation has to be preferable to any that relies on ghosts, secret societies, and tunnels that we were specifically told don't exist. No one believes that superstitious nonsense anymore. No offense, Esmé."

"None taken," she assured him.

"C'mon, admit it, Townsant," Bastian chided him. "You were just as creeped out as the rest of us when you saw that card show up here again."

"Creeped out, yes. And I'll admit I gave in for a moment to thinking that maybe, *just maybe,* something weird and sinister may be going on. But when you look at things logically …"

"I'm sick of looking at everything logically," Bastian interrupted. "Logic sometimes causes wars. It's used to justify racism and sexism. It reduces poetry to nothing more than a series of patterns and theories. Logic has probably killed at least as many people as religion has over the centuries."

"Now you're beginning to sound like Dittman," Townsant countered. "Everything logical and orderly is just a symptom of patriarchal oppression."

"Well, is she wrong?" Bastian challenged him.

The women looked on in horror as the men seemed to lapse into the sort of conflict that often occurs between two rival males—be they rams, gorillas, or Siamese fighting fish—as they try to establish their alpha dominance.

In the end, the study session broke up with nothing resolved and with most of the work due the next day left undone. Each of the students would have to study well into the night just to be ready when Garner closed the door and began his Greek class promptly at 8:00 a.m. the next day.

In one sense, however, Bastian did make a convert that evening. During their afternoon break, Mallory Warren-Whitehead walked up to Bastian as he was headed across the quad and said, "*I* believe you. There's something evil going on, and I don't like it. *I'll* help you look for answers."

And wherever Mallory went, Prudence would soon follow. So, in the space of less than a day, Bastian went from holding a minority opinion among the imminent scholars to having a majority on his side. Townsant had no idea that any of this was happening.

Buoyed by this first feeling of success, Bastian decided to spend an hour or so of the afternoon break doing research in the library. An idea occurred to him that, in all honesty, should have occurred to him or any other of the students much earlier: Why not search for *The Transmundane Codex of Berossus* in the school's *computerized* library system? If the book had indeed once been in the library's collection, surely its record would have been transferred over to the electronic catalog when that system was developed. Bastian could hardly believe that he hadn't thought of it before.

He thus sat down at one of the library's terminals and typed in the name of the book. A reply popped up immediately:

No such record

He then tried each word of the title individually and received the same result.

Not having the card with him, he couldn't recall its complete call number, but he remembered it began with 182.

Instantly, a long list of titles appeared, all of which had something to do with Greek philosophy. One by one, Bastian looked at the full record of each book, but none of them seemed to have any clear connection to Berossus or even to the Hellenistic Period in which he wrote.

"Can't monopolize a terminal all day," a voice said behind him.

Bastian was startled and turned around to see the sharp features of Barbara the Barbarian Librarian staring back at him.

"Um, sorry," Bastian stammered. "I was just looking for a book."

"*Obviously.* And it appears you weren't having much luck doing so."

"No, and I've tried everything I can think of."

"Have you considered the possibility that it's not in the Sutlinger collection? It's a very good collection for a college our size, but it doesn't have everything, you know."

"But it *has* to be here. At least a record of it has to be here."

"And why does the book 'have' to be here? Upon what are you basing your information, young man?"

Bastian suddenly realized that he couldn't reveal how he and the others had seen the mysterious card. They weren't supposed to be touching the card catalog and, if he admitted too much, he was sure they'd be banned from the room. "I mean, it *should* be here. It's an important book."

"Then say what you mean and mean what you say. What's the title?"

"*The Transmundane Codex of Berossus.*"

Winchester's face twisted in a strange expression. She hesitated a moment and then said, "Never heard of it. Write it down for me."

Bastian did so and handed the slip of paper to the librarian.

"Check back with me tomorrow."

"You mean you've got other ways of finding books in our library?"

"Of course, I do. I'm the head librarian, after all. But that's not what I meant. If this book is as important to you as you say, I'm going to request it via interlibrary loan."

Bastian's expression made it clear that he'd never heard that term before.

Barbara Winchester sighed. "I blame it all on video games and sugared cereals," she muttered. "Interlibrary loan is when one library requests permission to borrow a book from another library. We're connected to a vast network of college and university libraries. One of them is bound to have a copy of this book."

CHAPTER TWENTY-SEVEN

The Strategic Plan

If students quickly absorb the academic jargon of their disciplines and then insist on inflicting that jargon on an unsuspecting public (i.e., their parents and any of their high school friends who elected *not* to go to college), then so do academic administrators. Chief among these expressions prized by presidents and deans were the ones already scorned by the eminent scholars—*learning outcomes assessment, multiculturalism/diversity/inclusivity*, and *quality assurance*—plus the granddaddy of them all: *strategic planning*.

The basic concept of strategic planning arose in the late 1940s when business leaders wanted to adopt for commercial purposes some of the techniques that had made the United States military so successful during WWII. They wanted to move seamlessly from the corporate mission and vision to specific goals and objectives that they'd achieve through long-term strategies and shorter-term tactics. From the 1950s through the 1980s, strategic planning took its place alongside other business-world fads, such as Total Quality Management, Theory Z, Management by Objectives, Six Sigma, and Management By Walking Around. Then, sometime in the 1980s, executives began to realize that strategic planning rarely lived up to its promise. It brought about changes, certainly, but those changes often could have been achieved at lower cost and greater efficiency by other means. Besides, what good was a ten- or twenty-year plan when the world would have changed in utterly unpredictable ways by the time the plan was ever fulfilled ... if indeed it ever could be?

Ironically, just as the corporate world was turning its back on strategic planning, the academic world was discovering it. Strategic planning became such a *sine qua non* of higher education that accrediting bodies often required it, and new presidents or chancellors almost always made the development of a new strategic plan one of their immediate goals. The problem was that, as the tenure of most presidents and chancellors decreased, the length and ambition of most strategic plans increased, with the result that the faculty and administration ended up devoting countless hours and other resources to preparing a new plan every four or five years. There were colleges and universities that benefitted from such an approach, and governing boards loved to cite them. But, for every strategic plan that succeeded, twenty or thirty of them failed to create any significant change at all, and most of the rest produced a few moderate improvements at best. It became common practice for the CEO of a university simply to declare the plan a huge success before moving on to the next position at a slightly larger school but with a far larger salary. There the CEO would start the whole process all over again, announcing "This is one strategic plan that won't merely sit on the shelf!" before introducing yet another strategic plan that, like all its predecessors, ended up sitting on a shelf.

Both President Woolridge and Dean McDaniel were old enough hands at college administration that they knew how to play the strategic planning game like pros. Their peers at other institutions either went on to more lucrative positions after a few years or were removed by the board after a vote of no confidence for some act of poor judgment or another, but Woolridge and McDaniel seemed to go on and on. They had a supportive enough board that their jobs were safe and, despite the occasional hiccup, their track records had been successful enough that members of the faculty and staff alike simply assumed that they'd remain in their positions for as long as they liked.

The current strategic plan for Mersley College would expire by the end of that very academic year. The result was that the president and dean decided to make the spring semester a preparation period for the start of the *next* ten-year strategic plan. In truth, that plan was already written. Over the holiday break, Woolridge and McDaniel had brainstormed a list of accomplishments that were going to occur anyway and created a "plan" that set these inevitabilities as "stretch goals." The problem was that college administrators couldn't just *announce* a new strategic plan to the faculty. They had to provide the illusion that the faculty and other stakeholders had *contributed* to it. And so, early that spring semester, posters appeared in every classroom and residence hall, on every lamppost and exterior wall of Mersley College inviting members of the faculty, staff, student body, and community to volunteer for the school's new "Strategic Planning Task Force." What Woolridge and McDaniel hoped to do was to select a pliable enough group that its members could be persuaded they themselves had thought of all the goals that had actually been developed by the president and dean. That approach had worked well enough for them before that they had confidence in its ability to work again. If there was any real "strategy" involved in the planning, that type of deception was basically it.

A number of faculty members and department chairs had already contacted the president's office and asked to be considered for the new task force. These tended to be the same people who volunteered for nearly every opportunity that arose on campus, and the vast majority of them have no relevance whatsoever to this story. But one person who saw the posters is highly relevant to what happened next: Bastian Lewis. He wasn't particularly interested in volunteering to help shape the *college's* strategic plan, but the concept, which was new to him, captured his imagination.

On the Thursday of that week, during the long afternoon break, Bastian arranged to meet with the Warren-Whitehead twins at a quiet table in the Dugout. There he announced that what the three of them needed to do was to develop a strategic plan that would lead them to the Catacombs and ultimately to the ritual chamber of the Fraternity of the Broken Omen.

"I've been doing some research on this," he said, using the term *research* to describe the three minutes he'd spent searching online for a quick summary of strategic planning.

"An effective strategic plan should be based on mission. Our mission has been handed to us by the events we've all witnessed in Chudwell Hall. We need to find out why the spirit of Tolbert Fitzgerald still haunts the building and, in so doing, track down *The Transmundane Codex of Berossus*, which, I'm convinced, stands at the very heart of this entire mystery. Mission should always inspire vision, and our vision should be to gain access to the tunnels beneath campus and trace them until we find the location of the ritual chamber. Mission and vision should suggest more specific goals and the strategies we'll use to achieve those goals, and that's what we need to work on next. You in?"

Delighted by the attention and the thrill of embarking on an adventure, both Mallory and Prudence were most definitely "in."

CHAPTER TWENTY-EIGHT

The One-Hundred-Percent Solution

Garner was *not* one of the faculty members who volunteered to serve on the new task force. He'd endured more than his share of strategic plans before and believed that the best way to deal with them was to ignore them and hope they'd go away. Inevitably they did.

But that did not mean that he remained unaffected by what the president and dean had in mind. One afternoon, as he was reading Horace's *Satire* 2.4 on the art of fine dining, Dean McDaniel appeared in his doorway.

"Good Lord, I'd forgotten how badly this building stinks," she said by way of announcing her arrival.

"It's always that way when administrators are around," Garner replied, not looking up from his book. "You must be lost. You haven't returned to the scene of the crime, as it were, in ... what? twenty years? twenty-five?"

"I can't believe we actually once taught classes in this old heap," she sniffed. "It's like returning to the stone age."

"I'd repeat to you what I had to remind Professor Pope of not long ago about workmen and their tools, if I thought you'd understand it. Nevertheless, some of us *do* continue to teach here, and rather successfully, I might add."

The dean drew her lips back in a tight smile. Garner had just given her a perfect entrée for the real purpose of her visit.

"Interesting that you should say that, actually. I was just going over the metrics for last semester, and I have some concerns."

"In that case, I strongly suggest that you take them up with Professor Dittman. She's the one earning 'the big bucks' this year as chair."

"I'd hardly call Mersley's modest chair stipend 'the big bucks.' And anyway, I *did* try to see her. She's not in her office. *None* of the other Horsepersons of the Apocalypse seems to be in. Only you."

"Horseper- ? What are you prattling on about now? Do make it quick, will you? I'm trying to prepare for my Roman Satire course."

"Horace, hmmm?" she said, looking at his book. "Then perhaps I should have said Horace-men of the Apocalypse. What? Not even a smile, Winton? Have you really lost all sense of humor?"

"I'll let you know if I ever hear any. But do feel free to leave Professor Dittman a note. I don't want to delay you in doing ... whatever it is that deans do, anyway."

"Interesting that you should say that. I'd probably describe one of my most important duties as promoting efficiency and sustainability in our academic programs. Have you seen the posters around campus?"

"The ones bearing my picture and reading, 'Wanted: Dead or Alive'?"

"One could only wish. No, I'm referring to the posters announcing that we're about to wrap up the college's current strategic plan and are, therefore, looking for volunteers to serve on the task force that will prepare the new one."

Garner actually guffawed. "You see? I told you I can recognize humor when I hear it. You certainly can't imagine I'd volunteer to waste my time on an activity as dreary and pointless as that. Haven't you and President Bonehead already secretly drawn up the next plan, anyway?"

"Of course not," she lied. "You really don't understand how college administration works, do you? And no, I'm not here to ask you to serve on the task force. I'd rather have my fingernails removed with a pliers or, worse, read one of your articles. No, I'm here because, as I was reviewing the current strategic plan in preparation for the upcoming planning period, I noticed something interesting in it."

"What? That it failed to include some bit of administrative jargon. What was it? SWOT Analysis? Key Performance Indicators?"

"Those were both in there, actually. No, what I noticed is that we'd included a provision for fast-tracking the elimination of any program that failed to meet certain enrollment projections by the spring semester."

"Sorry. I must have nodded off during that last bit of administrative drivel. You were saying?"

"I was saying that the Department of Eminent Scholars is in very great danger of being shut down. And sooner rather than later."

"You know, if you say 'sooner,' it's redundant to add 'rather than later.' You're padding again."

Dean McDaniel adopted what she regarded as an ingratiating smile, but what, to any unbiased observer, would have been characterized as something far more malicious. Uninvited, she picked up a pen from Garner's desk and, for absolutely no reason whatsoever, began playing with it.

"It's unfortunate that you've chosen not to take the current situation seriously, Winton. It *is* serious. Your department has only five students enrolled in its major. Your former department, Classics ... "

"*Our* former department, Dawn. You were once a classicist yourself, remember? Not a particularly good one, I must say, but a classicist nonetheless."

Dean McDaniel started to protest that, like Garner, she had also been a recipient of the Covington Prize. But then she realized that he was merely trying to provoke her, and so she returned to her main topic. "As I was saying, *our* former department, Classics, has the second lowest number of majors: sixteen. More than three times the number of majors in *your* new program."

"Really? I'm surprised you were able to perform such advanced mathematics without a calculator."

"Contrast that to the 'big leagues': Business Administration with 256 majors, Biology with 194 ... "

"All of whom expect to make it into medical school and ninety-eight percent of whom will be disappointed."

" ... Psychology with 185 ... "

"What's your point, Dawn? My Horace is getting cold."

"My point, *Professor* Garner, is that Mersley College can no longer afford to keep you. I had blindly assumed, when the Department of Eminent Scholars was first created, that we'd need to give you the full three-year run specified in the faculty handbook to see whether you could develop a sustainable enrollment. But then I came across this statement in the current strategic plan ... "

She opened a document she was carrying to a dog-eared page. There, under a section labeled "Goal: Promoting the Sustainability of Mersley College," was a paragraph stating that programs failing to meet certain enrollment requirements between the fall semester and the spring semester would be subject "to immediate dissolution, with the faculty in those programs either reassigned to other departments or non-renewed, at the dean's discretion."

The last four words were heavily underlined in the dean's copy of the plan.

"So, you see, we really are at a crossroads, I'm afraid. Five students served by four professors? I don't know what your definition of *sustainability* is, but mine's certainly not that. Now, I don't mean to be unreasonable. If you like, I can allow you and your colleagues until the end of the year before we eliminate your department. But I think, in the best interests of the students, we ought not to wait so long. I'd like to call a meeting of your—how many students was it again? Oh, yes: *five*—students and work to transition them into new majors immediately, before they waste any more time on a program that certainly won't be around when they graduate. And we'll be generous to you and your colleagues, too. Although we won't be able to renew your contracts, we'll allow you to retain library privileges for ... shall we say, three months?"

The eyes of Garner and McDaniel were each fixed on the other. Hers said, "Gotcha!" while his merely seethed with a mixture of contempt and animosity.

Finally, Garner said, in a voice that sounded thin and weak, "Might I be able to see that, please?"

He accepted the copy of the strategic plan from her and read over the section in question. Then he asked, his tone now far more restrained, "How many majors did you say Business Administration had?"

"256."

"Was that their fall number or their spring number?"

"Spring. It started off as 328, but still, I think you'll admit, 256 majors is a healthy ... "

"And Biology? What was their fall enrollment?"

"231. Why? What's all this about?"

"I'm just trying to come up with a few figures in my mind. You can check these later with your calculator. I don't keep one myself. But I think your figures mean that Business had a seventy-eight percent retention rate, fall to spring, while Biology had an eighty-four percent retention rate."

"So?"

Garner closed the document and handed it back to Dean McDaniel. "One of the things we try to teach students in the Department of Eminent Scholars is how to analyze texts properly, and the first step in doing that is understanding precisely what they say. If you read over that section of the plan again, you'll see that the targets are all about reducing attrition. It doesn't say anything at all about overall numbers. The only thing that matters is the percentage of students a program *retains* from fall to spring. We had five students last fall. We still have five students this spring. That makes—and I'll spare you the difficult math—a one-hundred-percent retention rate for the Department of Eminent Scholars. In other words, our record is far better than either Business Administration or Biology. I imagine, if you'd 'run the numbers' as you folks like to say, that Psychology will have done even worse. So, if you're actually serious about fast tracking the elimination of non-sustainable programs, you might start with one of those three. Personally, I'd cut Business Administration. I mean, it's not *really* an academic discipline anyway."

"But ... "

"Hardly something that Plato would've taught in the Academy."

"You can't ... "

"Certainly not one of the four areas of study taught in mediaeval universities."

"Winton ... "

"In fact, I think if you choose to pursue this apparent vendetta you have against our program, I'll show this section of the strategic plan to the board and insist that they eliminate all three of the programs you named. Now, if you don't mind, my Horace?"

CHAPTER TWENTY-NINE

The Phantom

The first step that Bastian, Mallory, and Prudence had decided on for their own strategic plan was to obtain the copy of *The Transmundane Codex of Berossus* that Barbara Winchester had ordered through interlibrary loan and read it. The problem was that, not ever having acquired a book through interlibrary loan, they had no idea how long that process would take. So, although their usual practice was to avoid the head librarian as much as possible, Bastian decided that he had no other choice but to seek her out and ask for a status update.

"I was wondering when you'd have the nerve to come back in here," Winchester said as soon as he walked up.

"Ma'am?"

"From now on, if you're intent on pulling some sort of prank on a member of the staff, I trust you'll find a more appropriate victim. Your library privileges are revoked for two weeks. Now, if you'll kindly leave the premises."

"Ma'am?" Bastian repeated. "I don't understand."

"That wild goose chase you sent me on. I know you all think I have nothing better to do than to re-shelve the books you're too lazy to return by yourselves, but I do *not* appreciate having my time wasted."

"Wasted? But I don't see ... "

She froze him with a withering glance. "*The Transmundane Codex of Berossus* indeed. Where'd you come up with such a ridiculous title?"

Not wanting to talk about the mysterious catalog card, Bastian made up an excuse. "I overheard two students talking about it in the Dugout. It sounded interesting."

"Which students?"

"Well, I don't know their names. I'd never seen them before."

"Describe them to me."

Bastian had to think quickly. He hadn't expected this line of inquiry. What description could he provide that wouldn't seem specific to any particular Mersley student? Barbara the Barbarian probably knew just about all of them. If he gave too many details ...

"I don't know. Two women. Average height. Sandy blonde hair. They were still in their pajamas."

"You've just described two-thirds of our student body."

In other circumstances, Bastian would have beamed with his success. In the present situation, however, he thought it best to control his reaction.

"I'm sorry. As I say, I don't remember ever seeing them before. And I'm really no good at describing women's clothing. The pajamas were light blue maybe, and one had a top that was plaid?"

Winchester's stern look didn't waiver. Finally, she said, "Well, if you do find out who they are, email their names to me. They'll be suspended, too. It seems they were playing a practical joke on you."

"You mean there *is* no such book as *The Transmundane Codex of Berossus*?"

"That's what I said, isn't it? No one's ever heard of it. *No one.* The book's a figment of someone's imagination, a fabrication, a phantom."

"Oh."

"If I were you, young man, I'd spend my time studying or making myself productive in other ways rather than ogling young women in blue pajamas. And just where do you think you're going?"

Bastian had assumed the conversation was over and was heading toward the stacks to get a book he needed for Professor Dittman's course.

"I was just going to grab an assigned text by Judith Butler."

"Is your mind so warped by hormones that you've already forgotten your suspension?"

"But I thought that, since you realized I hadn't been the one who made up that book ... "

"Then you thought incorrectly, young man. Now, you are not to set foot inside Sutlinger for two weeks."

"Can't I appeal that to someone?"

"Of course, you can."

"To whom then?"

"To the head librarian. Oh, wait. That's right. *I'm* the head librarian. Appeal denied. Two weeks!"

* * *

Bastian tracked the twins down just outside their residence hall and told them what had just happened.

"A phantom?" Mallory said, replying to one detail in his narrative.

"Don't worry. I'll get the Butler book for you," Prudence added, replying to another.

Bastian, who had appointed himself keeper of the revenant catalog card, removed it from his backpack and looked at it with newfound awe. "The real question is: Where did this come from then?"

They quickly dismissed the idea that the card was part of some complex practical joke. "Who would be able to duplicate the style of the card catalog so precisely? And who would know where we found it?"

"I think it's a form of proof," Mallory said.

"Proof?" Bastian asked.

"Proof that you're on the right track. It's uncanny. *Literally* uncanny. It's like it had just been manifested for us from some other dimension."

"Or some other place and time," Prudence suggested.

As much as Bastian wanted to believe in his own paranormal theory about secret tunnels and arcane wisdom, he was having a little trouble accepting the idea that the card was delivered to them by residents of a parallel universe.

"I don't know," he said. "Maybe we were too quick to reject the notion that we're being 'had' by some fraternity or other."

"Oh, but I'm sure we are," Mallory said. Then, in response to Bastian's questioning look, she went on, "The Fraternity of the Broken Omen."

CHAPTER THIRTY

The Golden Ideal

Winton Garner was not the sort of professor who would typically be described as entering a classroom "with a spring in his step." Nevertheless, following his most recent skirmish with Dean McDaniel, there was something in his manner that those who knew nothing of Garner's personality and history at the college might almost mistake for something approaching *joie de vivre*. He'd bested an administrator in a battle of wits, his research on Bacchylides was proceeding apace despite his "impossibly heavily" teaching load, and he'd been promised at least a blissful year and a half before he'd have to take his turn as department chair. Yes, indeed. Things were looking up.

It's easy to imagine the professor's disappointment, therefore, when he looked out at the students in his Greek class and saw that they didn't share his exuberance. Bastian and the twins were behind in their work because they'd been distracted by a so-far-futile search to find the hidden Catacombs or locate a copy of Berossus's "phantom" book. Esmé and Townsant lacked those excuses for their failure to come to class that morning completely prepared, but the amount of work they'd been assigned in all their courses meant that *something* had to take the back burner. And that particular morning, the "something" in question had been their reading in Plato's *Crito*.

When Bastian had misidentified an aorist subjunctive as a nonexistent "future subjunctive," Garner decided enough was enough.

"*Mister* Lewis, *if* you are fortunate enough to continue your study of ancient Greek beyond the rather rudimentary level where we are currently forced to dwell, you will discover that, for any expression Plato uses, there exists one and only one perfect way of rendering that thought in English. In the past five minutes, you have managed to inflict on us the *worst* possible equivalent of each expression. Would you care to try again and at least *approach* a reasonably adequate translation?"

Flushing a deep red, Bastian returned to the passage in question and, with excruciating slowness, gave the text another effort.

"Miles to go before we sleep, Mr. Lewis," Garner said, trying to hurry him along. "Or perhaps not," he muttered under his breath.

The professor's last remark proved to be the tipping point. Bastian slammed his textbook shut and complained, "So much for 'moderation is best,' I suppose. We are *trying* to give you and all the other professors in this program our best possible work, but each day the assignments get longer and longer."

In a surprisingly mild tone, Garner replied, "Take that as a compliment, Mr. Lewis. We expect much from you because we have confidence that we'll *receive* much from you."

"And what about the Golden Mean? All that talk about 'Nothing too much.' Was all that just more hot air?"

It may be taken as evidence of just how close to feeling chipper Winton Garner was that morning that he did not eviscerate Bastian on the spot. Instead, he looked from one exhausted face to another in the classroom and decided it was time for another lesson in what he and his colleagues in the department were hoping to accomplish.

"You raise a valid point, Mr. Lewis. But I'd modify it only slightly. The Golden Mean is indeed a concept that many ancient Greeks saw as a guide to excellence, but so is the Golden *Ideal*."

He stepped toward the blackboard and wrote the word *asymptote*.

"No doubt in your study of mathematics in high school, you

came across this term. It has perfectly straightforward Greek roots. The initial *a-* suggests negation. The medial *sym* or *syn* means *with* or *together*. And πίπτω (*PIP-toe*), the verb meaning *I fall*, is one of those rare Greek verbs that contains very few irregular forms. 'I don't fall together': That might serve as an initial way of rendering the three morphemes of this word. An asymptote, you'll recall, is a line that continually approaches a curve, but can never quite touch it. It does 'not fall together' with the curve, no matter how far we extend it."

Garner drew a crude line and curve on the board to illustrate this concept. Then, wiping his hands together to shake off as much chalk dust as possible, he continued. "The ancient Greeks were fascinated by the ideal, by what was perfect. In the *Republic*, Plato tries to imagine the ideal state. In the Olympics and the other Panhellenic Games, athletes strove to approach physical perfection as far as possible. The poet Pindar celebrates this spirit, using such images as water, gold, and the sun in his *First Olympian Ode* as symbols of this perfection. Thucydides sought, in his *History of the Peloponnesian War*, to write what he called a κτῆμα εἰς ἀεί—a *k-TAY-ma ace IGH-yay* or 'thing that would last forever,' a perfect creation. And until the Hellenistic Age, Greek sculptors created very few portraits of individuals. Instead, they sought to depict the *perfect* athlete or the *perfect* female form. Imagine living in an environment where you had all these images of perfection surrounding you. You couldn't possibly live up to those ideals. No one could. But, to use the modern phrase, these ideals were goals to 'live into.' You yourself were the asymptote, approaching the ideal as close as possible even though you *knew* you would never quite reach it. *That* was the Golden Ideal."

He held up his copy of the *Crito*. "This work that we're reading right now, this dialogue by Plato. Some scholars even think it might be the first dialogue Plato ever wrote. We call it a *classic*. My academic training is in the Classics. But what do we *mean* by 'a classic'? A classic is a work of exceptional quality that has stood the test of time. Not time as we Americans see it. If you travel about the United States, you might tour a house that's two hundred years old and think, 'My, how ancient this is!' But two hundred years is *nothing*. Even a millennium is *nothing*. People sometimes forget that Cleopatra is closer to *us* in time than she was to the building of the pyramids. Now, the pyramids, *they're* ancient. They've survived the test of time. Are the works of Jane Austen and Charles Dickens 'classics'? Well, you tell *me*. They've survived many decades of being regarded as well-written, insightful books, but many well-written, insightful books from antiquity survived for *centuries* but now are lost or completely forgotten. We talk about American 'history.' America is too young to have a 'history.' All it has are current events. People are still arguing about the meaning of the Civil War and the merit or lack of merit of the so-called 'Founding Fathers.' These things are too recent for us to think of them alongside the true *classics*. Sometimes it seems to me as though we're *still* fighting the Civil War."

Garner opened the book to the passage assigned for that day's reading. "The *Crito*, however ... the *Crito*'s a classic. It truly has stood the test of time. Is it perfect? No. No book can ever be perfect. But it *approaches* perfection, and that's why we read it."

He paused long enough that Esmé was able to break in. "What about the Bible? The Bible's perfect, isn't it?"

"Well, it is the Good Book. But in the field known as Classics, we study the *Great* Books." He smiled, an expression that always seemed somewhat out of place on Garner's face. "And perfect? Perhaps you can enlighten me. The opening of the gospel attributed to Mark: 'The beginning of the gospel of Jesus Christ, the Son of God.' Then what comes next?"

For Esmé, the question was an easy one, far easier than any other assignment she's received from her professors that semester. "'As it is written in Isaiah the prophet, Behold, I send my messenger before thy face, who shall prepare thy way; the voice of one crying in the wilderness: Prepare the way of the Lord, make his paths straight.'"

"Ah, yes. The Revised Standard Version. Very good. But perhaps you can enlighten me: Where in the Book of Isaiah does that passage appear about sending a messenger who's going to prepare a way?"

Esmé appeared flustered. She knew a lot of biblical passages by heart, but Garner happened to ask her about one that she didn't have at her fingertips. "Um ... I could look it up for you, if you like."

"No, no. Let me save you the time. It doesn't appear in Isaiah at all. It's a quotation from Malachi. So, I ask you: How perfect can a book be that can't even quote *itself* accurately? And it's a good thing you didn't quote me the King James Version because that tries to plaster over the issue by not naming Isaiah but simply saying 'As it is written in the prophets.' I can assure you, though, that Isaiah is very clearly named in the original Greek."

He walked back to the blackboard. "Look. I know you all think I pick on Esmé for her beliefs from time to time. But that really isn't the case. Each of you is free to *believe* whatever you like. But in this course, as in all the courses I teach, simply believing something isn't good enough. It's like what I told you before: Plato makes a major distinction between δόξα, which is mere belief or opinion, and ἐπιστήμη, which is genuine knowledge, and we ought not to confuse the two. In my classes, we shall focus solely on the *evidence*."

Townsant gave Esmé a knowing look, since he had once said almost those exact words to her.

"Now, why do I mention the important of evidence in our discussion of the Golden Ideal?" Garner continued and wrote a new word on the board. "It's because of this concept: ἀρετή, *ah-reh-TAY*, commonly translated as 'virtue.' Today 'virtue' tends to bring up images of high-button shoes and sour-looking biddies telling you that drink and sex are sinful. But that wasn't the Greek sense of ἀρετή at all. It meant the *excellence* of something, the fulfillment of that object's intended purpose. If you wear glasses, and those glasses restore your vision to 20/20, they're excellent glasses. They fulfill their intended purpose. If you buy a bottle, and it holds its contents without leaking, that's an excellent bottle. It fulfills its intended purpose. But what makes a *person* excellent? Or, to revert to my earlier vocabulary, what is virtue when it comes to people such as you or me? I've already given you one answer that Aristotle provided for this question: the Golden Mean. The 'purpose' of a human being, Aristotle thought, was to achieve a middle way, being neither a beast nor a god. That's why he defined each virtue as a mean between two extremes. But *everything* must have moderation. We have to pursue even moderation in moderation. *That*, Mr. Lewis, is why I said that the Golden Mean has to be tempered by the Golden Ideal."

Garner drew a line on the board. "Many of Aristotle's concepts are responses to ideas he learned from Plato. And many of Plato's concepts are responses to ideas he learned from Socrates. Those ideas change substantially as you move from Socrates to Plato to Aristotle, but one thing remains: 'A human is an animal that *thinks*,' to quote Aristotle's version of this principle. The purpose of a human being is, not to surrender to emotions (that's what the Golden Mean was all about), but rather to use logic and evidence to understand the world, to understand the nature of reality. Thinking, learning, reasoning: *Those* are the Golden Ideal for a well-lived life. Can we ever get to the point where we think, learn, and reason perfectly? No. Like the asymptote, we'll never reach that goal, no matter how hard we try. But it's our human duty to *live into* that goal. As I said, we expect much from you because we are confident that you can accomplish much. Have we demanded *too* much this semester? Well, possibly. And I promise to bring that up at our next faculty meeting. But here's what I suggest. Take the weekend. Go back over the assignment I'd given you for today. And next Monday, reach for the Golden Ideal. Be prepared to translate and interpret the text, not perfectly, but as perfectly as humanly possible."

CHAPTER THIRTY-ONE

The Spirit of Tolbert Fitzgerald

None of the other faculty members at Mersley College is likely to have called Winton Garner a motivational speaker. And yet, his remarks to the class that morning motivated the students in a manner that even he couldn't have anticipated. Perhaps their response was due to his words, and perhaps it was due to the fact that he engaged in the unprecedented act of posting a sign on his classroom door later that day that read, "You said you needed more time, and now you have it: Go Study! Classical Mythology CANCELED!" Whatever the cause, it worked. The five students redoubled their efforts and, by late Friday afternoon, they were not entirely caught up, but they could definitely see the proverbial light at the end of the proverbial tunnel.

And tunnels, proverbial or otherwise, were most definitely on Bastian's mind when the group met that night for their study session in Chudwell 2B. He took advantage of the fact that Townsant and Esmé were running a little late to update the twins on his current line of thinking.

"Something about what Professor Garner said today struck me," he began.

"I thought *he* was going to strike you at one point," Mallory joked.

Prudence, of course, found this comment hilarious, while Bastian drew no humor from it whatsoever.

"The Golden Ideal," he said. "I think that's what the Fraternity of the Broken Omen was all about. I mean, you've seen what the other students are like here: It's Friday night, and half of them are back home with mommy and daddy while the other half are in town with fake I.D.s, getting drunk. I bet Mersley was always like that. Most of the students came here simply because it was expected of them and gave them a chance to party, but there was a small group that really cared about what they learned, that were hungry for wisdom, not just a degree. I'll bet that that's how the fraternity started. They were pursuing sort of an intellectual Golden Ideal, learning the most important things, no matter where they led. That's what drew them to Berossus."

"Maybe, but what was the omen that they named themselves after?" Mallory asked.

"And why was it *broken*?" Prudence added.

"I don't know. Maybe they just thought it was a cool name, or maybe that's one of the secrets we haven't discovered yet. Anyway, I think that, somehow, the Fraternity still exists."

"You mean, there are students and professors who still get together in the Catacombs?" Mallory asked.

"Perhaps," Bastian replied.

"Or do you mean that the ghosts of former members still haunt this campus?" Prudence asked.

"Perhaps," Bastian replied with an enigmatic grin. "Or perhaps it's not the either/or but the both/and. And perhaps *we're* being offered initiation into the fraternity."

"All five of us?" Mallory asked.

"Or just the three of us?" Prudence added.

"Well, at least the three of us. The others may come along later, but for now we're on our own. That's why I think we should ... "

"Should do what?" Townsant asked, opening the door to the study lounge.

"Should ... um ... start by going over our Greek and then, if there's time, talk about that Judith Butler reading."

"I agree," Mallory said, picking up on Bastian's cue. "Those are the two things that still confuse me the most."

Townsant looked from one of them to the other, not entirely convinced that they had told him the truth and still suspecting that he had walked in on a conversation he wasn't supposed to overhear. "Well, let's wait and see what Esmé thinks."

"Where is Esmé, anyway?" Mallory asked. "It's not like her to be late."

"Not sure," Bastian said. "But let's not waste time just sitting around before she gets here. Plato, anyone?"

* * *

In fact, Esmé was already in the building while this debate was taking place. She had gone to Professor Garner's office on the pretense of thanking him for understanding the students' need for extra study time but actually to tell him, as diplomatically as she could, that his continued taunts about her beliefs were upsetting her. She hadn't been entirely honest earlier when she'd claimed that challenges like those from the professor didn't bother her. In truth, they bothered her deeply, and she wanted them to stop.

Esmé assumed that Professor Garner would be in his office because he *always* seemed to be in his office except when he was in class or at a group get-together at the Diogenes Club. But that night was different somehow. His office door was locked. The lights were out. And that entire hallway seemed darker and more abandoned than usual.

Something in the air gave Esmé a chill, so she decided to head down to the study lounge the quickest way possible. Instead of using the main staircase, she opened a door across from Garner's office that led to a narrow set of steps supposedly used by maintenance crews ages ago. That staircase now bore a sign reading, "ENTER AT YOUR PERIL" because the steps were worn from decades of use, and a few of them even felt loose beneath your feet. Ordinarily, the extra ten or so yards she would have had to cross to get to the main staircase would have meant nothing to her, but the strange feeling of dread she felt in the dimly-lit hallway made her want to join the others as soon as possible.

It was only after she was already in the maintenance workers' stairwell and the door had closed behind her that she realized there was no light at all there. The darkness was absolute, with none even creeping in from under the door she'd just used. Slowly, she felt her way along the wall until she got back to the door.

It had locked when it had shut behind her.

Now, with no other alternative, Esmé nervously began her way down the decrepit, creaking steps. Each one sounded as though it would crack beneath her feet and cause her to plunge onto the concrete floor below. She could see nothing, and the staircase seemed so quiet that she almost believed she could hear her own heart as it began to pound more loudly in her chest.

After about four steps, she heard another sound, a whooshing or gushing as though a small blast of air had been released. Then she heard something else: the same banging of the pipes that the group had once heard in their study session. The banging of the pipes grew louder and louder and then she heard a voice moaning, "Cold ... soooooo cold."

When those words had been uttered the first time, they sounded as though they were clearly somewhere inside Chudwell Hall, but not inside the study lounge with the students. This time, however, the voice, while soft and plaintive, seemed to be right there in the stairwell with her.

Esmé Dawson did the only thing she could do.

She screamed.

Longer and louder than she'd ever screamed in her life.

Only seconds passed, but, to Esmé, they seemed like an eternity. A light flicked on down in the basement, and the sound of footsteps was heard. The face of Sexton appeared at the bottom of the steps.

"What are ya doin' up there?" he asked.

"I'm trying to get down," she told the caretaker. "There was no light, and there were these sounds ... this voice ... "

Sexton lit a flashlight and made his way up the steps to where Esmé was standing. "I've gotcha now," he said, and with incredible tenderness, he took her by the hand and led her down the remaining steps.

By the time they reached the bottom, the other four students were waiting for them. They'd heard Esmé's scream and rushed there as quickly as they could.

"What happened?" Bastian asked from the back of the group.

Before she had a chance to answer, Sexton said, "Youse wait here. I'm goin' to check the rest of the basement and then do a circuit around the buildin'. If there're any of them fraternity boys here again, they'll have to answer to me."

Sexton was no one's idea of a threat, but as he left to perform this errand, Bastian mouthed the word "Fraternity" to Mallory and Prudence. A fraternity may indeed have been responsible, he implied, but not the one the caretaker had been thinking of.

In great detail (and, it should be admitted, with a few embellishments), Esmé related the story of what had just occurred. By the time she was finished, Sexton had returned.

"They's no one down here," he said, "and if they was pullin' this stunt from outside, they seem to be gone now. But that don't mean they won't come back. Better gather your stuff and head back to the dorms. I'll lock the buildin' up tight and keep an eye out. If anyone comes back, I'm callin' the cops."

Townsant protested and said they still had studying to do, but Esmé insisted that all she wanted to do was to get out of Chudwell Hall. "Look, we're further ahead than we thought we'd be. And if you really want to do more work tonight, I can always open up Banworth."

"I thought you didn't want us to use the chapel except on Sunday nights," Mallory pointed out.

"I'll make an exception." Esmé spoke each word slowly and individually to underscore the fact that the idea seemed obvious to her.

Fully in keeping with past practice, the group debated their options for about fifteen more minutes before deciding to take Esmé up on her offer to open Banworth Chapel.

They walked back to the study lounge. The door was closed. "I could've sworn I left it open," Bastian said. "I was the last one out."

Hesitantly, he opened the door again, and the students entered Chudwell 2B to retrieve their books and backpacks, which had now all been rearranged in a circle.

There at the center was a small white card, the type of "social card" people once used when paying a formal call on someone. The card read:

PROFESSOR TOLBERT FITZGERALD WAS HERE

CHAPTER THIRTY-TWO

The Cabal

By the time they reached the chapel, Bastian had lost his terrified look of only moments before and seemed smug in his confidence that he'd been right all along.

"Well, do you believe me *now*?" he asked once the students were safely inside.

"Believe you about ... ?" Townsant asked.

"All of it. *Everything*. Something's going on here at the college that we have to look into. It's our *duty*."

Townsant arched his eyebrows. "'*Duty*?' Don't tell me you've started to believe your own B.S. about Chudwell Hall being cursed?"

"I never used the word *cursed*," Bastian protested. "I just said there are things going on at this school that shouldn't be happening."

Townsant chuckled. "Yeah, well, it's college. I imagine that pretty much every school like ours has 'things going on that shouldn't be happening.'"

Bastian sneered. "You're pretty calm for someone who was scared speechless less than twenty minutes ago. And don't deny it: I saw your face. When Esmé screamed and then again when Professor Fitzgerald's card appeared in the study lounge ... both times you looked as though you were about to leap out of your skin."

"You're exaggerating," Townsant said.

"No, he's not."

The voice that came from the corner of the room was as quiet as those of the two men had been loud. Its very softness caused it to carry more weight. It also stunned the others because the voice belonged to Prudence, the one member of their group who rarely said anything unless she was following the lead of her sister.

"Someone's just playing a practical ... " Townsant began.

"You were terrified," Prudence interrupted him. "I'm not saying you were wrong to be frightened. We all were. But you can't claim now that what happened back there didn't scare you. Bastian said he saw your face. Well, I saw it, too. There are only the five of us in this program, and we've got to stick together. Someone or something has summoned us. We have a calling."

Except when she was answering a question in class, Prudence hadn't ever strung as many words together as that. For a moment, it seemed, they were all stunned by the sheer peculiarity of her standing up to anyone, let alone Townsant who had persuaded them all to enroll in the new program and thus sometimes cast himself as the group's leader.

Bastian saw his opportunity. The right moment had come for the Bad Boy of the Scipionic Circle to become its new head.

"Look. Mallory, Prudence, and I have been working on this for quite some time now."

It was an exaggeration, if not an outright lie. The trio had joined forces only days ago.

"What do you mean?" Townsant asked. "Some sort of secret cabal, a Star Chamber? The three of you forming your own little clique?"

"It isn't like that," Mallory said. "You weren't interested, and Esmé wasn't interested, so we felt we had to go ahead and explore what was happening on our own."

"'What was happening,'" Townsant replied mockingly.

"Yes, the card from the catalog. The voice we all heard in the study lounge. Now this calling card from Professor Fitzgerald."

"I'm sure there's some logical explanation for all of it," Townsant insisted.

"You sound just like Garner," Bastian argued. "Everything has to be evidence and logic. Well, look. I'm here to tell you that evidence and logic only get you so far. There are just things in this world that they can't explain."

"'There are more things in heaven and earth, Horatio, than are dreamt of in your philosophy,'" Townsant quoted.

"If you like," Bastian continued. "Look, Esmé. You're a person of faith. I dare say you're the only one of us who's willing to accept something on faith alone."

"'Now faith is the substance of things hoped for, the evidence of things not seen,'" Esmé quoted. "To me, faith *is* evidence."

Just as Bastian had expected, a schism was forming between Townsant and Esmé. It was time to divide and conquer.

"'Things *hoped* for, Esmé," Townsant told her, "not things that actually are. We're not going to prove anything just by quoting things we've read."

"You're the one who started quoting Shakespeare!" she pointed out.

"I was being ironic! Remember what Garner said: You can romanticize it all you want, but faith is nothing more than the acceptance of something as true despite lack of evidence."

"So, I can't quote Paul, but you can quote Garner, is that it? And 'Garner says' proves everything?"

"At least Garner has a Ph.D.! I find what he says more compelling than what some Bronze Age tent maker said two thousand years ago."

"Iron Age," Mallory corrected him.

"What?" Townsant asked. In his argument with Esmé, he'd nearly forgotten that the others were there.

"It was the Iron Age, actually. The Bronze Age was over for eight or nine centuries by the time Paul was writing."

"Whatever," Townsant muttered. "The fact is that any of us can sit here and quote this person or that person all night, but if what they're saying isn't logical, that doesn't prove anything."

"But we *have* proof," Bastian said. From his backpack he pulled out the catalog card and Professor Fitzgerald's visitor's card. "You can take it on faith or you can take it by evidence, but someone's calling us to do *something*. And I, for one, want to know *why*."

CHAPTER THIRTY-THREE

Winter Refuge

The events of that Friday night had given Bastian a status within the group that no one had expected. As a scholar, he was, even by his own admission, the weakest of the five. He earned B's and B minuses on assignments that regularly earned the others A's and A minuses. By missing many of the group study sessions, he'd deprived himself of an advantage that could easily have been his.

But now he had a new advantage: He'd been the first to take the mysterious events at Mersley College seriously. He'd thought through their possible significance in a way the others hadn't. The result was that, every time one of the other four asked, "But what about ... ?" he had an answer ready. It may have been an illogical answer. It may have been an answer that none of them would have believed even a few months earlier. But it was at least *an* answer, and that was more than Townsant or the other students had.

They did, however, have one thing that Bastian Lewis *didn't* have: library privileges. For the next two weeks, he was forbidden to even set foot inside Sutlinger Library. But he somehow managed to turn this weakness into a strength. By using the others as his private research team, his *de facto* status as the group's new leader became even clearer. Over the course of that weekend, he sent one of the students after another on various "reconnaissance missions" for him. Several of these did, it is true, relate to the assignments that the students were gradually getting caught up on. Many of them did not. He used what he'd come to think of as his "research associates" as unpaid labor to find out what they could about Berossus, Professor Tolbert Fitzgerald, and the legend of the hidden Catacombs that ran beneath the campus.

Indeed, it was the last of these mysteries that provided at least some proof that Bastian's claims weren't based *solely* on his imagination. And, ironically, the person who made that discovery was Townsant, Bastian's own personal Doubting Thomas.

While searching the library's database for discussions of Toni Morrison's 2008 novel *A Mercy*, Townsant had absentmindedly typed the words *A Mersley* instead. He ended up with a screen full of citations that would prove absolutely useless for his assignment in Professor Dittman's Queer Theory and Feminist Theory course, but which would be invaluable, nonetheless. There before him were listed twenty-five campus master plan volumes, labeled *Mersley Plan A* through *Mersley Plan Y* and dating from roughly fifty years after the college's creation in 1826 right up through the school's current strategic plan. Unbeknownst to him, President Woolridge and Dean McDaniel had already drawn up *Merseley Plan Z* in secret and intended to manipulate the strategic planning task force into thinking that the ideas contained in it were their own.

One of those ideas was ignoring the decision of the city council about Chudwell Hall's historical significance and ordering the building's immediate demolition. Then a brand new "state-of-the-art" science facility could be constructed on the site. It would be the beginning of the end for any of the liberal arts and humanities to be taught at the college.

Townsant, of course, had no idea about any of this. He didn't even know what a "master plan" was. But the expression appealed to him, and so he copied down the call number of the first set of master plans and headed into the stacks to find it.

What he discovered was not the secret door to the hidden Catacombs, but a different kind of "door," one that led him to believe those Catacombs might actually exist.

The master plans turned out to be little more than sketches and suggestions for how the campus would develop. As the student body of Mersley grew, new buildings were constructed, old buildings eliminated, and a strategy of "paving the paths" ensued in an effort to prevent as much of the grass on the quads from being trampled by students as they walked between classes.

Townsant spread out the first five sets of sketches on a large table. The oldest one of the series was dated 1879; the most recent one before him was prepared in 1909. And a detail he noticed in the 1905 set caused him to cry "*Heureka*," his excitement in the discovery not overshadowing his awareness that the form of the Greek perfect tense uttered by Archimedes when he discovered the principle of density actually began with a rough, not a smooth, breathing mark.

The impetus for this (admittedly somewhat stifled) cry was a set of lines linking Old Main and at least six other buildings by what was labeled as a "Winter Refuge." This name was explained by a crumbling set of typewritten notes, apparently the minutes of the committee that had created the plan.

> Due to the ongoing threat posed by severe weather, beginning in early December and often continuing through mid-April, it is the desire of the Committee that as few class days be lost in the future as possible. The construction of an underground Winter Refuge will thus protect students and professors alike as they make their way underground to the main campus facilities. While it will not be possible for the Winter Refuge to link all buildings, it is estimated that over two-thirds of all inter-facility traffic would be protected by the creation of this new convenience.

His hands trembling, Townsant moved from one master plan to the next. The Winter Refuge appeared on them—it was even extended several times—up until the 1944 plan. From that point forward, the tunnels were neither depicted on any of the sketches nor mentioned in any of the accompanying text.

The problem was that the binder covering each set of plans was stamped NON-CIRCULATING. There was no way, therefore, that Barbara the Barbarian Librarian would let him check out any of these volumes. Since the mountain wouldn't come to Mohammed, this was definitely a case where Mohammed would have to come to the mountain. Checking to make sure no one was looking, Townsant re-shelved most of the plans but took the 1939 volume, which contained the most elaborate tunnel diagram, and hid it behind the Subject cabinet in the old card catalog room.

The next Saturday, little actual studying was done, but hours were spent poring over the diagrams and seeing which buildings still remained that were supposedly connected by the Winter Refuge. All the residence halls and dining facilities were built from the 1950s onward, so no access to the tunnels would be from there. Old Main, Sutlinger Library, and several classroom buildings *did*, however, appear on the plans.

And one of those buildings was Chudwell Hall.

"What I can't tell," Townsant told the others while reviewing his findings, "is whether these underground tunnels were ever actually built or whether they were simply *planned*. I've counted at least eight buildings on the 1939 plan that never reached the construction stage. Maybe that's why the tunnels don't appear after 1944. They were a good idea that proved impractical, and the administration just gave up on them."

"Either way," Bastian said, "it's the best evidence we've encountered to date that I was right about the Catacombs all along. And it tells me what the very next step in our strategic plan has to be: We've *got* to discover whether these tunnels ever made it from planning to actual construction."

CHAPTER THIRTY-FOUR

The Waiting Game

As that spring semester continued, each member of the Scipionic Circle experienced what is blithely referred to as "a learning opportunity." The faculty members learned that, as bright and committed as the five students were, it was counterproductive to push them too hard and assign too much work. If the students were required to read two hundred pages from one class period to the next, they found themselves overwhelmed and perhaps completed only fifty. But if they were required to read only thirty pages from one class period to the next, they often became fascinated by what they were learning and read over a hundred. Garner and his colleagues quickly realized what Lev Vygotsky had discovered a century earlier: People do their best work when they're just challenged enough to find the task engaging but not challenged to such a degree that they find it frustrating.

The students, too, were learning an important lesson: The easy part of creating a plan is setting the goals; the hardest part is figuring out how you're actually going to *achieve* those goals. That's the lesson that caused the vast majority of those institutional strategic plans to end up sitting on a shelf, and it applied to Bastian's own strategic plan as well.

The *goal* was clear. If the Winter Refuge tunnels had really been built, the group needed to find at least one entrance to them and then explore whether the stories of hidden Catacombs leading to a central ritual chamber were based in fact or were nothing more than a legend. But figuring out how to reach that goal was proving elusive. Barbara Winchester patrolled Sutlinger Library like a hawk. She would swoop down on any student who so much as unwrapped a stick of gum and suspend that student's library privileges for at least a week. Anything as dramatic as inspecting the walls for a secret entrance was certain to draw her attention and possibly incur a harsher penalty (not to mention a bit of withering ridicule). Banworth Chapel had no basement. It stood atop what appeared to be a foundation of solid concrete. There was no hope of finding any secret passageway there.

Only Chudwell Hall remained as a possible entry point to the tunnels. Its construction date fell within the right period, and it most definitely had a basement. In fact, the maze-like warren of hallways that surrounded the student lounge provided endless opportunities for access to the "Winter Refuge." And the students were often inside Chudwell Hall. The problem was that the faculty members were there each day, the caretaker was there each night, and owing to the work schedule that Sexton had negotiated with Sabrina Pope, the building was locked up tight each weekend.

The only solution, it seemed, was to wait for Spring Break when the professors would be absent from the hall during daylight hours and the students' exploration could occur in earnest. But Spring Break seemed so far away, and it was unclear how patient the spirit of Tolbert Fitzgerald or whoever was summoning them might prove to be.

And so began an uneasy waiting game. The five students tried to focus on their studies and put all thoughts of Berossus and the Fraternity of the Broken Omen from their minds. At times, they were successful. Often, they were not. During a discussion of the Eleusinian and Dionysian mysteries in Professor Pope's Art, Literature, and Music of Ancient Greece course, a series of side glances among the students revealed that all of them were thinking about other secret rites of initiation that may well have occurred in a chamber beneath their very feet. After Professor Briggs assigned a reading that used the expression *ontological temporality* in his course on Semantics, Semiology, and Semiotics, Bastian reminded the others that this same expression had supposedly been used in the title of Professor Fitzgerald's purloined manuscript.

College students often become skilled at operating in dual realities at once. Who they are when interacting with their professors may have little to do with who they are when interacting with one another. Usually, however, the goal is to make their professors believe they're much more studious than they actually are and their peers believe they're much more socially engaged than they actually are. But the students in the Department of Eminent Scholars were equally studious both in and outside the classroom. It's just that they were studious about different things.

"What exactly *is* ontological temporality?" Mallory asked when Bastian brought the phrase up during their study session.

Townsant, who fancied himself becoming more and more like Garner every day, offered the sort of response he could imagine coming from the professor's own mouth.

"Well, it's easy, isn't it? Just think about it for a second. The word *ontological* has Greek roots: *onto-* relating to the present participle of the verb 'to be,' and *log-* relating to the same root for reasoning that often means 'study of' in words like *biology*, *geology*, *psychology*, and so on. *Temporality* is purely Latin, with *tempus/temporis* being the word for time. So, ontological temporality would mean something like 'the study of being as conditioned by time.'"

Bastian rolled his eyes. "Well, that clears it *right* up," he said sarcastically.

Esmé had taken a different approach. As soon as Mallory had asked her question, she'd pulled out her phone and done a search on the Internet.

"I can find citations for *temporal ontology*, but *ontological temporality* isn't bringing up anything yet."

"Well, what's temporal ontology, then?" Mallory asked.

Esmé read from an article she'd discovered. "'Some scholars

use the expression *temporal ontology* to refer to when reality exists. Does only the present moment actually exist with the future nothing more than possibility and the past being completely irrecoverable except as memory? Do past, present, and future all exist simultaneously, even though the nature of human consciousness only allows people to perceive the present? Are the past and present somehow 'real,' either as memory or as experience, while the future is mere potentiality? Or are past, present, and future all equally illusory, mere products of the human consciousness?'"

"I can't believe that people actually earn a living making up stuff like this," Bastian said, shaking his head.

"*I* can't believe any of that has any relevance to semantics, semiology, and semiotics," Mallory added. "They sound like entirely different areas of philosophy."

"Unless Wittgenstein was right," Esmé pointed out, "and all philosophical problems, including ontology, are just linguistic 'blips.'"

"I don't remember Wittgenstein ever using the word *blips*," Bastian objected.

"No, Professor Briggs was right: *Slabs* were more his thing," Mallory agreed.

"But I do think there's a connection," Townsant said, once again doing his best to channel Professor Garner. "Think of such concepts as absolute versus relative time in linguistic or semantic terms. 'I already bought the book': a past tense verb with a perfect aspect. On the other hand, 'By the time the class began, I had already bought the book': a *plu*perfect verb that refers to the very same action. In the first instance, the reference was to absolute time; in the second instance, it was to relative time: *before* the class began. It's the whole basis for sequence of tenses in Latin. I think *that's* what ontological temporality is all about. In fact ... "

"Shhh," Prudence interjected.

"*Excuse* me?" Townsant asked, not necessarily surprised by the interruption itself, but definitely surprised by who had made it.

"I said 'Shhh,'" Prudence clarified. "I think I've found something more important than any of this."

Townsant was annoyed. "What can possibly be more important than figuring out the thesis of this article?"

Prudence ignored him. "While you were all arguing, I went onto WorldCat to look for that book you were talking about."

"Which book, Pru?" Mallory asked.

"The one that Professor Fitzgerald supposedly wrote and that was stolen by another professor."

"Yes, well," Townsant sniffed, "I'm pretty sure that, even if hidden tunnels do exist beneath Mersley College, *that* particular story is nothing more than an urban legend."

"No. No, it isn't. I *found* it. *The Deleuzian Rhizomatics of Ontological Temporality: A Deconstructionist Approach.* That's the one, right? Here it is."

Prudence passed Townsant the phone so that he could read the citation.

"Well, I'll be damned," he said. "She's right."

"But the big question is: Who's the author?" Bastian asked.

Townsant squinted at the screen and then looked back up at the others, his expression one of complete disbelief.

"Dawn McDaniel."

CHAPTER THIRTY-FIVE

The Best Kind of Research

Even the most conscientious guard must, at times, leave his post. Meals must be eaten, sleep must be obtained, and calls of nature must be answered. With this principle in mind, the students set up shifts in Sutlinger Library keeping an eye on Barbara Winchester in order to identify a time when she would not interfere with their plans. And it couldn't just be anytime, either. The stars would have to align in such a way that, not only was Barbara the Barbarian Librarian nowhere to be seen, but Mia Thornton had taken her place.

The casual observer might conclude that the library staff at Mersley College consisted solely of Ms. Winchester. In fact, there were seven other full-time librarians and five part-time members of the staff. Most of these other employees worked in back offices, however, and so few of them were highly visible to the student body. Nevertheless, the head librarian had trained them all with the result that they tended to imitate Barbara Winchester in much the same way that Townsant tended to imitate Professor Garner. If any student attempted to do anything that they felt they couldn't handle, all they had to do was call out, "Oh, Ms. WIIIIIIINchester!" and the nemesis of the Mersley College undergraduate community would soon appear.

Mia Thornton was the proverbial exception that proved the rule. She'd been hired suddenly over the Winter Break when Olivia Watson, who was universally known as "Old Miss Watson" because she was even older than Barbara Winchester, "took poorly," as she described it, and abruptly announced a long-overdue retirement. Mia had then been hired because ... well, primarily because she happened to be available and, although her credentials weren't, in the head librarian's words, "of Sutlinger quality," she would have to do until someone better came along.

It wasn't merely that Mia's library degree was "only from one of those 'community college' *things*" (once again to quote Barbara Winchester), but also that she lacked any semblance of common sense whatsoever and was as gullible as a substitute teacher at a middle school. You could tell her almost *anything*, and she'd believe it.

If those qualifications were only minimally acceptable to the other members of the library staff, they were absolutely perfect for the imminent scholars. They were in need of a librarian who asked no questions, did what she was told, and accepted even the most outlandish lie as an absolute fact.

The problem was that the Venn diagram representing Barbara Winchester's departures from the library and Mia Thornton's assignment to the front desk consisted of two circles with virtually no overlap. For several weeks, whenever classes were not actually taking place, at least one of the students sat at a table on the main floor of the library, ostensibly to study but really to keep an eye on the comings and goings of the various librarians.

At last, the seemingly impossible occurred. Esmé happened to be the one assigned to duty over a Thursday lunch hour when the opportunity arose.

"Elvis has left the building. Repeat, Elvis has left the building," she said into the walkie-talkie function of her smart watch, looking like nothing so much as a three-dimensional form of Dick Tracy ... if, that is, Dick Tracy had been a nineteen-year-old woman in a beige silk blouse and a plaid skirt.

"Message received," Bastian replied. "Authorization given to proceed with Plan K."

There were, as it happened, no Plans A through J, but the group thought that "Plan K" sounded more mysterious.

Esmé sidled up to the front desk.

"Is this where I can put in a request for interlibrary loan?" she asked. Mia Thornton drew a deep breath. She'd been hoping her responsibilities in the head librarian's absence would be no more complex than checking out a book or informing a student that "Regrettably, periodicals do not circulate."

Like a pilot on a dangerous mission, she gritted her teeth and told herself, "Remember: This is what all the training has been for." Then, switching on a smile as though it were one of the fluorescent lights deep in the stacks, she replied, "Why, yes. Yes, it is. How may I help you?"

"I need this book for research in one of my classes, and Sutlinger doesn't have it. Here. I wrote the name down. It's a bit complicated."

Mia Thornton read the title of the book, and her heart sank. Mistyping even a single letter would mean that the request would be rejected, and she might have to face Ms. Winchester's wrath.

Clutching at straws, she said, "Are you *sure* we don't have this book? It sounds like something Sutlinger would have. You know, if you don't spell every word absolutely right ... "

"I've tried. I've done a title search, an author search, and even a subject search. Then I looked up the call numbers of books on similar topics and browsed the stacks. We don't have it. I'm sure."

"Maybe you could try just one more time ... "

Esmé decided to switch tactics. "Well, I suppose I *could*. It's just that Ms. Winchester promised me that you'd be the best person to locate this book for me. She was going to handle the request herself, but I'm in a bit of a hurry, and she ... " Esmé left the sentence hanging as though she were searching for the next word.

" ... has that lunch meeting with the Dean's Council," Mia helpfully supplied.

"Has that lunch meeting with the Dean's Council," Esmé confirmed as though Mia were right about this, just as she was right about everything. "So, if you could simply place the request for me."

Mia bit her lip, but thought, "If Ms. Winchester really said I could handle this, then perhaps I shouldn't let her down."

She began to type the title into the interlibrary loan screen on her computer. She actually moved her lips as she mentally spelled out each letter.

"*T-h-e* space *D-e-l-e-u-z-i-a-n* space *R-h-i-z-o-m-a-t-i-c-s* ... "

When she finally got to the end and hit SEND, she asked Esmé, "What kind of research are you doing again?"

"Oh, the *best* kind."

CHAPTER THIRTY-SIX

When One Door Closes

Perhaps because it's located so far to the north, Spring Break comes early to Mersley College. It offers a chance for students and faculty members to escape the snows, which are bound to last at least until mid-April regardless of what the groundhog said that year, and flee to warmer climes. And flee is precisely what most of the students and roughly a third of the faculty did. The result was that, even though it had long seemed to the students of the Scipionic Circle that Spring Break would never come, it actually arrived before the shortest month of the year was even half over.

In the second week of February, Mersley College took on an appearance akin to one of those outdoor shopping centers that had seen better days. Foot traffic was light. The quads echoed with little more than the sounds of ropes clanging against flagpoles. Only one campus dining hall remained open, and the choices there were few and rarely varied from day to day.

The campus diehards, like Winton Garner and Barbara Winchester, remained at their posts, but doing so only added to their reputations as eccentrics. Even President Woolridge managed to slip away, joining the rest of his family for a few quiet days on a southern beach that, while somewhat chilly by local standards, seemed luxuriously warm to those who still had roughly two months of "real" winter to endure.

The result was that Dean McDaniel was nominally in charge of the college, the operative word here being *nominally*. With only one administrative assistant remaining on duty in Old Main, she had virtually no one left who could carry out any instruction she gave. She was even compelled to brew her own coffee each morning. Nevertheless, the corners of her mouth curled up in delight at her temporary eminence and, although the president had left no instructions that she could do so, she relocated her base of operations to what was grandiosely called "the executive suite," a cluster of three offices that were marginally larger than others in the building. She even prepared a handwritten slip of paper reading "Dawn McDaniel, Ph.D., Acting President" that she affixed over the nameplate on Jefferson Woolridge's desk with two small pieces of tape. "Every day should be like this," she thought as she leaned back in the chair she would briefly occupy.

As he'd predicted, Spring Break did turn out to be a highly active period for Bastian Lewis's "strategic plan." During the day, when Sexton had not yet arrived at work, he and the other students went corridor by corridor, floor by floor throughout Chudwell Hall, taking down portraits and running their fingers over the walls in search of levers or switches that might open a passageway to the long-forgotten tunnels. When Townsant pointed out that it was a waste of time to search anywhere above the basement for entry to the underground "Winter Refuge," Bastian merely scoffed.

"That's exactly what they *want* you to think. Look, if you were the head of a secret cult that wished to remain secret, you wouldn't place the switch that would open the door to your hidden lair in an *obvious* place. If it were me, I'd place it in the most remote corner of the highest level of each building, the very spot where no one would look."

"And then what?" Townsant challenged him. "Dash down the stairwell to the basement before anyone else saw your secret entrance? It's ludicrous. I don't even think we should spend time searching the *first* floor. If we concentrate on the basement ... "

"We'd be falling right into the trap that the Fraternity of the Broken Omen had prepared for anyone who was onto them. I've been doing a lot of thinking about this group, and I've concluded that they must have been devilishly clever."

"Based on what evidence?" Townsant asked. "I'll grant you that the references to this mysterious 'Winter Refuge' in those copies of the master plan mean that it's *possible* there are some tunnels beneath campus, but there was no indication on any of the plans that there was anything secret about them. Quite the opposite, in fact. They were there for anyone to see. We don't know that this Fraternity of the Broken Omen actually existed. We don't know that they were 'devilishly clever,' as you describe them. And we don't know that they had any sort of ritual chamber. *That*, you'll recall, was never on the plans."

They bickered like this back and forth while Esmé, Mallory, and Prudence did the actual work of searching. By Thursday of Spring Break week, they'd uncovered quite a lot of dust and a surprising number of mouse droppings, but nothing remotely like a hidden switch that would grant them access to an underground tunnel.

Late at night, as they sat in Chudwell 2B, actually doing some studying during their study session, their mood was morose, bordering on resigned. There was only one day left for their daytime search. Chudwell Hall would be locked over the weekend. The rest of the students and faculty members would be back for classes on Monday. They had wasted a great deal of time and had nothing more than a few spider bites to show for their efforts.

In the middle of their discussion of the Homeric Hymn to Demeter, Bastian suddenly threw down his book.

"I don't get it. We've looked *everywhere*."

For several seconds, no one said a word. Mallory was the one who finally broke the silence. "Not quite everywhere."

"What do you mean?"

She gestured to two portraits that hung on the wall of the study lounge. One was of Virgil Blanton, a now-forgotten president of Mersley who had served for only a few months in 1924. He was so insignificant that when the Hall of Presidents was becoming overcrowded with paintings back in the 1950s, his image was cast into exile in Chudwell Hall and had never been missed in the interim. The other was a rather amateurish painting of some Renaissance author or scholar. Some said it was supposed to be Shakespeare. Others claimed it was Francis Bacon. Still others identified the figure as Christopher Marlowe. Finally, there had been a small but highly vocal group that argued all three of those authors were really the same person, anyway.

"How about this?" Mallory asked. "Prudence and I will take down these two paintings. Then we'll search the wall behind them. If nothing's there, we'll just conclude—we'll *all* just conclude—that, if the tunnels ever existed, there's no longer any way for us to gain access to them. We'll have tried our best, but we can't keep ignoring our coursework for a mere hunch. What about it? Who's with me?"

"I am," Townsant said immediately.

"Sounds like a good compromise," Esmé added.

All eyes turned to Bastian. He looked from one of them to the next and finally nodded wearily.

"All right then. Prudence, shall we?" Mallory asked.

The twins approached the paintings and, with decorum that almost seemed ceremonial, they took down the two paintings.

In the very center behind each portrait was a small button that looked as though it had been painted over at least three or four times.

"We've found it!" Bastian exclaimed triumphantly.

"We've found *something*," Townsant admitted. "For all we know, they could be light switches."

"But hidden like that?" Bastian asked.

"Okay. Time to try them. Press the left button first," Esmé suggested.

Mallory had removed the painting that concealed the button on the left. So, with a tenuous finger, she pressed that button. The layers of paint caused the button to stick. Mallory kept exerting more and more pressure until finally the paint around the button cracked, and she was able to press it into the wall.

It snapped back immediately, and nothing else happened.

"Okay. Try the right one," Esmé said.

"You have to push it kind of hard," Mallory told her sister.

With considerable force, Prudence pressed the button on the right. Like the other, this button recessed slightly into the wall once the paint was broken, but it returned to its original position as soon as Prudence had removed her finger. Once again, nothing happened.

The group's excitement had been short-lived. A wave of disappointment swept through the room.

"Now what?" Prudence asked.

Softly, Townsant quoted Professor Garner. "Life isn't about the either/or; it's about the both/and."

"What?" Bastian asked irritably.

"Press both buttons simultaneously," Townsant replied with an almost eerie certainty.

The twins looked at each other. Holding each other's gaze, they pushed the buttons in at precisely the same moment. This time, the two buttons stayed in.

But nothing else happened.

"Good grief, are youse still here? It's Spring Break, y'know!" a voice called from the hallway.

"It's Sexton," Bastian said in alarm.

"Quick. Shut the door," Esmé said.

The five students had become careless over the week. Previously, they'd always closed the door to the study lounge as soon as they'd arrived. But despite the frigid weather outside, Chudwell Hall had been so hot that week—and the room had been so stuffy—that they'd taken to leaving it open.

Townsant rushed to the door to close it. For good measure, he turned the knob to lock it. As the caretaker, Sexton would, of course, have the key, but Townsant thought his actions might slow Sexton down just enough that they could get the portraits back on the wall and pretend that they'd been studying all along.

But something strange occurred as soon as the door was closed and locked.

At the other end of the room, a section of wall popped forward.

As the saying goes, "When one door closes, another one opens."

CHAPTER THIRTY-SEVEN

The Rat Pack's Pack Rats

Bastian's face said it all. His disappointment was unmistakable.

"It's a closet, not a tunnel."

After the students had pried open the hidden door—a task that had proved difficult even after the switches had been pressed—they found themselves confronted with a stack of bankers boxes, magazines, and old newspapers that formed a nearly solid wall only an inch or so behind the opening.

"Is everythin' all right in there?" a voice called from out in the hallway.

The students exchanged a panicked look. It was Mallory who kept her head.

"Everything's fine, Mr. Sexton," she replied. "We're just trying to make sense of this reading for Professor Briggs's class. Please don't open the door. We've got books open behind it and can't lose our place."

"Okay," Sexton grumbled. "But don't stay *too* late. I'm buffin' this hallway tonight, and youse can't walk on it for a few hours after I'm done."

"That's fine, Mr. Sexton," Mallory told him. "Another hour perhaps."

Even through the closed door, they could hear the old man sigh and mutter something about "entitled brats these days."

As soon as they no longer heard his footsteps, the students redirected their attention to the opening in the wall.

"Let's see how far back it goes," Townsant suggested.

"And just how do you intend to do *that*?" Bastian asked. "It's solid boxes and other garbage."

"Let's take out what we can and see where that gets us," Townsant replied. Without waiting for an answer, he pulled his chair up to where Bastian was standing and tugged at one of the boxes at the top of the stack. "Sheesh, this is heavy."

"Pass it to me, weakling," Bastian sneered. But even he nearly collapsed under the weight of the box after Townsant had slid it to the edge of the stack and begun to pull it down. "What did they put in these things?"

With Mallory's help, he managed to get the box over to the table. It was taped shut with several long strips of heavy tape but, after a few minutes, they'd peeled it open and looked inside.

Almost filling the box was a series of old ten-inch shellac records, each in a paper sleeve. Most of them seemed to date from the 1940s. On top of the records were various magazine clippings and other random pieces of paper. Whoever filled the boxes seemed not to want to leave a spare millimeter unused.

"Cliff Edwards. Paul Whiteman. Ted Lewis. Phil Harris," Prudence said, reading the names on various records she pulled out. "Are any of these names familiar to you?"

"Not me," Bastian said. "That stuff's worthless."

"Or *price*less," Townsant corrected him. "Some old records are collector's items. There might be a few thousand dollars worth of old 78s in there."

"Which are not ours to sell," Esmé pointed out.

"Finders keepers," Bastian replied. "But I still bet they're just junk."

"Do you remember what Professor Garner told us about Gustave Lefebvre?" Townsant asked.

"Oh, please," Bastian complained. "It's a little too late in the day for yet another Garner story. I mean, I know he's your hero and all ... "

Townsant ignored him. "When Gustave Lefebvre found the Cairo Codex, it had been torn apart as worthless and used as covers for the personal papers of someone or other who thought his own files were important, but the texts of Menander and Eupolis had no value. Today those texts are regarded as *in*valuable, and that sixth-century Egyptian's personal documents are just so much detritus."

Earlier that week, Garner had used the word *detritus* in his mythology course, and Townsant so liked the sound of it that he used it whenever he could.

"One man's trash," Mallory said, expressing the same idea as Townsant but with a saying so familiar she didn't even have to recite its second half.

"Exactly," Townsant agreed.

"None of which has anything to do with what you said you wanted to do: see how far back the closet goes," Bastian pointed out.

"Think of it as archaeology. I'm doing sort of a 'dig.'"

"When there are so many other more important things we could be doing," Bastian grumbled.

"Look. You're the one who insisted there were secret areas beneath Chudwell Hall. Well, we've *found* one. You should be happy."

"What we've found is a *closet*."

"A closet containing archaeological evidence," Townsant said. "Could one of you start looking up the names on those records? They'll give us a *terminus post quem*, the earliest possible date for all this stuff to be placed in the closet."

"I'll do that," Mallory offered.

"And I'll help," Prudence added.

As the twins searched for the various names on the Internet, Townsant and Bastian hauled down several more boxes. Within half an hour, they'd cleared enough from the front of the stacks that a sort of rough staircase was formed. Since Esmé was the smallest of the group, she climbed up the boxes and, using her phone as a flashlight, peered over the topmost boxes to see as far into the storage area as she could.

"If it's a closet," she announced, "it's a very deep one. There're boxes and stacks of newspapers as far as I can see."

"And there are some newer records here," Mallory said, opening another box that contained a number of thinner, vinyl albums of the "high fidelity" type. "Frank Sinatra. Dean Martin. Sammy Davis Jr."

"The Rat Pack," Townsant declared. "Well, that proves one thing: This closet was at least used into the 1960s. Maybe later."

"Okay, let's put this stuff back," Bastian said.

"*What*?" Townsant asked. "We just hauled it all out of there."

"And we can play with it again some other night, if you like. But we told Sexton we'd be gone in an hour, and it'll take us the rest of the time we have to get things put back together. For now, this discovery has to be our little secret."

Townsant couldn't bear to think of replacing all the heavy boxes they had just taken down. "Why? Why not just leave it all out here? No one comes into this room."

"Sexton does. And as soon as he knows what we're up to, *everybody* will know what we're up to."

"And exactly what *are* we up to?"

"We're looking for answers. Why were the tunnels abandoned? Why doesn't anyone seem to know about them now? Are they actually connected to the Fraternity of the Broken Omen and the legend of their secret rites? You thought I was just imagining things but, in one case after another, my ideas keep being proven correct. And we're still just at the start of it all. Mark my words: Somehow, behind all these old records and outdated catalogs, there're going to be more mysteries waiting to be unearthed than we could possibly have imagined."

CHAPTER THIRTY-EIGHT

"Painful and Divisive Experiences"

It was after 2:00 a.m. by the time the students got back to their residence halls. Most of them were simply delighted to get some sleep. Bastian, however, stayed awake for hours, fleshing out his fantasy about what other secrets the hidden closet in the study lounge might reveal.

And Esmé, too, discovered that she could not yet rest from her labors of the day. A note had been folded and taped to her door. It read:

> *Come see me at your earliest opportunity.*
> *B.W.*

There were no exclamation points, no furious underlining, and no other indications of hostility or rancor, but still, somehow Esmé could tell that the person writing the note had been furious at the time. "B.W." could be only one person: Barbara the Barbarian Librarian. And it was clear to Esmé that she'd somehow violated one of Ms. Winchester's innumerable rules and that remorse (whether genuine or illusory) would need to be shown and some type of penance would need to be performed.

What was *not* clear to Esmé was when the note could have been affixed to her door. After dinner, she'd met with the Warren-Whiteheads to discuss a group project they were working on for Professor Pope's class. Then she'd done some reading by herself in the nearly-empty student union and finally gone to Chudwell Hall for the "study session" that had led the group to their momentous discovery. As a result, the note could have been delivered at any time from 6:00 p.m. onward. Sutlinger Library normally closed at midnight, but its hours were limited during Spring Break. In all likelihood, therefore, the librarian had probably dropped off the note herself after locking up the library at 9:00, leading to two conclusions that left Esmé uncomfortable. First, she'd now have to wait until at least 8:00 the following morning when the library opened before she could discover the reason behind the note. Second, she wasn't at all pleased at the thought that Barbara Winchester knew exactly where she lived.

Those two conclusions deprived Esmé of several hours of much-needed sleep, nearly causing her to turn off her alarm when it rang at 7:00 and simply roll over again. But then it all came back to her in a flash. Ms. Winchester. The note. The violation of some unspecified policy. Better, she thought, to get the inevitable over with and perhaps salvage *something* from her last weekday of Spring Break.

And so it was that a freshly showered and breakfasted Esmé Dawson passed through the library's main entrance as soon as one of the assistant librarians unlocked the doors at 8:00 a.m. Barbara Winchester's glower struck her from the moment she entered the lobby and didn't waver as Esmé walked the twenty or so steps that brought her to the main desk.

"Well, you're prompt at least. I'll give you that," the head librarian began.

"What was it that you wanted to see me about?" Esmé asked as cheerily as she could, belying her true feelings.

Barbara Winchester tossed a white sheet of paper in front of her. "What do you call *this*?"

"It's an interlibrary loan request," Esmé replied after glancing at the paper.

"And why have you requested this particular book?"

"Because our collection doesn't have it."

"Don't be impertinent. I meant, of course, why should you happen to need the *dean's* book?"

"Did it come in?"

"Answer my question."

Esmé did her best to generate a convincing story. "Well, it was something of an accident, really."

"'An accident.'"

"Yes. I'd been doing some reading for Professor Briggs's semantics class and came across the expression *ontological temporality*. Neither I nor any of the other students in the class had come across that term before, and we weren't sure what it meant. Naturally, I did an Internet search."

"'Naturally.'"

"And that's when I discovered that our very own dean had published a book on that topic. So, I looked for it in the stacks and, when I couldn't find it, decided to request it through interlibrary loan. I mean, it's kind of exciting, isn't it, to find out that the college's dean happens to be an expert in a topic relevant to one of your classes?"

"Is it?"

"It is. Anyway, I was hoping to read the book while I had some extra time during Spring Break. Did it come in?"

"It did."

"May I have it?"

"No, you may not."

Esmé's brows furrowed. "But why not?"

"Did it ever occur to you, young lady, that, even though we very prominently feature the books published by Mersley College faculty, there might be a reason why the library does not happen to stock *one* of those books?"

"No, I never ... "

"'No, you never' is correct. There is a very good reason why that book does not now and will never exist in the Sutlinger Library collection."

"And that reason is?"

"One that I need not share with you."

"But if the book has already arrived, surely it can't hurt ... "

"It can hurt, and it *would* hurt. If I'd been on duty at the time you'd made your request, I'd never have processed it for you. In fact, I was completely unaware that the book had been requested until it arrived in yesterday afternoon's post. I, of course, immediately returned the book to the lending library. It's no longer here."

"But *why*?"

"I believe I've already made it clear that I do not owe you any further explanation. I have no desire to put this college through one of its most painful and divisive experiences yet again. Good day, Ms. Dawson."

"But ... "

The implacable look on Barbara Winchester's face suggested that further protest would be futile. So, Esmé turned to leave and, in doing so, saw Mia Thornton through the door of the back offices. She was packing a box with her things, a tear rolling down her cheek.

Apparently, Mia Thornton had paid the price for the group's strategic plan.

CHAPTER THIRTY-NINE

The Nightly Excavations Continue

Once Spring Break was over, a new routine became established for the imminent scholars. Their weekend study sessions in the chapel and library remained unchanged, as did the rest of their days as far as outside observers were concerned, but reality was far different from the illusion they created.

Formerly, the times the students were not in class had been divided between solo study and leisure activities, such as trips to the Dugout, quiet afternoons with books read purely for pleasure, and, on days when the weather was reasonably temperate, walks across campus or quiet moments on the park benches that were placed randomly about the quads. Weekday evenings had, of course, been devoted to group study sessions in Chudwell 2B.

Now, however, there was no time for solo study periods, no time for leisurely strolls, and precious little time for recreational reading. Any spare moment throughout the week was devoted to group study—in the student union if it was quiet enough, in the common room of one of the residence halls if it wasn't—with the result that, if one student made a mistake in Garner's Greek class or misunderstood a passage by Jean Baudrillard in Briggs's semiotics class, they *all* did. Even the most routine assignments were no longer completed by individuals. They were completed by committee.

What was once a study lounge in Chudwell Hall now assumed the appearance of an archaeological site, beginning about 9:00 each evening and continuing until roughly 2:00 or 3:00 when Sexton began knocking on the door, reminding the students that he still had work to do on that hallway and, "Shouldn't youse be gettin' to bed anyways?"

The problem was that, at a typical archaeological site, dirt and artifacts are removed as work continues. In Chudwell 2B, that was simply not feasible. The result was that the students spent the first hour or so removing boxes from the secret passageway and stacking them up along the walls of the study lounge and then spent well over an hour at the end of their "excavations" putting everything back as it was.

Not everything, it is true, made it back into the tunnel behind the wall. Papers that were clearly useless, like the mounds of old Faculty Senate minutes that someone had apparently used to test the nibs of new pens, were regarded as safe to remove. But it was impossible, even late at night, for the students to leave Chudwell carrying huge bags of garbage to leave in a trash bin somewhere. *Someone* would see them and think their actions were suspicious. As a result, each student stuffed no more than an inch or two of what Townsant continued to call "detritus" into a binder, satchel, or book bag and removed the garbage bit by bit from the room. That slowed the process drastically and caused Esmé to remark that the five of them would be dandling great-grandchildren on their knees before they ever reached the back wall of the storage area or whatever it was.

For some reason, it took nearly a month before it occurred to one of the students—and Mallory gets the credit for having this blinding flash of insight—that they had been wasting valuable time by removing *everything* from the storage area each night and then putting it all back again. "If we simply focused on extracting the boxes from the *middle* of the tunnel, we could move much faster. It wouldn't be a *large* opening for us to go through, but I think that someone small, like Esmé, could turn sideways and squeeze between the remaining boxes, then crawl on top of those at the end to see whether the back wall was yet in sight."

Townsant grumbled that he enjoyed seeing what was in the boxes as they removed them and didn't think it was a good idea simply to ignore whatever was stacked along the sides of the closet. But Bastian pointed out that the goal was to discover whether what they'd stumbled onto was the mysterious Winter Refuge, the secret passageway that led to the ritual chamber of the legendary fraternity, both, or neither; it wasn't simply to have fun looking through a bunch of bankers boxes.

Passageway. Tunnel. Closet. Storage area. Catacombs. Winter Refuge. Even the terms the students used to refer to the site of their nightly labors revealed that they weren't all of the same mind about what lay behind the walls of Chudwell 2B. By late March, it had become clear that, if it was indeed something like a closet or storage facility, it was a very deep one indeed. By making more rapid progress through only the middle row of boxes, the students estimated that they'd already reached about fifty or sixty feet behind the lounge's wall, and it appeared that the floor was now gradually sloping downward. Bastian took this as confirmation that his theory about the secret tunnels and the Fraternity of the Broken Omen had been correct all along.

But as the work proceeded, the anxiety of the other four students began to increase. Prudence noted that, if the tunnel had been blocked off and sealed up, there must have been a very good reason for it. "Perhaps it's unsafe. We don't want to get so far underground that we can't get back if the ceiling collapses over us."

Esmé, who'd not thought of that possibility, now seemed more hesitant to continue her role as the vanguard of the group or, as Bastian callously put it, "our canary in the coal mine." Townsant thus took over for her. He wasn't as slim as Esmé, so it was a tighter fit for him to squeeze through the opening between the boxes, and it was absolutely impossible for him to climb up the stack at the end each night and peer over the boxes to make out what could be seen (which, as Esmé had discovered, was simply more rows of boxes anyway). But, at least, progress continued.

One night, having nothing else to do since she couldn't squeeze into the tunnel and there were no new boxes to open and explore, Mallory made the mistake of doing an Internet search of the phrase "secret tunnels beneath campus" on her phone and found references to a number of stories similar to the one that Dean McDaniel had told them the previous fall. These legends, it seemed, were told about campus after campus, and many of them shared similar details.

Usually, it seemed, a group of students was said to have been alarmed by sights of ghostly figures appearing in various old buildings at the school. At night, when returning from the library, the students would often discover a shapeless, glowing blob, hovering outside an abandoned residence hall, but the mysterious figure would vanish whenever one of them drew too near. At last, they became concerned enough that they decided to explore a series of old tunnels connecting all the buildings on the campus, tunnels that, the legends said, had been sealed off and forgotten many years before.

As she read the various stories she had found, everyone except Townsant (who was already too far down into the tunnel to hear) became quiet and recognized the obvious similarities to what they themselves were doing.

Armed with flashlights, the stories continued, the students spent night after night venturing into the dank, odiferous tunnels, their sense of dread increasing the further down they went. One night, after entering an area far beneath the college's administration building, they began to feel that they weren't alone. Simultaneously, their flashlights went out, and they were plunged into absolute darkness. Chilling breezes brushed past their cheeks, and a low rumble began to be heard.

"We need to get out of here!" one of the students cried.

They ran in the direction they believed would lead them to safety but, in the blackness, they frequently stumbled and fell. From time to time, a flash of glowing, malevolent eyes would appear in the dark, increasing their terror. Eventually, one of the students felt the claws of some type of animal scratching at her clothing. She screamed, but it was too late. Whatever the creature was had already reached her, and her calls for help were suddenly cut short as the being's fangs plunged into her flesh.

One by one, the other students fell victim to the creature who inhabited the tunnels beneath the campus. Only one member of the group made it out alive, his clothing torn to shreds, and his face bloody with the signs of a desperate struggle. Shaken by the experience, he could barely tell those who then found him what had just occurred.

The administration of the college, desperate to avoid publicity that they knew would be their ruin, ordered that all the entrances to the tunnels be sealed up. The bodies—or what was left of them—of the students who had died were never even recovered. Their parents were told merely that the students had vanished from campus, and the school disclaimed any responsibility for what may have happened to them.

Students at a college campus come and go. The incident was eventually covered up. But still, it is said, ghostly figures sometimes dart between the buildings of the school, and echoing cries for help may occasionally be heard as though they emanated from the ground itself.

The one surviving student never regained his sanity. He remains, the story concludes, as Patient Number 6873 in the state hospital for the hopelessly insane, staring off into nothingness and muttering only the words "Cold ... soooooo cold" over and over.

When Mallory reached the last line of this story, the other students themselves felt a chill and looked at each other in turn, silently wondering whether the legend may indeed have had some basis in fact and whether other schools may simply have adopted a tale that had actually occurred at Mersley College.

They stood in silence, and Bastian felt himself jump uncontrollably when he heard a voice behind him.

It was merely Townsant, emerging from the tunnel and saying, "So, what did I miss?"

CHAPTER FORTY

The Strange Interlude

Despite the progress being made during their nightly explorations, Esmé couldn't help feeling guilty about the dismissal of the (admittedly incompetent) Mia Thornton. She set out to find the now-unemployed librarian so that she could apologize. And yet, doing so proved more difficult than she'd anticipated. Even for a town as small as Mersley, there were a surprising number of people named Thornton. Plus, if you also looked in the nearby towns of Northwich, Wintervale, and Ashborne Commons, that number swelled impressively. Add to Esmé's difficulty the fact that, since the nightly "study sessions" were now almost totally devoted to exploration of the passageway behind Chudwell 2B, and her time for doing research on the Thorntons was quite minimal.

The first thing Esmé discovered was that Mia Thornton didn't live alone. In fact, as far as the Internet was concerned, she didn't exist at all. Mia had no noticeable presence on any of the standard social media platforms, and all the Mia Thorntons who could be found otherwise were too old, too far away, or both. Two possibilities existed. The first was that Mia still lived with her parents. If that were true, she might be found by calling up any family in the area who shared that surname and asking if Mia were home. The second possibility was that Mia lived with one or more roommates and that her name wasn't listed on the rental agreement for the house or apartment. If that were the case, the chances of ever finding her were slim to none.

With the limited time available to her, Esmé figured that she could call at most one or two families on Mondays, Wednesdays, and Fridays, and three to five families on Tuesdays, Thursdays, and weekend days. That made her progress similar to what the students were encountering in their advance into the tunnel: painfully slow and not particularly productive.

Esmé had come to appreciate the people who, when asked if Mia were there, simply said, "No one lives here by that name" and slammed the phone down. Although rude, such an approach was at least efficient. It told Esmé what she needed to know and allowed her to move quickly onto the next call. But people in the area surrounding Mersley were the sort who tended to be "helpful." They kept Esmé on the phone by speculating whether their second cousin or maybe the estranged wife of their nephew's brother might know someone of that name. They continually suggested that Esmé call this person or that, usually naming people whom she'd already contacted. On more than one occasion, the person on the other end of the line simply wanted to talk and, being intensely polite, Esmé was loath to hurry a lonely senior citizen off the phone.

It was thus only in the first week of April that Esmé hit pay dirt.

"Hi. Is Mia there?"

"Speaking."

The answer came so suddenly and unexpectedly that Esmé nearly forgot what she'd planned to say next. After a few moments of uncomfortable silence, followed by a bit of stammering, she was finally able to get a few words out.

"I'm Esmé Dawson. I'm a student over at Mersley."

"Yes?" Mia replied, a note of suspicion rising in her voice.

"Um, we met once. Briefly. You took an interlibrary loan request from me."

"Yes?" Mia repeated, the note of suspicion becoming even more pronounced.

"I'm worried that, by doing so, I inadvertently cost you your job."

"And?"

"And I'd like to apologize."

"Okay."

"Well, I mean more than just *say* I'm sorry. I'd like to take you to lunch."

"Oh, I really don't think ... "

"*Please!* I feel so guilty. You'd actually be doing me a big favor if you'd let me."

Esmé was met by silence on the other end of the line. Eventually, Mia said, "Do you know The Strange Interlude?"

"The Eugene O'Neill play or the movie with Clark Gable?"

"What are you talking about?"

"*Strange Interlude*. That's what you said, isn't it?"

"I'm talking about the vegan restaurant over on Highway 86."

"Oh. Yes, well, I think I've seen it. Do you want to have lunch there?"

"I work there now."

"Oh."

"I do split shifts. I get a break from 3:00 until 4:30 most afternoons. Can you meet me there tomorrow?"

Making that appointment would mean that Esmé would have to miss Professor Dittman's Queer Theory and Feminist Theory class, and Esmé was *not* a student who skipped classes. On the other hand, if there was one thing Esmé had learned in that course it was that women needed to stick together, supporting one another rather than just looking out for themselves. And what could be a more practical example of someone who needed support than Mia Thornton?

"Sure. Oh, and Mia?"

"Yes?"

"Thanks."

* * *

The Strange Interlude occupied a building that had first been a piano and organ showroom, then divided into three stores that sold various "New Age" items like crystals, incense, and unattractive clothing made from sustainable materials, and finally a tax preparation center, a chiropractor's office, and the vegan restaurant where Mia Thornton worked. If the goal of the decorator who designed the interior of The Strange Interlude was to stress the importance of recycling, then that goal may be said to have been achieved admirably. Everything about the restaurant seemed to have been recycled from one of the building's earlier incarnations. The stools for customers to sit on were all mismatched. The tables may have been an appropriate height for the display of merchandise, but some of them were far too low for comfortable eating. Even the air appeared to have been recycled. A vague odor of frangipani and patchouli hovered as a reminder of the incense once there on display.

The restaurant's menu did little that would persuade carnivores that vegans gave the taste of food anything more than a passing consideration. Each item available at The Strange Interlude was described in terms of what it *didn't* contain and the health benefits it promised to convey, rather than the pleasure it might give. If you were looking for a lactose-free, gluten-free, preservative-free "food product" that promoted heart health and promised to align your chakras, you were most definitely in luck. If you were looking for a meal that might cause you to say, "My word, that's tasty," it was probably better to keep moseying down Highway 86.

As soon as Esmé stepped inside, her nostrils were struck by the faint traces of incense mentioned earlier that blended with an earthy, yeasty, and malty scent emanating from the natural vitamins that, in powdered form, you could have sprinkled on your kale salad or added to your spinach and mushroom wrap. She recognized Mia at once, standing as she was behind the cash register with a bored expression.

"Ready to get a coffee or something?" Esmé asked her.

"Sure. Let me tell my manager I'm clocking out."

Esmé expected that Mia would then disappear into some back room and re-emerge without the apron she was wearing, but that didn't happen. Not moving from the spot where she stood, Mia simply shouted to a man who was wiping down one of the tables, "Hey, Phil! I'll be back after break." Then, without waiting for a reply, she joined Esmé on the other side of the counter.

"My treat, remember?" Esmé told her guest. "Do you want to stay here or ... ?"

"Oh, God, no," Mia replied. "The food here's horrible. I know a better place only a few miles away."

From the look the manager gave Mia, Esmé wondered whether she may not have just cost the woman yet another job.

The "better place" Mia knew about turned out to be the Wintervale Burger King. She took Esmé up on the offer of a full lunch, with Esmé herself settling for a black coffee. "I had to eat on campus today," she excused herself, stretching the truth in that, while she did indeed have lunch in one of Mersley's dining halls, there was nothing mandatory about it. It was merely the cognitive dissonance of the fast-food restaurant having a menu that was, it seemed, the photographic negative of the meals served at The Strange Interlude that, according to the colloquial expression, "put her off her feed."

As soon as they had received their order and found a seat, Esmé got right to the point. "I just wanted to talk to you face-to-face because I feel so awful that my interlibrary loan request got you fired."

"Don't worry about it," Mia assured her. "If it hadn't been that, it would've been something else. Winchester was a terror to work for. By far the worst boss I ever had."

"So, you've had a lot of bosses, then?"

"Well, there's Phil," Mia replied, not having expected that her casual remark would lead to a follow-up question.

"Right. What you're saying, though, does confirm what all the students think about Ms. Winchester. She seems absolutely awful."

"You'd think Sutlinger Library and everything in it were her personal property."

"Exactly."

"Frankly, I'm glad to be out of there. Something's just not right."

"About the library, or about Ms. Winchester in particular?"

"About both. I mean, why does she insist that everything's gotta be done exactly the way *she* did it back around the time of the Civil War ... "

"I don't think she actually ... "

"And why get so upset just because I entered a simple interlibrary loan request without asking her first?"

"Yeah. What's up with that?"

"You tell me. All I know is that it was a big deal. First, she was royally pissed that I used the interlibrary loan system at all. Then she absolutely *exploded* when she saw what book you'd requested."

"Really? What was her problem with the book?"

"Some huge uproar that happened years ago. I don't know all the people involved. You may know more about them than I do."

"I doubt it. Tell me whatever you can."

"Apparently, at one time, there was this professor named Fitzpatrick or something like that."

"Fitzgerald?"

"Could be. As I say, I don't know any of the people she was going on and on about. Anyway, the author of that book ... "

"Dean McDaniel?"

"Sounds right. So, she and this Fitzpatrick or Fitzgerald or whatever got into some heated debate about whose ideas were whose. She said the basic concept and research were her own. The other guy said they were his. Sounds like it was a huge commotion over originality. The word *plagiarism* was being tossed around, Winchester said. The upshot is the campus broke out into something like an armed rebellion, part on McDaniel's side, part on the other side. Then McDaniel won some sort of prize ... "

"The Covington Prize?"

"Got me," Mia shrugged. "Some sort of prize, anyway, and what was already a bad situation became an absolutely horrid situation. Some professors resigned in protest. This Fitzgerald guy disappeared. The campus was even shut down mid-semester for a few weeks. And the whole affair was so awful that there was this agreement never to talk about that book again. Copies were removed from the library and God knows where else. That's why Winchester was so angry. She thought someone—well, *you* really—decided to stir the pot and bring up all this ancient history. 'I will *not* go through all that again,' she kept shouting. Long story short: You're in the doghouse; I'm out of a job; and the world still keeps on spinning."

Esmé looked thoughtfully into her coffee for several minutes. "When you say that Professor Fitzgerald 'disappeared,' did Ms. Winchester give you any idea of what that meant? She didn't mention the word *suicide*, did she?"

"Not that I remember, but, by that time, I gotta admit, I wasn't listening to everything she said. I'd just been fired and ... well, that pretty much took up all my attention."

"Of course, of course. Well, all this is, for me, very interesting. I mean, when you're a student at a college, you never really know what the faculty and staff are up to behind closed doors, do you?" She took a piece of paper from her backpack. "Here's my cell phone number. Call me if you remember anything else. I'll treat you to another lunch. I mean, it's the least I can do. Speaking of which, is there anything else you need right now?"

"Well, I wouldn't say no to some soft serve."

CHAPTER FORTY-ONE

The Covington Prize

As unbelievable as Bastian's ideas had been about hidden tunnels and secret societies, all of which were somehow connected to the suicide of the former professor, Tolbert Fitzgerald, every new discovery seemed to confirm them. That night, while the students were engaged in their nightly exploration of the storage area behind Chudwell 2B, Esmé filled them in on what she'd learned from Mia Thornton.

The news had a strange effect on Townsant. He almost seemed to resent it. Having first formed the group early the previous autumn, he regarded himself as the natural leader of the five. And the fact that he also believed himself to be the most naturally intelligent student at Mersley only confirmed this conviction. He had frankly never seen Bastian as much of a rival, even if Bastian viewed the matter quite differently. For months, it had been easy to ridicule all the "outlandish" talk about the Fraternity of the Broken Omen and its supposed ritual chamber. When one of his companions seemed to imply that Bastian might actually be onto something, Townsant would sigh, cock a condescending eyebrow, and say, "I don't know. That's all a bit outré, as far as I'm concerned. Bastian's a nice enough lad and all, but he'd be out of the program by now if the rest of us hadn't constantly helped him. He's indolent and, if you'll pardon my saying so, a bit of a naïf, don't you think?"

That Townsant was able to work the words *outré*, *indolent*, and *naïf* all into the same speech was, he believed, proof of his own intellectual superiority. Needless to say, he was also the only one of his contemporaries who ever called anyone a "lad" without a trace of irony, a habit that he was convinced gave him some sort of extra credit in the eyes of others.

But now the Bad Boy of the Scipionic Circle appeared to be

more of a visionary than a fantasist. It was bad enough that the Warren-Whiteheads were looking up to him with some sort of admiration, but, when Esmé began to do it, Townsant felt that his own status was rapidly diminishing. He had to do something ... and fast.

Esmé's account of her meeting with Mia was barely concluded when Townsant said, "Well, then it's perfectly obvious what we need to do."

"And what's that?" Mallory asked.

"It's time for another delegation to the dean's office. Don't worry. I'll organize the whole thing. Shall we say tomorrow at 1:00? Bastian, if you need that time to catch up on your Plato, that's perfectly all right. The rest of us can go."

Townsant had not been in the least bit subtle about what he was hoping to accomplish by arranging the visit. "No, that's fine," Bastian said with a tone of false amiability. "I'm all caught up. Wouldn't miss it for the world."

* * *

And so it was that, at precisely 1:00 p.m. that Thursday, all five students appeared in Dean McDaniel's outer office and asked to see her.

"Do you have an appointment?" the administrative assistant asked.

"No, but the dean will want to meet with us, I can assure you," Townsant replied.

"I'll have to check. I'm not sure she's back from lunch yet."

"It's fine, Katie," the dean called from her office. "Send them in."

The full effects of sitting in the president's chair over Spring Break had not completely worn off. Dean McDaniel leaned back as the five students approached her desk, feeling as though there was no problem too large for her to handle.

"Well, well, look what the cat dragged in," she began. "Or should I say five cats? Five cats who'd swallowed canaries to judge from your expressions. What are you all feeling so smug about today?"

"Oh, not much," Townsant replied. "Just a little something called *The Deleuzian Rhizomatics of Ontological Temporality*."

To their dismay, the dean didn't bat an eye when confronted with the name of the book.

"What of it?" she asked.

Townsant had thought he'd played a trump card only to discover that he'd been outplayed. He had to resort to Plan B.

"Why is there no copy of it in the library?"

"I'm sure you all think that here in Old Main we have such large pots of money hidden somewhere that we can buy any book in existence. I don't really blame you. That's what the faculty thinks, too. But if you haven't done any comparison shopping lately, I'll let you in on a little secret: Books are expensive. Harvard may be able to purchase any book their faculty and students desire. Mersley can't. It's as simple as that."

Townsant had by this time recovered sufficiently that he could spot a hole in the dean's argument. "That may be so, but why can't we request a copy through interlibrary loan?"

"Who says you can't?"

"Barbara the Bar- ... I mean, Ms. Winchester."

His remarks brought a smile to the dean's face.

"Ah, I suspect she's just trying to protect me."

"Protect you from what?"

"Oh, from things we try to keep concealed from students."

Dean McDaniel almost seemed wistful. "Your college years ought to be a very special time in your lives, a threshold experience as you pass from adolescence into adulthood. *Limina Luminis*, as the college motto says, 'the thresholds of light.' No one needs to know how the sausage is made, how legislation is passed, or how a college's faculty members treat one another behind closed doors. That book reminds people of a time we still refer to as 'The Troubles.'"

"Like in Northern Ireland?" Mallory asked.

"Similar. And, in its own way, just as bitter. That book won me the Covington Prize, you know."

"We know," Townsant said. "Which makes it doubly strange that there's not a single copy on campus."

"That's not true," the dean corrected him.

She walked over to a cabinet not far from her desk, took out a key, and opened a door. Behind it were what must have been fifty copies of the same book. Dean McDaniel removed several of them.

"Here's one for each of you, since you're so interested. This book established my reputation. Until your Professor Garner came along, I was the only one here who'd ever won a Covington. You're too young yet to realize that award's significance. In the Classics, it's roughly the equivalent of a Nobel Prize and a MacArthur Genius Fellowship combined. The expression *paradigm shift* is used too frequently these days. It seems to have lost all meaning. But you don't receive a Covington Prize—you're not even nominated for one—unless your research produces a complete paradigm shift in the Classics. Alas, fame is fleeting, and academic achievement doesn't always translate into having written a bestseller. Apparently, the reading public wasn't quite as interested in a completely new interpretation of Eleatic philosophy as the prize committee was. Hence the cabinet full of unsold copies. The publisher was only too glad for me to take them off his hands. Today, I can't imagine there are more than a few hundred copies of this book left in existence."

"But The Troubles ... ?" Townsant reminded her.

"Indeed." The dean's wistful expression vanished. "There was a professor here at the college at about the time I was writing this book."

"Tolbert Fitzgerald?" Esmé asked.

"Ah, yes, that's right," the dean answered her. "I'd forgotten we'd talked about him before. Tol we called him. He was the one you thought had gone crazy and hung himself. Silly college legends. No, you see, the truth about Professor Fitzgerald was, as I told you, much simpler than you imagine: He just wasn't very good. Mersley may not be one of the big research universities, but we do expect our faculty to be able to publish *some* research. Tol never could."

"What does he have to do with your book?" Townsant wondered aloud.

"That's where The Troubles come in. It was a long time ago, you must understand. A lot of water has passed under the proverbial bridge. But we older lot, like myself and Ms. Winchester, have no desire to see our campus torn apart once again."

"But the book ... ?"

"I'm coming to that. I'd been at work on *The Deleuzian Rhizomatics* for quite some time. I knew it was going to be an important work. *How* important, I had no idea, but important, in any case. The five of you have a study group, I'm told. Is that right?"

"Yes. Every night."

"Well, faculty members sometimes do something rather similar, especially when they're just starting out. I was young. Tol was younger. I made the mistake of reading him some sections from my manuscript. I thought he might help me 'punch things up,' as it were. Frankly, I thought it might also light something of a fire under him. He was coming up for tenure in a few years and had virtually no publications to show for it. And he was helpful. Too helpful, perhaps. A few weeks later, he offered to give a departmental colloquium. A chance to talk about some research he had in progress. No one thought anything of it when the announcement came out. As a department, we did that all the time, and Tol was long overdue at sharing with us what he was working on. So, when the day arrived, there was some rather good attendance, not just classicists but sort of a cross-section of the entire college community. He got up to read his paper, and the words just seemed to spill out. *My words.*"

"He stole your research."

"That he did. Well, it was a scandal of the first order, as you can imagine. But you also have to remember when this was all happening. Mersley was still something of an Old Boys Club in those days. There were a lot of people who believed him and thought that *I* was the one who was guilty of plagiarism. Huge uproar. It was terrible. Tol claimed he could prove the ideas were his. He said he had a full manuscript of a book he was going to call *The Deleuzian Rhizomatics of Ontological Temporality: A Deconstructionist Approach.* Only problem was he never produced it. Claimed it had been 'lost' somewhere. The Faculty Research Committee held a hearing. There were actually protests all over campus on the day of the hearing, half claiming Tol was right, half claiming I was. Personally, I can't imagine that happening these days. But back then, people just seemed to protest *everything.* There was vandalism. Some of the windows of Chudwell Hall were shattered. It's just a good thing no one was hurt. Anyway, seven hours later—*seven* hours; it was the longest meeting in the committee's history—the committee announced its decision. Tol was declared to be guilty of plagiarism … by a single vote. Naturally, that didn't end it. If anything, that made things worse. It was all anyone talked about for days. Faculty members threatened to quit. Students threatened to transfer. It was a disaster. Finally, the governing board decided to get involved. It terminated Tol's contract, and he left. Heaven knows where. But no, there was no mysterious hanging in the bowels of Chudwell Hall. For years afterward, I kept thinking I'd run into Tol somewhere at a convention or something. But it never happened. I have no idea what happened to him. No one does."

"So, he never passed a bookshop window and saw the book published with your name on it?" Bastian asked, deflated.

"Oh, you've heard that one, too, have you? What kind of bookstore would put a work of academic research in its window?"

The confidence with which the students had entered the dean's office had by now evaporated.

"I'm sorry," the dean explained, "but the world just may not be as bizarre and mysterious as the legends out there say. Anyway, enjoy the book. It did win me the Covington Prize, so it's pretty good, I must admit. Not a page-turner perhaps, but it put me on the road to the deanship."

"I see," Townsant said.

"Oh, and on your way back to Chudwell Hall, you might want to pop into the library and apologize to Ms. Winchester. It sounds as though you've badly misjudged her. There's no conspiracy at work here. She's just a good person who has no desire whatsoever to relive a bad time in the college's history."

CHAPTER FORTY-TWO

The Aurelian Club

Chastened by their latest conversation with Dean McDaniel, the five students temporarily abandoned their nightly excavations behind Chudwell 2B. "I mean, we haven't really found anything useful," Prudence observed, fully living up to her name. "And even though our workload isn't nearly as heavy as it was, I, for one, could really benefit from our group study being more like it was last semester."

"Frankly, I could, too," Mallory admitted, for once following her sister's lead rather than vice versa. "We've got that paper due on the Platonic Theory of Forms coming up for Pope's class, and I've barely started it."

The two young men felt compelled to agree, Townsant because he'd been embarrassed as the spokesman for the group in the dean's office, and Bastian because the whole "conspiracy," as the dean had called it, was really the fruit of his own imagination.

And so, as April began to fade into May, the student lounge was once again filled with discussions of genitive absolutes, the conquests of Alexander, the writings of Judith Butler, and the differences among internalist, inferentialist, and expressivist semantics.

Despite what a closed circle the faculty members and students in the Department of Eminent Scholars had become, the group had drawn a bit of attention from the rest of the Mersley College Community. Much of that attention consisted, sadly but predictably, of ridicule. The students didn't dress, act, or socialize like others at the school. The four faculty members, three of whom were the type that caused other professors to grimace when they learned that they were seated beside them on the same committee, were appreciated largely for their absence from most campus gatherings. Nevertheless, it couldn't be denied that the group had considerable strengths, at least in certain areas.

Perhaps the most obvious of these areas was their established achievement in Latin, combined with their growing facility with ancient Greek. The Classics Department that had served as the former home of both Professor Garner and Dean McDaniel could not long ignore the rumors of what was going on in the new department's classes. Most of the other students at Mersley, if they arrived at the college with any knowledge of Latin at all, had studied the language for no more than two years in high school. They could decline a noun or conjugate a verb with only a few errors and read passages from Caesar's *Gallic Wars* if those passages were somewhat simplified and highly annotated. More than that was, however, beyond their abilities. And absolutely none of the new majors that year had taken even a single year of Greek.

So, when stories began to emerge about five strangely dressed first-year students who met occasionally in the Dugout to read bits of Plato, Horace, and Juvenal together that those majoring in the Classics would find challenging in their *fourth* year, the remaining professors in the Classics Department were filled with both envy and admiration. They also found themselves faced with something of a dilemma.

Each May, Mersley sponsored what it called the Examen Maximum or "Really Big Test." This competition consisted of five passages of Latin and five passages of Greek, all of which had to be translated at sight and without use of a dictionary or any other sort of aid in no more than three hours. Typically, the passages were all taken from authors that were commonly regarded as easy: Aulus Gellius, Cornelius Nepos, Xenophon, Lucian, and the like. As the date of that year's Examen Maximum drew near, the question debated by the classicists was whether they should allow the five students in the Department of Eminent Scholars to compete as well or limit the event only to those students who'd declared a major in the Classics.

That question proved more vexed than it may initially appear. Excluding the five students taught by Garner might look as though the classicists were simply trying to protect those in their own department. On the other hand, if the reports about the level of work being done by the five students were even close to the truth, the typical passages appearing on the Examen Maximum would prove to be no challenge at all.

The top three finalists on the exam each received a certificate and a cash prize, but these were not the factors that most worried the classicists. The top quartile of the finalists was invited for admission into the Aurelian Club, the classical honor society of Mersley College. Membership in that organization wasn't permanent. Students who scored in the top quartile one year but not the next were then dropped from the membership rolls. And the numbers participating in the event that year were a cause for concern. There were currently sixteen Classics majors. In the past, that would have meant that the Aurelian Club would consist of four students the following year. That was certainly a decrease from the glory days of the 1950s when the Aurelian Club annually had more than thirty members and was vying with Phi Beta Kappa as the most distinguished intellectual body on campus. But even more troubling was what might happen if the competition were open to *any* student taking Latin and Greek at Mersley. If all five imminent scholars sat for the exam, it was conceivable that next year's Aurelian Club might not have a single member of the Classics Department in it, and that was a humiliation that the classicists were loath to face.

So, the choice was between humiliation and being accused of protectionism. One of the classicists suggested that the sensible thing to do would be to declare that the Examen Maximum had served its purpose and retire it. But the competition had already been announced, and the current members of the Aurelian Club were unwilling to give up their status. They weren't afraid of a group of weirdos in tweed jackets and pleated skirts. "*Ludi incipiant!*" ("Let the games begin!"), Chester Hoffacker, the club's current *imperator* declared, and that, most of the classicists agreed, should be that.

But Madison Caldwell, the chair of the Classics Department, was still nervous. "If we include passages from authors we typically use, what's it going to look like if some of those 'outsiders' finish the exam in only fifteen or twenty minutes while most of our majors don't complete it in the full three hours? And you know there's always a group that can't finish the test in the time allowed. We've got to make the exam harder this year."

"What're you thinking?" Harper Blake, one of the other classicists, asked. "Tacitus and Thucydides?"

Caldwell chuckled. "Well, maybe not *that* extreme. But mix in some poetry with the prose. Make it a real challenge. That way, things won't look quite so bad if *none* of the students finish the exam when we call 'Time!'"

"But there's something else we haven't thought of," Blake continued. "How can we be objective in grading the results? Even if some of our students *do* qualify for the Aurelian Club, won't it simply look as though we went easy on them?"

"Simple," J. Harley Hurwit concluded. "We grade the exams anonymously."

"Won't work," Blake countered. "I can recognize the handwriting of every student in the department. No, there's got to be a better way."

"How about if we give them all tablets?" Zea Harvey suggested.

"Which kind?" Hurwit asked. "Cyanide or the Ten Commandments variety?"

"Don't be daft," Harvey told him. "Obviously, I was thinking of the computer kind. They *type* in their answers, and submit them under a randomly assigned pseudonym. There's no way of knowing then whose answers are whose."

"I like it," Caldwell concluded. "I'll call the I.T. Department and get it set up. And I think I can take it a step further. You know that Baz Hill College always has its own Classics competition on the same day we do the Examen Maximum. What if I suggest to them that, this year, they grade our students' papers, and we grade theirs? That way, there's no chance of anyone playing favorites."

"Could work," Blake agreed. "At least we'd have an out if anyone accused us of skewing the results."

* * *

In most of the United States, the first Saturday in May is primarily known for the annual running of the Kentucky Derby. But at Mersley, Baz Hill, and several other colleges in their region, the first Saturday in May had been designated as Academic Challenge Day. In addition to the Examen Maximum, similar competitions were held in mathematics, modern languages, history, and other disciplines. Students would sit for exams that were designed to separate the genuine scholars from the "also rans." Prizes were then awarded on Scholars Night, a major ceremony that took place on the evening before graduation.

The students in the Department of Eminent Scholars initially thought that they'd be exempt from participating in Academic Challenge Day. The disciplines they studied were too diverse, and the students in the program were too few, for a departmental test to be either coherent or meaningful. But on the Thursday before the exam, Garner announced in Greek class that he'd arranged with the Classics Department for all five of them to sit for the Examen Maximum. He held out both carrots (any student admitted to the Aurelian Club would be exempt from *both* the Elementary Greek and Roman Satire final exams) and sticks (any student who failed to show up for the test would have to complete an additional fifteen-page paper on myth and ritual in the tragedies of Aeschylus) in order to encourage complete cooperation.

Esmé briefly considered opting out of the competition because she found the paper topic interesting, but even she, in the end, showed up for the test that was scheduled to begin at promptly 9:00 a.m. that Saturday in Bryant Hall.

Wynn Parry, a faculty member from Baz Hill, would proctor the test.

"You will each have precisely three hours to complete the exam. Remember that we're looking for accuracy in translation, not necessarily artistry, so don't think that you can fool us by obscuring your lack of knowledge with some flowery circumlocutions. 'Purple patches' were not amusing to Horace, and they won't be amusing to the judges either. So now, if there are no questions, you may begin."

Chester Hoffacker opened the exam booklet, and his heart sank. There, instead of the simplified and heavily annotated passages he was used to, were whole swaths of Propertius, Juvenal, Euripides, and Demosthenes with nary a note or vocabulary word in sight. Yet even as he stared at the blank screen on his tablet, the five imminent scholars were already tapping away at their screens. He thought for a moment of giving up, but then the prospect of surrendering his role as *imperator* of the Aurelian Club seemed too bitter a pill to swallow. He took a deep breath, straightened his back, and began to give the test his best shot.

CHAPTER FORTY-THREE

La Tanière Dorée

Unexpectedly, it was Sabrina Pope, not Madison Caldwell or Winton Garner, who divulged the results of the Examen Maximum. But she did so unintentionally, assuming (as people often do) that what had been revealed to her alone was already common knowledge.

"So," she said at the end of the next Wednesday's Art, Literature, and Music of Ancient Greece course, "have you decided yet whether to oust Chester Hoffacker? Or are you going to throw him a sop and let him retain his *imperium*?"

"We won't know that until the scores are announced," Bastian replied.

"Oh," Pope said with genuine surprise. "I thought you'd all heard."

"What?" Esmé asked. "Do you know the results?"

Pope was a better professor than she was an actor. "No, no," she said, trying to cover her faux pas. "I was just wondering is all."

"You *do* know!" Bastian cried out. "Come on, don't keep us hanging here!"

"No, I really couldn't. That news has to come from the Classics Department. I've said too much already."

"*Pleeeeease*," Mallory begged, followed by the others in turn.

After what seemed an eternity of begging (but was, in fact, no longer than four or five minutes), Pope gave in. "All right. All right. Here's the email I received. But act surprised when the results are announced officially. Professor Caldwell likes to do that in person."

She set a sheet of paper down on the table at the front of the classroom, and the students gathered around it to see what it said.

> TO: faculty@mersley.edu
>
> FROM: mcaldwell@mersley.edu
>
> RE: Examen Maximum Results
>
> Wynn Parry of Baz Hill has just sent me the results of this year's Examen Maximum. Out of a total of 100 points, the scores are:
>
> | | | |
> |---|---|---|
> | 1. | P. Bradford Townsant III | 96 |
> | 2. | Esmé Dawson | 92 |
> | 3. | Chester Hoffacker | 83 |
> | 4. | Mallory Warren-Whitehead and Prudence Warren-Whitehead [TIE] | 79 |
>
> *[There then appeared a list of students from the Classics Department, followed by:]*
>
> | | | |
> |---|---|---|
> | 17. | Bastian Lewis | 61 |
>
> *[Four remaining names, all those of Classics majors, rounded out the list.]*
>
> On Scholars Night: this year, Townsant will be recognized with a certificate and a $250 cash prize, Dawson will be recognized with a certificate and a $150 cash prize, and Hoffacker (last year's first-place finalist) with a certificate and a $75 cash prize.
>
> A total of 21 students participated in this year's competition. Since the top quartile of the competitors consists of Townsant, Dawson, Hoffacker, M. Warren-Whitehead, and P. Warren-Whitehead, they will be the members of the Aurelian Club for the coming academic year. Congratulations are to be given to them and to all those

who participated in this year's Examen Maximum."

When the students had finished reading the email, Townsant said to Bastian, "Sorry, old man. That's a tough break."

"Is it? And are you?" Bastian replied. Then he stormed out of the classroom, his face a brilliant crimson, although whether it was from anger or humiliation was impossible to tell.

* * *

As Professor Pope had predicted, Madison Caldwell made the rounds later that week, informing each of the five new members of the Aurelian Club that they had been successful on Academic Challenge Day. He also presented each of them with two gold keys, reciting what had become a well-worn speech as he did so.

"Now, both of these keys are for you to keep, but only one of them is to be displayed publicly. The first is your emblem of membership in the Aurelian Club. Wear it proudly. In the old days, students used to attach it to the chain of a pocket watch ... or attach *them*, I should say, since members receive new keys each year they qualify for membership. Nowadays, women tend to attach their keys to a charm bracelet, and men tend to use them as lapel pins or ornaments on a key chain. But that's entirely up to you. The second key you must never give or even show to anyone who's not been inducted into the Aurelian Club. It provides you with access to *La Tanière Dorée*, the club's private meeting room. Entrance to *La Tanière Dorée* by means of these keys is permitted only by current members and faculty advisors like myself. And nothing that you ever see or hear within the clubroom may ever be repeated outside of it. Repeating those secrets or, even worse, lending the key to a guest or even one of the Aurelian Club's alumni is strictly prohibited. Any books, writings, or printed materials found in *La Tanière Dorée* must remain there. Removing or making copies of them will result, not only in expulsion from the club, but will also be reported to the College Honor Board as a Class C offense. So, use your keys and your year in the Aurelian Club wisely. One final note: Although you may keep this second key as a souvenir, it will only be useful beginning on Scholars Night this year and ending on Scholars Night next year. The locks are changed annually, and this rule is very strictly enforced. Any member who uses his or her key to grant a non-member access to *La Tanière Dorée* will immediately be removed from the club and disqualified from future membership. Do you have any questions?"

At this point in the dialogue, Chester Hoffacker, of course, had no questions. He was a rising senior and had been a member of the Aurelian Club for the past two years. But the other new initiates all had precisely the same question: "Where is this *Tanière Dorée* of which you speak?"

"As to that," Professor Caldwell told them, "you will receive all the instructions you need when you are also taught the club's secret handshake in a private ceremony after the Scholars Night festivities have concluded. Until then, I bid you good day."

CHAPTER FORTY-FOUR

Scholars Night

The annual ceremony for academic awards at Mersley College was practically identical to other such ceremonies at any college or university anywhere in the world. A group of administrators and faculty members sat on the stage of an auditorium, each of them wondering why the ceremony seemed to be lasting even longer than the one last year. The rear of the auditorium was reserved for parents, all wishing that the event would move much more quickly when the awards being announced did not involve their own children, but much more slowly when the names of their sons and daughters were called. The first five rows of the auditorium were cordoned off for the students, who processed in with a line that was more or less straight and then spent the rest of the ceremony playing with their phones and wishing they were anywhere else.

The sole exceptions to this general pattern were the four students from the Department of Eminent Scholars who were about to be inducted into the Aurelian Club. Unlike their peers, they seemed fascinated by the events taking place around them, and their garb—tweed jackets or pleated skirts instead of t-shirts and "my *good* jeans"—made them seem as though they were almost from a different school. In a sense, they were. No other students at Mersley would ever have considered setting foot inside Chudwell Hall, and both the faculty and student members of the Scipionic Circle mingled with the rest of the campus only when absolutely necessary.

Chester Hoffacker did not sit with them. His nominal reason for avoiding the imminent scholars was that he was also receiving a bronze medal that evening for outstanding composition in an English course and thus "had" to sit with the other students from the English Department. In truth, there was no regulation about where the students had to sit. He merely resented the fact that he hadn't placed first on the Examen Maximum and now had to spend his senior year in the Aurelian Club with four students he regularly referred to as "freaks."

Each presenter of the awards was allotted two minutes to describe the honor being bestowed and was instructed to read the names of all the honorees "in a measured but rapid cadence." The audience was told to hold its applause until all the names had been read and all the recipients were on their way to the stage. Not a single person, of course, adhered to these guidelines. It was only the rare administrator or faculty member who spoke for fewer than five minutes, and Baldwin Dolton, the senior member of the faculty of German Language and Literature, droned on for more than twenty before announcing the name of that year's sole recipient of the Varnhagen Medal. The very first award that was presented that evening—to Eva Walton, the first of six recipients of the Bettmer Prize in Sociology—caused her family to whoop and cheer so loudly that they must have assumed they were at a Monster Truck Rally rather than an academic recognition ceremony. Their actions set the tone for the evening. From that point forward, as soon as each name was called, the family and friends of the recipients seemed to compete with one another as to who could cheer the loudest.

At first, Dean McDaniel cast a jaundiced eye toward the worst offenders in a vain hope that "the look" might discourage their exuberance. But, in the end, even she realized that her efforts were futile. The academic world had changed, and Scholars Night, like the graduation ceremony itself, had become more a scene of unbridled revelry than the somber and sober acknowledgment of intellectual achievement it once had been.

The event started at 8:00 p.m. and was intended to conclude by 9:30. But a late start and verbose speeches meant that it was already 10:45, and the induction to the Aurelian Club was still three items away on the agenda. By this time, the auditorium was far emptier than it had been hours earlier. A number of parents had stayed only until their own children had received their awards and then left. Even one or two members of the faculty had excused themselves from the stage for "a prior commitment" (that typically involved the consumption of at least one adult beverage and extended conversation of how "this year's Scholars Night was the worst *ever*"). Only the students remained in their seats, held prisoner by President Woolridge's stern admonition that their honors would be instantly revoked if they departed before they were formally dismissed. That this threat would never have been carried out seemed not to detract from its effect. The students squirmed. They yawned. They checked the time almost compulsively. But they did not leave.

Finally, it was time for the results of the Examen Maximum to be made public. Madison Caldwell approached the podium, cleared his throat, and gave what he considered to be an abridged history of "the distinguished and noble fraternity of the *Societas Aurelia*, commonly known as the Aurelian Club. He mentioned the names of several past members who had gone on to successful careers in classical philology, including Dean McDaniel herself. He emphasized the club's exclusivity and noted that only current members and faculty advisors, all of whom themselves must have once been members of the society, were given keys to the "inner sanctum" of *La Tanière Dorée*. He painted a picture of the lofty intellectual conversations that "we must imagine occur nightly within these hallowed precincts," ignoring the fact that, for years now, the room had chiefly been used for games of Dungeons & Dragons or Magic: The Gathering.

At last, he got to the primary purpose of his remarks: the announcement of the names of the group's current members. For the first time that evening, there wasn't a single shriek of joy or burst of applause at the mention of each name. The parents of Townsant, Esmé, and the twins weren't in attendance. Those of Hoffacker had left an hour earlier. And no one else seemed to care.

The event concluded not with a bang, but with a whimper. The president announced, "This concludes the awarding of honors at this year's Scholars Night. Thank you for attending, and good evening." Before his final words were even spoken, the majority of those in attendance began moving toward the exit. While the students had been instructed on how to process *in*, no one had bothered to explain how they should recess *out*. As a result, the exits quickly became clogged with a mixture of students, faculty, administrators, and parents, all headed to their cars, their homes, or their residence halls. Orderly it was not.

In the parking lot, Madison Caldwell was about to enter his battered blue Volvo when he heard a call, "Professor, wait!" He turned to see Townsant and the others proceeding toward him. "Haven't you forgotten something?" he was asked.

"Forgotten? What?" he replied, annoyed that his departure had been delayed.

"The handshake? The keys?" Mallory asked.

"Oh, that. Well, the secret handshake is easy enough. Here." Starting with Townsant, he demonstrated the ritual to each of the students in turn. He reached out as though to engage in a traditional handshake but, at the last moment, curled back his ring finger and pinky. Then, once his remaining two fingers were clasped with those of the other person, he used his thumb to tap rapidly three times against the back of the other person's hand.

"Got it? Easy, isn't it?"

"And we use this handshake ... for what?" Esmé asked.

"To recognize other members of the club and so that they can recognize you."

The students looked at each other. "But we already know who's a member. It's just us and Hoffacker."

The professor sighed. "Yes, well, I guess it all made more sense when the club was larger. Anyway, you wanted to know the handshake, and there it is. Now, if there's nothing else ... "

"But there is," Townsant pointed out. "*La Tanière Dorée?*"

"What about it? I already gave you your keys."

"Yes, but when can we start using it? Can we go there now?"

Caldwell was tempted to say, "You can all go to blazes for all I care," but he judiciously edited his remarks, saying instead, "I'd wait until tomorrow after the graduation ceremony. The maintenance crew has to change the lock. They're supposed to do that while the rest of us are attending Scholars Night, but ... well ... sometimes they're slow."

"But you haven't told us where it is," Townsant reminded him.

"Oh, yes. Well, you know the candy machine down in the basement of Old Main?"

"I think so."

"It's easy enough to find. There's only one in the entire building. Find it, and to the left of it is a metal door. The sign says, 'Warning: Electrical Closet,' but that's just a ruse. Use your keys to open the door, and there's a long, winding ramp behind it. It's quite dimly lit, so be sure to let your eyes adjust to the light before you start to descend. At the bottom you'll find another door, this one larger and more ornate. Your key unlocks that door, too. Once you open this second door, that's it. You're in."

"And what'll we find there?"

"The secrets of the world, son, the secrets of the world."

CHAPTER FORTY-FIVE

The Peeling of the Belles

Technically, the Sunday following Scholars Night was known as "The Annual Mersley College Commencement." More idiomatically, the day was referred to as "The Peeling of the Belles." The explanation for that custom requires a bit of history.

Back in an age when Mersley College's enrollment was limited to men—even before Elisabeth Banworth, the chapel's namesake, could complain about the pearl-less outfits worn by the "coeds" of the 1960s—many of the school's soon-to-be graduates would invite their girlfriends to join them for that weekend's festivities. A substantial number of these women were from either Westside Girls Seminary or the Athena Academy, institutions that are now, alas, extinct, but at one time provided advanced education for what was quaintly referred to then as "the weaker sex." That expression, like the schools themselves, has now been mostly forgotten but, in their day, Westside and Athena did serve something of a purpose: They provided dating opportunities for the students at Mersley who would one day become their husbands. Only a minority of those enrolled at the women's colleges actually graduated. The joke, common enough in its day, was that students only attended these schools to earn their "M.R.S. Degree." As unfortunate as that attempt at humor was, the statement was largely true. The number of marriages arising from attendance at the three colleges represented a success rate that any online dating app would today envy.

The graduates-to-be were thus joined by their brides-to-be at the college's annual baccalaureate service (a religious ceremony later superseded by Scholars Night) and then by a great graduation banquet, held in clement weather out on the South Quad immediately following graduation. But stuck in its outdated tradition, only faculty members, graduates, and members of their immediate families were permitted to attend the actual commencement ceremony. That left the girlfriends with nothing to do for several hours on Sunday morning ... nothing to do until an informal tradition of its own arose.

It started with an impromptu croquet match on the North Quad that took place in 1872 and then gradually morphed through several different formats until it became a "Beach Party Without the Beach" sometime in the late 1960s. By that time, of course, girlfriends (or anyone else for that matter) who wanted to attend graduation were free to do so. But the more festive atmosphere of the North Quad appealed to some of them more than the stodgy and seemingly endless performances of *Pomp and Circumstance* on the South Quad. In addition, not all the women who attended Mersley College had yet moved out of their residence halls. Those who were returning to their homes for the summer had until Wednesday of the following week to vacate the premises, and anyone who was enrolled in one of Mersley's summer sessions didn't have to move out at all. Since the weekend of graduation was often one of the first truly hot and sunny times of the year in that part of the country, the primary activity of the "Beach Party Without the Beach" consisted of several dozen young women, lying on beach towels and sunning themselves in the expectation of a quick tan and drinking tall glasses that were reputedly filled with "lemonade" but obviously weren't.

Rather than getting a head start on their tans, however, the majority of the fair-haired, blue-eyed women in attendance simply ended the day with a terrific sunburn—and probably raised the likelihood that they'd all be getting skin cancer several decades later. The 1960s and 1970s were, however, times when such future dangers were far from people's minds, and so deep red burns and peeling skin were often regarded as badges of honor.

In the week following graduation, those badges were so commonly seen on campus that one of the local wags began referring to the "Beach Party Without the Beach" as "The Peeling of the Belles" and, by the early twenty-first century, that name had stuck.

Since attendance at summer sessions was practically a required component of the curriculum in the Department of Eminent Scholars, all five students remained on campus that weekend. Their plan, initially, was to stroll through the North Quad as something akin to tourists, taking in the sights of "The Peeling of the Belles" (which, for some reason, seemed to appeal more to Townsant and Bastian than the others) and then, once the graduation ceremony was over, head to *La Tanière Dorée* and make use of their freshly-issued keys to this mysterious inner sanctum.

As so often happens in life, however, anticipation proved far superior to reality. Far from the modern bacchanal that many at the college described, "The Peeling of the Belles" turned out to be a somewhat subdued affair. Illicit alcoholic drinks were there, to be sure, and about a dozen or so young women had been present since breakfast, "soaking up the rays" as one of them put it. But, on the whole, the event was something of a disappointment. At least half of those in attendance were actually asleep and, those who weren't, engaged in conversation on topics to which the five students were decidedly indifferent. If Townsant and the others had imagined that they would be taking the role of anthropologists, investigating a strange and inexplicable culture, the reverse seemed to be true. They appeared to the "belles" as something like visitors from another planet or, at least, another century. Their ties, collared shirts, and baggy trousers contrasted sharply with the implicit dress code of the event, and they quickly grew uncomfortable.

"Surely they must have changed the locks by now," Esmé said, as they made their second pass through the quad.

"Only one way to find out," Mallory agreed. "Let's head over to Old Main and see if our keys work."

"Great," Bastian said. "I wanna see this place. There are all sorts of rumors about it, and ... "

"Um," Townsant interrupted. "I'm afraid you can't come with us."

"Why not?" Bastian asked angrily.

"Members only."

"Nonsense," Bastian protested. "I only want a look. I won't trespass on your *sanctum sanctorum*."

"I'm not prepared to risk it. Are you?" Townsant asked Esmé.

"No, I'm not, and I can't imagine the rest are either. Look, Bastian, Professor Caldwell was very strict about this rule: current members only. Even alumni can't be admitted if they didn't qualify for that specific year. I'm sorry."

"Oh, come on," Bastian complained. "It's not like anyone is going to find out."

"That's a chance I'm not willing to take. I don't want to be expelled from the Aurelian Club on the very first day I'm a member."

"That's just bullshit," Bastian replied.

Prudence tried to make a compromise. "We can take *photos*, can't we? Professor Caldwell never said anything about not taking our phones down there. Why can't we show Bastian the room afterward?"

There was a keen debate of the sort that can only occur among a group of students who'd recently taken a class on semantics on whether doing so would violate Professor Caldwell's decree that "nothing you ever see or hear within the clubroom may ever be repeated outside of it."

Negotiations, such as they were, continued for another twenty minutes until Bastian finally said, "Oh, go do whatever you want," and stormed off.

"The fox has declared the grapes to be somewhat sour, it seems," Townsant concluded as he watched Bastian head back toward his residence hall. "Anyway, let's go. Times a-wasting."

* * *

None of them had seen Old Main as empty as it was that Sunday. Usually, the halls were filled with people heading to or from one of the administrative offices, their footsteps echoing in the white-and-black-tiled hallways. But that Sunday, the four students had the building to themselves, an experience that made them feel as though, despite the keys they'd been issued, they were about to enter some forbidden territory.

They walked down a central stairway into a dank and dusty cellar. Stacks of chairs stood here and there, too worn to use but too good to discard. Huge, outdated boxes, which had been there since the 1950s when the basement of Old Main served as a Civil Defense shelter, made the passage through the hallways narrow at several points. In another corner, three ping pong tables were stored, folded, and forgotten, causing Townsant to wonder how in the world such large objects were brought there without an elevator and how they could ever be removed through the corridors of the cellar now made even more narrow by all the "detritus" (he still loved that word) that had been left there.

Eventually, they came to an old vending machine, its glass as cloudy and yellowed as the headlights of an old car. There, as they'd been informed, was a metal door to the left that bore a rusty sign reading "Warning: Electrical Closet," with a stylized lightning bolt beneath the words.

"You know, it's interesting how we depict lightning today," Townsant observed. "The ancient Greeks saw it as looking more like a trident or ... "

"Just open the door, Townsant," Esmé directed him.

He slid his key into the lock, turned it to the right, and the door swung open. Immediately behind the door, the floor began to slope and curve, rendering what lay only a few yards ahead completely invisible. Tentatively, the group entered the passage and began to allow their eyes to adjust to the gloomy darkness. Within moments, the door swung closed behind them without any action on their part, and the lock clicked shut firmly and, it seemed to them, threateningly.

Professor Caldwell had said that the passage was poorly lit, but his warning was, if anything, an understatement. The only thing the students could see for several minutes was the dim, flickering glow of a candle at some distance ahead of them. Feeling their way along the damp wall, they crept ahead toward this faint beacon. It was only when they were directly in front of the light that they could see it wasn't a real candle after all, but a tiny electric bulb containing a carbon filament that oscillated inside the glass and created a flickering effect.

"Our parents have a couple of these in our den," Mallory explained when she saw the light. "They're really intended for decoration only, not to provide any real light."

"Someone must've thought otherwise," Esmé said.

"Look, there's another one down there," Prudence added.

And once again, they began making their way hesitantly down the passageway.

About a third of their way down, the air around them seemed to change dramatically. It grew cold and heavy, giving the students a sense that they had left one world behind and were about to pass into another.

Inch by inch, they made their way down the winding hallway until they came to a massive oak door bearing a sign written in no language that any of them had ever studied. Cryptic symbols conveyed a message that they could only assume threatened death and destruction to anyone who dared enter the secret chamber without permission.

His hand now trembling almost uncontrollably, Townsant inserted his key into the lock and, before he could even turn it, the door creaked open.

The room in front of them must have been somewhat dark. But their eyes, having adjusted to the near-complete blackness of the passageway, made them feel as though they were staring into a blinding light. Eventually, they could discern the outlines of a vast circular room with a high, domed ceiling supported by ornate pillars carved with images of serpents, harpies, and other grotesques. Five statues stood before five secondary doors that led heaven knows where. These statues were identical: tall gargoyle-like creatures, made of a dark red stone that appeared to be jasper. Along the wall stood massive shelves laden with books, all bound in leather and all looking as though they contained, as Caldwell had said, the secrets of the world.

At the center of the room was a large table, its top simply a flat sheet of masonite on which it would appear that the games so dear to Chester Hoffacker and his cronies were played. It was the base of the table that was far more interesting. Intricately etched with sigils and encrusted with precious gemstones, this trapezoidal pedestal, fashioned from obsidian, at one time almost certainly had some other use than to provide a surface for the playing of fantasy games. Around it, other images were carved into the floor and, although they were mute and stationary, it was easy to imagine them pulsating with some sort of otherworldly energy.

"The ritual chamber of the Fraternity of the Broken Omen," Townsant whispered. "Bastian must've been right all along."

"Prudence, you've got the better phone," Mallory said. "Snap some photos. I don't think I want to stay here very long."

As Mallory simply looked about, Townsant and Esmé also took out their phones and began taking pictures. The gold lettering on many of the books was cracked and faded, but it was clear that the lore they contained was not the sort that one was likely to encounter in Sutlinger Library.

Esmé was about to remove one of these dust-laden volumes from the shelf when suddenly the room burst into a brilliant light.

"I figured you losers couldn't wait to get down here," a voice announced. "Cringing in the dark like rats? Why didn't you idiots just flip on the overheads?"

The four of them blinked and realized that they'd been so focused on the decor that they hadn't noticed a fifth person enter the room.

Chester Hoffacker was now among them.

CHAPTER FORTY-SIX

The Consuls

Immediately upon seeing Hoffacker, Townsant tried to mend fences. "Oh, sorry, Chester. You're right. We just couldn't wait to see the clubroom. Pretty spooky, isn't it?"

Hoffacker looked around as though he'd been there so often he'd begun to ignore the peculiarity of the place. "'S'all right, I suppose," he said. "No one bothers you down here. Anyway, I just stopped by to grab some of my stuff. I'm off to Bermuda for the summer."

"Study program?" Esmé asked.

"'*Study* program'?" he asked sarcastically. "Yeah, that's it exactly. I'm gonna study the local anatomy down at the beach. You guys heading out soon?"

"No, we're here for the summer. Our program runs year-round," Townsant told him.

Hoffacker shook his head. "Loser. Summer school, eh? Yeah, well, enjoy that. Just don't wreck the place before I get back."

Mallory, who'd been studying some of the books on the shelves, asked, "You ever read any of these?"

"Those dreary old things? Nah. They're just part of the decoration."

She read the names of some of the authors. "Annie Besant. Carl Reichenbach. Arthur Machen. This is all pretty occult stuff."

"Pretty *boring* stuff, if you ask me."

By this time, Townsant had joined Mallory and was examining the shelves. "Very little of it seems related to the Classics. Seems like an odd collection for a classical honors society."

Hoffacker shrugged. "I think they were here even before the Aurelian Club took over this room." The four other students exchanged glances. "Anyway, I presume you're going to want to be the next *imperator*, Townsant, since you scored highest on the test."

"What exactly does the *imperator* do, anyway?"

Hoffacker looked even more bored than he had before. "Basically, it's just a fancy name for being the club president. Look, you want it or not, 'cause I'm happy to continue if ... ?"

"There's got to be some kind of constitution or set of bylaws for the Aurelian Club, hasn't there?" Townsant asked. "Wouldn't that spell out the duties of the *imperator*?"

"Not that I ever saw. We pretty much just made things up as we went along."

"An oral constitution?" Townsant said, thinking aloud. "Kind of like most ancient Greek and Roman cities." He suddenly had an idea. "That means we could change the governmental structure, couldn't we?"

The very suggestion made Hoffacker suspicious. "What d'you have in mind?"

"I mean, these are unusual times, right? The Aurelian Club has consisted solely of Classics majors before, hasn't it? And now the members are from two different programs. Why not have two different leaders?"

"*Two* people in charge?" Hoffacker asked. "That'll never work."

"Worked for Sparta," Prudence pointed out. "They had two kings."

"And more importantly," Townsant said, fleshing out his idea, "it worked for the Roman Republic. Two consuls, each with equal power."

"But what happens if we disagree?" Hoffacker asked.

"Look around you. We have an odd number of members. If our consul wants to do one thing, and you want to do another, we hold a 'plebiscite.' As long as everyone votes, there has to be a majority for one of the proposals."

"Yeah, *your* proposal," Hoffacker muttered. "Everyone else in the club is one of your cronies."

"We don't work that way," Esmé said. "The whole point of our program is to develop our critical thinking skills. We disagree with one another in class *constantly*. And sometimes we even change one another's minds. I think Townsant's idea might work."

Hoffacker thought it over. "Okay, I guess. So, what, then? You and me as the two consuls, Townsant?"

"No, I was thinking more you and Esmé."

"*Me?*" Esmé asked in shock.

"Oh, yeah," Hoffacker said. "I heard you get an earful of all that feminist crap from Ditsy Dittman in your major. Bad optics if the two men are in charge while the three girls are simply members, eh?"

The word *girls* caused the others to bristle. But, before anyone had a chance to respond Townsant said, "No, I just think Esmé's the better candidate. She's more diplomatic than I am, for one thing. And I've seen what's going on in our department. The chair, Professor Dittman—who's the furthest thing from 'ditsy,' by the way—has major portions of her day eaten up by administrative details. Professor Garner, on the other hand ... "

"Ah, yes, I've heard Grumpy Garner's your hero."

Townsant ignored him. " ... devotes all his time to teaching and scholarship. Frankly, those are more my thing than having a title I can list on a résumé someday. I'm more than happy to be a member of the *plebs*. So, I nominate Esmé Dawson and Chester Hoffacker to be this year's consuls of the Aurelian

Club."

"Second!" Mallory called out.

"All in favor?"

Before Hoffacker had a chance to do or say anything, Townsant and the twins raised their hands.

"The motion carries," Townsant announced. "Move that nominations be closed."

"Second!" Mallory repeated.

"All in favor?"

Once again, Townsant and the twins cast the deciding votes.

"So there you have it," Townsant concluded. "Congratulations, Esmé and Chester on your new eminence."

"You guys are all nuts," Chester said, shaking his head. He grabbed the few objects he'd come down to *La Tanière Dorée* to retrieve and headed out of the room without a further word.

"Well, *that* was rude," Townsant said as the heavy wooden door banged shut. "But no matter. Madam Consul, what's our first order of business?"

For several seconds, Esmé looked like a deer in the headlights. But then, almost before the very eyes of the others, she seemed to "grow into" her position.

"Let's clear away these game pieces and move this sheet of masonite aside. I'd like to take a look at what we really have here."

CHAPTER FORTY-SEVEN

Bloodstains, Bound Books, and Bastian

Brushing the remnants of the various games from the tabletop took mere seconds. Lifting the board from the pedestal, however, proved to be a far more formidable task. What had initially appeared to be a large sheet of masonite was actually glued to a disk of granite or marble that was well over a foot thick and nearly three feet in diameter. If each of the four students took a corner and lifted, the masonite would merely buckle and tear off in large chunks. None of them wanted their first day in *La Tanière Dorée* to be known ever after as "that time the four weirdos trashed the room." And so, they very slowly and carefully began to slide the table top off the pedestal so that they could support the part of it made from stone and thus carry the structure intact to one side of the room.

None of the imminent scholars was likely to excel at any weightlifting competition. As students, they had put all their eggs into the basket of the *mens sana*, leaving none for the *corpore sano*. (Or as Townsant might point out, "Actually, that would be *corpus sanum*, if you're going to omit the 'in'.") Indeed, that was one of the reasons they'd all applied to Mersley College in the first place. While other institutions of higher learning were adding physical education requirements to their curricula during the early 1960s as a result of John F. Kennedy's President's Council on Physical Fitness, Mersley had decided to buck the trend. Twenty years later, during one of its many cost-cutting measures, it had eliminated intercollegiate athletics entirely and greatly reduced its annual spending on intramural sports. The result may have been to create precisely the sort of intellectual home that would appeal to the five students in the Department of Eminent Scholars, but it hardly prepared them to be effective at shifting a 130-pound tabletop ten feet from the center of the room.

By the time they'd completed their task, the Mersley College Orchestra was winding up its vastly inflated version of *Pomp and Circumstance* and shifting to a lively rendition of the triumphal march from *Aïda* for the recessional. As faculty members, graduates, and their parents poured forth onto the South Quad, Townsant, Esmé, and the Warren-Whitehead twins at last gazed upon their handiwork.

Before them stood an intricately carved trapezoidal block of obsidian. With the tabletop removed, the four were able to get close to the stone in a manner that hadn't been possible before. Into the side of the object had been etched enigmatic runes and images of twisted serpents, their scales curling sinuously, almost as if they'd been frozen in mid-motion.

The top of the pedestal bore traces of wax, the last vestiges of candles that could have been burned there decades before any of them had been born. At the very center of the altar was a large, thick slot that perhaps served as a depository for whatever unsavory material remained there after a sacrifice. Then, radiating out from this slot, four channels had been cut, each one leading to a different corner and ending in what appeared to be something like a spout.

Mallory examined the channels closely and then leapt back as though she'd been struck by a bolt of lightning.

"What is that? Blood?" she cried, pointing to the stone.

The others approached the object and saw the source of her reaction: small stains, each perhaps an inch or less in diameter, left behind by some liquid that had dried and left an irregular pattern.

"It's an altar," Townsant said, somewhat gratuitously since all the others had drawn the same conclusion he did.

"So, we've found it, then," Esmé said. "The ritual chamber of the Fraternity of the Broken Omen."

"All this time it's been here," Mallory observed.

"And yet, no one has known," Prudence added.

"Or perhaps they *did* know," Townsant said.

"What do you mean?" Mallory asked.

"Well, hear me out. A room this strange would be almost impossible to keep a secret. People on a college campus gossip about *anything*. Surely, at least one member of the Aurelian Club would have spilled the secret, even if it was nothing more than a 'You'll never guess what *I've* seen.'"

"What're you suggesting?" Esmé asked.

"I think the Aurelian Club *is* the Fraternity of the Broken Omen. Or at least the fraternity morphed into the club over time. Think about what Professor Caldwell told us when he gave us our keys: 'Nothing you ever see or hear within the clubroom may ever be repeated outside of it.' We've all been sworn to secrecy, just like every member before us."

"What? You mean like a cult?" Prudence asked.

"Something like that. We've been inducted into an occult fraternity without our permission or even our knowledge."

"But why us?" Mallory wondered.

"I don't know. Maybe you have to understand a good bit of Latin and Greek in order to perform the rituals. Or maybe that was the case at one time, but the Epigoni ... " The term was one that Townsant had picked up from Professor Pope's class on ancient Greece. Originally referring to the less capable descendants of the great heroes of mythology, the term was, Pope said, now applied to anyone who was a mere imitator or who represented a decline from the greater accomplishments of the past. " ... stopped engaging in rites they could no longer understand and devoted themselves to fantasy games instead. Maybe we've been chosen because we're supposed to restore the fraternity to its former greatness."

Instead of listening to this explanation, Esmé had been examining the rest of the room. "Well, if this *is* the ritual chamber that Bastian was talking about, shouldn't these five doors lead to the tunnels that connect the campus buildings?"

"Let's find out," Townsant suggested.

He walked up to one of the large jasper gargoyles and tried to move it away from the door. But it proved to be even heavier than the tabletop.

"Here, give me a hand with this," he called out to the others.

Straining with all their might, even the four of them together were able to "walk" the stone monstrosity less than a yard to the left. The result wasn't perfect, but it was enough to get the door open a few inches.

"Give me your phone," Townsant said to Esmé.

"What's wrong with yours?" she asked in reply.

"I wanna use your flashlight app."

"Your phone's got one. All ours do."

"Yeah, but yours is brighter. Are you going to give it to me or not?"

"Hold your horses," Esmé told him as she rummaged through her handbag.

Once he had Esmé's phone, Townsant flipped on the light and peered into the darkness behind the door.

"Why didn't we think of that when we were creeping down that dark passageway?" Prudence asked her sister.

Mallory shook her head. Like the others, she'd been too frightened to think of anything as obvious as using her mobile phone for light.

"Can you see anything?" Esmé asked.

"Yes, wonderful things!" Townsant replied, repeating the exchange between Lord Carnarvon and Howard Carter when the latter first peered inside King Tut's tomb.

"Really?" Esmé asked excitedly.

"No," Townsant replied, stepping back. "Just more bankers boxes."

"But that really is wonderful, isn't it?" Mallory said.

"How so?"

"Well, think of what we found behind the door in Chudwell 2B. If *that* space was filled with bankers boxes, and *this* space is filled with bankers boxes ... "

" ... the two tunnels are probably connected," Prudence added, completing her sister's thought.

"I don't see where that gets us," Townsant replied. "We had a hard enough time getting fifty yards back into the tunnel from the other end. It'll take us *months* to get the same distance from *this* end, and that's only *if* we can shift this gargoyle back further."

"Yes, but think about it," Esmé told him. "We could only move slowly before because each night we had to put the boxes back where we found them. Now we don't have to. We've got a whole *room* to store the boxes we take out of the tunnel and all summer to do it: a full summer when no one can come down here and see what we're up to."

"And besides," Mallory noted, "it's all just further proof that, yet again, Bastian was right. There *was* a secret cult with a secret ritual chamber constructed beneath the campus. All that stuff Sexton and the dean told us about the tunnels not existing was just wrong."

"Or lies," Townsant suggested.

"Either way, we've got our summer project cut out for us," Esmé concluded. "But first, let's take some photos and tell Bastian what we've found. We may not be able to bring him down here, but I'm sure he'll have a plan for how we should all get started. Give me back my phone. I want to see if I can get a picture of those boxes."

"Esmé," Prudence called out. She'd drifted away from the others during the last arc of this conversation. "I think you may want to get a photo of this first."

"Why? What is it?"

Rather than answering, Prudence pointed to a row of identical books standing side by side on one shelf. They were all richly bound in burgundy leather with raised hubs and their titles inlaid with gold foil. Unlike most of the other books in the room, these titles were not worn away, and they gleamed out from the bright overhead lights:

The Transmundane Codex of Berossus

CHAPTER FORTY-EIGHT

Suite 16

P rudence took down several of the volumes, opened them, and spread them out on the top of the altar. The books were not printed but had originally contained blank pages that had been filled in by hand. A wide variety of different writing styles appeared, but all the entries were formatted the same.

The following entry was typical:

> Department of Classics
> Minutes of Weekly Faculty Meeting
> Friday, October 14, 1983
> Suite 16, Chudwell Hall

Members Present: Becker, J. (head); Clifford, M.; Thornton, T.; Fowler, Q.; Platt, K.; Schumann, D.; Turner, H.; Duncan, C.; Manning, T.; Jordan, I.; Foster, L.; Harvey, F.; Arnold, P.; Tucker, D.; Peston, E.; McDaniel, D.; Hodges, L.; Pangborn, H.; Fisher, D.; Francis, Z.; Lindsey, A.; Goodwin, M.; Hoffman, M.; Robinett, S.

Members Absent: Blanton, J.; Fitzgerald, T.

The meeting was called to order at precisely 4:00 p.m. by the head of the Department of Classics, John Becker. The main purpose of the meeting was twofold: 1) to ratify departmental and collegiate committee appointments made at the prior week's meeting; 2) to consider for adoption the introduction of a new course, The Aesthetics of the Archaic Period ...

The set of minutes went on for several pages summarizing a

long list of arguments for and against the two items under consideration (with several of the arguments made nearly verbatim by different members of the department) and concluding with ratification of the committee appointments and adoption of the course with only one slight change to the phrasing of the syllabus. Other minutes in the volumes were similar: long discussions of what appeared to be fairly insignificant issues, plenty of repetition of key points, a final vote that almost always included one or two faculty members abstaining ("out of principle," it was sometimes noted), and then a discussion of the agenda for the following week's meeting.

"Man, the Classics Department was *huge* back then!" Mallory exclaimed as she glanced at the list of names.

"And look who was present," Townsant said, jabbing a finger down onto the page. "Dean McDaniel before she was even dean."

"Where's Garner?" Prudence asked.

"A few years before his time, I imagine," Mallory told her.

"More to the point, look who else was absent: T. Fitzgerald," Townsant pointed out. "This meeting must've taken place around the time of 'The Troubles,' as Dean McDaniel called them."

"Maybe we'll get the full story from these minutes," Esmé suggested.

"Maybe," Townsant agreed, "but why keep *handwritten* minutes? Surely there were typewriters back in 1983, even some of the first word processors."

"Tradition?" Esmé proposed.

"If so, then it must've really been important to them. The sheer effort required to write down all these notes by hand ... " Townsant left the thought unfinished.

"Here's a volume that starts in 1975," Mallory said, glancing through some of the other books that Prudence had placed on the table. "I wonder how far back they go."

"I'm more curious about this reference to 'Suite 16,'" Townsant remarked. "We've spent the whole year in Chudwell Hall and never seen a room of *that* name."

"That isn't even the strangest thing," Esmé pointed out. "All these books have the exact same title: *The Transmundane Codex of Berossus*. Doesn't it seem odd that that's the precise book we've been trying to track down?"

"A book that Barbara the Barbarian insisted doesn't exist," Prudence noted.

"And yet a book with a catalog card that *twice* seemed to materialize in our study lounge," Mallory added.

"Let's take a few of these books back to Bastian and see what he makes of them," Esmé proposed. "He's been pretty good at connecting all the dots so far."

"No!" Townsant objected. "Don't you remember Professor Caldwell's warning? We're not supposed to remove or copy any of the books or other written materials *in* here. It would be an honor code violation."

"Well then," Esmé conceded, "let's just photograph some of the entries."

"Wouldn't that be the same as copying them?" Townsant asked.

"Look, we've already snapped a few dozen photographs, including some of the book titles and the carvings on the altar. That might be considered 'copying texts' as well. In for a penny, in for a pound, I say."

"This whole consul thing has already gone to your head," Townsant chuckled. "Okay, take a few more photos that we can show Bastian. We can always delete them later. Maybe they'll help us figure out what this place is doing here and why the Classics Department considered these volumes of minutes so valuable."

* * *

It took until mid-afternoon before they'd completed their initial investigation of *La Tanière Dorée*. Then they found Bastian, sulking in his room and reading *The Secret History* yet again, even though he knew whole passages of the work by heart.

"Get off your butt, Bastian," Townsant began, "and stop living in Fantasy World. We've got a *real* mystery on our hands."

Breathlessly, they explained what they'd encountered down in the clubroom and showed him the photos they'd taken.

"I *knew* it!" Bastian shouted, suddenly excited. "There really *was* a Fraternity of the Broken Omen (maybe there still *is*), and now you've got proof. They've engineered this whole thing: luring us in with the catalog card, enticing us with the story of this lost volume by Berossus, making sure that I was the only one who didn't qualify for admission to the Aurelian Club ... "

"Well ... " Townsant said, dubiously. He was all too familiar with Bastian's poor study habits and less-than-perfect language skills to feel that any supernatural explanation was needed for his performance on the Examen Maximum.

But Esmé was not about to let the issue pass by in silence. "Why was it so important for *you* not to be a member of the club?"

"Isn't it obvious?" Bastian asked. "I'm the one who's been onto them all along. They want us to *work* for access to the secrets they're hiding, not make it too easy. Still have your keys? Let's go back there now. I bet I'll understand things that you guys didn't."

"Whoa there, Champ," Townsant objected. "What we said before still stands: We're not going to risk our membership in the

Aurelian Club by sneaking you in. Sorry."

"But surely things are different now," Bastian protested.

The two men continued to argue this point for several minutes until finally Esmé said, "I think I know a way."

"How?" Townsant scoffed.

"I've been trying to recall Professor Caldwell's exact words. Correct me if I'm wrong, but didn't he say, 'Any member who uses his or her key to grant a non-member access to *La Tanière Dorée* will immediately be removed from the club and disqualified from future membership'?"

"How does that help us?" Townsant asked.

"'Any member *who uses his or her key* to grant a non-member access.' We simply don't use our keys."

"And how exactly do you suggest we do that?"

Esmé brightened with the cleverness of her own idea. "Easy. We use the Catacombs."

CHAPTER FORTY-NINE

Faith and Confidence

Summer Session A at Mersley College began less than a week after Commencement Weekend. Garner, who'd planned a research trip to Greece for later that summer, agreed to offer the first of the three courses that students in the program would have to take. In Summer Session B, Professor Briggs would be teaching De Saussure, Bloomfield, and the Meaning of Meaning, while Summer Session C would be reserved for Professor Dittman's course on *Gravity's Rainbow* and the Literary History of Post-modernism.

Garner's course was designed to be a more typical Latin reading course. The students would read Augustine's *Confessions* in its entirety, along with passages from *The City of God*.

"Not my favorite author," he announced on the first day of class. "The Latin's a bit turgid for my taste, and the reasoning's sometimes convoluted. But these are works that, as a well-educated person, you'll need to have read. And you'll have one advantage over 99.99% of the population: You'll have read them in the original, so that means you'll actually know what you're talking about. Of course, if you *do* ever find yourself discussing these works out there in 'the wider world' ... " Garner waved his hand vaguely in the air to designate everything outside of Chudwell Hall itself. " ... I have one bit of advice. Refer to the author of *Confessions* simply as 'the bishop of Hippo' until your interlocutor actually says the name. Then use whatever pronunciation *that* person is using. Believe me, it'll save you endless hours of pointless arguing whether he's 'aw-guss-TEEN' or 'aw-GUSS-tin.' In the end, it really doesn't matter, and you're probably better off simply conceding the point on this one."

He continued to explain why Augustine was the appropriate author to be reading at this particular point in the students' courses of study. "The works we'll be reading this summer will allow us to pull together concepts that you've encountered, not only in my own courses, but in those of my colleagues as well. For example, we'll have ample occasion to discuss Augustine's notion that what we experience in this world consists of phenomena that may be divided into 'things' (*res*) and 'signs' (*signa*), an idea that I'm sure Professor Briggs must have mentioned at least once or twice. Plus, in addition to Plato's distinction between 'knowledge' (γνῶσις or ἐπιστήμη) and 'belief' (δόξα), Augustine adds a third mental category: 'mere opinion' (*opinio*). This framework allows him to distinguish between beliefs that are based on assumptions or credulity and beliefs that he regards as fundamental to faith. We'll want to explore whether you conclude that that distinction is valid or simply a bit of verbal legerdemain used to salvage the concept of faith, something that some may regard as a virtue while others regard as a great intellectual vice."

That Sunday in *La Tanière Dorée*, Townsant had observed a change that was occurring in Esmé. She had always been the polite one, the diplomatic one. If Prudence at times held her tongue because she didn't want to create a stir, Esmé did so because she regarded being gracious when others state their views as the civilized thing to do. That, after all, was one of the reasons why he thought she'd make a good consul for the Aurelian Club. But in their debates about how to proceed once they'd discovered the altar and the volumes of departmental minutes, Esmé had begun to demonstrate true leadership qualities. And leadership often requires one to proclaim, like Luther, "*Hier steh ich. Ich kann nicht anders.*"

Apparently, leadership required Esmé to do so at that precise moment because she did something that no one except Bastian had been foolish enough to do before. She contradicted Garner.

"Nonsense," she said.

The word was so unexpected, both in general and from Esmé in particular, that it completely interrupted the professor's train of thought. He stopped in the midst of his remarks and said, "Excuse me."

"I said 'nonsense,'" Esmé repeated.

Garner wasn't quite sure whether to be offended or amused. For whatever reason, he was inclined to indulge the latter tendency.

"And what, pray tell, Ms. Dawson, have I said that constitutes nonsense?"

"The idea that some people think faith is a vice. That's ridiculous."

Garner smiled indulgently. "I wasn't making a judgment, Ms. Dawson. As you know, I'm well aware that your faith is an integral part of who you are and, as long as it enhances and does not interfere with your progress in this program, I have absolutely no quarrel with it. I was merely making a statement of fact. To some—indeed, for historical and cultural reasons that I'm sure you'll explore in your courses with Professor Pope—probably to the great majority of people we encounter from day to day, faith is, as you say, regarded as a virtue. But for others, it is a vice. That's merely a statement for which there is evidence. I, for one, regard faith as a vice, and so my original observation stands. Now, as I was saying about Augustine's attempt to build upon the foundation laid by Plato ... "

"But you're wrong."

At this point, the atmosphere in the room shifted dramatically. Garner had made his point. Esmé had made hers. The others felt that it was time to move on. They were all too familiar with the professor's habit of making quick work of Bastian when *he* was unprepared or made a remark that Garner regarded as foolish. But they were loath to see Esmé receive the same treatment. And, rather than resorting to her typical diplomacy, she seemed intent on digging in her heels with regard to a point that, they felt, could easily be left for another day.

"How can I be wrong?" Garner asked, his voice now losing the trace of humor it had held earlier. "As I said, I am merely making an observation of a demonstrable fact: *You* regard faith as a virtue; *I* regard it as a vice. Both views exist. QED."

"But you're wrong when you say it's not a virtue. Faith, hope, and love: Those *are* the three virtues."

"The three *Christian* virtues. Don't forget the four *classical* ones: prudence, justice, courage, and temperance."

"That just proves my point. You just said it's one of the virtues."

Garner clicked his tongue. "You're logic chopping, Ms. Dawson. My point was that, in the Christian view ... "

"'These three remain: faith, hope and love. But the greatest of these is love.' Love is the greatest virtue, but faith is the first."

"All you've proved, Ms. Dawson, is that you can quote Saint Paul. 1 Corinthians 13:13, in fact, in case you doubt my familiarity with the text. But if we're about to get into a St. Paul quoting contest, how would you say he defines faith?"

"'Faith is the substance of things hoped for, the evidence of things not seen.'"

"Hebrews 11:1. Not a genuine Pauline epistle, I might observe, but I won't press that point. All right, if we define faith as the substance of things that we hope for and the acceptance of things we haven't seen, how is that any different from gullibility?"

"They're not at all the same. Faith ... "

"If you receive one of those emails from a 'rich Nigerian prince' who asks for a few hundred dollars today in return for many millions of dollars 'sometime very soon,' is it faith or gullibility if you wire him the money? You may *hope* for such a substantial return on your investment, and you certainly haven't *seen* it yet. So, I guess that makes it faith, by your definition ... or pseudo-St. Paul's rather. And do we admire the people taken in by this scam as demonstrating the 'virtue' of faith, or do we pity them for their naïveté, their credulity?"

Esmé advanced what she thought would be a winning argument.

"But you demonstrate faith every single day."

"Oh, heavens, I hope not. What makes you say that I do?"

"You come to class having faith that we'll show up and be prepared. You get up in the morning, having faith that the sun will rise as it always has. You flip on your computer, having faith that it will work, even though you've told us before that you have no knowledge of or interest in technology."

"You're confusing faith with confidence, Ms. Dawson. We have confidence in something or someone when we have an empirically established basis for trust. To rephrase your examples, I have confidence that the majority of you will be in class each day, ready to discuss the assigned material, because you have a reliable record of doing so. In other words, I have confidence in you because you've earned my trust. (I'm somewhat surprised you've done so, I must admit, but you have.) And in the same way, I have confidence that the sun will rise and that my computer will work because they have a long history of doing so."

"But computers do break down sometimes," Esmé objected.

"That they do. But it doesn't happen often and, when they do, there's a physical and demonstrable reason for it. If I can't determine that reason (and I'll grant you that I probably can't), a competent technician can. That's a far cry from just *hoping* they'll work or, as the author of Hebrews put it, 'the evidence of things not seen.' The fact of the matter is that I *can* see it, and that gives me confidence, not faith. But I'm actually quite pleased that you've raised this issue because it brings us to an interesting point that we'll have cause to explore during our study of Augustine."

Garner walked to the chalkboard and began to make a list. "Let's see if we can distinguish a number of these mental concepts, using the appropriate Greek and Latin terms. As we saw in Plato, γνῶσις is knowledge that's usually empirical in origin, ἐπιστήμη is knowledge derived from logical deduction, and δόξα, or what Augustine will call *opinio*, is mere belief. In the texts we'll read this summer, Augustine will also talk about faith (*fides*) which he regards as a different kind of belief from *opinio*, one that is somehow higher and better. In light of our discussion just now, however, I think we can make another distinction: *opinio*, which, as Augustine says, is mere belief; *fides*, which is belief stemming from some underlying assumption, such as that God exists; and what I've been calling *confidence*, which is belief stemming from either γνῶσις or ἐπιστήμη."

Townsant spoke for the first time during what had seemed like a private conversation between Garner and Esmé. "And which Latin or Geek term would you say comes closest to *confidence*?"

Garner reflected for a moment. "That's something of a problem, actually. Most Roman authors would use the word *fides* to mean either faith or confidence. If I were to suggest the word *confidentia*, that seems like a cheat, and it violates my cardinal rule of not translating Greek or Latin words by using their English derivatives since that never tells you whether the translator truly grasps the concept behind the word. *Fiducia* comes close, but that's just a cognate of *fides*, so I'm not entirely happy with that. As a temporary solution, let's say that *confidence* is something akin to the Latin word *ascentia*, which gives us 'assent' in English. Later Christian authors distinguished *ascentia* from *fiducia* on the grounds that *ascentia* implies mental or intellectual acknowledgement, while *fides* or *fiducia* implied something more visceral, which they regarded as more profound. The basic idea is that *fides* or *fiducia* had what we might call 'salvific value' while mere academic acceptance of a religious truth did not."

Esmé thought she'd spotted another opening. "But don't you see? Once again, you're just proving my point. If faith has what you're calling 'salvific value,' then it *must* be a virtue. You simply won't admit it because you don't want to believe in salvation. Or maybe you just don't want to be saved."

"I believe I said that later Christian authors ascribed to that view. I didn't say I did." Then Garner paused and thought for a moment before continuing. "Ms. Dawson, let me try to illustrate my point in another way. Suppose I were a supremely wealthy but supremely savage eccentric. Suppose, too, I were to tell you that I intend to put you to death by the most painful and brutal means I can imagine, unless you can do one simple thing. If you can believe—and, by that, I mean really, truly *believe*—that right beside you at this very moment stands an eight-foot-tall spotted purple unicorn named Harold who speaks fluent Spanish, I'll not only let you live but I'll give you wealth beyond your wildest dreams, could you believe in Harold? Could you tell me truthfully and honestly that you have faith in Harold? You might assent to my assertion in order to save yourself and reap your reward, but would you genuinely *believe* what you said?"

"That's a ridiculous example."

"Is it? Isn't that very similar to the world that Paul describes? Eternal agony for those who can't believe, but eternal joy for those who can? And doesn't that strike you as quite immoral? You can't *make* yourself believe in something. You can *say* you believe it ... "

"But that's all God wants: a tiny mustard seed of faith. 'I believe; help my unbelief!' Mark 9:24."

"Ah, now *there's* a verse that's much more impressive in the King James Version: 'Lord, I believe; help thou mine unbelief.'"

"But the meaning's the same. All you have to do is *say the words. Pray.* The belief—the *genuine* belief—comes later."

"Does it? You imagine that there's an infinitely powerful, infinitely wise deity who'll save me because I *claim* to believe in him, because I essentially *pretend* to believe in him? I thought Jesus hated hypocrites."

"You're twisting all of this. It's about *grace*. You're making a very beautiful, very loving concept sound ugly. God loves you enough to save you from death and give you the gift of eternal life. In return, all he asks is that you accept him and love him in return. What could be more beautiful than that?"

"A great many things, I imagine. Now, I'm absolutely sure you believe in a god who loves us all unconditionally. But we're also told that, in order to be saved, we have to *believe* in this god and *love* him and *obey* his laws. Ms. Dawson, *those are conditions*. There's nothing the least bit unconditional about it. You see, my point is that, if you're going to believe, you can't simply choose certain passages of certain texts to believe and reject those that don't fit your preconceived ideas. Remember Revelations 3:16: It's all or nothing. And when you do read the *whole* text, not just the nice, 'happy' bits, the Christian god doesn't sound very loving at all. Cruel and vindictive, rather."

"God. Is. Love," Esmé said, carefully articulating each word. "He loves us. All we have to do is love him back."

Garner paused again. "Perhaps I'm not making my point clearly. Let me tell you a story ... a parable, if you will. There are two men who live in neighboring houses. Both of them have very large families. One night, a tragedy occurs. The two houses catch fire. The first father only rescues the children who have told him they love him. The second father rescues *all* his children, even those who rejected him or who believed he wasn't really their father. Which of the two loved his children more? Do you see what I'm trying to say? Isn't what you're calling very beautiful something that, when you examine it closely, is really quite hideous?"

Esmé curled her fingers in frustration. "You're distorting everything. You're intentionally misunderstanding some very simple things. Faith isn't at all what you're saying it is."

Garner smiled. "And that brings us to a perfect place for our reading of Augustine. For tomorrow, please prepare the first fourteen chapters of Augustine's *Confessions*. That will bring us to the point where he starts to speak about his own studies of Latin and Greek. If you have time, finish Book 1. It's only six more chapters, and I don't think you'll find the Latin very challenging. In fact, the grammar's rather repetitive, you'll discover. Come to class ready to translate aloud and discuss what we might call the beginning of the author's 'pilgrim's progress.' Until then, keep the faith."

At the last word, he winked, although it wasn't clear whether he was making fun of Esmé in doing so or sharing what he thought was a witticism with the entire class.

As they walked back to their residence halls to drop off their books and get ready for lunch, Mallory sidled up to Esmé. "How're you doing?"

"All right," Esmé replied without any emotion in her voice.

"'All right' all right or *really* all right?"

"Oh, I'm fine. Really. I know I said I'm used to dealing with people like that but, for some reason, Garner always finds a way to get under my skin. I think he hates me."

"Actually, I think it's just the opposite."

"How d'you mean?"

"I think he regards you as the brightest among us. Even including … " Mallory pointed discreetly toward Townsant who, it was clear, always regarded himself as the group's intellectual star. "Garner doesn't challenge you because he thinks you're weak. He challenges you because he knows you can take it. He's just trying to get you to defend whatever position you happen to take. I bet he'd do exactly the same thing if one of us dismissed the concept of faith entirely."

"You know what they call that, don't you? Playing Devil's Advocate. Professor Garner may be the closest thing I've ever encountered to the devil. I think I'm going to find every logical argument I can to prove him wrong."

"Then you see? He's done his job. You've just participated in a real-life, modern-day Socratic dialogue."

CHAPTER FIFTY

A Fool's Errand

As Garner had predicted, none of them found Augustine's grammar or vocabulary to be particularly challenging. By mid-afternoon, they'd all read the first fourteen chapters in *Confessions*, and everyone except Bastian had made it all the way to the end of Book 1. Esmé, who found the text interesting and not at all "turgid," as Garner had described it, wanted the study group to keep going, but Bastian said he needed a break.

"And exactly what kind of break are you suggesting?" Mallory asked.

"How about we tackle *that* again?" he replied, gesturing toward the back wall of the study lounge. He turned to Esmé. "You said yourself that the Catacombs all seem to lead to *La Tanière Dorée*. Why don't we see if we can get there from here?"

"We tried clearing the boxes out for *weeks* last fall," Townsant objected, and never got even a hundred yards back. What makes you think this time'd be any different?"

"Last time we just *hoped* the Catacombs led somewhere. This time we *know* they do. Faith and confidence, baby. Before, it was just a matter of faith. This time I'm *confident* I know where we're going."

"Oh, don't remind me of that horrid class today," Esmé said.

Bastian gave her a smile that verged on cruel. "So, what is it? When Garner jumps all over me, it's just a learning experience. But when he gives *you* a little bit of blowback, suddenly you can't handle it."

"It was more than 'a little bit of blowback,'" Esmé contradicted him. "What happened today was *personal*. He took something that he knew was very important to me and simply mocked it."

"That's not what I saw," Prudence said.

Esmé had been counting on the others for support and was angered when Prudence, of all people, didn't automatically take her side. "Oh, yeah? And what exactly did *you* see?"

"I saw him engage in what we came to college for. Garner was just insisting that you use your best critical thinking skills to defend your perspective. And let's remember: You were the one who started by challenging *him*, not *vice versa*. If he got you out of your comfort zone, isn't that what all the professors have told us this program was about from Day One? We've all had experiences something like the one you had today, and we've all survived them. In fact, I think we've all become stronger *because* of them. Are you really upset because Garner criticized your beliefs or because you don't yet have an answer for him?"

"I'm going to have an answer for him. I'm going to work twice ... no, three times harder because of it."

"Then I'd say that Garner achieved his purpose."

"That's what I told her," Mallory said.

While all this was going on, Townsant was jotting down some numbers on a piece of paper. "Speaking of critical thinking," he began, looking up from his calculations, "I don't think what Bastian is suggesting is feasible."

"You just don't like the idea because I suggested it," Bastian told him.

"No, I just think that it's literally impossible. You saw how high we had to stack the boxes before just to get as far as we did. So, here's what I figure: The standard dimensions of a bankers box are 12.5" wide by 16.3" deep by 10.5" high."

"How do you figure *that*?" Bastian asked.

"Easy," Townsant said, holding up his phone. "I looked it up.

It's called research. Anyway, if you multiply all that out, it comes to a volume of ... " He checked his figures again. " ... just over 2,139 cubic inches or roughly 1.23 cubic feet. Let's call it one-and-a-quarter because we want to accommodate the space between the boxes."

"Why do we want to do that?" Bastian asked.

"Just bear with me a moment. What do you estimate the dimensions of this room to be?"

"I can do better than estimate," Esmé replied. "The ruler app on my phone should tell me precisely." She opened the app and then moved her phone back and forth, then up and down. "This says the room is 10.4 feet by 20 feet exactly by 8.3 feet high."

"Okay," Townsant said, returning to his phone. "That means we've got just over 1,726 cubic feet to play with. Given the size of each box, that means that—even if the table, chairs, and everything else were removed from the room—you wouldn't fit more than 1,381 boxes in here."

"Well, that should be plenty," Bastian observed.

"Hardly. And remember: That would mean the study lounge is completely packed with boxes. Where would the furniture have gone? How would we get into or out of the passageway? It's a great idea. It's just impossible."

"Maybe if we just emptied out more of the boxes instead of putting them back," Esmé suggested.

"It'd still take you longer than we've got. And lots of that stuff we saw in the boxes looked valuable. I don't know about you, but *I'm* not going to be the one to dump it."

"Let's have a look anyway," Mallory suggested.

Townsant shrugged as if to say, "Fine by me, but you're wasting your time," and the five of them went through the procedure they'd discovered the autumn before. They opened the outer door, took down the two paintings, pressed both hidden buttons simultaneously, and then closed and locked the study room door. The panel at the back clicked open, and they saw once more the wall of boxes and stacks of newspaper they'd been ignoring for months.

"Okay," Bastian said. "Let's get busy."

Townsant took a deep breath, not wanting to devote any more time to Bastian's "fool's errand," but, because the others seemed eager to proceed, he reluctantly joined in, too. For more than two hours, they removed box after box, clearing a pathway down the middle and lining the walls of the study lounge with as many boxes as they could fit in.

They took a break for dinner, hoping that no one would enter Chudwell 2B in the meantime, then rushed back and continued working until the space beneath the conference table was filled with boxes, the top of the conference table was filled to the ceiling with boxes, and only a narrow space permitted movement between the doorway on one side of the room and the hidden panel on the other.

Exhausted, they took another break just after midnight. Townsant, annoyed by all the time they'd wasted, complained, "You see? I told you it was impossible. We're back further than we've ever been, but we're still nowhere near Old Main."

From behind the boxes, a voice was heard to say, "Mebbe I can hep'."

CHAPTER FIFTY-ONE

The Natatorium

The students had been so focused on their task that they hadn't heard Sexton come in. Their line of sight, blocked by all the boxes they'd removed from behind the secret panel, prevented them from seeing the scraggly old man until he came around the corner and stood directly in front of them.

"And here I was gettin' t'be convinced that all this talk about hidden tunnels were just a myth."

"*Getting* to be convinced?" Bastian said angrily. "You out-and-out *told* me there were no hidden tunnels here at Mersley and no secret ritual chamber. And yet, here's the tunnel, and my friends have found the chamber."

Sexton's face assumed a strange look. "They did?"

"We sure did," Esmé said. She went on to describe what they'd seen in *La Tanière Dorée*.

"And just where is this ... whatcha call it?" Sexton asked.

"*La Tanière Dorée*. It's the private clubroom for members of the Aurelian Club."

Sexton closed his eyes and emitted a sudden breath. "'Course. Shoulda knowed." Then he looked up at Esmé with an eager expression.

"Take me there. I worked here for over fifty years and ain't never seen it."

"No, we can't," she told him.

"Why?" he asked, both hurt and disappointed.

"*Strengsten verboten*," Townsant answered.

"Say what now?"

"Strictly off limits." Townsant went on to explain the severe restrictions placed on the members of the club regarding the use of their keys.

"That's why we're trying to clear out these boxes," Esmé continued. She told the caretaker about her idea of clearing the Catacombs far enough that Bastian could look into the clubroom without any of them using their keys. "We could take you there, too ... if we can clear enough of the clutter away."

"But I keep telling them it's hopeless," Townsant said. "The room here's as full as we can make it, but we're nowhere near *La Tanière Dorée*, which is directly below Old Main."

Sexton licked his lips a bit and then said, "Well, as I told ya, mebbe I can hep'."

"Help? Help how?"

The old man looked at all the boxes stacked about him. "I gotta forklift. Youse clear out the boxes and other junk, and I kin haul it away."

"Away where?" Bastian asked, suspiciously.

"Come. Follow me. I ain't never showed nobody this."

Sexton led the five into an area of the basement they'd never seen. There were so many twists and turns in the direction the old man took that they soon became hopelessly confused as to where they were. Even with all his years of work in the building, it seemed nearly impossible that Sexton could find his way through the twisting corridors beneath Chudwell Hall.

Eventually, they came to a large double door with a chain twisted through the door handles. Sexton removed a key from the massive ring he wore on his belt, opened the lock, and removed the chain. He swung the doors open.

"Mind yer step in here," he told them. He pulled a flashlight out of his pocket and cast a beam into the interior. "I only got one o'these. Any of youse got a flashlight?"

"We all do," Esmé said, lighting up her phone as the others did the same.

"'Course ya does. Anyway, mind yer step."

Sexton led them into a huge, dark room. "This here's what were once the natatorium."

"A swimming pool?" Mallory asked.

"See? And here I thought all that Latin's useless," Sexton chuckled. "Yeah, a swimmin' pool. It were part of the original structure back when Chudwell Hall were built. Hasn't been used in close to a century now, I'd say."

He directed his flashlight toward the wall. "See them holes? That's where a buncha stacked benches were once attached. For spectators."

"Bleachers?" Townsant wondered.

"Yah, but they didn't call them that. Anyway, they was removed and hauled away even afore my time."

Sexton then shifted his light to where the pool itself had been. About fifteen yards in front of them, the tile began to slope down. At the far end, the pool must have been eighteen feet deep.

"I kin move the boxes here. Pool's deep enough and ceiling's high enough ... I bet we got plenty of space."

"The corridors seemed rather narrow in places. Are you sure you can get a forklift through there?" Bastian asked.

"Just lemme worry about that. I gots my ways."

"So, whaddya think, math genius?" Bastian asked Townsant. "Is this place gonna work?"

"Should be fine," Townsant replied. "It'll still probably take us from now until Doomsday, but this should give us the space we need."

"Nah, won't take that long," Sexton objected. "With youse clearin' boxes and me movin' 'em over here, we'll get to Old Main by the end o' this summer. Probably even sooner."

"I wish I had your confidence," Esmé said.

"Just gotta have faith in me," Sexton replied. "Why don't youse skedaddle now? Looks like yur not used to physical work and are about ta collapse, anyways. Let me clear out the boxes from Chudwell 2B, and youse can start pullin' out more tomorrow. Why, if I get the room cleared fast enough tonight, I might haul out a few more boxes mesef'."

"We don't want you to hurt yourself," Prudence said, looking at the frail seventy-eight-year-old.

"Aw, don't worry 'bout me. I's a tough old bird. Now, kin youse find your way out whilst I go get the forklift?"

"I think you'll probably have to lead us," Townsant admitted, glad that the darkness of the natatorium wouldn't allow Sexton to see his blush.

"Yeah, fine," the caretaker said. "Back this way."

As they headed toward the study lounge, Sexton said, "Ya ever open them boxes? See what's inside?"

"Not all of them," Townsant said. "It got pretty boring after a while. But we did look in the first few. Lots of old records. Frank Sinatra. Dean Martin. Mel Torme."

"Ah, so *that's* where they went," Sexton muttered.

CHAPTER FIFTY-TWO

A System and a Schedule

For the next two weeks, a kind of daily routine emerged. The students would attend Garner's class in the morning, finish their homework by mid-afternoon, and then spend the rest of the afternoon and evening clearing boxes out of the Catacombs. Sexton then used the forklift to move the boxes into the natatorium overnight and, as he promised, sometimes even moved a few more boxes out of the tunnel himself. As a result, the work did indeed proceed much faster than they had predicted. Although the physical effort made them feel like a tiny hoard of Nibelungs, they sensed that they were closing in on *La Tanière Dorée* through the secret tunnels.

Townsant and Esmé, as the fastest translators in the group, usually completed their assignments far ahead of the others. For a while, they'd simply kept reading while the others completed the passages they'd discuss the following day. But they eventually had read so far beyond what Bastian and the Warren-Whiteheads had completed that they decided to stop reading early and put an extra hour or two into clearing the tunnel.

Weekends also took on an entirely different schedule from what they had during the academic year. Now that Sexton had become a co-conspirator, he gladly admitted them to Chudwell Hall even on Saturdays and Sundays. That meant the five students could each spend at least seven hours on a weekday and as many hours as they wanted on a weekend doing nothing but shifting boxes.

It must be admitted that, even before Summer Session A was complete, their fascination with this project had begun to flag. It was hard work, and it was boring work. Within a few days, walks about campus, reading, and snacks in the Dugout began to vie for their attention. As a result, they began taking turns at the tunnel-clearing project. Sometimes three of them would haul boxes while the other two did something else. Sometimes only two of them were at work. Not infrequently, only one of them would be in the tunnel.

"We need a system," Esmé finally said. "A system and a schedule."

"What do you mean?" Bastian asked.

"Well, a schedule would help us work more consistently and equitably. I hate to say it, but there have already been three days this week when I've been the only one down in the Catacombs."

"What does it matter?" Bastian replied. "Even in shifts, we're still getting as many boxes out of the tunnels each day as the study lounge can hold. Sometimes, we even have to stack them partway down the hall outside."

"You mean *I* have to stack them down the hall outside. Look, Bastian. This whole project was your idea to start with, and now it seems like the rest of us are doing most of the work. That's why I say we need a system and a schedule. The schedule will help keep things fair. We'll set up regular shifts of two or three people working at a time, and the others can do what they like. But that also means we need a system."

"What kind of system?" Townsant wondered.

"Well, suppose it's a time when only two of us are working, and we reach the door of *La Tanière Dorée*. We've got to have a way of notifying the others."

"That's easy," Bastian said. "Send a text."

"And say what? 'We're there'? That can mean anything. We must send one another texts like that five or six a day to tell one another we're in the classroom or the dining hall or the study lounge."

Bastian scoffed. "'We're at the chamber' or 'We're at the doorway.' We'll all know what that means."

"And so might anyone else if people suspect what we're up to."

"People?" Mallory asked. "Who'd care what we do? We're the weirdoes, right? No one gives us a second thought."

"Six months ago, I probably would've said the same thing," Esmé said. "But ... well, I don't know if I'm getting paranoid or what, but ... "

"What?" Townsant asked.

"Is it just me or have any of you felt that the further down into the Catacombs we get, the colder it gets?"

"Well, yeah, I noticed that, but I just figured it's cold underground," Townsant explained.

"But it *shouldn't* be. There's no ventilation down in the Catacombs. And have you ever seen miners coming up from a mine? They're always drenched in sweat. We should be getting hotter the more we work, not colder."

"So, what exactly are you saying, Esmé?" Townsant asked gently.

Esmé took a deep breath. She'd obviously been thinking about this issue for days but was reluctant to share her suspicions with the others. At last, she said, "Remember that voice? 'Cold ... soooooo cold'? I hate to be superstitious, but I think there's something malevolent going on here."

"The Fraternity of the Broken Omen," Bastian said.

"Right," Esmé agreed. "Think of all those symbols on the altar we found. Don't they all strike you as ... well ... 'unholy.' And all those occult books on the shelves. I don't think this is a *good* fraternity we've stumbled on."

"And become unwitting members of," Prudence added.

"*That's* what frightens me sometimes. What if we've been pulled into something sinister, something evil? We've been treating this whole tunnel-clearing operation like it's just another research project. 'Let's see if the Catacombs actually reach the ritual chamber. Let's find a way for Bastian and Sexton to see the secret clubroom.' Well, remember that there weren't just weird symbols on the altar. There was also *blood*. Something *died* there, or perhaps *someone*."

"Blood sacrifice has been a part of religious rites *forever*," Townsant pointed out. "I mean, even the Greeks and Romans ... "

"This isn't the time to perform your Professor Garner impression, Townsant," Esmé warned him. "I'm serious. What if we're in over our heads?"

"Well, *you're* the one who said 'in for a penny, in for a pound,'" Townsant reminded her.

"Maybe I was just being foolish then."

"Or maybe you're just being foolish *now*. Okay, look, how about this? We keep removing the junk from the tunnel, but once we reach the door on the other side—*if* we ever reach the door on the other side—no one goes in alone. We all go in together, or no one goes in."

"That's stupid, Townsant," Bastian sneered. "The four of you have been in that clubroom *lots* of times without me. And hasn't at least one of you gone there alone? Maybe just to be somewhere different when you were taking a break?"

"I have," Mallory admitted.

"So have I," Prudence agreed.

"Okay, okay," Townsant yielded. "But, so far, all of us have gone into *La Tanière Dorée* the *right* way, the *proper* way, by using our keys. Something may be weird about those keys. I mean, Professor Caldwell made such a big deal about them. And Esmé may be right. The doors here on campus can be weird. Think of what happened in the study lounge. The door to it is mostly just an ordinary door. But, when the two secret buttons are pressed simultaneously, the hidden panel opens. Maybe ... who knows? ... something like that happens when one of the five secondary doors to the ritual chamber is opened."

They were all silent for a moment, each with his or her own thoughts of what horrors might occur if one of the doors was opened *im*properly.

"Five doors," Bastian said, his voice almost a whisper. "And five of us. Can't be a coincidence."

"Well, it *could be*," Townsant countered.

"But I, for one, would rather not take that chance," Esmé said. "So, let's agree: No one goes into the ritual chamber from the tunnel side unless we *all* go in. We have to think of some sort of text to use to signal the others. Something that no one but us is likely to understand."

"But what *kind* of message?" Prudence asked.

"I don't know yet, but I'll think of something."

CHAPTER FIFTY-THREE

Back at the Diogenes Club

At some point in the course, Garner and Esmé came to a kind of unspoken truce. He would discuss Augustine's concept of faith-with-reason in terms that implied no judgment. She would refrain from comparing Augustine's faith to her own and would do her best to use evidence and reason to support her statements, rather than simply quoting scripture. The tension in the air that had existed since the first day of class began to dissipate.

They completed *Confessions* in even less time than Garner had allowed and so were able to cover large portions of *The City of God* and even a few passages from Boethius' *The Consolation of Philosophy*.

"Together," Garner told the class, "these works should give you a good preparation for The Art, Literature, and Music of the Middle Ages, which Professor Pope is scheduled to teach next spring. I know it can be kind of a slog at times, but you may also want to read Gibbon's *The History of the Decline and Fall of the Roman Empire* between now and then. With Augustine, Boethius, and Gibbon all under your belt, you'll have a lot to consider when asked why and when the Roman Empire actually fell."

Then Garner proceeded to describe what would be on the final exam. In addition to the usual translation exercises, he noted there would be five essays on a range of issues dealing with Augustine's concept of time, the existence or absence of free will, the structure of the *Confessions* as a spiritual journey, and the imagery of Babylon in *The City of God*.

"Naturally, I'd be remiss if I didn't ask you at least something about the concepts of *opinio* and *fides* since that issue arose on the very first day of class. If you'll recall, in response to a question from Mr. Townsant on how I might render into Latin the concept I was calling 'confidence,' I proposed the term *ascentia*. There'll be extra credit for anyone who can come up with a better term. Either Greek or Latin, I don't care. There is no right or wrong answer here. I'm really just curious as to how your minds work after one year in our program."

Garner started to gather up his papers in preparation for leaving when another thought occurred to him.

"Oh, I nearly forgot. Professor Briggs mentioned to me that, in all the excitement about the results of the Examen Maximum, the Scipionic Circle neglected to have an end-of-year celebration. That was a rather unfortunate oversight. So, as chair of the Department of Eminent Scholars, Professor Dittman has graciously offered to sponsor a sherry reception this Friday at 6:00 p.m. in the Agalma Lounge of the Diogenes Club. A variety of soft drinks will be available for those of you not of an age to drink sherry ... which, I imagine, is most of you. Be there or be square, as you young people say."

"Oh, Professor Garner," Esmé said with an indulgent smile. "*No one* says that."

* * *

At the appointed time, the nine members of the Scipionic Circle were all present for Professor Dittmer's belated end-of-year reception. It was a singularly hot and muggy June day, and Townsant, Bastian, and Mallory, who'd been assigned by Esmé's schedule to shift boxes from the Catacombs into Chudwell 2B that afternoon, had to end their work early to shower and dress for the party. As cold as the passageway was, it was a further distance each day that the students had to carry the heavy bankers boxes back to the study lounge. The constant exercise was increasing their endurance, but it was also leaving them exhausted and, after every three- or four-hour shift, drenched in sweat.

Before heading out, however, the students retraced the complicated route to the natatorium to examine their progress. Although they felt that they must be within a hundred yards or so of reaching *La Tanière Dorée*, the pool was not even close to being full of boxes. The natatorium would easily hold all the boxes necessary to ensure a clear path from Chudwell 2B to the rear door of the secret ritual chamber. Mallory even predicted that they'd complete their work before the second summer session was over.

The Agalma Lounge was one of Professor Dittmer's favorite places on campus. Its subtle lighting, provided by two dozen Art Deco sconces recessed into the walls, cast flickering shadows across the velvet curtains that draped the Gothic windows and kept the lounge in eternal twilight. The furniture, all made of dark mahogany and covered with aged leather, is the type on which it is easy to sit but hard to rise from once you're there. More than one visitor to the Agalma Lounge later claimed that the furniture refused to let go of them, almost as though it were imprisoning in its grasp whoever was foolish enough to venture too near.

In one corner of the room, a grand piano has now awaited the arrival of a musician for more than a decade. Badly out of tune, it emits a haunting and dreary tone each evening as the building's caretaker wipes the dust from its keys. Like the books that stand in cases along the walls of the lounge, the piano remains there more for visual effect than for practical use.

At the center of the lounge stands a life-size statue of Apollo, a tribute to the generations of scholars who have taught or studied at the college. Carved from a single block of Parian marble, Apollo looks with mute disdain at those gathered about him, enjoying the fruits of Dionysus rather than availing themselves of the cultural opportunities he himself could easily provide. Perhaps intimidated by Apollo's haughty stare, the visitors to the lounge typically speak in hushed voices that are interrupted only occasionally by the clinking of glasses.

At the far end of the lounge, an imposing stone fireplace is kept ablaze year-round, as out of keeping with the June weather outside as are the tweed jackets and skirts of the students who had gathered there that evening. These students made small talk, uncomfortably, each of them feeling more intimidated by the professors *out* of class than they were *inside* the seminar rooms. There was something vaguely incongruous about a professor who wasn't actively professing, and even Bastian, who was rarely at a loss for words, often struggled to keep the conversation going.

At last, Professor Dittmer tapped an empty glass with a spoon, and the soft chatter inside the lounge ceased entirely.

"I'd like to thank you all for coming here today. Last summer, when the idea for the Department of Eminent Scholars ... "

"That's *Imminent* Scholars, Wilda," Professor Briggs called out, in an effort to make a witticism of which everyone in the room had long grown weary. Nevertheless, they all chuckled politely before the department chair continued.

" ... when the idea for our new program was first suggested, there were those here at Mersley who believed that such an endeavor was doomed to failure. How, after all, could one take four such accomplished academicians from four reasonably diverse fields and then weld them into a cohesive unit that could teach—at the undergraduate level no less!—advanced skills in critical thinking by use of original sources in their original languages and relying on cutting-edge pedagogical concepts. Many assumed we were doomed to fail. Indeed, some, I trust, *hoped* we were doomed to fail. Well, I am here today to assert my firm belief that those naysayers were wrong!"

A discreet but heart-felt cheer went up from those assembled.

"We have done what people said we could not do. We have taught and conducted research this year, not with the aim of preparing our fine students for a career, but with the aim of preparing them for *life*. And in this endeavor, I say we were entirely successful. And so, I'd simply like to take this opportunity to express my appreciation to my colleagues and my gratitude to this, our inaugural class of students."

A round of applause then ensued.

"And now, I'd like to offer the opportunity to any of my colleagues who wishes to add a few words of his or her own."

One by one, the other professors recited a few of the highlights of the year. Professor Pope retold yet again the story of "Esmé's little concert" and her success in reconstructing the Near Eastern lyre. Professor Briggs tried to parcel out his praise equally, recounting a moment in which each of them (even Bastian!) made a contribution to the class that he regarded as remarkable. And Professor Garner drew the event to a close by offering the following short speech.

"I have developed a reputation, I know, for always demanding as much as possible from my students but rewarding them with little, if any, praise in return. Well, perhaps it's the influence of the Diogenes Club's excellent sherry, or perhaps I'm simply growing soft in my old age, but I'd like to deviate from that custom tonight. As the students know, but perhaps my colleagues don't, I had set my Augustine class the challenge of rendering the concept of confidence, as opposed to mere belief or religious faith, into Latin or classical Greek. The successful student would, I promised them, receive a small amount of extra credit on the final exam. Well, I have spent this afternoon grading those exams, and I'm delighted to share the results with you."

He cleared his throat and paused for effect. "In addition to some excellent translations and perhaps the finest batch of essays it's been my honor to read as a college professor, they also taught this old Classics master a thing or two about how to 'reconceptualize,' as I believe Professor Briggs might say, what may, in the end, be a modern concept while being restricted to an ancient vocabulary. Mr. Lewis proposed the Latin term *con-*

fisio, which I'll excuse as being a cognate of *fides* because, as Mr. Lewis points out, Cicero himself used this very word to define *confidentia*, the direct ancestor of our word *confidence*, in his *Tusculan Disputations*. '*Confidentia*,' the orator says, '*id est firma animi confisio*.' 'Confidence, that is to say, an unwavering assurance of the spirit.' So, well done, Mr. Lewis. Ms. Prudence Warren-Whitehead suggested *securitas*, the origin of our word *security*, stating the following: 'In Quintilian and elsewhere, *securitas* sometimes has the negative connotation of carelessness or *false* confidence, so why could we not extend it in a positive sense to mean something a bit more like our English word *confidence*?' To which I say, 'Why not indeed?' Her sister, Ms. Mallory Warren-Whitehead follows a similar logic but in Greek instead of Latin, proposing μεγαλοψυχία, a term that literally means *greatness of soul*. Like Prudence, she points out that this word at times has a negative connotation—arrogance or *over*confidence—which could well imply that its positive connotation would include much that we encompass with our term *confidence*. And Mr. Townsant and Mrs. Dawson similarly preferred to seek a Greek expression rather than a Latin one, the former offering me the term θάρσος, which, as he says, often refers to boldness or overconfidence in battle, so we might metaphorically apply it to the boldness we have in making assertions. And Ms. Dawson put forward the word ἐμπιστοσύνη, which, I'll admit, puzzled me at first."

Garner sipped from his sherry. "Not the meaning, of course. That's rather straightforward. The prefix means *in-* or *into-*. The suffix is used to create abstract nouns. And the root, πίστις, is the New Testament word for *faith*, the very word used in Hebrews 11:1. So, ἐμ-πιστο-σύνη would mean the abstract notion of putting your faith in something ... or perhaps in someone. No, it wasn't the *meaning* of the term that puzzled me. It was the fact that I couldn't find a single citation of it in the entire Liddell and Scott lexicon. So, I thought, what would my students ... what would Esmé do in a situation like this? The answer seemed rather straightforward: I typed the word into a browser and looked it up online. And do you know what I found? The word ἐμπιστοσύνη isn't ancient at all. It's *modern* Greek. It *looks* ancient. There's no reason why it *couldn't* be ancient. Certainly, in our discussions of Plato, we talked about δικαιοσύνη, justice, often enough, and, linguistically at least, δικαιοσύνη and ἐμπιστοσύνη are structured almost identically, so why *not* treat it like an ancient word? After all, we only know the words the Greeks wrote down. It's not impossible that *someone* between Plato's time and Augustine's had used the term ἐμπιστοσύνη in conversation."

He looked at his glass, seemed annoyed that it was empty, and then continued. "As I told the students when I posed this problem to them, I wasn't looking for one right answer. In fact, there *is* no right or wrong answer to the challenge I gave them. I just wanted to see how their minds work. And their minds work *beautifully*. Some find what they need by scrolling through dictionaries. Some think of words that mean one thing and wonder why, metaphorically, they couldn't be used in some other, more unexpected way. And some see the works we're reading, not as outdated artifacts of the past, but books filled with living, breathing ideas, ideas that form a continuum extending from the ancient to the modern world."

Garner glanced up at the statue of Apollo. "I bet *he* knew that. Any- ... anyway ... I'm straying far from my point. I have a tendency to do that. You may have noticed. My point is that I gave *each* of the five students extra credit. Not that any of them needed it. Their exams were all wonderful. There's not one of them who hasn't come a long way this year. And that means that I want to change which course I'll be offering next fall. The dean will be annoyed. But when *aren't* deans annoyed? I'd simply called the course I was going to offer Intermediate Greek I, and I thought that we'd read some of the Attic Orators and, after all the Plato we read this year, mix in some Aristotle just for variety. But, as I read these exams today, I thought, 'No. That's not ambitious enough. This group needs to read Sophocles. They need to read *Oedipus*. It may be a little hard going at first. I'd originally planned it for the fourth year of the program. But these students ... they're ready. So, buckle up, everyone. Next fall, we're going to be asking some of the most challenging questions you may have encountered yet."

CHAPTER FIFTY-FOUR

The Tabula Rasa

When the end-of-semester celebration was over, some of the other faculty members quibbled with Garner over whether *any* of the terms the students had suggested accurately captured the essence of the English word *confidence*. But he, still feeling the effects of at least three glasses of sherry more than he needed, simply waved them off.

"They'll get there. They'll get there eventually," he told the other eminent scholars. "Reaching the goal wasn't the point of the exercise. As I said, my whole purpose was to see, after just one year of studying with us, *how* each of them attempted to reach that goal. Maybe their answers were pretty good. Maybe they weren't. But what I was giving them wasn't like a story problem in Sixth Grade Math. It was a conundrum: a mystery that has no answer or perhaps no one *perfect answer*, just a challenge to see how close you can *come* to an answer."

Like the other faculty members, the students may not have understood exactly what Garner had been trying to accomplish with his extra-credit question, but they were pleased by the result. The most frustrating, irritating, and, at times, downright frightening instructor they'd ever known had just called their minds "beautiful." And *that*, more than any A they would ever receive in any course, had them walking on air.

"You know what?" Bastian said as they approached the residence halls. "We should celebrate. Professor Briggs's course doesn't start until next Wednesday. We should take a long weekend and *go* somewhere!"

"Home, you mean?" Prudence asked.

"No, somewhere *together*," he replied. "I'm thinking like Philadelphia to see Independence Hall and the Philadelphia Museum of Art. You know, Whistler's Mother."

"Nashville has a full-scale reproduction of the Parthenon," Mallory suggested.

"Yeah, but it also has country music," Bastian countered.

"Okay, so there's that," Prudence agreed. "What about Chicago? You've got the Art Institute, the Museum of Science and Industry ... "

"Well, if it's museums you want, why just go to one? The Smithsonian in Washington has *twenty-one* museums, *plus* the National Gallery."

For the next twenty-five minutes, they considered one destination after another, finally settling on Minneapolis because it was drivable, more affordable than some of the suggestions that were made, and home of the Guthrie Theater, which had performances all year round.

"You've been rather quiet," Townsant said to Esmé. "Not excited about going to Minnesota, or still on a high from all that praise Garner heaped on you?"

"Oh, neither." Then she thought about it a bit more. "Or perhaps both. I really can't figure it out myself."

Esmé looked up at Townsant with a pleading look that suggested he might not understand.

"Would it be okay if I said I just wasn't quite up to a road trip right now?"

Townsant was concerned. "Are you feeling all right?"

"Oh, yes, I'm fine. I just want ... well, a little less 'togetherness,' if you know what I mean. The five of us have barely been out of one another's sight—or, at least, it seems that way—since last fall and ... "

"Say no more," Townsant told her, holding up a restraining hand. "I get it entirely. You just want a little time to decompress without the rest of us looking over your shoulder constantly. Don't worry. I'll square it with the others. You've earned a bit of time by yourself. You've earned a good deal more than that, if I'm being honest."

"Aren't you always honest?" she asked with a chuckle.

"Oh, at times *painfully* so."

* * *

The immediate problems facing the four students who wanted to spend a long weekend in Minneapolis were: 1) how to get there; 2) where to stay; and 3) how to get back.

The first and third problems proved the easiest to solve. Esmé's car, a champagne-colored 1993 Ford Thunderbird she'd inherited from her grandfather, was fine for trips around town but not at all "road trip ready," as Bastian put it when he saw it. None of the others had a car on campus, and a couple of them didn't even have a driver's license. But the town of Mersley did have a somewhat reasonable bus station and, if you were willing to transfer as often as necessary, you could use it to get wherever you needed to go. Checking the schedules, Mallory found that, if they caught the 5:15 a.m. bus to Chicago and waited around for an hour, they could meet up with a bus that would get them to their destination before it was even dark on Saturday night. Taking the same route back, they would arrive on campus even earlier, reaching the bus station in town just after 4:00 in the afternoon and getting back to the college a short time later.

That left them all day Sunday and Monday to attend *The Duchess of Malfi* at the Guthrie, spend some quality time at both The Minneapolis Institute of Art and The Walker Art Center, and rest their legs by popping into the Basilica of Saint Mary.

Getting to the bus station that early, however, meant that they'd have very little sleep that night. They still had to do a bit of packing and, most important of all, solve their second looming problem: Where would they stay once they reached Minneapolis?

None of the four could come up with a solution. Bastian proposed that they simply not stay anywhere but go back to the bus station or find somewhere else that was open twenty-four hours and pass each night there. The faces of the other three, coupled with Mallory's single-word reaction ("Nasty!"), proved that this idea was a non-starter.

It was finally Esmé who came to the rescue.

"Look. I've got an aunt who lives in Eden Prairie. It's about twenty or thirty minutes outside of the downtown area where you want to be. It's late, and she's probably already in bed, but, if you like, I can give her a call."

"Won't she find it strange that four of your friends are staying with her but you're not?" Mallory asked.

"Maybe, but I'll think of something. I mean, it's either that or do what Bastian suggested, and I don't think ... "

"Call her!" Mallory replied.

* * *

Esmé's primary motivation was, as she'd told Townsant, that she just wanted some time to herself. But she had a secondary motive as well. When she'd last been in the Catacombs, she'd become convinced that the tunnel had been cleared nearly all the way to *La Tanière Dorée*. Then, while the group had been walking to the Diogenes Club on the night before, the report that Townsant, Bastian, and Mallory had given convinced her that there may only be a day or two of work left.

Some deep-seated need inside her made Esmé want to be the one who cleared away the last few rows of boxes and found the door they were looking for. She was too principled to go back on her promise: They'd all go in at once, or none of them would go in. But it was somehow very important to her that *she* report to the others that their goal had been reached.

So, after contacting her aunt as she'd suggested, making the arrangements, and getting a few hours of sleep, she drove the others to the bus station and impatiently waited for them to leave so that she could return to the study lounge and start carrying out a few boxes.

It was just after 6:00 in the morning when she entered Chudwell Hall. Sexton was nowhere to be seen, but there was evidence he'd been there overnight: All the boxes set in the study lounge the day before had been cleared away.

The caretaker hadn't trusted the students to drive the forklift themselves, citing a college policy on who could and could not use heavy equipment on campus. But, for the last few days, he had been letting them borrow one of his hand trucks so that they wouldn't have to carry each box individually out of the tunnel.

The hand truck just barely cleared the channel they'd made through the middle of the boxes. None of them wanted to waste effort by removing anything from the Catacombs that wasn't absolutely necessary. And so, maneuvering the hand truck down the long narrow passageway, stacking three or four boxes on it, and then guiding it back was a challenge of its own. Many times, Esmé had to stop when a wheel of the truck got stuck on the corner of a box that hadn't yet been cleared, causing her to back up, reorient the hand truck, and then push onward.

After three hours of work, she was exhausted and badly in need of a break. She collapsed into a chair inside the study lounge and found herself on the edge of sleep.

But then she snapped suddenly to attention when her phone

rang. She didn't recognize the number but, fearing that something had happened to one of the other students, she immediately answered it.

"Hello? Is this Esmé?" she heard an unfamiliar voice say.

"Yes. Speaking," she replied hesitantly.

"Oh, hi. This is Mia." Then, when Esmé gave no response, the voice continued. "You know, Mia Thornton. I used to work at the library."

"Oh, yes, *Mia*," Esmé replied, finally recognizing who the caller was.

"You told me to call you if I remembered anything else. You said you'd treat me to lunch. So, I was thinking, how 'bout today?"

The suggestion promised to put a real crimp into Esmé's plans. Not only would she have to sacrifice some of the time she'd envisioned working in the Catacombs, but her idea of being off by herself for a few days would now be delayed.

"Oh, I don't know, Mia. We just finished our first of three summer sessions, and ... "

"It's important."

"Well, then, just tell me what you need to tell me over the phone."

"It's not something I can just tell you about. You really need to *see* this."

Esmé sighed. "Okay. Where d'you want to meet for lunch?"

"There's this place called the Tabula Rasa. It's out in a strip mall past ... "

"I know where it is."

"Can you meet me there at 12:30?"

Esmé checked the time on her phone. If she forgot about the break she'd started to take, she could probably get a couple more hours of work in before heading back to the residence hall and taking a much-needed shower.

"Sure. Fine."

"See you then!" Mia said with a chirpiness that Esmé herself did not feel.

***

The Tabula Rasa was certainly a step up from both of the restaurants Esmé had visited the last time she was with Mia. Its outdoor seating area was crisscrossed with string lights and separated from the stores on either side by a box hedge. Earth tones characterized the interior, where the walls were adorned with abstract paintings interspersed with posters bearing inspirational quotes like "'Be yourself; everyone else is already taken.' - Oscar Wilde" and "'The only place where success comes before work is in the dictionary.' - Vidal Sassoon."

An open window allowed patrons to peer into the kitchen, creating a modified open kitchen concept. To the side of the window was a dusty chalkboard listing the day's specials ("Chicken Alfredo Pasta: $8.99; BBQ Pulled Pork Sliders: $6.50"). Esmé couldn't figure out why these dishes were "special" since they also appeared on a stack of laminated menus at exactly the same price.

The back of the menu explained the name of the restaurant:

> *The Tabula Rasa, a Latin phrase meaning "blank slate," captures the essence of what the Ogley family has offered here for three generations: a fresh canvas for our guests to savor new flavors and create lasting memories.*

Among the "new flavors" the author of that passage must have had in mind appear to have been the Tabula Rasa's "Famed Sushi Burrito ($12.99)" and "Tandoori Poutine ($10.99)," neither of which Esmé was tempted to try.

Mia arrived late and sat down across from Esmé without apology.

"I'm surprised you knew about this place," Mia said. "It's supposed to be one of Mersley's best-kept secrets."

"Maybe they should've kept it a secret a little longer," Esmé was tempted to say, but instead she replied, "I couldn't help noticing the name when I first drove into town last fall. It's Latin, after all."

"Well, if you're interested in Latin food, you might want to try their Bolivian gyro. I've never had it, but it's supposed to be very authentic."

There were so many things wrong with that statement that Esmé didn't even know where to start. "I think I'll just have a BLT," she said.

"They're good, too. But I always get the meatloaf."

Esmé smiled politely. She waited for the server to take their orders and then asked, "So, what was it you remembered that you wanted to tell me?"

"Oh, well, glad you asked. You remember how I used to work in the library?"

"Of course."

"Well, when I first got there, I was looking for something to write down all of Winchester's instructions on. And she gives a *lot* of instructions, let me tell ya. Anyway, she was kind of annoyed I didn't bring my own notebook with me. Like anyone would actually do that. I was going to use the notepad app on my phone, but that seemed to annoy her even more, so she sent me into the storage room to find some scrap paper, and that's when I found a big box of these."

Mia removed from her bag a burgundy leather volume with a

gold title that Esmé could read all the way across the table: *The Transmundane Codex of Berossus*.

Esmé's eyes widened, and she reached eagerly across the table. "Let me see that."

She grabbed the book and paged through it. It was identical to the others she'd seen in *La Tanière Dorée*, except this one was completely blank.

"Talk about a *tabula rasa*," she muttered. "Ms. Winchester let you *keep* this?"

"Not even close," Mia replied with a smirk. "In fact, she blew up when she saw I had it. Then again, she was always blowing up at *everything*. She said those books were 'artifacts.' That's what she called 'em."

"'Artifacts'? Did she explain what she meant by that?"

"Apparently, it's all part of some big private joke from back during the Stone Age or something. There was this department chair named Becker."

"Yes, John Becker. He was chair of the Classics Department. I've seen his name in a book just like this one."

"That's the guy. According to Winchester, he did his research on the works of this Barrel- ... "

"Berossus," Esmé corrected her.

"As I said. Anyway, there was this other guy in the department, Peston or something."

"Edward Peston. He was a big Cicero scholar in his day."

"If you say so. And Peston keeps riding Becker because almost none of this Barrelossus's works survives, so how could he, like, do much research on him?"

Esmé thought about what Mia was telling her. It actually made a bit of sense. Only fragments of Berossus's works are known, and that would seem like nothing to a scholar of Cicero for whom nearly a thousand works remain.

"Where does this book come in?"

"That, Winchester said, was part of a practical joke that Peston was playing. He had *dozens* of these blank books printed with the name of some fake work on it and pretended to 'donate' them to the department. They were supposed to stay blank. The idea was something like, 'In this book, you'll find everything you really need to know about Barrelossus,' and then you'd open it and find nothing. It was intended to humiliate this Becker guy. In the end, though, the department started using them for notepaper."

"Departmental minutes, actually."

"Oh, yeah? Well, I guess the joke wore pretty thin eventually because they stopped using the books for notes and gave them to the library."

Esmé tried to take it all in. If what Mia was telling her was in any way accurate, it meant that Barbara Winchester knew all along where the title *The Transmundane Codex of Berossus* came from. If the librarian had simply *told* Bastian the book's history when he asked about it, instead of pretending to search for it through interlibrary loan, the students could have avoided wasting a great deal of time that year.

But it was typical of Barbara Winchester to hoard information like she hoarded the books in Sutlinger Library. It was as though the less she shared with others, the more powerful she felt.

That was probably why she was keeping the rest of the blank books in her supply cabinet. Someday, she must have thought, it will be a piece of Mersley history that only she knew about.

"I don't get it, though," Esmé said to Mia as their meals arrived.

"If Ms. Winchester wouldn't give you this book when you found it, why do you still have it?"

"Ain't it obvious? I was so mad when she fired me that, when I was packing up my stuff, I swiped it."

CHAPTER FIFTY-FIVE

Thalatta! Thalatta!

Mia refused to let Esmé keep the book. She seemed to regard it as her "due" because of the way Barbara Winchester had treated her. Even so, Esmé thought the price she'd had to pay for Mia's meatloaf (accompanied by a large Coke and followed by the most ample serving of apple pie à la mode that Esmé had ever seen) was well worth it for the information she'd received in return. A major piece of the puzzle had now fallen into place.

As soon as she got back into her car, Esmé sent a text to the others, saying merely, "Berossus mystery solved. Will explain later." The fact that none of them replied immediately suggested that they were still on the bus and had entered some part of the state where cell coverage was sparse.

Heading back to campus, she switched into clothes more suitable for her work down in the Catacombs and headed back to Chudwell Hall. Even though it was still early in the day, she thought she might run into Sexton. She'd supposed he would be as excited about their discoveries as they were. At least, that was the impression he'd given when he'd first taken them to the natatorium. But ever since that time, he hadn't crossed their paths even once. In fact, the only sign he was still at work was the regular removal of the boxes each night and their transfer into the long-empty pool.

It was the thrill of potentially reaching the door of the clubroom that kept Esmé going. The actual work was deadly dull. And more than once, she thought she may have made a mistake in not going on the road trip. She'd remove three boxes from where she'd left off, hope to see evidence of the door ahead, and be disappointed. So, she'd load the three boxes onto the hand truck and pull it back through the long, dark passageway to Chudwell 2B.

To help pass the time, Esmé listened to music on her phone. Her standard playlist included the prelude to *Lohengrin*, Schubert's "Winterreise" and "Erlkönig," Saint-Saëns's "Danse macabre," and about two dozen other works she often listened to while she studied. At first, she'd listened to the music through ear buds because she preferred the sound quality that way. But, when one ear bud or the other kept falling out as she moved this way or that in her "excavations," she finally just gave up and let the phone play the music aloud. Who, she thought, was she going to disturb down there anyway?

When her phone finally rang sometime after 4:00 p.m., her ringtone—a low, repeated tolling of the bells at Rouen Cathedral—startled her. It was such a sudden change from the Chopin nocturne that had been playing. Mallory was calling.

"What's all this about the Berossus mystery being cleared up?" Mallory asked her without even saying hello.

"Where *are* you?" Esmé asked.

"Some god-forsaken part of Minnesota I've never seen before. So, quick, before our phones go dead again, tell me what your text was about. We're all dying to know."

"That former librarian, Mia Thornton, wanted to have lunch today," Esmé began.

"Wait. I'm going to put you on speaker. Okay. There. Start again."

In as much detail as she could manage, Esmé retold the story she'd learned at lunch that day. Edward Peston. His ridicule of John Becker. Peston's cruel attempt at a practical joke. She ended with, "So, that's why they were taking minutes of their meetings in those books. Mia said that Edward Peston'd had *dozens* of those blank books prepared. Apparently, there's still a box of 'em in one of the storage rooms at the library."

"So, it was all just some sort of silly prank?" Townsant a̶s̶

"Apparently so."

"I still don't get it," Bastian said. "If those books are all just fakes, why was there a library card for it? And why didn't Barbara the Barbarian just *tell* me that when I was looking for the book?"

"As to that, Mia didn't say. You'd have to ask Ms. Winchester."

"Oh, I intend to," Bastian continued. "I don't care how long she'll ban me from the library this time. I want answers from her."

"Well, good luck with that."

Mallory was back on the line. "You asked me where *we* were. Where are *you*? Your voice sounds all muffled and weird."

"Oh, I'm just down in the Catacombs. I didn't feel like reading," Esmé lied because there was never a time when she didn't feel like reading, "so I thought I'd clear away some boxes."

"Yeah, well, don't get *too* carried away," Townsant said. "If you get up to the door, *stop*. Either we all go in, or none of us goes in. That was the deal."

"Not even close to being a problem," Esmé replied.

"What was that?" Mallory asked. "You're breaking up."

Mallory's words, too, were filled with static and barely audible.

"You must be going into a dead zone. Why don't we ... ?" But, by that time, the call had dropped, and the phone simply beeped in Esmé's ear.

Since the call had already interrupted her work, Esmé thought about stopping and heading for an early dinner. Her phone, however, revealed that it was still a long way from 5:00 yet, and her lunch from the Tabula Rasa was sitting a little bit heavy, so

boxes after the phone call, Esmé saw some-
n yet another stack of bankers boxes. A bat-
surrounded a wooden door. The door had
e, while those she'd seen inside *La Tanière*
ural wood. But this *had* to be one of those
doors. Esmé wondered whether perhaps, years earlier when
the tunnels were still being used, the maintenance staff may
have painted the sides of the doors on the Catacombs side so
that they'd be more visible in the limited light there. She considered several other reasons but could come up with no better
solution than that one.

Suddenly, she began to feel as though she were more of an observer than a participant in this discovery. "Esmé Dawson!" she
said to herself. "What are you doing *analyzing* the situation
when you should be *excited* about it? You've been trying to
reach this point for months, and now you've made it. But what
are you doing? You're *intellectualizing* when you should be *feeling*. Is that what Professor Garner and the others have turned
you into? A hollow academic who mistakes every life experience for a possible research topic? Stop trying to figure out *why*
the door is painted that way and congratulate yourself on
achieving the goal you set yourself!"

Esmé removed the last few boxes in front of her and began to
stack them on the hand truck. She knew that she could carry
only three at a time back to the study lounge, and there were
five boxes in the stack she'd just cleared. Even though she must
have made several dozen trips back and forth that day alone,
the thought that she'd have to make two more such runs
seemed to overwhelm her.

"To hell with them," she thought. She left three boxes stacked
in the hand truck and pushed it back about ten feet or so. Then
she slid the final two boxes behind her so that the door could
swing fully open and stared at her handiwork. Like Pandora,
she desperately wanted to open what she'd sworn would, for

now at least, remain closed. But in Professor Pope's class that semester, she'd learned all about the story pattern known as the Theme of the Violated Prohibition. The one thing that a character in a myth was forbidden to do would prove simply too tempting and become the one thing the character would do. It wasn't just Pandora. Ask Eve, Lot's wife, Patroclus, the daughters of Cecrops, Phaethon, Persephone, Eurydice, Odysseus's crew, and Icarus. Indeed, Esmé had a hard time thinking of a prohibition in ancient literature that *hadn't* been violated.

Almost unthinking, she reached out and placed her hand on the knob. It turned easily. As they'd found when they opened the door from the inside, none of the secondary doors appeared to be locked. She drew a deep breath and tried pulling the handle toward her.

The door wouldn't move.

"That's right," Esme chastised herself. "I should've remembered from the time we opened this door from the other side. It swings *into* the clubroom, not into the tunnel."

Considering this discovery an omen, she decided that it was better to leave well enough alone and simply report her discovery to the others.

She remembered that the plan was to text out some kind of code that only the imminent scholars would understand and would be meaningless to others. But they'd never agreed on the precise nature of the code. She'd have to text something immediately obvious to the four other students but couldn't think of what that might be.

Esmé initially considered Archimedes' famous cry of "*Heureka!*" But wasn't that too obvious? And besides, it had already been done. That's exactly what Townsant had shouted back when they were searching through the campus master plans. Esmé wanted something that would both be original to her and yet meaningful only to the imminent scholars. She knew there *had* to be a better solution.

As she stood before the door, considering her options, the air around her began to grow far colder. Perhaps that was due to the fact that she was no longer struggling so hard at moving the boxes, and perhaps that was due to something far more sinister. Either way, however, it made Esmé shudder.

After several minutes, she remembered the passage of Xenophon's *Anabasis* they'd all translated on Professor Garner's fall semester final. That, too, involved a cry of joyful discovery, as the despairing Greek troops finally caught sight of the sea in their march. Waiting no further, Esmé sent a group text message to the others, reading "*Thalatta! Thalatta!*" ("The sea! The sea!"), knowing that they (and perhaps no one else) would understand it. Then she waited.

One minute went by. Then two. Then five. There was no response. Even if, for a reason she couldn't imagine, they didn't understand the allusion, they would at least have sent back *something*. A question. Perhaps even just a question *mark*. But no reply came back at all.

The door stood before her, mocking her or perhaps begging her to open it. She waited several more minutes and then decided that "just a brief peak" might be all right. After all, she wouldn't be *entering* the room, just looking in. In fact, she rationalized to herself that she had an *obligation* to open the door a crack. Otherwise, how could she be sure that she'd really found one of the secondary doors to the ritual chamber? Sure, it had the same basic shape and design as the door they were looking for, but there was that matter of the white paint. She really needed to check and make sure she was in the right place.

Esmé turned the knob again and pushed the door ahead of her. It swung a little more than a foot forward, but then it would go no further. She took her phone, switched on the flashlight app, and peered through the opening she'd created.

She could see books lining a number of shelves and the piece of masonite they'd removed from the altar. It was definitely the right place. But why wouldn't the door open further?

She slid her head through the crack and discovered what had happened. She'd reached *one* of the five secondary doors, but not the one from which they'd removed the tall gargoyle. The stone statue was blocking her entry.

"Probably a good thing," she thought. "This way, I won't even be tempted to go inside." But she peered around the room, using her flashlight. It had been several days since she and the others had been in the clubroom, and it all looked as bizarre and spooky as it did the very first time.

All at once, a voice boomed out. "COLD ... SOOOOOO COLD!"

The first time Esmé had heard this voice, it had been far softer, almost as though it were coming from a great distance. In the stairwell, it had seemed quite near her. But now the voice sounded almost like a shriek. It hurt her ears and appeared to surround her on all sides.

"COLD ... SOOOOOO COLD! COLD ... SOOOOOO COLD! COLD ... SOOOOOO COLD!" the voice echoed over and over.

Esmé echoed a shriek of her own and jumped back from the room. But in doing so, she banged her head hard against the door frame. She stumbled and then, in her confusion, forgot about the boxes and hand truck behind her. She tripped again, struck her forehead against the handle of the hand truck, and collapsed onto the boxes at her feet.

CHAPTER FIFTY-SIX

No Arguments

When Esmé woke up, she found herself inside the study lounge, lying on the table with some sort of blanket beneath her. She couldn't remember how she'd made it back to Chudwell 2B, however, or where the blanket had come from.

Her first thought was that Sexton had moved her there. But, if he had, why hadn't he called someone for help? And why would he have simply abandoned her after bringing her out of the tunnel?

But then she thought it couldn't have been Sexton after all. The boxes she'd moved into the lounge earlier that day were still scattered about. There was no sign he'd been there at all. Perhaps his shift hadn't started yet.

What time was it, anyway?

The red flashing battery icon on her phone indicated that it was nearly out of charge. In fact, it stayed on only long enough for Esmé to see the time—1:26 a.m.—and then shut down completely. The only light in the room came in from the hallway. The door was open, just as she'd left it, but neither the haunting voice nor any other sound could be heard.

Gradually, and with her head throbbing wildly, she inched herself off the table and made her way into the hall. If it was the middle of the night, the caretaker should be on duty, so she made it her first priority to find him and see if she could get an answer to all her questions.

The lights in the hallway always buzzed, but they never seemed quite as loud as they did to Esmé that night. Her head still throbbing, she kept one hand on the wall as she made her way to the places where she regularly saw Sexton. He was in none of them. "Perhaps," Esmé thought, "he's down in the tunnel near where I collapsed." But, if that were the case, she had no desire to return there. The voice and her accident cured her of ever wanting to enter the Catacombs again. Her priorities had changed. Now, her greatest desire was for fresh air, followed perhaps by a glass or two of cold water.

Slowly and painfully, she climbed back upstairs and headed outside from the main entrance of Chudwell Hall. Despite the heat of the day, there was a briskness in the air that Esmé found refreshing. But as cool as the breeze was, it lacked the sinister chill she'd felt when she'd cracked open the door to *La Tanière Dorée*. That had been a morbid chill of death. Now, as she made her way back to the residence hall, it was almost as though each breath filled her lungs with the healing air of life.

Esmé's residence hall, named for one of the state's industrialists who'd made a contribution to the college in the 1950s, lacked an elevator. Her room was on the fourth floor, and each step she took seemed to make her head pound even worse. She reached her doorway, went inside, and placed her phone on its charger. Then, without even changing her clothes, she collapsed on her bed and fell into a deep sleep.

In what felt like moments later, a repeated clanging woke her. It took several moments before she realized that it was her Rouen Cathedral ringtone. Groggily, she reached out for the phone and answered it.

It was Mallory.

"Where have you *been*?" Mallory asked, her voice filled with concern. "We've been calling you all night."

"My phone was out of charge. Then I fell asleep."

"Have you been drinking? Your voice sounds funny."

As briefly as possible—she desperately wanted to return to her dreamworld where her head didn't hurt quite so much—she explained the events of the previous day.

"Yeah, we figured out your reference to Xenophon," Mallory replied. "Pretty exciting, isn't it? Bastian's ideas were right on target again. But your accident sounds terrible! Are you sure you're all right? Do you need to go to the infirmary?"

"I'm fine. I was just clumsy. That's all. I'm going to take it easy today and sleep in."

"Well, we're coming back as soon as we can."

"There's no need ... "

"It's already been decided. We're at the bus station now."

"Now? What time is it?"

"Just after 10:30."

With her blinds pulled tight, Esmé had assumed it was still the middle of the night. "10:30?" she said in surprise. "That bang on the head must've affected me worse than I thought."

"Well, don't do *anything*. In particular, don't go back down to the clubroom ... either with your key or through the tunnel."

"No need to worry about that."

"Our connection back won't be as convenient as on our way up here. Apparently, there aren't as many buses on Sunday. It may be close to midnight by the time we see you."

"You really don't *have* to ... "

"No, listen, Esmé: We *want* to. Prudence's eager to get back to the clubroom. Townsant wants to confront the dean about all the lies we've been fed this year. Bastian says that Barbara the Barbarian owes him an explanation. I'm worried about you ... "

"Don't."

"Well, I do. So, end of story. Bastian's standing here with the tickets. It's all taken care of."

* * *

It was dark again when Esmé's door opened. A thin beam of light from the hallway woke her from a sound sleep.

"Oh, my God, you're bleeding," Mallory said as she rushed into the room.

"Am I?" Esmé replied, still half asleep. "What time is it, anyway?"

"1:15 Sunday night. Well, Monday morning, actually. Did you sleep all through Sunday?"

"Yeah, I guess. Bleeding, you say?" Esmé reached up and touched her forehead. Her fingers immediately met some dried patches of blood.

"Well, you *were*, anyway. It looks like most of it's dried now. Did you go to the infirmary like we talked about?"

"Not yet. I was going to ... "

"You're going *now*. No arguments."

Mallory slipped an arm around Esmé, and the two of them headed out into the darkness.

CHAPTER FIFTY-SEVEN

Lillian Hawthorne

If you were to call up Central Casting and ask them to send you a stereotypical college nurse, you would be expecting the arrival of someone precisely like Lillian Hawthorne. Unmarried, unassuming, and unyielding when challenged, Nurse Hawthorne lived on campus in a small apartment on the upper floor of Howell Infirmary. Her residence there allowed her to tend to ailing students at any time of the day or night, a duty that she had now fulfilled for more than thirty years.

When Nurse Hawthorne first arrived at Mersley, her chestnut hair had been pulled back into a neat bun, and her piercing blue eyes gave promise of knowing anything that was necessary to treat the ill or mend the lame. These days, her hair was streaked with gray, but the style in which she wore it had never varied. A pair of horn-rimmed glasses now covered those piercing blue eyes, but, if anything, they had assumed a look of even greater confidence from her experience of dealing with a seemingly endless series of bumps, scrapes, hangovers, and stomach ailments as the infirmary's sole full-time employee.

The fact that she never talked about her past allowed each person she met to fill it in however he or she wished. Rumors swirled as randomly as did the campus leaves each autumn. Some claimed she'd once been a battlefield nurse, serving at the height of the Vietnam War and then seeking the more tranquil environment of a college campus when she could no longer endure the horrors she'd witnessed. Others speculated that she'd begun her career as a nurse in some large city— Chicago and St. Louis were most commonly mentioned—tending to the poor and needy before suffering from a nervous breakdown that drove her to apply for the first position she saw in a college town far away from her origins.

In truth, none of these rumors—including more bizarre stories that she'd once been a spy, the illicit lover of a famous politician, the heiress of the inventor of a mass-marketed shampoo, or all three simultaneously—were true. She had grown up not far from the college in the town of Ashborne Commons. Her father, Walter Hawthorne, had been the town's leading doctor, and Dr. Hawthorne always hoped that Lillian would follow in his footsteps and, one day, take over his practice. But the headstrong Lillian Hawthorne had other ideas.

From an early age, Lillian had fallen in love with words, and she dreamed of becoming a successful author. Beginning at the age of eleven, she would spend long summer days in her family's garden, crafting stories about faraway places and mysterious people. For several years, Lillian's father tolerated these pastimes but, once his daughter entered Ashborne Commons Country Day, the most prestigious private high school in the county, he found himself increasingly annoyed when she preferred classes in literature and creative writing to what he regarded as "more serious subjects" like biology, chemistry, and physics.

Throughout the Hawthorne family (but no further), it was common knowledge that the doctor's heart broke when she turned down admission to the pre-med program at Duke and enrolled instead in English and Creative Writing at the University of Iowa. "Iowa, of all places!" Dr. Hawthorne grumbled to his wife, Larissa. "And a *public* university at that!"

Gritting his teeth, he tolerated Lillian's choice of major the best he could. But he did so only under certain conditions. (He was, after all, paying her tuition.) "After you graduate, I'll give you five years. No more. And I'll support you during that time as you seek to establish yourself. But no graduate programs in 'creative writing' or anything else like that. And no extension to the five years I'm allotting you. If you can publish a novel during that time—or even sell a single short story to a national magazine—I'll admit I was wrong, and you can continue your career as a writer with my blessing. But, if you *don't* demonstrate at least some success in your field, then I expect you to do the right thing: Go back to school and learn a practical career in some branch of medicine. I believe I have enough pull at Duke to get you in. Now, I don't want to hear another word about it. This is just how it's going to be."

Perhaps surprisingly, Lillian agreed to her father's terms with good grace. She believed in herself, and the praise she'd received for the short stories she'd published in her university's undergraduate literary magazine gave her confidence that in even less than five years, she'd demonstrate to her father that her dream had not at all been a mere illusion.

But in this hope, Lillian was badly deceived. Getting her first novel published proved far more difficult than she'd imagined. Nearly four years went by, and all she'd collected for her pains was a collection of letters from various publishers beginning with the words "We regret to inform you ... " Her narrative was regarded as too bizarre even by editors who typically liked bizarre stories. She continually revised her story and resubmitted it, all to no avail. In the fifth and final year of her agreement with her father, she tried cannibalizing parts of her novel and turning them into short stories. Unfortunately, this attempt proved no more successful than any of her others, and her time was up.

With a mixture of condescension and sympathy, Dr. Hawthorne informed Lillian that she now had to make good on her promise and go to medical school. But Dr. Hawthorne's "pull" turned out to be far less impressive than he had believed. Duke refused to accept Lillian into the medical school, saying that the courses she'd taken as an undergraduate were inadequate preparation for their program. He tried again to get her accepted into the school's physician assistant program and had no more success than before. Finally, the nursing program agreed to admit Lillian on a conditional basis, provided that she take a number of remedial courses and then do well enough in her first year to merit continuation.

Unmarried, unassuming, and unyielding: It was the last of these three qualities that enabled Lillian to receive straight A's, not only in her remedial courses, but in all her nursing courses as well. She graduated from the program with honors and returned to Ashborne Commons to begin her career as a nurse in her father's practice.

Then the unexpected happened.

On the very day Lillian was to begin work, Dr. Hawthorne complained of a sudden pain in his left arm and collapsed facefirst into his plate of scrambled eggs. By the time the emergency medical team arrived, he was dead. As he was the sole physician in the practice, the office was forced to close, and Lillian found herself without a job and with certification and a degree in a field she'd never really wanted.

The money she inherited from her father would keep her afloat for a while. But it also had to be shared with six siblings and her mother. Frantically, Lillian returned to her novel, sending out prospectus after prospectus, and meeting with no greater success than before. Her allocation of the inheritance was almost gone when one morning she saw an ad in *The Ashborne Commons Daily Herald* that began as follows:

> WANTED: CAMPUS NURSE. Mersley College, a private college of about 2,000 students, is seeking a full time nurse to staff its Howell Infirmary. The infirmary serves as the first line of health care and partners with nearby Ovalton Medical Center to provide ...

Lillian drew in a deep breath, made her resolution, and then wrote a letter of application for the position. In less than a week, she received a letter letting her know that she was the college's leading applicant. (She was, in fact, the *only* applicant.) After driving to nearby Mersley and being interviewed for less than half an hour, she was offered the job. Lillian had been the school nurse ever since.

Being back in an academic environment, Lillian thought it might be safe to show others her novel again and even believed it might meet with a favorable reception. But the Mersley College faculty was, for whatever reason, far more unforgiving in its tastes than her advisors had been at the University of Iowa. Her writing was openly ridiculed and then quickly forgotten. Only one member of the faculty was at all complimentary, and Lillian had always suspected that was only because the two of them were in the midst of a short-lived romantic relationship. And so, she tucked her novel away in a drawer and did her best to try to forget it was ever her dream to become an author.

It was in that very drawer that Mallory found the novel on the night she brought Esmé to the infirmary.

Some explanation is, no doubt, needed. Mallory Warren-Whitehead was not, by nature, a snoop. She thought she had good reason for looking inside that drawer, and the last thing she ever expected to find there was an unpublished novel.

What happened was this.

Because the summer session at Mersley is far less well-attended than the rest of the academic year, and since that particular weekend fell during the break between Summer Session A and Summer Session B, the infirmary was completely devoid of patients when Esmé and Mallory arrived in the middle of the night. They had to ring the buzzer to wake Lillian up and, when she opened the door, she was wearing a thin nightgown covered by a simple cotton robe and had her hair drawn back even more tightly than usual. Mallory explained briefly what had happened, and Lillian quickly ushered them inside.

She had Esmé sit down and began to examine her in order to determine whether a call to the Ovalton Medical Center emergency room was in order.

"This could take a while," she told Mallory. "In fact, I may want to keep her here at least until the morning. You can stay, too, if you like. The 'ward,' as I call it, has plenty of beds. In the meantime, why don't you go upstairs to my apartment and put on some water to make tea? There's an electric pot in the kitchenette, and tea bags in a drawer somewhere."

It was that expression "drawer somewhere" that led to all the confusion. Filling the pot with water and turning it on to boil was the work of a moment. But the tea bags were nowhere to be found. Mallory went through every drawer she could find in the kitchenette, and then thought they might be in one of the drawers in a room that Nurse Hawthorne used as a sitting area.

In the third drawer Mallory opened, she saw the manuscript: *The Rites of Alcabaz by Lillian Hawthorne*. That title alone merely roused Mallory's curiosity, but what caused her to nearly drop the pages in shock were the opening lines.

> The ritual chamber of the Fraternity of the Broken Omen was known to only a select few. Buried deep beneath the earth of a tranquil village, none of the residents ever suspected that the very heart of evil beat in their midst.
>
> None suspected, at least, until one day when a thoughtless girl opened a door that should forever have remained closed.

CHAPTER FIFTY-EIGHT

Front of House and Back of House

If people checked the schedule posted on the door of Sutlinger Library, they would find that it was advertised as open between summer sessions. But it was open only in the sense that the recipient of an honorary doctorate is technically a doctor or that the "keys to the city" actually unlock anything.

During the academic year, even when the vast majority of Mersley College students had fled campus, the library retained its most loyal patrons, typically assistant professors who were coming up for tenure review soon and still had a number of publications to complete. But in the summer, these professors were off doing research elsewhere even if it was only to nearby cities with universities that boasted larger libraries. As a result, Barbara Winchester, in a rare act of generosity, gave the members of her staff time off between summer sessions. Her act was not entirely due to altruism, however. If anyone *had* seen what the head librarian was up to during these breaks, her secret habit of reading the latest romance novels purchased for section 813.08 ("Genre Fiction") of the library would have been exposed. But for years now, indulging in a bit of summer escapism had become part of Winchester's annual routine.

That is why, shortly after she had unlocked the doors that Monday morning, she was surprised to see *any* student enter Sutlinger Library. And she was even more surprised to see that the student who had violated her sacred routine was Bastian Lewis, whom she regarded as the Scipionic Circle's weakest link.

"What are you doing here, Lewis?" she asked the young man as he strode confidently toward the circulation desk. "I would've thought you'd still be licking your wounds as the only member of your little group *not* to be offered admission to the Aurelian Club. Certainly, *that* had to sting."

Winchester's remarks had been intended to irritate Bastian and, she hoped, drive him from the library so that she could get back to the copy of Lizzie McKinney's *A Wallflower Bursts Into Bloom* that lay open on her desk. But her words had an effect opposite to her intent. They caused Bastian to become almost eerily calm. He knew he had information that Barbara the Barbarian didn't know he had and that information, properly used, provides strength.

"Just couldn't keep myself away, Ms. Winchester. You're right as always, of course. It *was* a bit humiliating not scoring as well as I might have liked on the Examen Maximum, so I thought I'd do a little extra reading this summer."

"Very commendable," she said warily. Bastian's study habits had never seemed that diligent before, but perhaps recent events had proved to be precisely the wake-up call he needed. "Well, don't let me stop you."

"That's just the thing, Ms. Winchester. I asked Professor Garner for a summer reading list," Bastian lied, "and I'd never heard of half the authors he recommended. I searched through our library's catalog online, and I was hoping you could get at least some of these for me through interlibrary loan."

Winchester breathed out heavily. Processing a stack of interlibrary loan requests was most definitely not how she'd intended to spend her morning. On the other hand, she could take the list from Bastian, send him on his way, and have one of the other librarians process the requests when they got back to work on Wednesday.

"Give me the list," she said, reaching out her hand impatiently.

"Oh, I haven't written it out yet. You know me: lazy to a fault. Say, where's the supply room? Maybe I could get a sheet of paper from there and ... "

"This'll do," Winchester said, handing him an advertisement that had arrived in the mail and was destined for the trash. "Just write the names on the back, and be quick about it. Or even better, go back to your room and do it."

"No, that's fine. I remember all the names."

In Sabrina Pope's class that spring on the Art, Literature, and Music of Ancient Greece, they had talked about a number of ancient works that, although they had survived, were not commonly read. Bastian wrote down the titles of as many of these texts as he could recall. The mimes of Herodas and Sophron. Gorgias of Leontini's *Encomium of Helen* and *Defense of Palamedes*. Pseudo-Homer's *Batrochomyomachia*. The *Carmina Priapeia*. Claudius Aelianus's *De Natura Animalium*. Ennius's *Euhemerus*.

When Winchester read over the list, her face displayed an almost comical grimace. "Professor Garner gave you *these*? I think he must've been having you on. I can't imagine you can handle most of these Greek works after only a single year of language study. Not to mention that some of them survive only in fragments. And as for the Latin works, one of them is actually obscene. But we may have several of these here in Sutlinger, not that you'd know where to look, of course."

She gave Bastian a condescending smile.

"Ah, that's right. I almost forgot. There's another relatively obscure work that I *know* you've got here in the library. Hand me that list back, would you?"

Bastian took the piece of paper, added one more title, and handed it back.

Winchester looked at the addition. Her smile instantly vanished. "*The Transmundane Codex of Berossus*. I'm afraid I don't like your sense of humor, Mr. Lewis. I don't like it one little bit. You sent me on a wild goose chase once for this book, and I told you it's a phantom. It simply doesn't exist. Now, get out of here. For wasting my time yet again, I'm suspending your library privileges for the rest of the summer."

"Yeah. About that," Bastian replied casually. "I don't believe you'll do any such thing."

"And why not?"

"Because you've got a whole box of these books back in your supply closet."

To the extent it was possible for Barbara Winchester to blanch, she did so at that very moment. "Who told you such a thing?"

"That's not important. The important thing is that I know you have it."

"I most emphatically do not."

"Then you won't mind if I go back to the supply closet and ... "

"You will do no such thing. Now leave immediately, or I'll call the dean."

"Oh, I invite you to do so. That'd be wonderful. In fact, why not call the president while you're at it? Perhaps you can explain to them why you lied to me about searching for this book when you knew its history the whole time."

"I know no such thing."

"No? You've never heard of Edward Peston and the contempt he felt for John Becker, who'd established a reputation as a scholar on the works of Berossus? Any of this ringing a bell?"

Winchester fixed Bastian with a steady stare. "What is it that you want, Mr. Lewis?"

"I just want to know *why*. Why didn't you simply tell me the story when I first asked you about the book? All the time we wasted ... *I* wasted. Why'd you do it?"

"It wasn't an attempt to be cruel, Bastian," she said, surprising him by the use of his first name.

"What was it, then?"

She wondered exactly how to begin.

"Have you ever had a job in a restaurant, Bastian?"

He frowned. "No. What's that got to do with ... ?"

"Well, I did once. Back when I was paying my way through school. And, in a restaurant, you learn pretty quickly that there's what's known as 'back of house' where all the food is prepared and 'front of house' where the customers actually eat. All kinds of arguments and chaos can be occurring 'back of house,' but servers are never, *ever* supposed to let that spill over into the 'front of house' environment. There everything is supposed to be calm, tranquil, the best possible atmosphere for the best possible meal."

"Why are you telling me this?"

"As a student here at Mersley College, the goal is for you to be 'front of house' at all times. Faculty members quarrel. Staff members get into raging shouting matches sometimes. But all that is kept 'back of house.' We want nothing at all to interfere with the best possible learning environment for you, even if we don't tell you the complete truth at times."

"Get to the point."

"Within a college, there's a very rigid hierarchy. Oh, colleges and universities *pretend* that hierarchies don't matter, that only ideas matter. But socially, the hierarchies are very rigid. Full professors ... they see themselves as entirely different species from lowly assistant professors. And, as for those of us on the staff ... why, we hardly exist at all. You've heard of that period the college went through that they call 'The Troubles'?"

"Yeah."

"Well, that was only one occasion that nearly tore this school apart. The way in which Professor Becker was treated, that ... that was another such time. And none of us want to relive those days. None of us want the stupid, cruel things that faculty members have done to one another make you feel any less respect for your professors. You *should* be in awe of them. *We* want you to be in awe of them, even if, in the end, they're only human."

"Yeah? Well, how's that workin' out for you?"

"Would it help if I said I was sorry, Bastian? You know, I don't apologize much."

Bastian looked steadily at Barbara the Barbarian Librarian, and she seemed to shrink almost visibly before his eyes.

"No," he said. And then he simply walked out of the library, leaving Ms. Winchester to read as much romantic fiction as she liked.

CHAPTER FIFTY-NINE

The Clearinghouse

While Esmé and Mallory were at the infirmary, and Bastian was at the library, P. Bradford Townsant III and Prudence Warren-Whitehead had a different mission. They were in Old Main, sitting on a bench outside the dean's office and waiting for Dawn McDaniel to arrive. Of all those who had misled the five students since their arrival at Mersley, Townsant regarded the dean's deceptions as the worst, and Prudence had come to the conclusion that it was no longer enough simply to exist in her sister's shadow.

Expecting a quiet Monday, Dean McDaniel sighed when she turned the corner and saw the two students waiting for her. Before she even reached them, she called out, "What? Only two of you today? Where are your compatriots?"

Then, before they even had a chance to answer, she continued. "You know, there are those who'd consider it cruel to harass an old woman first thing in the morning before she's even had her coffee." As she unlocked the door, she added, "I'll bet I see more students from your program here in my office than I do from all the others combined."

She dropped her keys on her desk. "Well, what is it this time? The blackboards in Chudwell not black enough for you? One of your professors say something that hurt your wee little feelings?"

Townsant prepared to answer, but it was Prudence who spoke first. "The Fraternity of the Broken Omen."

"What?"

"The Fraternity of the Broken Omen," Prudence repeated.

"Well, what of it? I told you myself about that old urban legend back in the fall. Don't tell me someone's now convinced you that it's true. I thought you were brighter than that."

"It *is* true," Townsant insisted. "We've found the ritual chamber."

The dean broke into a laugh. "Of course, you have. I almost forgot. You'll have been to the clubroom of the Aurelian Club by now. That's, of course, how all those rumors got started. But you're idiots if you've actually started believing them."

"The altar ... ," Prudence began.

"Ah, yes, the 'altar,'" Dean McDaniel interrupted. "Do you know where that came from?" When neither of the students said anything, she answered her own question. "It's actually a relatively new addition to the clubroom. Back in the 1960s, we had this art professor by the name of Edie Bird. A sculptor. Bird was a good name for her: She was flighty. Anyway, the campus was changing back in the '60s—It's always changing, I suppose. —and Elisabeth Banworth, one of our alumni board members, decided that what Mersley needed was 'a good, old-fashioned revival.' Her words, not mine. She was practically alone in this opinion, but she was the sort of person who got what she wanted. She had offered to pay for the building of a new science center and a much-needed classroom building on the North Quad. But suddenly her stipulation was that she'd fulfill these pledges *only* if we'd also build a chapel. A chapel that she'd pay for."

"Hence Banworth Chapel," Townsant said.

"I see Professor Garner's emphasis on critical thinking hasn't passed *you* by, Mr. Townsant," the dean said sarcastically. "This being the '60s, there were protests. People said that Mersley had no business privileging one religion over any other and that the college had greater needs than a chapel no one would use, anyway. Lizzy Banworth thought she had a solution: It wouldn't be a chapel just for the Protestant faiths, but would be open to *all* believers. She thought that meant that the Catholics might use the building, too, and maybe the Jews might use it as a synagogue if there ever were enough of them on campus. She never thought it would ever be used as a mosque. Back then, there were no Muslim students at Mersley. Well, that's changed, too, and I'm rather proud of that. But Edie Bird did something that she thought would really call Lizzy Banworth's bluff."

"Which was?" Prudence asked.

"Being a sculptor, she carved what she thought an old, pagan altar might look like and insisted that, if Banworth Chapel were really open to *all* religious beliefs, certainly there could be no objection to the occasional animal sacrifice being performed there."

"So, that's why there's blood on the altar," Townsant speculated.

"My, you really *are* naïve, aren't you? That's just paint, Mr. Townsant. That altar was never used by anyone, not the imaginary Fraternity of the Broken Omen and not anyone else either. But Edie Bird kept insisting that either *all* religions or *no* religions be given a facility on campus, and that meant that Banworth Chapel would need to accept her pagan altar. She was really trying to block the whole idea of building a chapel on campus, though things didn't work out that way."

Despite herself, Prudence found that she was fascinated by the story. "What happened?"

"Oh, precisely what you can imagine. Elisabeth Banworth blew a gasket and threatened to cancel all her funding. Edie Bird refused to back down and threatened to go to court. The president at that time, Tristan Fisher, finally worked out a compromise. Miss Banworth got her 'non-satanic chapel,' as she called it, and Miss Bird's pseudo-pagan altar got moved down to the clubroom of the Aurelian Club. Good location for it. Fits the atmosphere."

"So, it really was a ritual chamber," Townsant said.

"*Nooooooo*," the dean scoffed. "That space was what we once called 'The Clearinghouse.' All the tunnels under campus fed into there. The 'Winter Refuge,' they called it. So, in inclement weather, you could get from any building on campus to any other building simply by going down into one tunnel, heading to The Clearinghouse, and then heading off in the direction you needed by choosing the appropriate tunnel."

"Tunnels that you specifically told us didn't exist," Prudence pointed out.

"Well, what can I say?" the dean replied. "If the student body knew there were tunnels under the campus, they'd tear up half the buildings trying to find them. And heaven only knows what they'd be getting up to down there if they ever found them. So, all of us on the faculty decided to tell anyone who asked that the Mersley College tunnels were no more real than was the Fraternity of the Broken Omen."

"But why *aren't* the tunnels still being used?" Townsant asked. "They sound to me like a pretty good idea, especially after slogging my way to and from Chudwell Hall in the rain and slush."

"They *were* a good idea ... back when the campus was small, and they could connect all the buildings. But each new building would mean digging a new tunnel, and there are, I'm proud to say, *three times* the number of buildings on campus as there were back when the so-called 'Winter Refuge' was first conceived. So, the tunnels were turned into storage space. All kinds of garbage plus a good bit of stuff that I imagine has some value was stuffed in there to block them up. And The Clearinghouse stood unoccupied for several years until finally, the Aurelian Club needed a space to meet, and it was given to them. With Edie Bird's altar in the middle of the room, the first members to use it decided to enhance the rather macabre atmosphere of the place and ... well, you've seen it, so you know what I'm talking about. More recent members of the club had decidedly different interests, so they insisted that overhead lighting be put in and that the altar be made into a game table by covering it with a piece of masonite. I'm still an advisor to the club, so I get the key each year. I went down there ... oh, maybe six months or so ago, and it's not what it was. Maybe your lot can change that."

"I still don't understand," Townsant said. "Filling up the tunnels must've taken *tons* of material, thousands and thousands of bankers boxes. Where did it all come from?"

"Wait until *you* become a professor someday, Mr. Townsant, and you'll see just how much waste, how much ... " She struggled for the word.

"Detritus?" Townsant suggested.

"Ah, yes. The *mot juste*. How much detritus a college can produce in even a single year. Professors move out and leave most of their stuff in their offices. Students do the same in the residence halls. But that's not even the half of it. The sheer amount of paperwork a college can produce in a year is practically mind-numbing. No, the tunnels weren't that hard to fill. They must be something like a time capsule now. Someday, I imagine an archaeological team will clear them and find all sorts of interesting historical documents from the '50s, '60s, and '70s."

"We've already started," Townsant said.

"Yes," Prudence added. "We found the entrance into the tunnel from beneath Chudwell Hall and have been moving the boxes out to clear the way to *La Tanière Dorée*."

"Ah," the dean chuckled. "*La Tanière Dorée*. 'The Golden Lair.' Sort of a glorified name for a student clubroom that was once little more than a passageway, isn't it? Well, good luck with that. I know the sheer quantity of boxes that are down there.

You'll be lucky to get even a tenth of the way there."

"Oh, but Esmé told us she already finished clearing the tunnel on Saturday," Prudence told the dean.

"Saturday? How'd she manage *that*?"

"We've had help," Townsant said.

"Help? What kind of help?"

Townsant was reluctant to get the old man into trouble, but he realized that he'd backed himself into a corner. "Sexton," he replied.

"Sexton? Who the hell is Sexton?"

"Mr. Sexton," Prudence said. "He's the caretaker for Chudwell Hall."

"Chudwell Hall doesn't *have* a caretaker. Why on earth would we waste money on maintenance staff for *that* old relic?"

CHAPTER SIXTY

Sexton

The dean just looked at them blankly. "I don't suppose it ever occurred to you that the term *sexton* is simply another word for *caretaker*. You've been had. The person who's helping you is some sort of thief. No doubt he's been stealing all the valuable material you've managed to clear out of the tunnels for him."

"You mean, like the vinyl records?" Townsant asked.

"The records and whatever else he could find in the boxes. You idiots! You believed a silly little story and probably aided and abetted a criminal."

"I can't believe Sexton's a criminal," Prudence objected. "He can be prickly at times, but I believe his heart's in the right place."

"Yes, well, let's just see about that." The dean grabbed her keys back off the desk and headed out of her office.

"Where are you going?" Prudence asked.

"I'm going to see just how much damage the five of you've caused."

Despite the dean's age, she practically flew down the main staircase and continued until she reached the musty cellar. Then she walked over to where the vending machine was and used her golden key to unlock the door marked "Warning: Electrical Closet." By the time Townsant and Prudence reached her, the door had already swung shut behind her.

Dean McDaniel had no need for additional lighting. She had gone up and down these slippery, stone stairs so many times that she knew them by heart. The two students remembered this time to light up their phones and use them for guidance in the dark stairwell. But even so, Dean McDaniel was already inside *La Tanière Dorée* by the time they reached the door. Using her key, Prudence opened the door, and the students went inside. There they found an unexpected sight.

Sexton was standing behind the altar with all the volumes of minutes from the Classics Department opened up in front of him. It's clear that he'd been going through them one by one.

Surprised by the dean's entrance, he froze in place, looking at her. She, in turn, looked back at him with a strange expression.

"Well, Tol," she said. "It's been rather a long time, hasn't it?"

* * *

"How'd you get in here?" the dean asked. "You don't have a key."

"The tunnel," the former professor who'd been calling himself Sexton replied, nodding toward the secondary door he'd used. "One advantage of not being able to afford every meal is that it leaves you skinny enough to get through even the narrowest opening."

The first thing Townsant and Prudence noticed is that the man spoke with none of the strange accent and poor grammar they'd always heard him use. Although heavily bearded and unwashed, he sounded almost like any other faculty member on campus.

"Mr. Townsant and Ms. Warren-Whitehead," Dean McDaniel said, "I'd like to introduce you to Dr. Tolbert Fitzgerald, one of Mersley College's less successful former members of the professoriate."

"Where is it, Dawn?" Fitzgerald asked. "I know it's down here somewhere."

"I have absolutely no idea what you mean."

"You know *exactly* what I mean."

"Where've you been keeping yourself for ... what's it been now, Tol, eh? Thirty-five years?"

"More, as you well know."

"I thought you'd died a long time ago."

"You'd have liked that, wouldn't you? You know, you ruined my career. Where've I been keeping myself? I'll tell you where: little private schools, community colleges, anywhere I could get a job, and those are hard to find once you've been turned down for tenure. All of them temporary positions, most of them not even full-time. But I managed. I worked until finally I couldn't get hired at all. So, I came back here. Four years ago last November. And I decided I had to find it. Chudwell Hall wasn't even that hard to break into it. You'd abandoned it. All of you'd abandoned it. So, I'd come here at nights and search."

"Search for what, Dr. Fitzgerald?" Prudence asked.

The old man ignored her. "No one ever even knew I was in the building. I camped out here. After a few months, when I could no longer afford my apartment, I started living here. Then one day that Professor Garner of yours saw me in his office. He asked me my name and what I was doing there. All I could think of since I was holding a trash can at the time was to say that I was the caretaker."

"And *caretaker* suggested the name Sexton, didn't it?" McDaniel asked.

"Not my best idea, I admit. Pretty transparent. But it seemed to work, even though my attempts to *sound* like a janitor were appalling, at best, I imagine. I just made up my accent on the fly. And, you know, at first, I thought my access to the building was going to be pretty limited, but then I thought, 'Who would object to the building's caretaker being on the premises all night?' Emptying out the garbage and sweeping the halls gave me a chance to look everywhere, to *be* everywhere, to search for a way into the Winter Refuge and ultimately get *here*. That's when I had my really brilliant idea."

"Which was?" the dean asked coolly.

"How much faster I could find the tunnels if I had five eager, little helpers. I've got an old computer I keep back in the room where I was staying. It isn't much, but it was enough for me to print out a fake catalog card: *The Transmundane Codex of Berossus*, the title stamped on the cover of the leather notebook I was looking for. I even had my own little joke on it. The catalog number: 182 Fit. 182, the section where early Greek philosophy books are found. Fit, the first three letters of the author's name: Fitzgerald. Because I *was* the author, you know. You're aware of that, and I'm aware of that. And, as soon as I find it, *everyone* will be aware of that."

"Aware of what, Professor Fitzgerald?" Townsant asked.

"I just needed help finding the tunnels and then clearing them. Help that the students willingly—I might even say *greedily*—supplied. Why, they even managed to turn up those old Sinatra albums I left behind in my office."

"But you denied the tunnels even existed," Prudence said.

"The old 'Theme of the Violated Prohibition,'" he told her. "It's all a matter of reverse psychology. The quickest way you can get someone to do something is to tell them not to do it. Anytime I thought your efforts were flagging, all I needed to do was to leave a fake calling card or provide some other reference to 'the Fraternity of the Broken Omen.' You know, I came up with that name because I happened to see it in a dreadful story written by a woman I once dated here a long time ago. Some nurse, I believe. Can't recall *her* name now, though. Oh, and if I ever needed an immediate response, I'd simply whisper 'Cold ... soooooo cold' into the air ducts and let it echo throughout the building. Ghosts are always cold, right? In fact, just the other day, that short one, Esmé, was about to come in here, so I had to shout into the air ducts to frighten her off."

"You caused her to go into the infirmary!" Prudence protested. "You're lucky she doesn't sue ... "

But she never got to finish her threat because, at that very moment, there was a huge crash. One of the large stone gargoyles tipped over, striking the altar, with the result that both the statue and the altar smashed into pieces on the floor.

The crack in the secondary doorway that Esmé had opened was wide enough for the emaciated Tolbert Fitzgerald to slip through, but it wasn't nearly wide enough to accommodate Bastian who'd put on a few pounds more than the typical "freshman fifteen" that year. He'd pushed the door open, knocking over the statue. Mallory and Esmé followed him into the clubroom.

Everyone looked on in horror at the disaster Bastian had caused. But then, as the dust settled, something else became visible in the chunks of obsidian and jasper that lay strewn about them. It was another leather-bound book, identical to the volumes of departmental minutes that Fitzgerald had been searching through on top of the altar.

No one wanted to say a word. Finally, Bastian, the Bad Boy of the Scipionic Circle, broke the silence. "I'm sorry. I'm just so, so sorry."

"It's all right, son," Fitzgerald replied. "Just hand me that book, will you?"

Almost mechanically, Bastian took the book, dusted it off, and passed it to the man he still thought of as the building's caretaker. Like the other volumes that Edward Peston had printed, the title on the cover read *The Transmundane Codex of Berossus*. But as soon Fitzgerald he opened the cover, he saw that the once-blank book was filled with his own handwriting.

On the first page was written:

> The Deleuzian Rhizomatics
> of Ontological Temporality:
> A Deconstructionist Approach
> by Tolbert J. Fitzgerald, Ph.D.

CHAPTER SIXTY-ONE

The Troubles

For many years, the faculty and staff had used the expression "The Troubles" to refer to how divided the campus had been as to the authorship of the book for which Dawn McDaniel had been awarded the Covington Prize. For the future, however, it would be well known that The Troubles had never really ended. They had simply taken a brief hiatus, destined to break out again when Tolbert Fitzgerald returned to claim what was rightfully his.

The unique penmanship style made it indisputable that Fitzgerald had indeed, as he'd always claimed, written out the book in longhand and given the manuscript to McDaniel for review. The blank volumes prepared by Edward Peston as his ill-fated practical joke proved convenient scrap paper for the poor young assistant professor to use while preparing his draft. McDaniel hadn't written the book. All she'd done was type it up and add her name as the author. She'd hidden the original manuscript in her office until she became dean. Then, when workers were about to move her belongings to her new space in Old Main, the newly-promoted Dean McDaniel became worried that the purloined book might be found. Taking it down to the Aurelian Club, she discovered that the student members were about to cover Edie Bird's altar with a sheet of masonite that they'd glued to a heavy stone base. She slipped the book into the slot at the center of the altar and allowed it to fall deep inside. The piece of masonite was placed over the slot the very next day, providing the perfect hiding place.

None of this would have come to light if she'd simply burned the manuscript. And, in the campus hearing that occurred that July, even she couldn't explain why she hadn't done so. But Fitzgerald, who knew the future dean well enough to intuit how her mind worked, always suspected she'd have hidden it somewhere in *La Tanière Dorée*. But he was wrong about one thing. He'd assumed it would merely be among all those volumes of departmental minutes that no one would ever be interested in reading. If Bastian hadn't barged his way into the room at the moment he did, the manuscript might be hidden there still.

The result of the hearing was that Dean McDaniel lost her deanship, her tenure, and her job, in that order. Perhaps what hurt her the most was an announcement by the Covington Commission in *The Chronicle of Higher Education* that, in its first such action ever, it was revoking the prize it had awarded her. In the aftermath of these events, President Woolridge first offered the deanship to Wilda Dittman, who refused it on the spot. She'd had more than enough taste of administrative work serving as department chair the year before and no desire to partake of it further. "Besides," she reminded the president, "I've still got to complete at least six more faculty hires for the Department of Eminent Scholars before the fall semester begins."

"New hires!" the president sputtered. "I'm not authorizing any new hires. Your department is still the smallest one on campus!"

"Smallest maybe, but also the fastest growing. We've had four requests for transfers from the English Department, three from Classics, two from History, and two more from Humanities. I imagine they were attracted to us by the results of the Examen Maximum and all the notoriety this summer's 'Troubles' have brought to the program. Plus, the five students who joined us last year have each contacted their high schools, and I suspect the new students and transfer students will bring our total enrollment to more than thirty. That means that this year's new students will be over five times last year's and, if you read the faculty handbook, any department with a student enrollment that grows more than fifty percent from year to year is entitled to a new position. And we'll need those new faculty members, too. After all, the four of us now in the program will have to teach *second-year* classes in our curriculum. We'll need new blood to teach the first-years. But don't worry." At this point, Dittman leaned in close to President Woolridge as though the two of them were part of the same conspiracy. "I'll make sure that every single one of the new hires is just like us."

* * *

None of the students, and very few on the faculty, ever expected Barbara Winchester to retire. And yet, at the very beginning of August that year, the head librarian distributed an email message, stating her intention "to embark immediately on a long overdue vacation and then retire from my position at Mersley College, effective September 1."

Since the three summer sessions had just ended, and the fall semester had not yet begun, the college's rumor mill was not yet in full gear, and speculations as to the cause of her sudden announcement were far more subdued than they would have been if she had made her announcement two or three months later. Nevertheless, Bastian would forever be convinced that it was his confrontation with the librarian that "put her over the edge," as he put it.

But that was not the reason.

It had begun roughly half a year earlier when Mersley College was still on its Winter Break. Out of the corner of her eye, she had caught sight of a bearded old man who, at first glance, might have been Father Christmas's far more rawboned brother. He was carrying what appeared to be a card from the old card catalog that he had somehow removed from the cabinet and was boldly about to carry out of the library. Ms. Winchester blinked and thought—just *thought*—that the gaunt senior citizen bore a slight resemblance to a young Classics professor who had still been on the faculty when she was first hired. But why would he have taken such a card from the cabinet, and where was he taking it?

If her mind hadn't been swirling with such questions, she no doubt would have instantly demanded that the thief stop and explain himself. But by the time she had recovered her composure, the man had gone. She ventured out the main entrance of Sutlinger Library to look for him, but saw no one. Any theft, even of a useless artifact like an old catalog card, annoyed Ms. Winchester, but, at the time, she had concluded there was little more she could do.

When, however, the story of Tolbert Fitzgerald's return to Chudwell Hall and his forgery of the catalog card had been revealed, the head librarian blamed herself. Dean McDaniel had always been one of "the good ones," in her view, and she thought that, with the former dean's departure, the last vestiges of the Mersley College she had known would be gone forever. Besides, if she had failed to stop Fitzgerald when he had walked directly in front of her, what else might she be missing? The Sutlinger Library collection was too precious to leave in incapable hands, even her own. And so, with no further thought than that, she scheduled an appointment with President Woolridge and informed him of her plan to retire.

* * *

As for the president himself, he briefly considered filing a complaint against Tolbert Fitzgerald, charging him with breaking and entering. But when word of his intention was made public, the Mersley College Faculty Senate held an unheard-of emergency meeting in the summer and considered whether to pass a vote of no confidence against the president.

Even the possibility that such a vote might occur caused Jefferson Woolridge to walk back his remarks immediately. He had, an official statement claimed, merely been speculating about what some hypothetical president *could* do, not what he himself had any intention whatsoever of actually doing. "Tolbert Fitzgerald has already suffered enough from the mistreatment he received from Mersley College. I have no desire to incommode the poor man further. Let us, therefore, consider this matter at an end."

But the Faculty Senate, as faculty senates are wont to do, was unwilling to leave the injustices committed against the former faculty member unaddressed. In a meeting that, to everyone's surprise, managed to get something done within the maximum one-hour timeframe, it voted to grant Fitzgerald the college's first-ever status as *professor emeritus honoris causa* and, in a tweak to the proposal added by Winton Garner, to award him what Socrates himself had proposed as his punishment when placed on trial by the Athenians: free room and board for the rest of his life.

The proposal passed unanimously, but then created another problem: Where should the college house Professor Fitzgerald? Should it rent an apartment in town? Allocate one of the rooms in a residence hall? Inquire whether some generous member of the faculty or staff has a spare room available?

"That should be no problem whatsoever," Garner continued. "There's one building on campus that's badly in need of renovations, including a brand new HVAC system, anyway. Despite the rapid growth of our program, there remains a good bit of space in Chudwell Hall and ... "

Other Novels by Jeffrey L. Buller

The Private Grimoire of Payvand Reed

1. *Payvand Reed's Curiosity Shoppe*
2. *Payvand Reed's Cabinet of Mysteries*
3. *Payvand Reed's Academy of Secrets*
4. *Payvand Reed's Museum of the Macabre*

Mysteries on an Operatic Scale

1. *Die, Meistersinger!*
2. *The Barbara Seville*
3. *Car Men*
4. *The Married Widow*
5. *Tsar Wars*
6. *Infidelio*
7. *The Battered Bride*
8. *Hot Salome*
9. *Monty Verdi*

The Secret Memoirs of Anton Krait

1. *Yesterday's Tomorrow*
2. *Moebius Strip*
3. *Premeditated Spontaneity*

CHAPTER SIXTY-TWO

Count No One Happy ...

Construction work, even in the best of times, is rarely rapid. And with its ongoing budget problems, these were hardly the best of times for Mersley College. The registrar thus had a sizable challenge on his hands, rescheduling and relocating classes so that all the courses taught by the Department of Eminent Scholars might have a home while Chudwell Hall underwent its extensive renovation.

It was thus in Marleburg Hall, not Chudwell, that Professor Garner began his course on Sophocles several weeks later. He looked askance at the white marker boards and "smart desk" as he entered the room, set down a stack of books, and, out of habit, walked back toward the door to lock it. Less than three feet away, however, he did something he'd never done before in all his years of teaching: He shrugged, left the door unlocked, and returned to the lectern at the front of the room. From there, he took stock of the assembled students.

In addition to the five students from the previous year, three students who had transferred into the program from the Department of Classics were deemed to be proficient enough in Greek to handle that semester's text. Even more surprisingly, one of the first-year students came to Mersley after having graduated from a private high school where four years of Greek had been offered. As a result, the course's enrollment was nearly double that of the classes Garner had taught the year before.

"Ordinarily," he began, "I'd spend the first day of a course like this talking about the challenges of dialect that tragedy presents, since it's not written in the Attic dialect you're all used to, and to explain a bit about Greek prosody. But in light of the events that have taken place recently on our campus, I thought it best to start this course somewhat differently. Would you please turn in your texts to the very last page of *Oedipus the King*? Many of the words will look unfamiliar to you, I know, but don't worry: I'm here, like Antigone, to guide you."

For the next half hour, Garner called on student after student and assisted them in translating a few words from the text. As they translated, he wrote the English words they'd suggested on the board. By the time they reached the end, this is what they had said:

> You who dwell in ancestral Thebes, look upon this man, Oedipus.
> He solved famous riddles and was the most powerful of men.
> None of you who are citizens did not look upon his fortune with envy.
> See how he's now been utterly swept under by the tide of dreadful misfortune!
> And so, a mortal should always focus on the last day,
> counting no one happy until he's passed the limits of his life, free from suffering.

"Now, that last line," Garner said, stepping back to admire the group's handiwork. "You may have encountered that sentiment in its more familiar form: 'Count no one happy until they are dead.' It's a thought we come across quite a bit in ancient Greek literature, and I'd like to devote this course to trying to determine *why*. But, in order to do that, we must first agree on what that statement even means. Any ideas? Yes, Ms. Warren-Whitehead?"

Garner was nodding toward Prudence.

"I think it's a fairly grim sentiment, Professor. It means something like 'Life is suffering, and death comes as a relief in the end.'"

"The world's nothing but a vale of tears. Is that the general idea?" Garner asked.

"In a nutshell," Prudence replied.

Garner actually smiled at the colloquialism. "Well, you're certainly in good company, if that's how you interpret the passage. In fact, there are a fair number of authors who say almost exactly what you just did. Can any of you from my former classes recall a passage from last year that expressed a similar sentiment?"

The class was silent.

"Not from Plato," Garner prompted them. "Maybe from something you came across in one of Professor Pope's classes?"

After a few moments, Esmé raised her hand. "There was one story that was on this theme. Something from Herodotus, I think."

"Yes, that's it. Go on."

"Two brothers ... and their mother was involved, too."

"You're thinking of Anpu and Bata," Bastian said. "That was Egyptian, not Greek."

"No, no," Garner corrected him. "She's onto something. Go on, Ms. Dawson."

"I don't remember it in detail, I'm afraid. Something about a festival and a cart."

"Oh, that one!" Townsant said excitedly. "Somebody and Biton."

"*Cleobis* and Biton, actually," Garner told the class. "Now, who remembers any of the details of this story?"

Over the next few minutes, as the imminent scholars contributed bits and pieces of what they'd recalled from their discussion in Sabrina Pope's course the previous spring, the following tale emerged.

In the city of Argos, the local residents were preparing to conduct a festival of Hera during which one of the local women would ceremoniously ride to the goddess's temple in an oxcart. But the oxen didn't arrive in time. So, rather than allow the festival to be ruined, the woman's two sons, Cleobis and Biton, harnessed themselves to the cart and pulled it in the procession. When they reached the temple, the young men's mother prayed to Hera that she might bestow on Cleobis and Biton the greatest gift that mortals could receive. At the close of the festival, the two young men simply fell asleep and never woke up again.

"Herodotus calls this story a 'divine proof that death is better than life,'" Garner concluded. "That may sound rather grim to us, but it's a theme that the ancient Greeks came back to time and again. In a lost work by Aristotle, Plutarch says that the philosopher retold the story of the wise, old figure known as Silenus who'd been captured by King Midas. Yes, *that* King Midas. In this story, Midas asks Silenus how he might obtain the most desirable thing in life. Silenus scoffed and replied that the best thing of all is never to have been born; the second best is to die as soon as possible. That story particularly appealed to Nietzsche—well, it would, wouldn't it?—and he liked it so much that he repeated the entire thing in *The Birth of Tragedy*. So, perhaps not everyone in the modern world finds the sentiment there so distressing."

The students in the class shifted uncomfortably.

"Non-existence is preferable to existence," Garner continued. "Today, that sounds vaguely Eastern in its sentiment. And who knows? Maybe it was. Herodotus was writing at about the time the Greeks were making their first, tentative contacts with the peoples of India. But I should also note that, in that very same passage in which Plutarch was quoting Aristotle, he calls the observation so ancient that, even in the philosopher's own time, no one knew who said it first. So, maybe it's not an Eastern thought, after all. We do find traces of it as early as the *Iliad* where, it's said, the god Zeus keeps two urns on his doorstep and uses these urns to bestow 'gifts' upon mankind. One urn consists of blessings, the other of evils. And if you find favor with Zeus, he takes a handful from both urns and showers them down on your life. But if you're not one of his favorites, all you receive is what's contained in the urn of evils. The point of the story is that even the best life has as much suffering in it as it does happiness. So, maybe the world's just a vale of tears, after all."

Garner let the students absorb this somber thought for a moment and then continued. "But, of course, that's not the *only* way in which we can read the final chorus of *Oedipus*. Does anyone have any alternative interpretations of the conclusion that we should count no one happy until they're dead?"

Townsant and one of the former Classics students raised their hands simultaneously.

"Yes, let's hear from one of the newer voices. Your name is?"

"Ramona Peters, sir."

"Yes, Ms. Peters. How would you interpret that sentence?"

"I think it means something more like a life can't be judged by any one moment in it. You have to see it in its entirety to know whether a person was truly happy."

"Let's explore that idea, too. It may be useful to note that Herodotus himself seemed to be of two minds about what 'count no one happy ... ' means. He follows the story of Cleobis and Biton, which is a story that almost certainly suggests non-existence is preferable to existence, with the following statement. And I quote ... "

Garner took out a pair of reading glasses and then opened the Oxford text of Herodotus to a passage he had marked earlier, translating as follows.

" ... 'Someone who's very prosperous may be no better off than someone who's impoverished unless his wealth continues throughout his entire life. ... Before he dies, we should call him lucky, not happy.' That idea, it's always seemed to me, is rather similar to what Ms. Peters has just shared with us. A life must be judged as a whole. You're far too young, but I often think of Lady Diana Spencer in this regard. I'm sure that anyone who saw her on the day of her wedding to Prince Charles must've thought, 'There goes the happiest woman in the world.' But none of us knew what was going on behind the scenes, and none of us, including herself, knew what lay in her future. So, was her life a happy one or not? And who are we to judge?"

He walked back to the blackboard and wrote three Greek words: ὄλβος, εὐδαιμονία, and μακαρίτης.

"Let's say these all together: OHL-boss, eh-you-DIE-moh-NEE-uh, mah-kah-REE-tace. All three of these words we tend to translate as 'happiness,' and that's indeed what they all mean, although with subtle differences. The first of these, ὄλβος, means something like 'earthly happiness,' wealth, bliss, and the like. The second, εὐδαιμονία, literally means 'the state of having been treated well by some divine spirit.' The origin of our word *demon* is in the middle of that compound, but that's a conversation for another day. The idea is that this type of happiness isn't due to anything you deserve, but rather was given to you through the generosity of some god. Our word *fortunate* is derived from a Latin term meaning almost the same thing: Fortune, Fate, or Chance was involved in providing your happiness; it wasn't anything you earned. And the third, μακαρίτης, takes this a step further. It comes very close to what we mean today when we say that someone has been 'blessed.' Related to what I was saying before, the ancient Greeks sometimes used the adjectival form of this word, μάκαρες, 'the blessed ones,' to refer to the gods ... but also to the dead. Now, look back at the passage of *Oedipus*. Which term does Sophocles use? It's an infinitive, so look for that type of ending."

After scanning the page, Townsant said softly, "ὀλβίζειν."

"That's right. Literally 'to be happy in an earthly sense.' Or maybe even 'to be happy as a result of one's own efforts.' Sophocles says, like his contemporary Herodotus, that, for most of his life, Oedipus was lucky, not happy. But one of the things I'd like to explore with you this semester is whether we might count Oedipus happy in one of the *other* two senses, happy, that is to say, in the 'gifts' he'd received from the gods."

Garner looked out at the class and could see they were confused.

"I'm sure none of this makes much sense right now. And it may not even make much sense unless we follow our reading of *Oedipus the King* with Sophocles's later work … in fact, almost certainly his *last* work and most definitely his longest work: *Oedipus at Colonus*. That's quite a lot of Greek ahead of us, especially for those of you who've only studied the language for a single year, but I've learned to have confidence in you that you're up to the challenge."

He winked at Esmé.

"That's confidence, Ms. Dawson, not faith. But as for those of you who have just joined us and who did not learn their Greek with me, maybe she has a point. Maybe I've got some faith in you as well."

Suddenly, Garner grew silent. He simply stared at his book for several long minutes. At last, he said, "I don't know why, but I've been thinking a lot these last few weeks about the nature of happiness and its permanence. Our former dean. Our former colleague. Which of the two of them, in the end, shall we count as happy?"

He looked almost embarrassed when he reached this point. "I hadn't meant to share that particular thought with you today.

Let's ignore it for now and turn instead to the paradoxical last line of Aristotle's *Nicomachean Ethics* that, I believe, some of you encountered in Professor Pope's class last year: 'And so, let us begin.' That strikes me as rather fine advice right about now. Miss Dawson, if you would do us the honors? Please turn back to the *opening* lines of *Oedipus the King* and read them for us in Greek. And so, let us begin."

Acknowledgements

First and foremost, let it be said that I find something strangely appealing about the genre that's come to be known as Dark Academia. As a result, I'd hate to think that readers regard *Chudwell Hall* as a satire or lampoon of that genre. Rather, please think of it more as an homage, coupled with my own awkward attempt to answer the question, "How could we write a type of story that is both humorous and true to the contours of a genre that, let's admit it, sometimes takes itself a bit too seriously?"

The story of Chudwell Hall thus embraces many of Dark Academia's most common tropes: a self-isolated group of students who are serious about their study of the classical languages and literature, hints of a macabre (perhaps even supernatural) mystery from the recent past, a setting in which dark and ominous places are preferred to bright and airy ones, and a cast of characters dressed, even on the hottest days of the year, in way, *way* too much tweed. When I, like many others, first encountered these tropes in Donna Tartt's *The Secret History*—Dark Academia's *ur*-text and, as it happens, Bastian's favorite book—it reminded me of my own college years two decades earlier. In fact, when I first discovered the genre (and fashion choice) called Dark Academia, my immediate reaction was, "These are my people!"

As a teacher and administrator, I have always favored students who not only studied Greek and Latin as I had done at their age, but who also tended to over-intellectualize everything, to live more in the head than in the heart. You'll find traces of them (and perhaps traces of me as well) in Professor Garner, Townsant, and indeed almost everyone else in this novel. Most of the students I felt closest to may not have been able to tell you precisely what it was they were hoping to get out of college, but, *whatever* it was, it wasn't simply access to a job. They cared about learning for its own sake and discovered life lessons, almost daily, in the works of Plato, Herodotus, and

Sophocles.

One final note: For all those potential Winton Garner clones out there who, after reading Chapter Fifty-Five are tempted to say, "Well, *actually*, the story of Persephone's not *really* an example of the Violated Prohibition since she was never specifically told *not* to eat the pomegranate seeds," let me point out that it's not *that* myth Esmé was thinking about when she made this comparison. The relevant story has to do with Venus (Aphrodite) and Adonis. The young Adonis, we're told, was so beautiful that Venus wanted him all to herself. She hid him in a chest and entrusted him to Persephone with the instructions that, under no circumstances, should she ever open the chest, and ... well, you can guess the rest.

If my need to include that clarification in this afterword doesn't reveal into which department *I'd* be assigned at Mersley College, then I suppose nothing will. Perhaps I *am* a bit Garneresque, after all. Be that as it may, I'd like to thank all the students who studied Greek and Latin literature with me—most specially those who also would themselves have been perfectly at home in Mersley's College's Department of Eminent Scholars—and hope that they like as much as I did the fictional curriculum I developed for them in the novel. I'd also like to acknowledge Vyara Pancheva, whose website "5 Creepy University Urban Legends" (https://www.topuniversities.com/blog/5-creepy-university-urban-legends) inspired the stories retold by Dean McDaniel in Chapter Sixteen and the tale Mallory read on her mobile phone in Chapter Thirty-Nine; Olivia Giovetti for her website "A Dark Academia Playlist," which inspired some of the music Esmé listens to in Chapter Fifty-Five; the members of the Dark Academia Facebook Group and The Secret Society Chat who read this work in a early form; and Sandra McClain, my devoted editor and life companion.

Jeffrey L. Buller
Raleigh, North Carolina
November 15, 2023

ABOUT THE AUTHOR

Jeffrey L. Buller lives with his wife, Sandra, in Raleigh, North Carolina.

Made in the USA
Middletown, DE
23 May 2024

54766016R00231